Origins
of Love

KISHWAR DESAI

SIMON &
SCHUSTER

London · New York · Sydney · Toronto · New Delhi

A CBS COMPANY

First published in Great Britain by Simon & Schuster UK Ltd, 2012
This edition published 2013
A CBS COMPANY

1 3 5 7 9 10 8 6 4 2

Simon & Schuster UK Ltd
1st Floor
222 Gray's Inn Road
London WC1X 8HB

www.simonandschuster.co.uk

Simon & Schuster Australia, Sydney
Simon & Schuster India, New Delhi

A CIP catalogue record for this book is available
from the British Library

PB ISBN: 978-1-47111-122-8
EBOOK ISBN: 978-1-47110-149-6

Typeset by Hewer Text UK Ltd, Edinburgh
Printed and bound in Great Britain by CPI Group (UK) Ltd, Croydon, CR0 4YY

Kishwar Desai is the author of *Witness the Night*, which won the Costa First Novel Award. *Origins of Love* is her second novel and she is currently working on her third, *The Sea of Innocence*.

Praise for *Witness the Night*:

'Terrific' *Telegraph*

'No "next-best-thing" novel has been as literary, bold and compelling as *Witness the Night* . . . it is a taut, gripping and complex thriller with two enigmatic heroines at its core . . . I dare you – woman, man, neither or both – not to love *Witness the Night*' *Huffington Post*

'A powerfully felt, shocking and moving indictment of cruelty and oppression' Maggie Gee

'[A] sad and thought-provoking tale' *Guardian*

Praise for *Origins of Love*

'As compelling as the stories of George Simenon's Maigret, Desai's Simran Singh novels are endowed with something else: the sense that she is delving not just into mysteries but into subjects that matter deeply. I cannot wait for her next adventure' *Independent*

Origins *of* Love

Chapter 1

SIMRAN

Let me tell you straight away that there are two things that fill me with dread: giving birth – and flying.

I have nothing against children. But, having grown up in a single-child household, I like my peace and quiet and am not anxious to jeopardize that for singing lullabies and wiping bottoms.

Even though I have recently adopted a 14-year-old girl, it's not quite the same thing as producing my own, and nothing to do with my biological clock – which my mother (who is a keen observer of such phenomena) assures me is not only winding down, but desperately needs oiling as well.

Does it bother me? No. But does it affect others? Yes, especially Ma, who could convince anybody that I should succumb to impregnation by any eligible and willing man and produce a grandchild for her. According to her, it will be beneficial all round. That is, it will both be 'good for me' and make me a more 'reasonable woman'. She also thinks that the very thought of 'real' parenthood will make me amenable to marriage. Open my eyes to the joys of a male companion, a family on a permanent basis.

1

The men who drift through my life like monsoon clouds are beginning to worry her. A child will also mellow me, tie me down. The wildness in me will be tamed and she will be able to curl her unfulfilled demands into those tiny hands and watch the lineage unfold, undisturbed . . .

The other day she showed me (only half-jokingly, I suspect) a newspaper report from Orissa which described an auction in which barren women bid for a pitcher of water from a magical well of fertility known as the Maricha Kunda, at the Linga Raja temple in Bhubhneshwar.

'Linga Raja, the temple of the Penis King?' I asked her. 'What a great idea. And what kind of water would that be?'

She seems to think that if I rush to Orissa and pour a bucketful of water on myself on the auspicious Ashokashtmi day she might hear her grandchild gurgle in her arms. It's a form of self-hypnosis, perhaps.

'It'll be a very wet conception, and less than immaculate. A priest or two may be involved. Are you okay with that?' I grinned.

She snorted, and briskly snatched the paper away.

Every year thousands of depressed, ill-treated, childless, accursed, unfortunate women flock to places like the Maricha Kunda. Here they fight an undignified battle for three pitchers of water, which are sold only to the highest bidders, by the high priests of fecundity. Shrieks of despair rise during the auction for the first pitcher, which is supposed to have the maximum potency and could provide deliverance from a lifetime of abuse and neglect. Many of these desperate women will soon be outcasts, ejected from their homes while their husbands install a younger, more fertile bride.

And what happened to all these women who won the great prize? Soaked, trembling with anticipation, they stood at the temple doors praying for the cosmic sperm to enter their wombs. Would the Penis King or the Linga Raja, the god Shiva whose erect phallus was worshipped by millions every day, oblige? Would he turn into a snake? Or would he appear in their dreams? There are many myths about the methodology of the Linga Raja, and each one is more mysterious than the last.

Auctioning water from these holy wells reinforces the irrefutable belief in India that being infertile is always the woman's fault. The men are infallible and so women beg and plead, shave their heads, starve, roll on the ground and tie their prayers in red threads of *mauli* that droop forlornly around the walls of shrines . . .

These millions of women have no choice. Luckily, I do. Unlike them, I can forgo the pleasure of a fertility rite.

But even for me, spiritual intervention is sought from every quarter. I know that my mother goes to the local gurudwara every day to ask the priest to say a special *ardas* for me. Her faith sometimes makes me wonder if one day all those unanswered prayers will be delivered to the right postal address – and by return mail a man will be dropped on to my obdurate head.

Meanwhile, I am quite content being plain Simran Singh, a middle-aged, meddlesome social worker and pre-menopausal single parent to a teenager.

Why I adopted Durga is a long story. Perhaps the urge for motherhood is not something we are born with but is a desire that can ambush you at any moment.

I know that Durga adopted me probably a little earlier than I adopted her. I was the first person she ever cried in front of when I met her in jail in Jullundur after she had been falsely accused of being a murderess.

It takes courage to cry in front of a total stranger. Certainly I have never been able to do it. I had felt a visceral connection with her, an impulse to look after her, to make her happy. I wanted to compensate her for all that had been snatched so cruelly away from her in her childhood. We grew to understand each other better and better as I slowly pieced together her tragic circumstances. After her release, I formally adopted her so that she could shut the door on those terrible memories of her past. Or so I hoped.

After long months of unease and suffering, just recently life has fallen into a quiet rhythm, with Durga, my mother and I sharing our evenings watching light-hearted movies and television, laughing over news (politicians usually provide the maximum merriment) and about our own, thankfully uneventful, lives.

Our conversation is mundane: about the woman across the street who wanted directions to the local metro. Or about the teacher who decided to make Durga's class enact a scene from *Othello* and wanted her to play Desdemona. Or what to cook for lunch the next day.

Occasionally, during a perfectly normal exchange, I still suddenly panic and watch Durga's face for any hint of tension, but even if troubled, she's beginning to put the trauma behind her. (Luckily, in her Delhi school very few people know about Durga's previous life. It is a very small and exclusive private institution – not one I would normally put a child into, but a perfect place to provide security.)

Around dinnertime each night, Durga's sister, Sharda, is brought downstairs by her carer to join us. She is staying with us, for as long as possible, in the hope that her condition will, eventually, improve. Her entry is always slow and reticent, her footsteps on the staircase almost inaudible – and it's always the encouraging, subdued voice of her carer that we hear at first. With her prematurely white hair in a neat plait, her face pale and still gaunt from the horrors of her own experience, she always stood at the edge of our group indecisively for a few moments: her unfocused eyes groping to recognize us. This is the moment when we plunge into an awkward silence, aware once again of the cruel journey which has brought us all together. Ironically, Sharda is luckier than Durga in that her memory of the past has been wiped away by the electric shocks she was given in the asylum. Perhaps as she begins to trust us she will be able to start completely afresh. That is something my teenage daughter will never be able to do.

A household with four women, all in various shades of disrepair. Durga, a damaged teenager; my mother, a widow in her sixties; and I, a cantankerous spinster in my forties. Whilst Sharda – well, it is impossible to say what age Sharda is now. I still hope she will wake from her nightmare one day, and let us know how old she really feels. She is fragile far beyond her natural years. Yet the drugs soothe her restlessness and she is gradually beginning to react to the world around her.

Our home might look odd to the outsider: but for me, feet on the sofa, surrounded by my 'family', my glass of whisky in one hand, a cigarette in the other, life could not be better. I have sighed more sighs of contentment these past few months than I have in all the past few years . . .

Alright, I know that none of this can really explain my refusal to have a child, nor my decision to adopt. But my aerophobia has a much more specific origin, the recollection of which is as tenacious as it is terrible. I have managed to wrestle many memories into forgetfulness, but this particular one is a formidable foe.

Imagine the scene: it is New Year's Day, 1 January 1978, and the balloons and streamers still dangle from the ceiling, bumping into the faux-antique mahogany furniture which crowds our flat in Bandra, Bombay. A double-decker chocolate cake is grandly crumbling into a half-eaten ruin on the dining table, the party hats are piled like a small mountain range on the sofa, while the champagne-and juice-glasses are an unwashed clutter in the sink. The maid has the day off and my mother has a 'headache': another euphemism for a hangover. My father, usually fastidious about his own appearance and belongings, always drew the line at doing 'women's work'. I was too much of a daydreamer to allow a messy room to upset me.

So he sits reading a catalogue on the latest technology in car parts and I am draped over the balcony railings, just outside the sitting room, where the large French doors have been opened up.

The flat was near Land's End, with a clear view of the night sky. We were living there briefly, while my father was trying a taste of 'big-city life' and setting up a factory in Bombay for small car parts. Though the business had been very successful, it was a dramatic change from our small-town life in Jullundur in North India, and we had struggled to find friends. And so the Maharashtrian family next door had meant a lot to us. But after our New-Year-cum-farewell party, they had just locked up their home, this evening, to catch a flight to Dubai. I was already missing them. Particularly my friend Abhinav, who was a few years older than me, a gentle bespectacled boy who understood my loneliness in a city which seemed consumed by haste.

I think I had a crush on him mainly because he did not mind spending time with me, easing my fear of school and of being different. On our daily walk to the beach, we ate *bhelpuri*, and in between sipping *narial pani* to temper the fiery taste, I would confide all my worries. Our short sojourn in Bombay was perhaps the only time I missed having a sibling, and Abhi, my 'boyfriend', filled the vacuum caused by my lack of confidence. I wondered what it would be like to kiss him. Someday, perhaps. He had long hair and soft brown eyes, with chocolate fudge centres. I spent a lot of time staring into them.

Abhi had grown up in Bombay while I was a 12-year-old still caught in the slowness of Jullundur, a town where I used to walk everywhere, or at most take a rickshaw. A small town where I did not have to pretend to be someone I was not. In Bombay I had to abandon my old cotton frocks and change into more swish, pleated, synthetic skirts. I struggled with my English accent as much as with the butterfly clips in my unruly hair. I also struggled to cope with competitive behaviour (a skill which would evade me for the rest of my life) but Abhi made it somewhat easier by being a buffer between me and this harsh new world which changed as rapidly as heroines changed their sarees in Hindi cinema.

And now he, too, had left, since his father, a journalist, had managed to get a job on a newspaper in Dubai. Those were the days when India's gold- and foreign-exchange ratio had finally begun to climb, thanks to the Dubai dollars.

Our high-rise building was in the flight path and I often used to watch the blinking tail lights of the planes slowly vanish as they joined the constellations in the sky.

I imagined that if I hung out on the balcony around eight at night, squinting against the sharp salty breeze, I could wave to Abhi as his plane went past.

So I stood staring mournfully out over the rough waves from the twentieth floor, face scoured by the rising wind, wondering which plane was carrying him away, and if I called out 'Abhinav' would he hear me ... when it happened.

My father had come out on to the balcony to hand me some leftover ice cream. I reached out for it and at the same time saw, from the corner of my eye, a plane juddering into view, veering sharply to the left.

I think I screamed and I still remember the ice cream splattering on the floor, as the *Emperor Ashoka* dived swiftly and neatly, like a phantom seagull searching for an underwater mate, into the Arabian Sea off the coast of Bombay.

The news reports said that all 213 passengers were killed instantaneously. The Boeing 747 should have been turning to the right, when in fact it was banking steeply to the left as the pilot lost control. It crashed within a few minutes of taking off.

For years the image of the plane nose-diving into a white foam-slashed sea remained frozen in my mind. Of course, Abhi must have been caught unawares, and would have been strapped in his seat – perhaps gazing out at the lights of Bombay, maybe looking out for me. 'Fasten your seatbelts,' the air hostess would have announced. When the plane smashed into pieces, and the water closed over his head and he struggled for air, there would have been no time for anyone to react. Perhaps he had tried to help his mother. I wondered if they had been holding hands, tightly, in those last few moments.

What if he had managed to break free and had survived – what if he had managed to grab a piece of the aircraft and come ashore?

I still have the newspaper cuttings, which said that the black box, later recovered, had recordings of the captain's last moments. The altitude indicator showed that the plane was in a right bank, when in fact the wings were level. The captain was puzzled, saying, 'What's happened here?' Was it already too late or was it too dark outside for them to see the horizon and get their bearings? Or was it something else? Some magnetic undertow that dragged the aircraft from the sky into the water, a few miles from my home?

Someone said the pilot lost his spatial sense. But I always wondered how everyone else on that flight also failed to notice that it was pitching forward at a forty-degree angle.

My father was an engineer and I drove him crazy with questions about engines and altitude and pilot errors.

The balcony door in our flat was now always kept open, and the moisture-laden chilly breeze constantly blew through our home. I kept a careful watch on the sea, using binoculars in case I spotted something on the coastline. I begged my father to go to the beach closest to the scene of the accident whenever we could, and questioned everyone for a sign of any survivor. And that is how we found him. If you could call him a survivor.

The fishermen pulled his bruised and battered body ashore. Abhi was still alive, but unresponsive to our cries, his face twisted in pain, one side of his head almost scraped to the bone.

We brought him home where my father quickly bandaged him. Calling an ambulance we took him to the Bella Vista hospital, considered to be the best for head injuries, even though it was in Colaba, quite far from where we lived. Till they took him away to the intensive-care unit, I gazed into his eyes. There was no recognition in them.

My father and I held each other closely. I couldn't stop shivering and he couldn't stop saying, 'He'll be alright.'

He would never be, of course, though we obsessively visited him every day, and asked the doctors impossible questions. They said he was in a coma from which he may never recover. Eventually his grandparents arrived and took over from us. A distance descended as more and more of our questions remained unanswered, till one day Abhi was shifted out.

No one would tell me where he had gone. Perhaps it was just as well, as I had stopped going to school and hung around the hospital hoping for a glimpse of my friend.

Within a few weeks, my mother stopped reasoning with me and thought it was time we went back to Jullundur. My father appointed a manager for his business and we locked up the flat. I refused to fly so we went by train, but I cried all the way, fearing that Abhi would think I had abandoned him.

So, flying is something that reduces me to complete terror. As a child I avoided it and even now as an adult I need to have a tranquillizer and several glasses of red wine (because they make me sleepy) before I can even reach an airport. The words 'pilot error' are emblazoned on my brain, and scare me more than terrorist threats. I don't mind dying messily, dismembered by a bomb. But I do mind a slow and painful struggle with my seatbelt while my lungs fill with water.

It's so strange, isn't it? I've just told you how much I dislike the thought of having children and that I hate, even more, the idea of flying. So you may well wonder how I now seem to have suddenly vanquished my own demons.

I have actually *flown* to London, and I am sitting in front of a man telling him I want to have a *baby*? It sounds a bit bizarre, doesn't it?

Believe me, it is.

But then I didn't have a choice, did I? You would have done the same thing in my place.

Nine months earlier

At half past eight in the morning, Kate was still in bed, staring out of the bay window on the first floor at the treetops outside. It was a quiet street in South London, with two rows of identical terraced houses facing each other across it, like foot soldiers ready for battle, prevented from lunging at one another, perhaps, by the thick oak trees growing through the pavements in front of them.

The double bed on which she lay was lower than the bay window. She could only see the trees and sky – and none of the neighbouring houses. Nor could the neighbours see her lying there with her patchwork blue duvet spread around her. In fact, on peaceful mornings she could imagine she was in an isolated forest, gazing at the treetops, her mind making a jigsaw out of the branches and the clouds. Today even this familiar view could not soothe her. She kept thinking of that unfortunate incident months ago. She pressed her face into the pillow.

Usually, she enjoyed the silent house when Ben was out jogging. It gave her a chance to dream. But today was different as she was far too tense. She did not want to move or even get out of bed. Hands clasped tightly together, she drew her knees up, face hidden behind her blonde hair, as she tried to escape from her thoughts. She was praying that perhaps at last this pregnancy would be successful, though the past did not promise a better future.

Ironically, when she had not wanted to be a mother she had fallen pregnant twice. And so effortlessly. The first time she had been celebrating her sixteenth birthday with some friends and bottles of gin. She had actually remembered the date of her periods, and knew that unprotected sex was risky, as her mother had warned her over and over again. But Jack (or Terry?) didn't put on a condom, and she had been too shy to stop him. He was an aspiring footballer, tall and muscular, and he had been flirting with her all evening, leaning over and whispering in her ear as though only the two of them could properly communicate with each other. Flattered by his attention, she forgot about being careful.

When she skipped her period she knew at once that she had to do something about it. She didn't want to drop out of school or be stuck at home juggling milk bottles and living off benefits like so many of her friends. Besides, Terry (or Jack?) had disappeared quite soon after their evening together. In a funny way, she didn't really mind too much, because the gin had made their encounter hazy and within a short time she didn't care about it at all. And she knew that even if she had tried to nurture the relationship, her family would have disapproved of him. He lived in a council house, and had dreadful manners. Why bother? It was astonishing, though, that she could not even remember his name.

Thinking about her 16-year-old self always made her uncomfortable. She had been so very lost and so easily led. In fact the mistakes she made as a child seemed to be more important and sadder than the blunders she made later on in life. Perhaps she had always been a misfit, a rebel in a highly conservative household, and had never acknowledged it.

Her next pregnancy was many years later, when she fell in love with her boss, a prize-winning documentary film-maker and a married man. But at least she remembered his name. Harry Cameron. Smooth as butter, with a smile that began in his eyes. Photographs of his wife and children on his desk.

'Why don't we go through the script together?' Harry had asked her as she handed him the fourth draft for a documentary on Margaret Thatcher. Even though she had studied her subject thoroughly, she wasn't satisfied. Or perhaps it was just that Harry made her terribly self-conscious.

The love affair and the documentary fell into place simultaneously. Harry would call his wife and tell her he was held up at work.

And Kate avoided the sly glances from their colleagues who looked deliberately unsurprised if she and Harry took a little longer to come in for meetings or lingered in rooms after everyone else had left.

Finally, he asked her to accompany him to South Africa to shoot a documentary on Nelson and Winnie Mandela. After a day's hectic filming in Johannesburg, he invited her back to his hotel room. Within a few moments the script was all over the room, along with their clothes. It was fabulous: intense and passionate.

She was prepared for the consequences, secure in the knowledge that he loved her. When, a few months later, he actually made an appointment for the abortion, she should have wondered why he was so *au courant* with the whole process. But she continued to think they had something special and that the magic would return very soon.

Only when she saw the sheer relief on his face, a few days later, did she finally understand that not only had she lost her baby, she had probably lost her job as well.

'I don't think *we're* going anywhere,' he said, printing out his tickets for an assignment in Brazil, which he had 'forgotten' to tell her about.

'But . . .' Kate began nervously and then realized that perhaps it was time she took stock of the situation. 'Are you taking Kelly with you?' This was the twenty-something assistant they had just hired.

'You weren't too well, and this gig won't wait.' He walked out casually, giving her a quick hug.

Kate drew a sharp breath, aware of a feeling she wasn't used to: heartbreak.

So why bother with relationships anyway? She was in her mid-thirties, a successful independent film producer who had over-committed to multiple assignments. After Harry, sex would happen only when she could find the time (which was rare) and was treated as a pleasant diversion. She was careful not to get involved.

That was before Ben took away all her defences.

So now her heart was breaking for a different reason, as she thought of the children she could have had. If only she could make her body remember to do what it seemed to have forgotten.

Her hands opened and closed, trying to grasp that magic and bring it into the room with her. Just a bit of luck from those days, she whispered. I only need a bit of luck, and it will all be okay.

She was staring at the trees outside without really seeing them. She hadn't moved for the past hour. To lessen the stress, she imagined a biology film running through her mind . . . '*And look, here the zygote becomes an embryo and eventually a foetus . . .*' It was a foolish little trick, but it soothed her. She closed her eyes and focused on the tiny beginnings of a child inside her. A pleasurable warm glow spread through her body. She breathed slowly, inhaling and exhaling, imagining the baby breathing in sync.

The door slammed downstairs and Ben whistled as he

ran up the stairs after his morning jog, but she lay still, at last lost in her favourite daydream.

When he sat by her side and cradled her close she thought he understood her fears perfectly. His hands moved gently over her abdomen and he rested his palm over her hands, which were clasped together, as though in prayer.

'Don't worry. It'll be okay . . . Are you planning to stay in bed for longer? Shall I make you some coffee?'

She looked up at him, unconsciously yearning, looking for reassurance: 'Tell me you think it will work this time.'

In her heightened state of anxiety she felt him withdraw from her just that tiny bit. Lately, as she grew more needy of his love, she had begun to notice that he wasn't as sympathetic as he used to be. He had also said, over and over again, that he wanted the child to bring them happiness – not this unending worry. She sometimes wondered whether he still wanted to be a father.

But before she could ask him anything, his expression lightened. He leant forward to kiss her eyes and mouth, bringing her clasped hands up to his lips. Her own love for him was, in that moment, indescribable.

Ben stooped to perform a pretend examination.

'Hmmm . . . the bump is getting bigger and bigger, isn't it?'

A slow smile spread over Kate's face.

'Maybe it's more than one baby?' she said teasingly, falling into the game.

'I only went away for half an hour – how did you do this?' He brushed the hair away from her face, tracing her upturned mouth with a finger. 'Come on, darling, maybe you'd feel better if you got dressed and I got you that coffee and some breakfast?'

As Ben stood, pulling her after him, Kate got up, but very slowly and carefully, still hoping that nothing would disturb the mating of the egg and the sperm, which formed the zygote and then the embryo and then the foetus inside her. It was amazing to think that, even while she was eating, sleeping, making love, their child's tiny hands, legs, feet, eyes, were all growing . . . a complete miracle.

It was only two months. But if something went wrong yet again, she wasn't quite sure if she could cope. She had barely survived the shock the last time. If only she could give Ben a real, living sign of her love. A baby with his brown eyes and curly black hair.

She put her arms around him and hugged him tight.

Turning her head, she looked at their reflection in the mirror on the wardrobe. How well they fit together. But then she saw the smile leave Ben's face as his expression became serious again, and his mouth straightened into a thin grim line. The sadness which she had seen creep into his eyes was now clearly visible. He frowned, and if he was thinking of their future he clearly did not like what he saw.

How long could they carry on like this, she wondered.

He was hiding something from her.

She also knew she was likely to fall apart if he walked out on her. Why couldn't he realize she was only going through all this pain for him?

Her arms tightened around him. She was never going to let him go.

And she was *going* to have this baby, come what may.

GURGAON

Dr Subhash Pandey sat back in his chair and tried to push away his tiredness. He was still jet-lagged after his seven-country, nine-city roadshow. The stopover in Berlin was the only time he had actually found a hotel he could sleep in. The rest of the accommodation had been fixed for maximum access and minimum comfort. So in all he must have slept for less than twenty hours in ten days. Two hours a night – and sometimes not even that. He looked out of the window and was cheered by the sight of the newly built hospital, its glass-and-steel structure glowing in the warm Gurgaon sunshine. The state-of-the-art Madonna and Child Clinic, just on the outskirts of Delhi.

It had taken years of toil, but now that India was a hospital-tourism zone, investment (and easy loans) flowed in. He stretched and carefully rotated his neck to release the tension, and took a few deep breaths to slow down his caffeine-loaded pulse.

He looked at his laptop: there were twelve couples in the queue already, so there was no time to waste. He brought up their photographs and details one by one: three American, one French, five British, one German and two Australian. Most of them were easily dealt with, except for the two gay couples, one from Britain and the other from Germany. The only reason he was doing it was because he was charging them double. The normal fee of twenty lakh rupees rose to forty lakh rupees, because dealing with homosexual cases in India was still so complicated. It was largely a taboo subject, and the laws did not help either. Since marriage or civil partnerships between gay partners were not recognized, there were problems when issues of adoption or parenthood came up.

Even normal heterosexual cases weren't straightforward. Countries like Germany, Spain, Israel, France and Belgium had already issued notifications that IVF clinics in India should not entertain surrogacy for citizens of their country. Yet the demand was pouring in, and hopeful would-be parents came to the clinic, quite prepared for the legal battle which often lay ahead. This meant careful negotiations upfront, explaining the possible risks.

So the process became doubly fraught when the couple was gay as well. And doubling the fee was, he thought, justified.

In fact he was concerned about the gay French couple already registered with them. The egg donor and gestational mother was carrying twins for them, but early indications were that it would be very difficult for them to take the children back and give them French citizenship.

He still felt a bit uneasy about homosexuals being given children to look after, but, as his wife Anita often told him, he was only a doctor, and not a priest. Why should he impose his 'morality' on them? He thought of his own daughter Ramola being brought up by two men. It made him shudder. Perhaps it would be better if the men got boys and the women got girls. Yet even that thought didn't reassure him completely. Could nature really outweigh nurture? His own experience as a medical practitioner had left him unsure about everything in life, except, of course, death.

Perhaps Anita could sort it out for him; she was far more relaxed about these things. Even the threats from Swami Ganga and the Pratha Suraksha Sansthan, an organization which claimed to be working towards preserving the 'moral traditions' of India and opposed children being given to gay couples, did not upset her. She shrugged them off and said briskly that 'Indians had to modernize'.

But as he argued back, 'Modernity isn't the issue. As far as I know homosexuality is a grand old Indian tradition, and is even in the Kama Sutra. It's this, this whole business of children being brought up by two fathers or two mothers. Is this a "normal" family?'

Anita smiled. 'Grow up and get used to it, baby.'

He tore up the latest hate mail from Swami Ganga predicting hellfire and damnation and threw it in the wastebasket. There was a similar-sounding protestation from Father Thomas on his laptop and, as he deleted it, he was amused that for once the Hindu and the Christian priests seemed unified, in their condemnation of homosexuality. Usually they were at loggerheads over everything.

He rang the bell and the receptionist peered in.

'Sir?'

'Have the women arrived? '

'Only two. One is still sick.'

'Is that fellow Sharma with them? He better be there. I don't want it to be a mess like the last time. I want all their personal histories, and have they had the tests done? They should be totally clean. No TB, no HIV, and, for God's sake, no hepatitis. What happened to the third one? I hope she doesn't have anything infectious?'

The receptionist looked a little nervous.

'Mr Sharma will tell you, sir. I've already sent them to the clinic for a thorough check-up, and their files are with Mr Sharma.'

Subhash shrugged.

'If he screws it up again, we'll just get someone else to source the women for us. Send him in.'

Dark-skinned and pot-bellied, Sharma came in chewing paan, carefully herding two women in front of him. The women both wore brightly coloured polyester sarees. One of them seemed to hang back while the other entered confidently – she was quite fair and passably good-looking. Subhash looked at her curiously. Good, firm breasts, and a little heavy around the waist; she was probably married. The other one was thin and better-looking but dark, which was always a problem. Most foreigners preferred fair women – it made them feel less like old colonial exploiters. She also seemed more nervous, pulling her saree *pallu* over her head and looking at the ground, whilst the other one sat down casually and gazed at the objects in the room and at Subhash without any coyness. She even wore lipstick and a slight touch of rouge. She reminded Subhash of someone. He looked at her closely, while she stared right back at him.

Preeti, of course! She was already pregnant and admitted to the hospital. Except Preeti was better looking.

She had come in two months ago and had almost immediately been used for a British couple, Mike and Susan Oldham. Subhash hadn't seen her for a few weeks now since he had been away; he wondered how she was.

He made a note to check on her; his colleague and partner, Ashok Ganguly, would have been looking after her.

Subhash looked at Sharma, in his white safari suit, two hairy feet with yellow nails and cracked heels thrust through leather sandals and planted firmly on the ground.

Sharma was the archetypical supplier. He was the guy you called when you needed foreign liquor at short notice, a driving licence without passing the test, a file pushed in a government office, or a new building given clearance without the proper fire-and-safety regulations being adhered to. He could get you medical supplies, oxygen cylinders, expensive perfume, imported cameras . . . No one knew his first name or where he came from, but he had made a small fortune from his ability to supply whatever the client wanted. His connections were many, and everyone supported him. He was invaluable in a city like Delhi. Subhash had even attended his daughter's wedding, though he hated going to Karol Bagh and eating greasy *pakoras*, sitting on plastic chairs, listening to loud bhangra music. A quiet drink at the golf club was more his style. But this was the price one paid to keep Sharma on side.

'Have you checked them this time?' Subhash asked.

Sharma gave a wink.

'Personal inspection, sir.' He laughed, sure that the two women would not understand English. 'But one has a little flu, so I've sent her home. Will bring her back next week.'

'What's their background?'

Sharma produced two official-looking files from his synthetic-leather briefcase and placed them in front of Subhash, pointing out the details with a stubby finger.

'This one is Shobha.' He nodded at the more confident woman. 'Like Preeti, she is from Uttar Pradesh, from a village near the Nepal border. Her husband stays in the village. She has one child, but needs the money because they want to build a house.'

'I hope she knows there is very little money upfront and she may have to stay here for nine months before she gets the entire amount? Who will look after her child while she's here?'

'Her husband.'

Subhash remembered the last fracas.

'But what about the community? What if they find out she's pregnant, it's not her child – and that she can't keep it?'

'They won't know, sir. Her relatives are all in the village. Her husband couldn't come but we have explained it to him. No physical *ghapla* – you know – he knows it will be all done in a tube, and then an injection.' Sharma chuckled as he spoke, almost as though he didn't quite believe it himself.

'Remember I don't want the TV cameras in here and people all over the place asking whose child it is. And the other one?'

'She's local, sir. Sonia. No husband. He ran off with someone. So she is totally free. She has had three children. One died in an accident. Two are still alive. But she's working as a maid in Delhi, next to the Health Minister's house. She says she is living with her cousin till she can earn enough money to get her children back; they are in the village, with her parents. She wants to give them a good education.'

Subhash looked at the photographs. With more expensive clothes, a protein-rich diet, bleach to lighten her skin, and maybe some makeup, Sonia could do. Better photographs would have to be taken (especially for the website, which was designed to appeal to Western tastes), in soft pastels and with floral borders. He had personally been keen to put in a few chubby cupids, but this had been vetoed by Anita who thought they were more suitable for matrimonial sites. But everything could be photoshopped these days, so he was sure that the final, slightly out-of-focus photographs of Sonia and Shobha on their website, would make them look more middle class.

'Call the nurse. Before we go any further I want to examine them myself.'

Sharma bustled out, after telling the women to wait. They looked at him and then carried on sitting quietly. He had prepared them well.

Subhash flicked through the brief files. Both the women, in their mid-twenties, were barely educated, though surprisingly it was Sonia who had studied till Class 6. This might be a problem, as high school-levels were usually asked for. Not that it made any difference, but the commissioning parents often thought that if the woman was educated the child would have a better start. It was hopeless explaining to them, especially the Americans, that the womb was immune to educational degrees. All that mattered was that the woman was well-fed, given her vitamins and got enough rest.

They had now built a wing to the clinic where the women were kept for the nine months and carefully monitored. Six women were in there already: three from the northeast (and that included Preeti, who was now one month pregnant), two from Punjab and another from Maharashtra, all carrying children from an international clientele and one local couple as well. But the extra rooms needed to be filled – and apart from the dozen queries on Subhash's computer this morning, there were bound to be more in response to his global marketing blitz.

Thank God Sharma's arms encompassed all of India; he boasted that he already had a list of five hundred women, all prepared for the task. Subhash wondered what Sharma's relationship was with these women – did he have a go at some of them himself, as he had often hinted, or was it only some macho posturing? They still needed ten more women, urgently. Sharma was falling behind his targets, despite his grand talk.

It was the same situation for egg donors. But the last time he had pointed out that they needed to pump up the numbers, Sharma had brought in younger and younger women, who were very keen on going in for the harvesting. It was apparent that some of them had not even had children as yet and were only doing it for the money. It was another issue he was getting increasingly concerned about. He did not like this trend – though Ganguly, his partner, was quite sanguine, and even at times, pushed for it.

The nurse came in and drew a curtain around the bed, beckoning Shobha.

Shobha walked behind the curtain and lay down, and, as the nurse instructed her, pulled up her saree and spread her legs wide apart. Subhash put on his gloves, hoping hers would be a clean womb. He was pleased to find she had been shaved, so that he could do a thorough examination. She seemed fine, with no scars or lesions, and good child-bearing hips.

'How old is your child?' he asked her in Hindi.

She hesitated before she answered, and seemed a little tense as she replied.

'Five years.'

'Any pain anywhere?' He pressed her abdomen. The ultrasound had been clear, but you never knew. She shook her head, though she gave a funny little smile.

'Periods are fine?'

A slight blush was spreading on her face.

'On time.'

'I have to examine your chest, so unbutton your blouse.'

Perhaps he pressed a little harder than he should have as he searched for lumps; but her smile remained unchanged. The nurse was busy with the blood-pressure instrument and ignored it all. She was a discreet woman from Kerala who very rarely spoke unless she was asked something.

He checked Shobha's heart and lungs with his stethoscope and then returned to his desk. Oddly enough, his own heartbeat seemed to be racing even faster than it should have been but that may have been due to his jetlag. He was tired and his hands were clammy.

Or was it due to her? The only other time he remembered his body reacting recently was when Preeti had first been brought in by Sharma. Subhash had liked the look of her breasts. Cream with pale-brown nipples.

It was a funny business. Most people thought that experienced doctors were indifferent to human flesh, but even now, after ten years, he felt an occasional tug of passion. That, he knew, was a dangerous sign, and he must restore the mask of neutrality to his working life.

After all, that woman, though she did not know it, was worth at least twenty lakh rupees. Or even, he reminded himself reluctantly, forty lakhs.

As he noted his observations on a piece of paper attached to the top of the file, he wiped the beads of sweat from his forehead. Perhaps the air-conditioning temperatures needed to be reduced.

The nurse came out and summoned Sonia.

Subhash drank a glass of water.

For some reason, he remembered Preeti again, sitting in front after her examination, a few months back. She stood out from the rest of the surrogates because of her voluptuous charm. Straightening her saree, Preeti had given him one last glance from beneath her lashes, a glimmer of excitement in her eyes.

'Is everything okay, sir? Sharmaji said you will pay us five lakhs for the baby?' she had asked outright.

'That's right. But has Sharma met your husband and explained it to him?'

'Yes.'

'I know his consent is on the file, but I have to be certain. You're sure he won't object?'

Subhash had wondered how her husband could live without her for nine months. She seemed almost combustible!

'Absolutely, sir. My sister will be there.'

The way she said it made Subhash wonder if this was a family enterprise. After all, she would bring in more money with just one pregnancy than her husband would earn in his entire life.

'So he's okay with it?'

'Sir, he's the one who went to Sharmaji and suggested that I come here. What's the problem, sir? I'm very good at having children. Other women have problems but I produce them so easily. My husband has come with us, sir, do you want to meet him?'

Subhash had shaken his head. Not just yet. He had a feeling he would have many interactions with Preeti in the future.

'Sir,' the nurse interrupted his reverie. 'Sonia is ready for her examination.'

He got up, quickly realizing that he hadn't heard the nurse the first time round. He was beginning to feel very tired.

Sonia may have appeared shy at first glance, but the way she lay down had no awkwardness in it. He looked at her face briefly. Her hard, still eyes startled him – and then she looked away. Subhash decided that his jet-lag was definitely getting the better of him.

Dismissing the two women after Sonia's check-up was over, he wearily closed the files. At least these two women were alright. He should also discuss with Ashok Ganguly when the next batch of embryos were expected from the UK, so that they had everything in place. Sharma needed a deadline to bring the rest of the women in. He had a feeling that soon there would be a deluge of demand, as India had become the destination for outsourcing wombs.

He picked up a phone and called Ganguly to ask about Preeti's pregnancy. Though Ganguly had just joined them as a consultant last year, he was enthusiastic about the whole business and eager to be involved in everything. That was good, because Subhash was equally keen to offload more and more on to him, so that he could take an occasional holiday with Anita.

And play golf.

Right now, though, that seemed an impossible dream.

MUMBAI

Sub Inspector Diwan Nath Mehta knew it was not his lucky day. It had begun badly with his wife Malti getting angry that he had not got his promotion this year. She had hoped that his work at the Customs and Excise Department at the international airport in Mumbai would bring him into contact with the *Who's Who* of Indian society. He knew she had visions of him nabbing a Mafia don smuggling drugs into the country, or at least a Bollywood star who had refused to pay duty on his latest car. She dreamt of gory encounters between him and the 'underworld' (though most of its members regularly had their photographs published in newspapers in the company of the city police and politicians at parties). Even when the Taj Mahal hotel was attacked she kept hoping her husband would unearth a fresh load of arms and ammunition or perhaps arrest a terrorist or two, despite the fact he was miles away from the action.

She dreamt that there would be a Pakistani invasion of the airport that would make her husband a national icon.

Mehta was hard pressed to satisfy her wild imagination and every day when she laid out his neatly ironed uniform he could see the longing in her eyes: perhaps today would be the day when his sniffer dog would lead him to a haul of heroin – and international recognition.

'No smuggler today?' she would ask, disappointed, in the evening as she took his empty tiffin box and put it on the side of the kitchen counter in their tiny flat in Dadar, in the heart of Mumbai.

It was quieter these days because his parents, who lived with them, were away. And though they had been married for ten years, there were no children, a fact which often upset Malti. She was a stout, formidable woman with a firm view of the world: things should go the way she wanted them to, and she was distraught if they did not. Her husband was her pet project for improvement, but since it was a life-long effort she hoped that one day he would achieve the perfection she desired. If she had children perhaps she could have been distracted from her mission, but without them Mehta was constantly under a microscope and, like a dissected frog, feebly flapped his limbs about to show signs of life as he was being prodded and poked.

So when he came home, he would take his shoes off and sit on the sofa wriggling his unfettered toes, sipping his tea and wondering how he could embellish his account of the day to make her feel he had saved the nation from a major calamity.

But then, of course, there was the question of rewards.

Recently his colleague Satish Bhonsle had managed to catch a smuggler with gold bricks in a suitcase. A minuscule percentage of the total worth of the gold bricks was given to him as a reward – making him comparatively rich as well as a local celebrity, with his interview published in the Marathi papers, and a local channel even covering his home with a special 'A Day in the Life of Satish Bhonsle'.

That evening Diwan Nath Mehta decided to go home as late as possible because he knew he would find his wife seated tearfully in front of the Shirdi Ka Sai Baba statue in the sitting room, next to the TV (given to them by her father), her hair open and hands raised in lament and prayer, asking her god plaintively why it had to be Bhonsle and not her husband.

She *knew* Mehta was meant for higher and better assignments – it was what her father, a shopkeeper in Nagpur, had saved up for. Her dowry, which included this flat, a scooter and three lakhs' worth of gold jewellery in the bank, was an investment in Mehta's career. Two years ago her father had given them the fridge and before that the television set. Mchta was supposed to at least double the money represented by that investment. When he didn't, her father had given them one lakh rupees in cash (no doubt black moncy he had collected from the sale of some property) and she had no intention of mentioning to her family that Mehta had not even opened the envelope.

It lay in their cupboard, untouched, and Mehta knew her biggest fear now was that she might have married an honest man. Or even, horror upon horror, a man with no interest in making money. In which case, the flat, the scooter, the cash and the jewellery was all she was ever going to have. And no children on top of that, *hai bhagwan!*

Given the dimensions of Malti's ambition, Mehta constantly wondered how he could break it to her that his was quite a lowly back-office job, and his boss, Nazir Ali, dealt with any contravention of the law.

Usually, in fact, his department relied on the importers to confess to any misdemeanours and, of course, once in a while there were tip-offs. Very rarely did a case really get noticed or even come up for discussion among the higher authorities – and even then, a 'commission' would often be charged to hush it up. However, occasionally something would need to be done for the credibility of the department and so a carefully executed raid would be conducted on a suspected contraband consignment. Ninety per cent of the time, these raids led to smiling pictures of the Customs and Excise officers in the following day's papers with the seized contraband arranged in front of them. Their connections with the media were very good, because of the number of times they had allowed computers, cameras and other equipment to go through with a minimum of paid duty or fuss. In a few rare cases, the 'tip-off' turned out to be a dud, and then it was better never to mention it again.

Today, he was not quite sure which category his current assignment would fall into, though he strongly suspected it could be quite small in the scheme of things. Rather than winning him instant fame and fortune, it was probably one of those ambiguous moments when everyone would turn on him and yell, 'Mehta, why the bloody fuck did you want to open that cargo, you banjo?' (The last was really supposed to be *behenchod*, i.e. 'sisterfucker', but its overuse had shortened it to the colloquial 'banjo'.)

Because his father, thinking that he would become rich and powerful, had grandly given him the title of 'Diwan' when he was born, Mehta was quite content to be abused for another reason once in a while. It was preferable to being teased about being a feudal landlord, as 'Diwan' implied, when he clearly was not.

That morning was the first time, ever, that his boss, Nazir Ali, had asked him to 'check' a 'suspicious' consignment. Here he was staring at a bunch of steel containers, which looked like mini rockets or shiny milk cans. He walked around them gingerly, wondering if they were going to explode. That wouldn't be a good start, would it?

He saw the consignee was a hospital in Gurgaon. Why would a hospital import steel containers? Perhaps they contained chemicals for medical use? He began to peruse the file – when his boss walked in.

Nazir Ali was a tall, well-built man who worked out every day. He had confiscated a consignment of gym machines many years ago and they had lain in his office, sleek with a brand-new gloss, as the importer had been unable to pay the duty. For some reason, the machines could not be auctioned at the asking price, and so Ali had gradually begun to use them and now he spent most of his time pounding on the treadmill and lifting weights. It took away some of the tedium of a job which ran according to a master plan of give and take. As Ali was fond of pointing out: the idiom was 'take from your hand and give into mine'. However, to be fair, Ali shared the loot and was very particular about giving his boys a chance at bodybuilding. A few of them had become so muscular that they were now participating in 'Mr India' contests all over the country. Mehta was still too lowly and too shy to demand that he be allowed either a workout or even a tiny cut of the financial pie.

Nonetheless he was flattered that Ali had asked him to help him out this time – perhaps because most of their other colleagues were involved in another case of cocaine smuggling. That was a frequent problem and required special expertise. The stakes were also very high and so Ali could only use his really trusted men. This was, in comparison, obviously a minor assignment.

'Why have we stopped this lot?' Mehta was bewildered. The milk cans must be harmless, he reasoned, because if there had been any suspicion that they contained explosives they would have been sent to the bomb squad and not brought in here.

'Read the document carefully. This banjo *saala* is cheating us. This is human trafficking.'

'These are only milk cans, boss.' Mehta's bad feeling about stopping this consignment came back with a rush. Why did he have to face an irate boss over a bunch of worthless containers? 'Shall I put them through the X-ray machines?'

'Have you read that paper? X-rays are prohibited because it can damage the content.' Ali towered over him. 'What's in the cans? Read it.'

Mehta tried to stop shaking (Ali was known to crush the bones of men who disagreed with him) and forced himself to read the document carefully. On the third page, he finally understood. In the cans was liquid nitrogen, within which were frozen embryos. These embryos had parents who all bore foreign names: Betty and

Alexander Smith, Susannah and Peter Wimpole, Kevin Franzen and Hannah Jacobson, and so on. Each container was separately marked. They had been sent from the UK by a company called 'Mybaby.com' and were headed for 'BirthingBabies Company' in Delhi who would further route them to the Madonna and Child clinic in Gurgaon.

He tried to remember his biology lessons in school.

'Boss, these are only embryos – not yet a human being.'

'I say they are human beings. *Saala*, baster, banjo, do they think they can bring in little American babies and make us into a white-white *gora* nation?'

'*Gora English* babies, boss, not American,' Mehta started to say, though he quickly regretted it.

Suddenly Ali went very still, and a glow of understanding dawned in his eyes. He snapped his fingers under a startled Mehta's chin.

'Perhaps not even just *gora* babies – but Christian babies! That must be it. *Saala*, these *goras* are always thinking how to grab us by our balls.'

Mehta protectively grabbed his own groin, and was reassured that everything was as it should be.

He wondered why his normally cool boss was overreacting so much, and how could this small number of embryos lead to a change in the colour and religion of the whole nation. He had heard of all kinds of arguments against the Church, but this seemed fairly improbable.

'Those *goras* are having fewer babies than us, you see. They are getting older, while we have a young population. So now they want to reverse that, get it?'

Ali had obviously worked it all out. 'They want our women to stop having babies for us and have them for those *goras* instead. *Our* women do the work, and *their* population goes up. Don't you see it's a plot? A new way to colonize us.'

Mehta was bewildered at the thought that this global conspiracy had been just been unearthed in Room 22 in the Customs and Excise Department.

'Boss, let's call this BirthingBabies company and find out. Are you saying it is illegal because these are human embryos? I've seen similar consignments coming in for the last one year and no one has stopped them.'

'This time I will.'

Ali's phone rang, and he reached to pick it up, irritated at the interruption.

But as he listened, a beatific expression spread over his face.

'Yes, I have them. Don't worry, you will get them when you want them.'

He nodded and then smiled mysteriously at Mehta and shut his phone.

To Mehta's surprise Ali abruptly dropped his evangelistic argument about the embryos.

Instead he mused aloud how they could be used to earn some cash. That, at last, was familiar territory – but it was the first time Mehta had been included in any such endeavour.

Ali looked at the milk cans rather fondly now.

'It is a simple formula. Now that I've said I won't release them people are interested. Economics, banjo, economics. The moment a commodity becomes scarce, the price goes up. Call the press for a meeting and we will tell them that we have confiscated the lot.'

'And then what do we do with them? Boss, these babies can't last forever like this – we will have to store them somewhere?'

'Don't worry, Mehta. It's all been worked out. Do you know how much each *gora* embryo is worth? At least fifty thousand. And as long as I make them illegal they will continue to earn money.'

Mehta was startled. He had no idea that the embryos conceived by Patricia and Scott Ramsfield, Zenobia and Gerald Mathews – he scanned the list, there were at least twelve different couples on it – were so valuable.

'But why?'

'Banjo, fucker – who cares? For us, it will be Eid! They will still be used – the only difference is that instead of Delhi they will be used right here in Mumbai.'

So the embryos were still valuable for people other than the consignees? A confused Mehta began to protest when an image of his long-suffering wife swam in front of his eyes. She had been praying every morning and evening for two hours, and had been fasting on Tuesdays for six months.

She had even refused to sleep with him, saying that only her abstinence and prayers would make him into a sensibly corrupt individual with an instinct for survival. An astrologer had told her this. With a full money-back guarantee.

Perhaps the black magic was working already.

Mehta's brow uncreased and, battling with his principles, he realized that even if he only got 1 per cent of the total amount, he would be elevated in Malti's eyes.

'Alright, boss, what do we have to do?'

Ali strode into his office, followed by Mehta. He sat down behind his desk and put his feet up.

And then he told him.

Chapter 2

SIMRAN

So here I was across the table from Edward Walters talking about babies, in a crowded Leicester Square restaurant in London. We sat outside because a very pale, almost white, liquid sunshine was spilling out slowly, very slowly, from behind a wall of grey clouds. A striped awning had saved us from the mandatory drizzle. The air was crisp and I was grateful for my light tweed jacket and freshly bought (though tight) knee-high suede boots. The airline food had killed my appetite but the smell of fried eggs and bacon, an inevitable 'full all-day English breakfast with coffee' was comforting. I suppose this was the equivalent of our *poori-aloo* breakfast. Why does most of the world always want to start the day with the greasiest meal imaginable?

Perhaps because of the familiar aroma of fried potatoes, I immediately felt at home.

As people passed by, I saw a few women turn around and look at Edward. And to be honest, he cut quite a dashing figure in his black jacket and Lycra pants. The proper attire for a dedicated cyclist.

I could see why many would think he was the ideal father. He had clear skin, dazzlingly white, even teeth, dark-blue eyes and soft golden-brown hair that fell over a broad forehead. There was something terribly clean and healthy about him. He had even cycled to our rendezvous and was now, much to my despair, drinking a glass of cold milk, while I sheepishly sipped red wine. It was barely afternoon, and I suspected he already disapproved of me.

He had probably been expecting a demure Indian woman, dressed in Tanjore silk and draped in a pashmina, with her hair swept back in a high chignon. Just like the joke photograph on my Facebook page, put there by Durga, taken one day when I'd dressed up to attend a wedding.

Instead he found a brown-skinned, jean-clad, middle-aged woman, whose curly hair had not been brushed since she stepped off the plane. I wished I had remembered to apply some lipstick, and wondered if it would look too vain if I whipped out a compact and put on a more acceptable powdered and rouged face. Thankfully, he was kind enough not to show his disappointment. On the other hand, I could certainly say he was better-looking in real life than in his photographs.

He wasn't too tall, but was slim, and had a deep voice, with an accent I could understand without saying *Ibegyourpardon* every few minutes. He was also very polite.

Yet, despite his kindness, at the back of my mind was the reminder that we had met to make a deal, an indication of how businesslike my life has become. On my first day in London, I could have been wandering around looking at the Picasso collection which was being displayed at the National Gallery or drifting down to Selfridges to buy handbags for my mother, or shopping at M&S for underwear for Durga and me. Instead, here I was, at a pavement restaurant, talking about making babies.

I wasn't quite sure what he thought of my coming all the way from Delhi to meet him. Perhaps he was intrigued by the whole idea of fathering a transnational, mixed-race baby. I had already informed him on email that I wanted to have a child by someone who did not live in India as that was safer for me. My story was that I was fairly wealthy and did not want any macho alpha male suddenly turning up to claim either me or the resulting child.

'On your website – you've quite openly spoken about helping women who want children. All for free! That makes you a philanthropist, of sorts, doesn't it? Amazing.' I began with blatant flattery. It always works.

'Started more than twenty years ago,' he said modestly, sipping his milk.

I had met various kinds of do-gooders but this was the first time that I had met someone who 'spread his seed' and women were actually grateful for it.

'One should categorize it as much-needed social work – especially for women like me. Not having a partner shouldn't stop me from having a child.'

'And then there are all kinds of other reasons – there are gay and lesbian couples who want children, and you'd be surprised how many men these days have a low sperm count,' he pointed out.

'Not a problem you've ever faced,' I said, piling on the praise still more generously. Admire everything, even his sperm count. I needed him to like me, trust me.

Because there was a child back home for whose sake I had fixed to meet him. A very sick child who needed him more than he would ever know. Each time I thought of her lying so very tiny and helpless in her cradle in the hospital, it strengthened my resolve to do whatever was required to help her.

'So what's the final tally? How many children?' I asked him as casually as I could. In our email exchange we had not discussed the total number of children he had fathered.

'I haven't kept track of every one of them. It can become a problem, you know, both for them and for me.' He stopped and was quiet for a minute. 'Shall I give you an honest answer? It sounds bizarre but it may be around forty or fifty. Probably more. I used to do this maybe once or twice a month, so even if you look at a ten per cent success rate over twenty years . . .' Now his voice trailed off.

I widened my eyes in amazement.

'The father of fifty children . . .? Aren't you worried you might meet them, somewhere – and you may not even know they are your kids . . . and what if one of them wants to meet you?'

He took a sip of milk and frowned, licking the white moustache off his upper lip.

'Actually up to a few years ago, I could be clear with the women that I did not want to be involved with the children. But now, as you know, the law has changed here, so in the next decade or so, my cover will be blown. The child will have a right to know I am the father – which is why I have stopped being as liberal with my . . .' He paused and looked at me, wondering perhaps if I would be offended.

'Sperm.' I supplied the word as blandly as I could.

He gave a grateful nod, and continued: 'It can become problematic if a child wants to visit me, though thankfully it hasn't happened so far. Even with the new law it won't matter for another fifteen years, but I don't want too many surprises. I only do the rare case now – someone who really needs me, and has tried everything.'

One-shot Walters! His confidence almost made me grin, till I remembered why I was here.

Did I look terribly needy? Or at least needy enough? I tried to arrange my features into a suitable expression. Now would he agree to 'father' my child? I saw him slide a glance towards his watch. Suddenly, I did not want him to reject me.

That's how I am: I always want the men who don't want me. I wanted him to pay attention to me.

And in this case it was essential.

'You know, you're like the sadhus in ancient India,' I told him. 'In the old days, we had our own form of sperm donation. If a woman couldn't have a child from her husband, the local sadhu or holy man would visit the house, and it is said he gave the woman a potion, and muttered some mantras over it – usually in a closed room, and in secret. Now that we're all smarter we know that the potion and the mumbo jumbo was probably just solid sex – and so these men were in great demand. The good thing was that, since it was all done by a spiritual leader or a pundit, it was condoned; no one in the family minded. It was better than getting one of the family men to sleep with the bride – though that also happens.'

Edward looked intrigued, and there was a wicked twinkle in his eyes.

'So though I'm not exactly a spiritual leader, I could fit in very well in India?'

'Definitely in ancient India . . .' I laughed.

'Not any more?' The corners of his mouth turned down comically.

Perhaps this was my moment to let him know the real reason I was there – but I thought I should be cautious and not reveal my hand, just yet.

'Actually there are quite a few IVF clinics who may be

interested in you because of the colour of your skin! Nobody wants babies who are brown like me.'

I smiled at him reassuringly.

'Of course, *talking* about sperm donation may be a problem, but *doing* it shouldn't be a problem. We know all about it because our mythological texts are full of similar cases.'

'Such as ?'

'Such as the Mahabharata. You've heard of it ?'

Edward nodded.

'But do you know that almost every single male figure in that epic was illegitimate? That is, their own fathers were impotent?'

He looked intrigued.

I was in full flow now: showing off. Despite my scruffy exterior he could appreciate my epic knowledge!

'That's right. So our mythology is full of surrogate fathers, who were usually gods, or maybe just potent macho men, who, er, supplied the . . .' I hesitated, teasingly.

He supplied the word.

'Sperm.'

I smiled back over the rim of my wine glass.

'Thank you. Bit odd, isn't it? So historically we've actually got this so-called new fertility rite already well ingrained in us. Which is why I guess I can be so relaxed with you.'

I tried to look as cosmopolitan as I could. A woman of the world, I did this every day.

My tactic seemed to be working. He seemed slightly more interested in me. For a moment I imagined what our child could be like if I gave up my reluctance to be a full-time mother to a bawling infant.

He or she would be quite lovely, probably paler-skinned than me, and with Edward's blue eyes and our shared darkish hair. The thought came to me unbidden – would she look like baby Amelia?

Even as I tried to concentrate on the present, I had to admire the ease of assisted reproduction.

It was such a simple way of doing things. No strings attached. We didn't need to go through the whole mating ritual of wooing and wedding; we just jumped straight into baby-making mode. I imagined my mother holding our child and she looked very happy. Very, very happy, indeed.

I was miles away from home, but already acting as though I could slip into motherhood. This was dangerous territory. Even if this were a proper discussion about making a child with Edward, the prospect, though tempting, was riddled with risks.

Yet my enthusiastic endorphins were getting in the way of my real reluctance about becoming a parent. I knew he was the last man I should be attracted to – and he could even be dangerous – but there was something oddly appealing about this sperm donor. His secret weapon was his charm – which did not, frankly, manifest itself on the Internet. Could I have been mistaken about him, after all?

I indulged in another fantasy. Edward wearing the traditional turban, with the *sehra* of flowers veiling his face, cantering up on a horse to marry me . . . somehow it didn't quite work. On the other hand, I could imagine us surrounded by a sea of babies – but what if he wasn't the man he appeared to be? In that case any involvement with him might hurt not just me – but baby Amelia, as well.

I imagined my mother once more, and this time she was no longer looking pleased, instead she said sternly, '*It's ridiculous to smile and flirt like this*', as she shook her finger at me. It worked. It always had, since I was five years old.

Blinking, I forced myself back to reality. Perhaps the flight and the wine I had made me lightheaded. I had to focus on why I was here.

'So what happens next?' I asked.

'Well, depends on what you're looking for. Have you had yourself checked up in India and are you already taking the drugs to induce, umm, ovulation ? Sorry, I have to say these things. It might be very disappointing if you're not prepared.'

I looked away and nodded. I didn't want him to guess that I was lying.

'Then let's meet on any day that's good for you – and I can do the necessary . . .' He sounded slightly bashful but matter-of-fact.

'You mean we should meet on my most fertile day?'

The red wine was helping me say things I never thought I would say to a man, let alone on our first meeting.

'Exactly. As I said in my email.'

'Do I . . . do we . . .' I stopped because I was so embarrassed. I wanted to ask: *Do we have to sleep together?* According to his website, he was flexible about his methods. He could try 'natural insemination' if I wanted, or he could provide me with his 'fresh' sperm, which I could then inject into myself, a kind of do-it-yourself fertility rite. I had checked. The 'ejaculate' would be given to me in a bowl and I would then quickly transfer it into a syringe and push the plunger between my thighs straight into my waiting womb. No human contact required. What had the modern world come to? Two total strangers would meet over a glass of wine (and cold milk) to plan their future child, who would start his or her journey to life in a plastic bowl.

He misunderstood my hesitation.

'Simran.' He now looked at me very carefully. 'I have to spell out a few ground rules. Because, you know, I've had a couple of bad experiences. Remember this is not a romance. Therefore, even if we go ahead, we mustn't meet too often or get involved with each other. I know that women from your, er, culture may get easily hurt because you've been brought up in a much more cloistered environment . . .' His voice trailed away, and he stared into the distance. Obviously he had prepared this speech before coming here. I was touched by his assumption that I was emotionally vulnerable. Where had he got his idea of Indian women from? And if only he knew why I was really here. He would have got up and fled.

However, in a way, he was right. It had to be said. I knew of one woman who thought she could handle it when a friend offered to father her child. She forgot it was like a business transaction and actually fell in love with him. But after getting her pregnant the man wasn't interested any more. Now she is an emotional wreck, looking after a child without a father. There was a very good chance that Edward had experienced everything, with all kinds of women (a hundred at least, by my rapid calculations!): the women who were simple and easy, the others who were more complicated and clung to him, and then others who never wanted to see him again.

I rubbed my tired eyes. My God, had he guessed that I had, fleetingly, imagined an involvement with him? Though I wouldn't blame him. Why else would I have travelled thousands of miles to see him?

Suddenly cool-headed, I forced a detached look at him. I needed to remember about baby Amelia and that this was nothing more than an act. To ensure he was trapped, pursued and prosecuted.

I shrugged.

'I'm no chicken, as my mother would say. And don't get me wrong – but I wouldn't fly halfway around the world to find a lover . . . this is an arrangement, nothing else – to get a specific outcome, as you know.'

I forced a soft tone back into my voice, which was beginning to sound harsh, even to my own ears.

'So you haven't told me as yet . . . why did you start on this . . . philanthropic pursuit?' I took another sip of wine.

Hopefully he would tell me what I wanted to hear, and then I could catch the next flight home.

'A friend asked me. She was desperate for a child and she and her husband just couldn't have one. In those days there was no Internet. She couldn't Google a sperm donor – and IVF wasn't so well known or freely discussed. She came home one afternoon and we slept together

'I didn't know what I would feel if she had a baby and how I would react when I saw the child. So we made a pact that in case she had a child we wouldn't meet again. We said goodbye and I never saw her again.'

'And then?'

'Because I didn't hear from her, I assumed that the experiment had worked. A year earlier, my own girlfriend had died in an accident. After her death, I don't think I ever wanted to be in a relationship with anyone. But when I helped my friend have a child a new meaning crept into my life. In a strange way, I think it made me a better person. So the word got around – and now I've put my name on a donor website, to be more accessible.'

'It's strange that you never fell in love again,' I couldn't help remarking.

'I still miss my girlfriend – she was one of a kind. Had we frozen her eggs, her memory would have lived on in our child. That's the thought that kept me going and why I wanted to help others. My own loss was the motivator.

So I suppose I did my best to survive, and all this . . . grew into a vocation.'

I sympathized with his grief, reminded of my own childhood friend, Abhi, lost possibly forever, trapped in an endless sleep.

'I know what it is to lose someone close to you.'

He looked at me, surprised.

'So you do understand?' he said.

I didn't want to speak about Abhi so I changed the subject.

'I'm still puzzled why someone like you doesn't donate to clinics.'

I wondered if he was connected to Mybaby.com.

'I prefer being, literally, a freelancer.'

There was a moment's silence as I realized that now could be the time to tell him the real reason behind our meeting. I began to put the right words together in my mind. I didn't want to scare him away.

I started to say something and then stopped. I remembered baby Amelia's face, pale and wan. Her helplessness. The oxygen incubator that kept her alive. All that came in a furious rush into my mind and in stark contrast – this man sitting across from me, his insouciance annoyed me.

'Shall I call you and fix our appointment?' I asked, finally, gulping down my anger. I knew I had to learn a lot more about him before I could tell him what I suspected. I still had to pretend I wanted a child from him.

Edward may have sensed my slight withdrawal. He raised his eyebrows, picking up his sleek helmet to strap it on. Now he looked like a long black beetle, about to fly away on his bicycle.

Did he realize I was hiding something from him? To my relief, his smile said it all – he didn't really mind my obvious reticence. Why should he? His whole life was comprised of brief encounters.

'Take care, Simran. But I hope you've planned to be here for some time?'

'Just for around ten days.'

He raised his eyebrows.

'Don't you want to stay on and see if it's worked? I don't want to be rude but the older you are the longer it takes. Have you ever done this before?'

I could be completely truthful, for once, and shook my head. 'Maybe I'll stay on if it's required.'

He waved cheerfully, and then he was gone.

The last few moments with Edward had made me feel exceedingly uncomfortable.

Something wasn't quite right today. Or was it my own guilt for having flirted with him, however briefly? I ordered another glass of wine.

My phone buzzed. It was too early for anyone in India so I assumed it was a message from my phone provider, welcoming me to London. I glanced at it – and my blood ran cold. Someone was definitely unhappy seeing me in London.

The SMS said in capital letters: 'YOU'RE WASTING YOUR TIME. GO HOME BEFORE ITS TOO LATE.'

Not only was the apostrophe withheld, so was the number.

Suddenly London didn't feel so friendly any more. I looked around, wondering if someone had seen me with Edward. It was odd that the message arrived after he left. Had I fallen into a trap?

My thoughts went back to the baby in the hospital in India. I no longer felt confident I could help her or even sort out the mystery behind her birth and her illness.

I quickly drained my glass and decided to leave along with a bunch of tourists, feeling safe in the crowd. But I still felt uneasy – very few people knew I was here. And I had kept my meeting with Edward highly confidential.

This message sounded like it could be dangerous both for me and for baby Amelia. What had I stumbled on to?

Eight months earlier

AUGUST
LONDON

Kate stood outside the Baby Gap store on Long Acre and, just to calm herself, walked in to look at the fresh stock of baby clothes for the autumn. It was crazy to do this, because in the bottom drawer of her wardrobe and in a suitcase upstairs in the attic were a whole variety of children's garments, from frilly caps to fur-lined boots for newborns. She had frocks and shirts and shorts and tiny coats. Even milk bottles and cuddly toys. She had hidden it all from Ben because she knew her obsession would worry him. He did not realize how much it soothed her to walk into a shop which contained the stuff of her dreams.

She picked up a shopping basket and automatically began filling it with all kinds of baby wear. Fluffy mittens and trousers no bigger than a palm. Pink frocks and ribboned socks. Slowly her anxiety receded. She had almost convinced herself that she was going to have the baby this time. Just that morning she had rearranged the living room to make space for a cradle near the sofa so that she and Ben could watch TV in the evening while the baby slept, and had even checked online for the nursery schools nearby. She had registered herself with a child-minding agency. In fact, she had done everything to reassure herself, including wearing a lightly cross-stitched loose smock, even though she was only three months gone and it was far too early to show.

Maternity-style jeans were next on the agenda. She was looking forward to the growing 'bump' which would change her life. Perhaps she would even get herself photographed, posing like Demi Moore did for Annie Leibovitz for the cover of *Vanity Fair*, naked, with a huge pregnant belly.

Ben would love that; she could plan it as a surprise, later in the year. Perhaps she would do it for his birthday? Later in the day she planned to meet a friend, Marie, who had three children, and chalk out the next six months with her, so that she could organize a good diet-and-exercise regime and not gain too much weight.

In the evening, her mother had asked her to come over for an early dinner. Kate did not go over too often, but she knew that she would not have much time after the baby was born. And since her father's death she'd felt a little more responsible for her mother. Her mother who had never really forgiven her for leaving home early and plunging into a fulltime television career. It had created a distance between them that was difficult to bridge, but Kate knew that her mother was hoping that the baby would bring them closer together again. The child was important in so many different ways.

The fact was that Kate had even given up her job last year so that she could spend all her time planning this new 'production'. Prior to that she had been making programmes exclusively for Channel Four, mostly on multicultural themes. It had meant frequent travel to India and Pakistan, though now Kate did not want to go anywhere. She missed her career, but her pregnancy was a mission and, like everything in her life, she felt compelled to achieve 100 per cent success.

Ben shared her interest in Asia, partly because he was a financial consultant and the Asian economies were booming, and partly because his grandfather had been in India with the British Army in the 1930s. He had carefully (and proudly) preserved the memorabilia and photographs of his grandfather's sojourn. Major Mark Riley had been an intrepid explorer and someday Ben planned to go back and retrace his footsteps. Perhaps even publicize his exploits a little, as he had learnt that he was quite a hero – fighting almost singlehandedly to suppress a rebellious mob while posted at Ambala, in India. He had been severely wounded in the skirmish and then forced to return to England with his newly wedded wife.

But there were other things which intrigued Ben about his grandfather's life in India.

There was a whiff of a scandal. Fleeting references in his grandfather's diary – about an Indian woman, the nightmares he had about her – made him curious. Could she be the reason that he had so rarely spoken about the five years he had spent as a bachelor in Ambala?

It was whispered in the family that, before his grandmother arrived in India on the infamous 'fishing fleet', along with other single women searching for British husbands, he had had a *bibighar*, as did so many of his colleagues.

In this 'house for a wife' he had kept a beautiful, dark woman, whose eyes were the colour of honey, who was his first and only love. His grandmother had alluded to it, with some bitterness, after his grandfather's death. But she said it was a closed chapter – and she wouldn't speak about it. The whole thing was a mystery.

Ben's mother had often wondered if they would, one day, stumble upon some Indian cousins. Or indeed, if they themselves had Indian blood in them. Kate sometimes teased Ben that his brown eyes and curly black hair might be a throwback to that woman his grandfather had left behind.

There was only one sepia-toned and fading photograph of the woman, standing at the entrance of an arched veranda, wearing a knee-length shirt over loose pyjamas. Her head was covered but there was a fragile silver ornament just visible, dangling from her hair like lace on the left side.

On one of her trips to India, Kate had discovered that this piece of jewellery was called a *jhaalar*, and she bought one: an intricately carved silver piece that, when pinned on to her hair, gave her a rather rakish look. She had plaited her golden hair and wrapped a dupatta around her face and even put a small red dot between her eyebrows. But for her blue eyes and fair skin, she looked very much like the mistress, that mysterious resident of the *bibighar*. Ben immediately took a photograph of Kate and placed it next to the one his grandfather had taken. They looked oddly similar.

'Women in love,' he observed teasingly. 'They all look the same.'

And it was true that, after meeting Ben, something changed in Kate: she just knew that her search for love was over. But this time round she had wanted to take it slowly. Savour every minute and allow the relationship to mature.

Like almost all her recent relationships, this had begun at work, as Ben was a consultant on her documentary about the rise of Asian markets. Even though she hadn't planned on marriage, it seemed perfectly normal when he proposed to her in the editing room, barely three months after they had met. While they were viewing some shots, he had suddenly caught her hand and slipped on a diamond ring. Why would she have refused? It was perfect.

He had also brought a bottle of champagne. They wandered out of the editing suite on to the balcony and drank straight from the bottle, staring out at the lights of London reflected on the Thames. Later he confessed that he knew there was no need to spend so much time with her, editing a show in which he only played a tiny role. After all, he had a fulltime job as a financial analyst. But he knew this was one way they could get to know each other. It was better than spending time in noisy pubs and restaurants. They could talk and discuss ideas; find out if they could spend the rest of their lives together.

'Even if we have children, you mustn't ever give up working,' he told her.

'And since both of us will be travelling so much, no chance of ever having kids, I think!' Kate laughed, holding out her hand to see if the diamond on her finger caught the glitter from the neon lights blazing around them.

Sometime around her thirty-sixth birthday, however, she became broody, aware that her fertile years were soon going to be over. She approached her 'baby project' with the same fervour with which she had launched her documentaries.

Ben was surprised, since he knew how much her work meant to her.

'Remember, kids can be demanding – you may have to take a very long break,' he pointed out.

'So will you, buddy,' she retorted, attempting to chuck him under the chin.

He ducked the left hook.

'So how many kids have you planned?' he asked, hastily closing his book as she pushed it on to the floor and sat on his lap. She was already unbuttoning his shirt.

'Two, to begin with? One for you and one for me?'

It was only when Kate had her first miscarriage that they realized that maybe they had been a little too complacent and that she needed to take more care of herself. Had she been overdoing things?

The second miscarriage last year was even more depressing for both of them – but to Kate it felt like a strangely personal blow, as her mantra until then had been 'you can always get what you want'. How had this happened? She looked around and saw her brothers and their toddlers, as well as her own friends with children, and her heart became ice cold with envy, though she had never been jealous before of anyone or anything. Her life had been challenging but she had always managed to beat the odds. This was a huge, unexpected setback, and one over which she had no control. It enraged her. How could her body let her down like this?

The investigation showed up an ectopic pregnancy, and the doctor had warned her that more problems could lie ahead. But she convinced herself that things would be better the next time round. Ben, who had been very distressed by it all, was much more reluctant about trying for a child again, and so soon. He needed more time to mourn the death of their unborn baby. She, on the other hand, thought that the only way she could overcome her grief was to try to have a child, no matter what.

Ben realized how serious the situation was when he came home one night to find her in the room they had kept for their unborn child. It had been painted a primrose yellow and filled with every possible toy a child might ask for. She had thoroughly enjoyed decorating it.

But now she sat on the floor, carefully taking out the baby clothes that she had bought, folding them into neat piles and putting them back into the cupboards. Her fierce concentration was frightening.

He sat down next to her, still in his office suit, while she continued to work her way through the clothes. She barely noticed him.

'Are you looking for something?' he asked her, hesitant about breaking her trance, but worried.

Kate tucked her hair behind her ears absently.

'No, it just makes me feel . . . better. One day we will use these for our child.'

'Of course we will.' He reached out and stilled her hands as she folded the clothes over and over again. 'Why don't you give these away? We can always get new ones.'

'Why should we do that?'

Because I hate the thought of you just sitting at home and doing nothing but making lists – of baby names, baby clothes, baby food. When will you go back to being my wife? He wanted to say all of that, but stopped himself.

She could not bring herself to give away her maternity dresses, and continued reading books about the various stages of child development as though she were still pregnant with their lost child. It made him increasingly nervous, but he said nothing, as telling her that their dream was over was even more difficult. He couldn't bear her silent tears when she saw other mothers walking with their children, or nursing them.

In the end, he realized that it would be healthier for her if they tried for another child, but it was no longer fun. Sex had become like a routine practised in a factory environment, with temperature charts and scientifically selected dates. If he had to travel during a fertile period, he knew there would be hell to pay. Without letting Kate know, he began to juggle assignments so that he could be in town during those crucial dates while his colleagues went in his place. He lost some lucrative work – but what the hell, it would be worth it in the end.

But somehow he always knew he was fooling himself.

So today, when the call came, he knew he would have to skip the board meeting he had been preparing for all week. He tried not to think about why he had to rush to hospital. He hated to think of her face, and the unhappiness trapped in her eyes like dying embers just before the rain came down. This time it would be much worse. He just knew it.

Still on Long Acre, Kate had actually ignored the cramps at first and had continued shopping. Then she asked for a chair and sat down, breathing deeply. She would not allow the baby to go. She called her doctor, who was an old school friend, and in between her ragged breaths explained the agony.

Luckily, he happened to be at the hospital and asked her to come immediately. But Kate could not move. She knew that if she went to the hospital the baby would be jinxed. Her dream would end.

It was actually the shop assistant who found her, bent over, trying to stop herself from crying. It was she who picked up Kate's mobile phone from the floor and called Ben. At that moment Kate hated her – she was quite sure that if she had been left alone she might have saved her child. It was only when a small crowd began to gather around that she was finally persuaded to get into the waiting cab and head for the hospital where Ben would be waiting.

Ben missed his board meeting and spent the next two nights sitting next to her hospital bed.

She refused to speak or eat anything, and lay there with her eyes closed, loathing the unfairness of it all. This time she had done everything correctly. She had followed all the rules, so why had the child been snatched from her again?

GURGAON

Subhash opened the door and walked into the long corridor, which in turn opened, on either side, into the special rooms. The passage in front of him was sleek and curved and the lighting soft and natural, creating a sense of buoyancy. It looked like a happy place. Even the benches and chairs scattered about were designed with elegance and painted in bright colours.

He had always said that it was essential these facilities were properly planned. Marketing was very important these days. He had just seen some photographs of the other clinics coming up rapidly in the country, as demand was growing, and he felt that their standards were not as high as at Madonna and Child.

He was shocked to see that in one of the most popular and well-known clinics the surrogates were kept on rope *charpoys* in an open ward. They had no privacy. Nor were the donors or commissioning parents able to spend time with them on their own, and this was proving to be a liability. Therefore Subhash had insisted that each gestational mother in his clinic would get a separate room. Of course, the size and space would differ according to the rates charged, but at least he would try to avoid the comparisons that sprang to mind most often: of breeding stables, of bitches in kennels. He wanted to humanize this process, make it pleasant.

Some problems remained. The commissioning parents who lived abroad were unable to understand that there were cultural issues about what these women could or could not eat and that there were local replacements for certain kinds of Western food. So the food packets kept arriving along with clothes for the surrogates. It was impossible to explain that these women had little experience of tin openers and had never eaten baked beans, ham or tuna. All kinds of peculiar requests related to diets had to be dealt with, and sometimes it was better to just pretend that orders had been followed.

'Simon loves ham sandwiches. We are quite sure the baby would like to try some too.' The note still lay on his desk, though he had managed to persuade Simon and Harriet Perkins that their unborn child would get its protein mainly from lentils and eggs.

And the next problematic item on the list was corned beef. Why would anyone think that Indians liked beef? Most of them worshipped cows. The beef was usually just thrown out with the rubbish.

But barely would he have got rid of the last batch of unnecessary items than a fresh consignment of tins and assorted biscuits and clothes would arrive in his office. Even if the parents were thousands of miles away, they still wanted to think they were feeding their child, and looking after it, albeit through the woman who was carrying it. Even though she would never in her life wear a gingham mini skirt (which one American parent had sent!).

Expectations had to be managed constantly. And the women had to be groomed in many ways.

In the common room, he saw them crowding around a facilitator, Simran Singh, Anita's cousin and a social worker, who had helped them set up a support system by hiring unemployed teachers. Every morning there would be an inspection of personal hygiene. Basic skills like knitting and sewing were encouraged so that the surrogate mothers would have something to do while they were at the clinic.

Unaware that she was being observed, Simran stood in her crumpled cotton saree and equally crushed blouse, intent on turning the surrogates into eager students.

As Subhash walked up, the women retreated, smiling but unsure what the doctorsahib was doing there.

Simran beckoned Preeti forward. As usual Subhash could not help but notice a slight jump in his pulse rate at the sight of Preeti. The woman was so darned attractive, even though she wore no makeup today and just a simple polyester saree. She was pregnant and glowing.

'Show doctorsahib what you've learnt today.'

Preeti slowly wrote her name in the English alphabet. It was correct, but the letters were all uneven, very much like a child's.

Her effort made Subhash inordinately proud.

'Well done!'

Her shyly mumbled 'thank you' sounded more like 'thunk oo' but at least she knew the right response.

Subhash gestured to the rest of the women to sit down, and resisted looking at her again. He turned to Simran, who was also a good friend.

'Can I tell you how grateful we are that you're doing all this for us? Especially since I know how much you dislike the whole business!' His wry look was reflected in her eyes.

He did not say how very impressed he was with her, knowing that, as a wealthy woman in her own right, she could have either chosen a less altruistic, more comfortable career, or just lounged around painting her nails! Why she preferred to spend her time either working in juvenile-detention centres, or sorting out problems for them at their hospital was inexplicable.

'I hope matron has distributed the food and the other gifts sent for the women?'

Simran nodded – keeping a steady smile on her face. She had obviously decided that she wasn't going to argue about anything in front of the women. Fair enough!

'Oh yes – and they are thrilled. But I better tell you that on the weekend they are going to take them to the bazaar and sell the stuff.'

Subhash ignored the remark. He didn't mind if the women made some money from the gifts. Considering that most of the women received only 3,000 rupees a month while they were carrying the child, with the full amount being cash-on-delivery, all these little sums helped to supplement their income during the nine long months.

Simran hadn't finished yet: 'But I do think that some of the gifts should be shared with the nursing staff and the ward boys too. The nurses would like the ham and beef tins.' The nurses were mostly Christian and so would not worry too much about Hindu or Muslim taboos.

Subhash shrugged resignedly. 'Just give whatever instructions you think fit – only keep them all happy, that's all I say! Many thanks. And when do we meet for dinner? It's the only way we can repay you for your help!'

Simran was rueful. 'You know Ma is looking forward to meeting you soon. So we must fix dinner – I'll check with her and get back to you with some dates?'

Subhash remembered that Simran's mother was trying to persuade her to at least freeze her eggs before it was 'too late'. And he also knew of Simran's resolute resistance to the idea – especially since she had already adopted a teenager, Durga.

Waving to the women, who were now beginning to relax a bit, and with a special smile to Preeti, Subhash left the room.

As he walked out, he could hear Simran once again start the English classes, before handing over to the other teacher standing alongside her. Skill-improvement, thought Subhash, was a damn good idea, but the women had a long way to go.

He bumped into Ashok Ganguly in the corridor, accompanied by Sharma who had a sheaf of certificates in his hand.

'So what's this?' Subhash asked.

'Sir, for the women. School leaving certificates.'

Subhash took them and went through them swiftly, and noticed that they were incomplete.

'They are stamped but the names are missing. You'll have to return them to the school.'

Ganguly began to laugh.

'You don't get it, do you? We are the ones who fill the names in.'

Subhash handed them back fast. He hated being involved in any of Ganguly's schemes. Ganguly knew how the 'system' worked. But Subhash tried to stick to the straight and narrow – always maintaining that what you don't know can't hurt you. Besides, Anita would be furious .

'I paid for them—' Sharmaji began to explain.

Subhash held up a hand to halt the confession. Ganguly thought he was like Gandhiji's three monkeys: see no evil, hear no evil, speak no evil. Fucking weak bastard – controlled by that woman!

'That's fine – some other time,' muttered Subhash, quickly moving away.

Ganguly was still chuckling. 'Relax, Subhash, these aren't college degrees – because we can't possibly pass them off as graduates! Only school. And only to placate the commissioning parents – even they know that the girls are too poor to have gone beyond . . .' He looked quizzically at Sharmaji who quickly glanced at the certificates.

'Class Ten.'

Subhash walked past feeling sorry for himself and for the women who would accept the false certificates as just another means for them to earn large sums of money legitimately. They would not even question the web of lies which surrounded their new identities. It was how the country functioned.

Not that surrogacy was easy anyway. There were so many physical issues to overcome – and then there were emotional problems as well. Many of them really did get attached to the child after they gave birth. Sometimes it was a huge wrench for them to promise never to see the baby again.

Perhaps, as Anita had pointed out, it was all the more difficult when a beautiful white baby emerged from between their dusky thighs, as though they had given birth to a god or goddess. It was a miracle they would remember for the rest of their lives – and their excitement was palpable.

One woman was convinced that the baby would never drink milk from her dark breasts and was astonished when the child happily clung on with a hungry, rosebud-red mouth. She forgot the pain of the delivery and kept gazing at the child in wonderment – till the weary moment when he was taken away. But in a sense she felt connected to the child as she still pumped out breast milk for him, which was carefully packaged and then sent off to Australia where the child would feed from it for at least three months.

Subhash reflected that globalization had made motherhood complex almost beyond belief – and its boundaries were constantly shifting, as everyone searched for the immaculate conception and birth.

He knew that Anita was far less sympathetic towards the surrogates. She was not as trusting as he was and she even suspected that the crying and wailing from the women at the time of saying goodbye was often just to give the foreign couple value for their money. She did not believe, as he did, that these women were being exploited. After all, she said, most of the surrogates were mercenary and not maternal. He wondered about that.

The situation was completely different to that in the US or Europe, where women were more educated; they knew their rights and they knew what they were getting into. In India, no self-respecting, educated woman from a middle-class background would agree to have another couple's baby – not unless there was a very compelling reason. In his hospital last year a mother had given birth to her own daughter's child, since the daughter was unable to carry an infant to full term.

The case had shocked the country and Indian families had woken up to the fact that a mystifying social change had arrived. IVF had not only transformed the destinies of women, it had also completely disrupted the idea of a family. Subhash, along with many millions of Indians, had pondered over the fate of the father of the child in this case. He had tried to imagine the bizarre situation in which the man was caught. Not only was his mother-in-law injected with his sperm, she was the mother of her own grandchild. Did that make him both the grandfather *and* the father?

But the mother had told Subhash and Anita that since her daughter had been born without a properly function-ing womb or vagina, they had no other choice. And he took a conscious decision to help her in whichever way he could.

As Subhash walked away through the new wing of the hospital, Ganguly abandoned Sharmaji with the certificates and decided to take stock of his favourite part of the hospital: the basement, where all the future business lay ensconced in liquefied nitrogen. Sperm and eggs from clients who wanted to take out an insurance on their ability to have children.

Ganguly had studied the many aspects to the business of assisted reproduction, especially its secrets and methodology.

Even though he had extensive files on the clients who came here, he often wondered what the sperm and eggs were really worth. This clinic could store them for half the price of those abroad, with a nice profit as well. But what if he, Ganguly, decided to use that sperm and those eggs and create a child without permission? It would have the same DNA as its parents. What price, thus, could he charge to prevent the *possibility* of misuse? Could he, for instance, blackmail anyone? It was an interesting thought.

Today Sharmaji had brought a girl who wanted to donate her eggs; he had left her in the basement to await Ganguly.

Dressed in a salwar kameez, she sat uneasily near the bed, tension writ large on her face as she twisted her handkerchief nervously in her hands. Her long hair was tied loosely in a plait.

'How old are you?'

The girl was thin, with visible blue veins sticking out of her skin. But she was quite fair, and had curly hair just as the client had demanded. The eggs were for an infertile Indian woman who was in her forties. She did not want her husband to know she was unable to have children. The eggs would be stored under her name.

Fortunately this girl would not ask any questions about where the eggs were to go.

The nurse stood by her side, and helped the girl on to the prepared bed. She looked frightened, but was already a little sleepy from the relaxant that had been given to her.

Ganguly wore his spectacles and began looking at the details, relieved that Sharmaji had done his homework properly this time. He hoped she wasn't a virgin, as that would make his task a little more difficult.

Nonetheless, it might be worth it. His hunch was that adolescent girls had better eggs, and were perhaps more robust where IVF was concerned, with fewer miscarriages.

He had some evidence of the latter. Recently he had groomed Radhika, a 16-year old who was pregnant with twins for Ludi and Nicolas, the gay couple from France. They had been told that she was a 22-year-old mother who needed the money to buy a flat. Luckily, since Radhika was well-built, no one questioned the fact.

She was a labourer from Rajasthan, working on a construction site where her husband had suffered a head injury. Sharma had found her by the roadside, weeping and distraught, and reassured her that he would get her husband admitted to hospital. And she, meanwhile, could earn some money through surrogacy. As the months went by he told her that her husband needed very expensive treatment. Part of the money Radhika earned through her surrogacy would go towards that. Radhika was not allowed to meet her husband – but she knew she was going to pay for his cure, anyway. Like a bonded slave, she was trapped by Sharma into (what he hoped was) an endless cycle of surrogacy. Now passed over to Ganguly, she became an ideal candidate for his experiments.

The data of Radhika's pregnancy was being collected and stored along with that of other older surrogates Ganguly had monitored. He was going to create multiple embryos, using the eggs he had harvested from younger girls like this one, to see if there was a qualitative difference there as well.

'How old are you?' he asked again.

'Fifteen.'

Even better.

'Why do you want to donate your eggs?'

'Money. I need . . . the money.'

'For what?'

The girl was getting increasingly groggy and could not respond clearly.

The nurse held her hand soothingly. The harvesting would be done under local anaesthesia, and she hoped that the girl would not bleed too much. She had already been given the required hormones some time ago.

'My father . . . lost . . . job . . .'

Ganguly determinedly focused on the task at hand. And this was the real difference between him and the Pandeys. He genuinely wanted to push the boundaries of medicine, whereas they just wanted to make sure the current procedures were properly followed.

For instance, while Subhash and Anita stuck to their natural deliveries, Ganguly backed caesareans. He insisted that an international clientele preferred to schedule their vacation break along with the birth of their child. Besides, it was a neat operation with minimum stress. So regardless of the requirement, more and more caesareans were being built into the busy delivery schedule at Madonna and Child. Mostly by him.

He did not always tell the Pandeys everything. Just as the little experiment in the basement with this young girl would not reach their ears. He had already warned the nurse that this was a private matter. She knew better than to ask him any questions. The only person he worried about was that social worker, Simran, who was always snooping around.

The thought of Simran irritated him, and his normally cheerful expression was wiped out for just a moment.

He roughly injected the local anaesthetic into the girl. The relaxant was also taking effect, and she gently went off to sleep.

Ganguly put on his mask and began to harvest the eggs as the girl slept. She moaned occasionally with the discomfort, but she was still asleep when she was wheeled out.

Meanwhile, on the first floor, Subhash continued his tour through the new wing. He opened the rooms being freshly prepared for the 'gestational mothers' and admired the soft colours and pale-cream carpeting. These rooms were laid out in a circular fashion – very much like a womb itself – and each bore the name of a flower in English: Rose, Petunia, Magnolia, Daffodil and so on. They had the imprint of that flower on the walls, the bedspreads and the curtains. Here too, Anita had argued against the extra expense, stating that it would be completely wasted on the women who would occupy them for nine months. But Subhash felt that the decor was important, especially as Ganguly was now trying to get more international investment into the hospital, and they were looking for a financial tie-up between their hospital and the UK's Mybaby.com. Mumbai's Freedom Hospital, of which Ganguly often spoke, was also on the growing list of possible investors.

Admiring his own good taste, Subhash completed his inspection.

Then he spotted Anita at the end of the corridor, waiting impatiently as he emerged from the last room.

'When was the consignment of embryos from the UK due to arrive?'

He winced because more and more, these days, her voice carried a tinge of impatience, as though she were speaking to a confirmed idiot. He tried not to get angry, because he knew she was tense about their huge debts and the nine-month gestation for each child – which delayed any immediate return.

'They had said they would try to sort out the problem. It's odd that they are saying it's illegal. I know that we can't export but since when has importing embryos become an issue?'

'God knows!'

'Let me try the couriers once again. I thought I had given you the number this morning?'

'You did and I tried. They gave me some garbled story. They want us to go to Mumbai to identify the consignment.'

'Oh fuck!' Subhash felt a sudden sharp stab of anxiety. He looked around the beautiful womb-like space soon to be filled with expectant surrogates and the international couples who were going to pay for everything. 'We've been chasing this consignment for more than a month. What the bloody hell is going on?'

DELHI

Lying in the hospital bed, Sonia clearly remembered the day, one month ago, when her life altered forever. She had been thinking of her meeting with Dr Subhash Pandey and how the surrogacy would change her life.

Just as she had reached home from the hospital Rohit, the 'cousin' she lived with, had slapped her so hard she was knocked to the ground. Wiping her hand across her face she found blood on her palm. Her nose felt swollen. *Chootiya saala* – the *haramzaada* always hit her on the face. Her right cheek felt inflamed and her arm was hurting because it had taken the full weight of her body when she fell on the mud floor. As she attempted, slowly and painfully, to get up, the tiny room in which she lived swayed alarmingly from side to side.

'Who told you to leave the house?' Rohit stood, large, muscular and frightening in front of her.

'I had some work.' Her voice seemed far away and weak, even to her own ears. She sounded as if she was lying and she knew it would infuriate him.

Rohit grabbed her long hair and pulled her towards the light.

'You know I can burn you with this bulb – and you'll remember my words forever. Never, ever go anywhere without my permission.'

She nodded, almost fainting from the pain, feeling as though her scalp was on fire. When would she ever be able to escape him?

'Get ready. Someone is coming to see you just now.'

He threw a brightly coloured saree on the bed and walked out, slamming the door. She slid back on to the floor like a collapsed doll. She had thought the hospital visit would buy her some freedom, but this bastard had other plans. Yet maybe if she told him about the money he might be tempted not to pimp her any more. She had wanted to use the money for her children's education, but perhaps the money for the first surrogacy could be used to pay off Rohit and get rid of him. And then she could have another baby – and that money could be sent home to her children. She had tried to keep her surrogacy plans from him but it was becoming increasingly difficult.

Slowly Sonia opened her eyes and got up. Pouring some water out of a plastic bottle she washed her face, carefully cleaning around her nose and holding the wet end of her saree on it to stop the bleeding.

Changing her clothes, she looked into the mirror hanging on the side of the room. She patted some powder on her face to cover the discoloration around her eye. Having learnt to count every small blessing she thanked God he had only hit her face. Luckily, she still had something left to sell, she thought, putting her arms around her abdomen and pressing it as the doctor had done. She must protect her womb somehow.

Rohit pulled the flimsy plywood door open and stood there with another, thinner man.

'This is Anil, and here is the lovely Sonia. Take good care of her.'

He pushed Anil inside the tiny aluminium-roofed hut and shut the door again. Arrogant bastard. He had never even bothered to ask if she was feeling up to it. Sonia knew he would be sitting outside for the next hour, smoking and having a drink, before he would knock on the door again if Anil hadn't finished with her. She wondered how much he had taken from Anil and she was nervous – now more than ever it was essential that she did not pick up any disease or get pregnant. She dared not ask Rohit if he had remembered to give Anil any condoms. After the earlier violence she did not want to upset him again. Had Anil been one of her regulars, she would have persuaded him to be considerate, but she had never seen him before. If he walked out on her, she knew Rohit would beat her to a pulp.

She could not pretend to have her period, either, because Rohit would know it was a lie and embarrass her in front of this man.

As she began to undress she remembered the malt whisky 'borrowed' from the Health Minister's bar, still hidden under the bed.

She looked at Anil, who was gazing at her hungrily. He had sat down on the edge of the bed and pulled out his shirt from his trousers, unzipping them as he did so.

She stood near the bed and removed her blouse. He pulled her breasts to his mouth and began to suck her nipples.

'Are you thirsty?' she asked.

He looked up and smiled through tobacco-stained broken teeth.

'If the thirsty don't come to the well where will they go?'

She pushed his hands away from her breasts and then bent down to take out the whisky from under the bed. His eyes widened with excitement. This was far more than he had hoped for.

She put a finger to her lips.

'You can drink from both the wells – but slowly and quietly. He will get really mad if he thinks we are having too much fun.' She made a face, and wagged her finger at him. 'No fun. Not allowed. I am a bad girl, you are a bad, bad boy!'

Anil laughed as she poured him a stiff drink. She knew he would want another. She pretended to resist him and then with another 'Bad girl, bad boy!' she poured a little for herself and a large shot for him. She helped him remove his shirt and, as the *coup de grâce*, gave him the bottle to drink from. He lay there and gulped from it, while she slowly took her saree off. She took her time, knowing that he was getting excited watching her undress.

As he drained the bottle she came closer, and made him recline back with his head against the wall, pulling down his trousers a little. She groped between his legs and, finding him somewhat erect, started massaging him, hoping he would be too drunk to want to come inside her. He moaned under her steady ministrations and after shuddering a little, sighed, lay back and almost immediately fell asleep.

Sonia wiped his semen from her hands with his shirt and once again washed her face and hands. She swiftly hid the nearly empty whisky bottle again under the bed, trembling with nervousness. She had saved her womb this time round but she might not manage it another time.

'What have you done to him, *saala*?' Rohit stood at the door. He looked at the figure of Anil on the bed, half-naked and snoring, and laughed. 'You witch, you've sucked the life out of him.'

She smiled nervously, never sure if his remarks were actually meant as a joke or if he was going to get angry with her.

'You know he is the new assistant in Madam Renu Mishra's office. Keeping him happy will keep us all happy!'

Rohit was a peon at the home of the Delhi Health Minister, Renu Mishra, and so he knew most of the staff there. Sometimes when he wanted a special favour he would bring one of them from the house and make Sonia sleep with him. But he was careful not to do it too often as he did not want word to get around. He said she was his lucky mascot. He had no doubt that one day he too would be able to sit on a chair next to the Chief Minister; he had seen so many bag carriers make the jump from being a lowly peon to a political player. You only needed to know how to do it. Sonia was an important part of his plans.

He looked at her fondly and pushed his hand between her thighs, rubbing her roughly as he did so.

'You're not wet, bitch.'

'He didn't excite me – like you do,' Sonia lied, as she kissed his neck. She swiftly wrapped her saree around her and buttoned her blouse. 'Let's go out before he wakes up. I want to talk to you about something. I think I know how we can make a little bit money. I don't want to say anything in front of him just in case—'

Rohit's eyes narrowed. Sonia's breath stopped for a minute. She forced herself to laugh.

'You think only you can dream of a better future for us? I can too, you know. And you know what – you don't have to do anything at all. The money just pours down from America, from London, from Australia . . .' Her head was spinning again, but she kept laughing, her eyes fixed on his face. Rohit briefly looked at the sleeping Anil, then he shrugged and walked out.

She quickly followed.

He was always ready to listen to a way to make money, but she hoped he wouldn't lose his temper when he heard about this. She must remember to tell him that there was no body contact. Only an injection, thank God.

. . . All that was before everything went haywire, before she had her crazy idea, and lost her freedom. Why had she made such a foolish suggestion about the baby? Why hadn't she realized she would immediately become a pawn in a very complicated game?

Every moment of that fateful day played out in front of her eyes as she now looked around the hospital room.

This would be her new home for eight more months. It felt more and more like a prison.

MUMBAI

Malti's attitude towards her husband, Diwan Nath Mehta, had completely changed after his photograph appeared in the newspapers a few weeks ago. Even though it was almost as tiny as a thumbnail, it was something he took out of his desk drawer and looked at fairly frequently.

The photographers at the press conference had crowded around the table at the Customs and Excise office, gazing at the milk-can-shaped jars, while Nazir Ali flexed his muscles and smiled at the mystified reporters. Most of them were his regular pals, kept happy with occasional confiscated whisky and cigarette cartons. They came when he called and once a year he managed to tip them off about a good story to follow. Usually if the story was a success there would be an alcohol-fuelled party at a bar down the road, so when Ali invited them, they came. A bit of confiscated cocaine always found its way into the celebrations, to add that extra frisson.

Ali gestured to Mehta, who scurried out to the other room to bring in trays of tea and biscuits, which the office peon helped him pass around.

'Good. Good, banjo.' Ali slapped him fondly on the back. He had taken off his jacket and rolled his shirt-sleeves up so that the photographers could admire his biceps and triceps. Some of the cameramen began to shoot him.

'Better than Salman bhai. *Yaar*, you must have eight-pack abs . . .'

The cameraman winked at his colleague; it was an invitation to Ali to remove his shirt. Salman, the Hindi cinema actor in question, was well known for his penchant for pulling off his clothes and dancing to reveal his muscular physique. Ali looked tempted and then thought better of it.

He put on his jacket once more. The point had been made.

'We'll do a separate session for that. Today the focus is our haul of these . . . human specimens.'

A wave of shock ran through the room and cameras started flashing, while the TV crew began to zoom in on the gleaming milk cans, as though they expected a Frankenstein's Monster-like gnarled hand to suddenly smash its way through the blandly shining stainless steel.

'Do they contain body parts?' said a cameraman, creeping as close as he could to the top of one milk can, and cautiously shooting it.

'These cans contain human embryos . . . which will become human bodies . . . and their parts.'

There was momentary silence as the group absorbed the information.

'But I know that embryos have been imported in the past and there has been no problem with that,' one of the girls behind the camera suddenly spoke up. Ali jumped at her voice – he hadn't noticed her all this while. 'In fact, for the past two years at least, hospitals in Mumbai, in Delhi and even in Gujarat have been inserting these imported embryos into surrogate mothers. So why didn't you stop them earlier?'

Ali felt a little uneasy seeing this underage-looking thin girl among the thick throng of testosterone.

He had a very personal reason why he had to stop this embryo implantation and he wasn't going to allow anyone to deter him. He had to think very carefully and answer her without allowing his irritation to show.

He still hadn't got used to the idea that women report-ers were being sent to cover the really tough departments like Customs and Excise. It was difficult for him to build any closeness with them – and passing on confiscated liquor to them was unthinkable. He made a note of the TV channel she represented. He must talk to the boss. Thank God the *saala* had sent a banjo cameraman, at least – though these days these *chootiyas* were telling women to do everything. Fucking motherfuckers.

'Madam, that is a very good point.' He smoothly adopted a conciliatory, well-modulated tone. 'You are correct. But two wrongs do not make a right, *haina*? The fact of the matter is that, if I could kindly inform you – so far there has been no proper law given to us. Now please may we read you this very important document. See – the British may have ill-treated us and put Gandhiji in jail, but they knew that the law is the law. Am I correct? So in 1898 – mind you, more than a hundred years ago – they knew that they had to ban certain products from coming into the country. You know these things coming in can ruin the environment – spread disease. This law was only very recently amended – and if I may just pass it around . . .?' Ali nodded at Mehta. 'Read it to them.'

Mehta cleared his throat and began reading, manfully:

'The Liverstock Importation Act, 1898.'

Impervious to a few sniggers from the audience, he doggedly kept repeating 'Liver', and slowly the sniggers grew into a loud laugh every time he said it. Ali looked on benignly. Press conferences were known for their mayhem. This too would follow the time-honoured tradition. He knew it was 'livestock ' and not 'liverstock' – but Mehta could have said 'Woodstock' and it would have made no difference to the journalists. At the end of the day they would only refer to his brief press release, partake of the hospitality and write whatever they felt like. The rest was just fluff and 'time-pass'. *'The Liverstock Importation Act, 1898, has been recently amended vide the Liverstock Importation open brackets Amendment close brackets Ordinance, 2001, which was promulgated on five full stop seven full stop 2001.*

'Prior to amendment, the said Act was applicable only for liverstock whereas the liverstock products were not regulated under the Act. The amendment to the said Act has been made to regulate the import of liverstock products in such a manner that these imports do not adversely affect the human and animal

health population of the country. Under the said Liverstock Importation Act, 1898, the Department of Animal Husbandry and Dairying has issued a notification on seven full stop seven full stop 2001 to regulate the import of liverstock products namely firstly meat and meat products of all kinds including fresh, chilled and frozen meat, tissue or organs of poultry, pig, sheep, goat; secondly, egg and egg powder; thirdly, milk and milk products; fourthly, bovine, ovine and caprine embryos, ova or semen; and fifthly, pet food products of animal origin . . .'

He droned on, mispronouncing most of the words.

After he finished, he took a deep breath and exhaled slowly, looking around at the reporters with obvious relief. A few were nodding off, others were doodling, but most of them looked bored and uncomprehending, waiting for him to finish.

Ali tapped the desk and cleared his throat. Everyone looked at him.

'Now, I want to know: did this say anything about human embryos? Nothing, *haina*? Where is the mention? There should have been at least some mention, no? There should be a law about it. But there is no law. If there was we would have it – it is not mentioned anywhere in this document.'

'Well, does that mean it is forbidden?' It was that girl again.

Ali took a careful sip of his tea.

'It does not mean it is allowed, either, and this is the only law in front of me right now. Till this matter is clarified I will not allow these human parts to leave this office.' He sat back triumphantly. 'And what if these embryos are something else? You know the way they are packed we cannot even open and check them, otherwise you know the babies may get damaged. That will be like murder. So we assume that these are human babies and we leave it at that.'

'But what about the parents of these embryos? They've spent money, got them fertilized, and now they are stuck here in limbo,' another reporter finally asked.

'What sort of parents are these, anyway?' Nazir Ali leant forward sternly, at his moralistic best. 'Do they really care? Sending their children by courier class? Bloody commercial nonsense. You've heard of mail-order brides from Thailand? Now they want mail-order babies from India. This is of course off the record, you know. If they can spend money to courier these poor half-made kids all the way to India, surely they can come themselves? I mean – is this safe? Would you courier your child to another country?'

The reporters looked suitably chastised.

Camera flashes began to go off, and the TV lights came on again as the phone on Ali's desk began to ring. Mehta took the call.

'Sir, it's Dr Wadhwani from Freedom Hospital.'

Ali stood and drew himself up to his full height.

'Yes.'

No one could hear what the doctor said, but they could see a slight smile hovering over Nazir's face. He spoke into the phone, loudly enough for the reporters to hear his stern pronouncement.

'I understand what you are saying, and you are right. But the law has to take its own course.' He loved that sentence and the sonorous sound of it – he had loved it ever since he heard the Prime Minister use it against a minister recently caught in a land scam. The Law Has To Take Its Own Course. It was a mantra used by every scamster in the country. The meaning, of course, was exactly the opposite of what was being said.

The reporters respectfully noted it down.

As the cameras rolled for the final time, Mehta stood behind one of the milk cans and Ali stood behind another. The picture the next day in the papers made them look as if they had raided a particularly over-stocked dairy.

In fact, in a disillusioned country where over a million babies were born to die every year, the news story was barely noticed. The tragedy of a dozen embryos stuck in customs never even made it to the front page. In a few newspapers it was tucked away on the last-but-one page, just above the classified advertisements, so tiny you had to strain to see it.

A serious train crash in which fifty people died had taken up virtually all available media space.

But the word spread just enough to tease a black market into life.

Ali's original game plan was only to block the import of the gametes or blastocysts, and hope for someone to offer a decent amount to make it worthwhile for him. As he had predicted they now had a very saleable commodity on their hands – though despite his brave words to Mehta, he wasn't really sure how much he could sell these half-made babies for. It was a virgin market, completely untried.

Yet – Allah was great! Ali now realized he could open his shop to get money in exchange for the release of the embryos.

Even if in future he was pressurized about handing them over, he could always find a loophole somewhere. A form not filled properly. A question left unanswered. Once the department tasted blood they could suck the sector dry, as the money was shared all the way to the top.

Mehta had already gathered that Ali had another destination planned for these embryos. Freedom Hospital.

Strangely enough, Madonna and Child, the hospital in Delhi which had ordered the embryos, may have also been pleased that Ali's scheme for gaining publicity had been aborted. Especially as it prevented the 'parents' of the embryos from hearing about the problem. Thus there was no public outcry from anyone.

Ali often said that they could rely on their inefficient friends in the press for an inadvertent favour. Both when they reported the story and when they did not, as in this case. Even the story from the over-enthusiastic woman TV reporter had been killed by that train crash.

One problem still remained and Mehta had been struggling to deal with it. A very angry Dr Anita Pandey from the Madonna and Child clinic kept calling him up to find out where 'her' embryos were. She had extracted his number from the courier company.

He dreaded the day she would actually appear.

So while he sat admiring his minuscule photograph in the newspaper, and he heard high heels clicking along the corridor, he had a sinking feeling that another brilliant morning was going to be wrecked. He quickly put the newspaper away and began randomly punching numbers on his mobile phone to look busy.

A very attractive, long-haired, tall woman in lilac trousers and shirt and lilac lipstick stood in front of him. She was frowning and upset. As she began to speak he realized that this was Dr Anita Pandey in the flesh and blood. She had come to claim 'her' embryos.

'Why have you held them up? Don't you know that this is a matter of life and death? Keeping these embryos here in these conditions in Customs and Excise is dreadful. Why have you stopped answering my phone calls?'

Then looking around, she stepped closer and, dropping her voice, said,

'Listen, we are – er – willing to look after certain . . .' She looked at him meaningfully.

Mehta was impressed. He had never been offered a bribe before and he certainly had not expected it to come from someone who was so obviously sophisticated.

He asked her to sit down and rang for a cup of tea. After all, she had almost paid for it.

He went inside Nazir Ali's room to inform him. Ali was already on the phone. But even more worryingly for Mehta he saw that the milk cans were no longer on the side table next to Ali's desk. They had been there last evening. Where had they gone? He waited till Ali put the phone down.

'Boss, that lady doctor I told you about has come from Delhi. She wants to . . . er . . .' He rubbed his forefinger and thumb together.

Ali shrugged. 'These bloody doctors are making too much money from these *gora* babies. It's good if they share it with some more deserving people.'

He spun the round glass paperweight in front of him, and watched the snowflakes float over Big Ben. It had come along with a consignment of office furniture that no one had collected. When the furniture was auctioned, Nazir Ali was struck by the forlorn way the snowflakes fell and the poet in him was aroused by their soft drift, so he had quietly slipped the tiny glass ball into his pocket. It reminded him of his childhood in Kashmir. Someday he would go back there.

'Mehta, the problem is that we can't give them to her. Don't tell her though.'

'So what do we do? She wants her embryos!' Mehta felt sorry for Dr Pandey and even more sorry for the notional loss he and Ali had already suffered. It had caused him many pangs of conscience, but since that day when Ali had promised him that the embryos were going to generate income, he had been anticipating a windfall. Yet nothing had happened. And now another chance to please Malti with some cash may have evaporated.

Ali spun the paperweight a little more and then went through the files on his desk.

'They are no longer with us – but no problem. I think we can adjust her quite easily. She wants embryos? She will get them! Send her in!' He sat back in his chair and waited.

Anita had never imagined in all the years she had studied medicine in Bristol University that one day she would be sitting and bargaining for a bunch of embryos.

She sat down and gazed at the muscular Nazir Ali playing with the paperweight. She knew she should not seem too eager, but she needed those damn embryos urgently. Her handbag was full of neat bundles of thousand-rupee rolls, and she was worried that the room was bugged or had CCTV. She didn't want to be filmed giving a bribe to a government officer, however junior he might be. It made her feel extremely uneasy. Ganguly usually handled these things – but this time he had bluntly refused to come along.

'These embryos belong to my patients. I hope you've kept them safely – you confiscated them over a month ago. You know they're very valuable for them, for us.'

She suddenly realized she had made a mistake. The word valuable was wrong. It would send the price up. She tried again.

'By valuable, I . . . I mean emotional value. Otherwise I mean it's just basically two cells, mating, fertilized. Quite worthless if you're not the parents, ha ha!' She laughed nervously.

'Ha ha,' repeated Ali politely. Fertilized? Next she would explain to him that the parents had screwed each other but could not conceive a child. Did she think he was an idiot? The problem with working women was that they were unable to be feminine. Ali's own wife was the epitome of femininity. She stayed at home in a burkha. He didn't have to worry about her meeting strange men and discussing how babies are made.

But he could hardly tell her about his jihad against surrogacy. That he hated Dr Pandey and her tribe. May they rot in hell. It was because of them that his only sister had now been lured into hiring her womb out to a rich childless sheikh from Saudi Arabia. The requirement was for a young pious woman – and his sister fell for the ten lakh rupees bait. The mother of two children! The shame of it! Ali was furious with her and his conniving, unemployed brother-in-law, who was no better than a pimp! If he couldn't stop her, he was determined to somehow disrupt the business, anyway, for as long as he could get away with it.

Wombs to rent! What utter fucking shit!

He adopted his suave and soothing tone once more. It always worked on women.

'Madam, you are right. I am a father myself. I feel the pain of these parents. How sad they must be – they worked so hard to get these babies into these milk cans, sent them through so many countries and now . . . they are stuck here. Terrible. Terrible.'

'What shall we do? I mean I would like to take them back with me. How can I help? You know this means a lot to us.' Again Anita stopped herself. She must not sound so desperate!

'Madam, I am helpless. Already the newspapers have learnt about all this – so they can easily check up what happened, *haina*? Even if I want to give these to you, I can't. This is confiscated property – it belongs to the government.'

Mehta was impressed at Ali's fluent lies. He almost expected him to say 'The Law Has To Take Its Own Course', any moment.

Anita looked close to tears. This was going to mean complete disaster for their newly furbished fertility clinic. A straight loss of more than two crores and forty lakh rupees. How was she going to face Subhash? Last year when the TV journalists started asking whose children the hospital was really producing, he had wanted to stick to local clients. It was she who had said they should remain a global service. And now once again . . . In some ways this was worse. They said lightning never strikes twice but the Madonna and Child clinic was becoming a magnet for it.

'Isn't there anything at all we can do?' She deliberately opened her bag and hunted long and hard for her mobile phone, hoping that he could see the money inside.

Ali waited for a moment, till he knew he could lay out his terms. He leant forward and, still spinning the paper-weight, counted the bundles. Thousand-rupee notes – at least ten bundles. Maybe more. He decided to take a punt on it.

'Only one thing is possible. But the news of this must not leave the room.'

She nodded, still keeping her bag open.

Ali took the gamble.

'A little flexibility is required. We are expecting another batch of embryos in the next week or so. For a small consideration, because you are suffering so much, we can give you those?'

Anita's jaw dropped. How could he have the gall to suggest that?

'I'm sure your clients will be happy with quick replace-ments?' Ali continued smoothly, enjoying the glazed look in Anita's eyes, as she struggled for words.

Chapter 3

SIMRAN

The shrill ring woke me up as I fumbled through the bedsheets for the phone.

Anita sounded very upset. The clock said 6 a.m.

For a minute I did not remember where I was. Looking out of the window I realized I was in Southall, in a bed and breakfast. I had deliberately not told anyone I knew I was in London – and wanted to stay somewhere I could be fairly anonymous. After the shock of that threatening SMS, I wanted to merge into the crowd. Edward was unlikely to find me here.

The fact was I still wondered if he had sent me that message. I had not called him back, either, waiting to see if there would be any follow-up. Any more warnings. But even though I had checked my phone at least sixty times in the last forty-eight hours, nothing harrowing had arrived on it – apart from a few messages from Durga, and the usual annoying property-sales text commercials from India.

I was feeling slightly disoriented, so it took me a while to understand what Anita was saying. Obviously she had forgotten the time difference. It was midday in Delhi. I could only hear every fourth word, and her voice was cracking up.

It did not help that the last few nights I had alarmed some of the more conventional local residents by checking out the various pubs around the area.

I had never been to this part of London before, and since I had no intention of going into a gurudwara or of eating plastic-wrapped untouched-by-human-hand *golguppas*, it was nice to spend time at the Glassy Junction, the local pub. Last night I had had one too many 'glassys', though – swapping stories about 'back home' with the immigrant bar tender, who had been more than generous with his measure!

And so now, when I tried to sit up, my head effectively rolled off the pillow and on to the floor. The mobile phone followed, and soon I was lying on the carpet trying to find where Anita's voice was coming from.

Finally locating my ear, I gingerly placed a screaming Anita near it and began to understand her anger. When Anita got *really* worried (which was rare) she got angry.

'Why haven't you called us back and told us if you had met Edward?'

That was the gist, anyway.

It was an interesting question. I could answer it in a thousand ways, I was sure, but nothing came into my mind just yet. And I didn't quite understand why she was so agitated.

I had, in any case, decided I wouldn't tell her about the SMS. Anita had enough to worry about.

'Anita. Hang on. I need to wake up, wash my face, eat something and then call you back. It's only been two days since I arrived. I was waiting for some real news before I called you. I can't meet a man on Monday and jump into bed with him on Tuesday, for God's sake. Be reasonable. It will all take time. I know this is London, but I have to be subtle about these things. He has to be free to speak to me. Let me call you back.' I shut the phone and laid my throbbing head on the floor once more and went back to sleep.

Two hours later I dragged myself down to the café down the road and ordered some scrambled eggs on toast. I received some really strange looks from people who were all eating *poori-bhaji* and *aloo paranthas* in a civilized fashion. Quite a change from my breakfast at Leicester Square. This part of London is certainly not known for its scrambled eggs and baked beans. But I ordered them anyway. A strong coffee-to-go, and I wandered out on to a bench in the sun. Because of all the politically correct laws in the UK I hadn't been able to have a single cigarette for nearly twenty-four hours. So now I finally lit up, took a deep breath, and called Anita back.

'What's the problem?'

'One problem? There are so many! Even the problems with the customs carry on.'

'Unbelievable!'

Eight months earlier a consignment of embryos shipped from the UK had been held up at customs. Anita had tried, unsuccessfully, to get them released. However, then Ganguly had intervened – and had found out, after greasing a few palms, that some paperwork was not in order. The hiccups continued. Obviously the situation with the customs department had not changed, and a particularly annoying man called Nazir Ali in Mumbai probably wanted more money.

I sighed in irritation. I was here for Amelia – not to explore why couriers were goofing up with their paperwork and customs were putting up roadblocks. But Anita and Subhash were my friends. This was not the time to let them down.

'So now you want me to look into that as well?'

'That's right. I was wondering if you could go across to Mybaby.com and find out a little more. Because we may have to stop importing the blastocysts. What's the point of embryos arriving here so many months later? Every time I ask the customswallahs they say that they can give me replacements, for a price, of course. But this is not like the spare parts for a car. I need to sort it out. Do you have any suggestions?'

Suggestions? Yes. Why not pull out of this foolish business? But before I said it, I remembered that there were far too many couples already in the queue for surrogacy.

'Any news of the Assisted Reproduction bill? Issues like this can only be sorted once there is a legal route.

Otherwise they can always say it's illegal and block the embryos.'

Anita also sighed, loudly.

'Still no news.'

'How's Amelia?' I asked.

'She's slightly better every day. Does Edward know anything at all? Can he help?'

Anita was usually a cool and calm gynaecologist. The best in the business. If you ever wanted a baby delivered you couldn't be in safer hands. I had got to know her better when she helped a friend use a surrogate, after years of failed IVF treatment.

Apart from being a friend, Anita was also a cousin, which is why I had got involved in Madonna and Child. And of course, once my mother learnt about how ART can help even middle-aged women like me have children, she jumped on to the bandwagon. So Anita and her husband became regular visitors at our home in Delhi and I saw the 'surrogate' baby business grow from just one or two babies a year to more than a dozen. I knew that this year they were hoping to reach at least thirty or more. It was an ambitious plan.

Thanks to Dr Ganguly they had also begun storing sperm and eggs for their patients, as extra insurance for the future. It wasn't something I approved of; I thought they were getting far too deep into assisted reproduction, the full implications of which were still unknown. If they listened to Ganguly any more, they would even be building artificial wombs next.

There was something about Ganguly I had never liked, but then I've always been difficult to please where men are concerned. I remembered how he had nearly jumped out of his skin when I went into the basement to look at the sperm- and egg-storage facilities in Madonna and Child. He said I made him nervous. I wonder why?

He did nothing to boost my confidence in the procedure of harvesting eggs either. And if ever I was forced into it, I wasn't sure that I would like him to be involved. Ma was obviously keen that they store my eggs, so that if I did not agree to have a child, she could perhaps go ahead and 'order' one on my behalf. It had given rise to quite a few heated arguments. I was not yet prepared to have a child, much less make some other woman bear it for me.

To be fair, in the beginning the hospital had attracted fairly straightforward cases. As Anita and Subhash were finding out now, it was simpler when you had local patients. An international clientele brought in more money but it was still a developing market. And then, with the transfer and travel of sperm, eggs and blastocysts or embryos, anything that could go wrong usually did.

Which is where I came in. Anita knew that I thoroughly disapproved of surrogacy, but because she could trust me, she asked me to become an unofficial adviser to their new fertility hospital, working as a facilitator with the surrogates, and guiding her and her husband on social and legal matters. Since I had been working with underprivileged children (even so-called juvenile offenders!) and was a social worker, I had a few useful contacts in the local administration – especially the police and the health department. However, I performed the role reluctantly, continuously making it clear that I had very little sympathy or empathy for what they were doing. I had tried to talk them out of it many times.

I even gave them a presentation on the large number of unwanted children in the country, encouraging them to actively suggest adoption as a solution to would-be clients.

Anita, Subhash and Ganguly had sat around the table, looking at me with various degrees of bafflement.

Subhash was the least bewildered but, after a while, Ganguly began to look frankly bored and started sending SMS messages on his mobile phone. Probably saying: 'Help! Get me away from this mad social worker.'

'Okay,' I had said. ' So why don't you encourage infertile couples to simply adopt? I know that adoption laws are tough, but things can be managed. Don't you find something . . . something very self-indulgent and repellent about the whole business of ART?'

'No!' said Anita and Ganguly almost in unison. Subhash looked uncomfortable but then he also shook his head.

Anita added very gently, 'For as long as I have known you, Simran, you've never wanted children. You don't have an overwhelming maternal instinct so I don't think you'd understand these women. They are willing to do anything at all to have that child. *Anything.*'

'Some of the husbands are totally obsessed too – and what about those loony lesbians?' muttered Subhash, the last very much under his breath.

'Alright,' I said at my reformist best. 'In that case why doesn't Madonna and Child have a crèche for the children of labourers who helped build it? Or start an adoption centre for orphans or a shelter for street children? There are many things you could do for children – just producing them for profit isn't enough!'

Ganguly raised his eyebrows. 'It isn't? I must tell you, Simranji, that there is no way this hospital can run if I don't make children for profit.'

The moment he said 'I' both Subhash and Anita looked at him with a tinge of surprise.

He hadn't even realized what he had said. After all, he was only a junior partner. But it was the truth. Neither Anita nor Subhash really had a head for business; it was Ganguly who kept the hospital out of the red zone.

'He's right,' said Anita. 'This is such an expensive and complicated procedure, we have to make sure we make some money at the end of the day—'

'Exactly!' I interrupted. 'But how much money do you need to make? The basic price you charge for the IVF and the surrogates and the international travel of the commissioning parents alone could pay for the food and schooling of thousands of homeless, hungry, undernourished children in India. And you earn much more than the basic.'

Ganguly shrugged.

'One day, Simranji, we will look after all those children you're worried about. At the moment we are looking after potential parents – and now if you will excuse me . . .'

As he left the room, I realized I had sounded like a self-righteous prig. Worse, I felt like a fool.

Despite my vehement objections and gloomy predictions, the first year had run smoothly. Six local and ten international babies were delivered through surrogates. The profit was over 1,000 per cent because the main cost remained organizing the surrogate and monitoring her for nine months. This cheap rent-a-womb was, according to me, a sort of slave trade – and people were willing to pay. I hated every one of those smug parents who came and picked up the baby that some poverty-stricken surrogate had carried.

Anita was careful to steer me out of the room whenever I saw a rich wannabe mom who perhaps could have got pregnant normally but chose a surrogate in order to preserve her figure or her career.

'The celebrity syndrome,' I would say *sotto voce*. Anita nodded patiently at all my accusations. It only fuelled my annoyance. 'Why can't a woman be anything more than a vagina or a womb? And since men don't have either, they get away scot free!'

Anita and Subhash bore my grumbling as best they could. Perhaps some of my vitriol hit home, because they started to try to involve me in every aspect of the 'business', including when the child was being handed over. But while I could ensure the ethics (to some extent) it was the emotions which bothered me and about which I could do very little.

The look on the surrogate's face as the commissioning parents took the child from her was usually difficult to view.

'We'll be in touch. We'll remember you forever. We are so grateful, we will visit you every year,' the parents would tell Bimla or Sarla or Sita. But within six months of their going home, the letters would be down to a trickle, till all was forgotten, except perhaps a Christmas card with a photograph.

Perhaps they were comforted by the fact that Bimla or Sarla or Sita was not poor any more.

Sometimes I wished we could do some serious counselling for the surrogates but I doubted if Ganguly would allow me to, in case I made them too aware of their predicament.

I thought they were being completely and thoughtlessly exploited – especially when they were given cycles of hormones to produce donor eggs, and persuaded to carry multiple embryos.

A while ago I had nearly walked out when I learnt about the gratuitous caesareans performed on the surrogates to fit in with the busy schedule of the commission-ing parents.

I was once again persuaded to stay, as the Pandeys said they needed me, but on the condition that I would be involved only in the really difficult cases. After all, I had plenty to do at home – I had Durga to look after, as well as my mother. And, of course, Sharda.

Life at the hospital was never dull. Recently there was a near-shootout at the hospital over a baby. And then, of course, there was the case of the gay French couple who had to be rescued from a 'morally' outraged mob. But the third and most worrying was the inexplicably sad case which had brought me to London. The case of baby Amelia.

She had been born (through a surrogate) to a British couple, Mike and Susan Oldham. Before her birth, every-thing had gone smoothly.

Even the embryo, which had been sent in advance from Mybaby.com in London to Gurgaon directly, had arrived safely for a change, and the surrogate carried the baby almost to full term.

Placed in an incubator, the child was fine, though the surrogate, a very beautiful girl called Preeti, was nowhere to be found.

So it was a shock when Anita told me the truth.

'Baby Amelia is HIV positive,' she said.

I asked if the surrogate was the source of the infection. She had been the prettiest woman in the ward and I always thought Subhash had a crush on her.

'Preeti wasn't HIV positive when she was first tested. In fact Subhash had checked her himself. But she's gone home now and we can't contact her. It's really terrible.'

I rushed straight to the room where I had last seen Preeti. Only baby Amelia was there, asleep.

Ganguly and the child's parents, Mike and Susan, were sitting separately at the cafeteria. I thought they were arguing about something – but in hushed voices.

I went into Subhash's office where Anita and he sat, looking exhausted.

'I just don't know how this is possible; we've always been so careful,' said Subhash.

'Any news from Preeti?' I asked.

'No. It seems she took her money and left, without even giving us time to take a blood test again, or ask any questions,' he said, puzzled and perhaps even hurt. He had made no effort to hide his affection for Preeti. How could she do this to him? 'She lives near the Nepal and Uttar Pradesh border and we can't trace her. Her husband says she must be on her way and he'll let us know when she reaches home. Sharmaji has also tried to find her, but no luck, so far.'

The implication was that she had known about – or was somehow responsible for – Amelia's condition, and that was why she had rushed off. This was bad news for the Pandeys.

When Mike and Susan joined us they too were obviously shattered. Their blood test showed no HIV strains either, and so the mystery deepened.

I felt sorry for them, but urged them to feel relieved that, at least, Amelia was otherwise perfectly normal.

In fact, she was angelic, with dark blue eyes and brown hair, and though this was indeed a tragedy for her, we discussed how, with medication, it was possible to manage the illness in the long run.

But tension hung in the air. Questions remained unanswered. Had the blastocysts already been contaminated, or were the facilities in the hospital to blame?

Ganguly somehow persuaded the Oldhams to take a short break in Rajasthan to recover from the shock. Since the child was premature she was still in the incubator and there was little for them to do.

Mike, a balding, soft-spoken man, shook his head sadly, and leant over to hold his wife's hand. She was in tears. But I saw a flash of anger in her eyes as she looked at Ganguly. She was definitely upset with him. But why?

Mike seemed to sense it too.

'Perhaps we should take the offer. It will be good to work out things between ourselves,' he said quickly.

Subhash, perhaps still shocked about the baby's illness and that Preeti had left so mysteriously and without a word, nodded in agreement.

'It will be good for you to get away,' he said, unable to stop sounding miserable. I could see that somehow he felt responsible for the entire mess. Preeti, his favourite, had let him down.

I too spoke up. 'This is the best place right now for baby Amelia. She can be properly monitored and medicated. Then, when you're back, the formalities for adoption can be completed.'

Later I would regret my words, wishing I had not urged them to go. What a ghastly mistake! But how could we ever have known what was going to happen?

'I'd like to see her before we leave.' Slowly, leaning heavily on her husband, Susan left the room, looking suddenly much older. Ganguly accompanied them.

It was the last time I saw them.

Tragically, the couple died in a freak car accident while returning from Jaipur.

In fact, this was the greatest irony of it all. It was just a routine, complimentary holiday to Agra and Rajasthan, given by most fertility clinics to couples who came to India. Perhaps the Indian tourism department could even adopt it as a campaign slogan: *Pay for a Trip to Rajasthan and Get a Baby for Free* . . . But in the Oldhams' case the holiday proved fatal.

Ashok Ganguly rushed to Jaipur to deal with the fall-out, bringing back news of an avoidable tragedy. It seemed the car had caught fire following the crash and only the Oldhams' charred bodies were recovered. They had been killed instantaneously, or at least that's what the hospital told him. The driver, who miraculously survived, was still recovering in a clinic near Jaipur. The police said that the driver of the other car was on the wrong side of the road, in a rush to get home.

This was fast becoming the sort of weird story that the media would love, but between the three of them – Ganguly, Anita and Subhash – they managed to keep it out of the news. And for a while Ganguly seemed less like a villain and more like a hero, even to me, as he flew around the place, managing a really dire situation.

But worse was to come. The baby's citizenship became an issue. Where would the child go, and to whom did she belong, with both the parents dead and the surrogate missing?

Normally, 'commissioning couples' had to adopt their child formally before they left the country, or else the child would automatically be given Indian citizenship and the surrogate recognized as the mother. Now, all options for baby Amelia were closed.

It was an awful dilemma and our own search for a family for baby Amelia led nowhere. The London address given by the couple turned out to be incorrect. Everything they had was destroyed in the car crash, including their passports. Perhaps even their names were fraudulent. Who were they?

To me it seemed that this case showed up the biggest problem with many of these transnational deals: almost everything was done on trust and often on the Internet. Potential parents just arrived on the doorstep of the hospital with the required money, driven by their desire to have a child. In the case of baby Amelia it seems that, since the embryo had been couriered in advance, the couple had only come in time for the 'collection' of the child. So what had gone wrong?

In the past month, before coming to London, I had tried to help by checking and rechecking all possible solutions – to investigate where the blame could lie. But so many people were involved at every stage that it was impossible to guess. This could even be a conspiracy to malign the hospital.

Mybaby.com, the clinic in London that had couriered the embryo, had denied all knowledge of any wrongdoing and put the blame squarely on Madonna and Child. Further, they said that they, too, had relied on the integrity of the couple. They could not run a police check on parents who came to them, as they operated within a strict code of confidentiality.

They told the Pandeys that Mybaby.com would carry on supplying the blastocysts, but only if Madonna and Child accepted that the problem had arisen at the Indian end.

Left with very little choice, the Pandeys had to agree.

Anita did not want a police investigation. While she asked me to help in planning for baby Amelia's future and possibly getting someone to adopt her, she also wanted me to help search for her family. So, quite unexpectedly, I had to don my sleuthing hat again.

While scrutinizing the admission forms completed rather untidily by Mike and Susan, I found a glimmer of hope. In one of the columns – for people who should be contacted in an emergency – was the name Edward Walters, with an email scribbled next to it, almost illegibly. It was either an afterthought or added by someone in a rush. It was a small clue – yet I was confident it could lead us somewhere. There were no other phone numbers or names.

And so I looked him up on the Internet. I checked out quite a few who shared the same name – but the moment I read about him I just knew he had to be the one. His profession made him a very likely candidate. A large cog in the machine which led to the birth of baby Amelia. After all, he clearly stated on the website that he was a sperm donor, and available to assist anyone who needed help. Could he even be the father? I knew this was a very long shot, but every aspect should be explored. How else could his name have been on the form?

In which case, was he HIV positive too?

But Anita told me quite categorically that it wasn't probable because fertility clinics operated under very strict conditions. In suspicious cases they would actually quarantine the sperm or eggs for three to six months to give time for the infection to be detected.

We sat and talked about the possibilities. Subhash joined us, and after some time Ganguly dropped in as well.

Why had Edward Walters's name been on that form? Could there be a simple and linear connection?

And more worryingly, how had the poor child contracted HIV?

Anita had voiced her own concern: 'Could the samples have been deliberately contaminated by someone before they were inserted in the surrogate?' she wondered.

Subhash, too, suspected that someone else, a competitor perhaps, wanted to wreck the reputation of the hospital. He thought it could even be one of the fringe fundamentalist groups who wanted to shut the hospital down since it was helping gay and lesbian couples with fertility treatments.

They both wanted me to explore every option – but to keep it as quiet as possible. Not even to go to the police for fear that doing so might disrupt the confidentiality of the clinic.

'What I'm really worried about,' Anita finally admitted, 'is whether we are putting these innocent women at risk by using imported or even local embryos on trust? Are we now going to have to check each embryo yet again? And will we also need to run tests on each of the surrogates once more? Perhaps every month?'

Ganguly, however, was remarkably pragmatic ... Perhaps he wasn't as bad as I had thought – at least he was able to give us some reassurance!

He leant forward and looked at each of us in turn. 'Firstly, we need to calm down. This might be a huge mistake but, Simranji, let me tell you there are many such blunders in IVF and ART. If you go through the list of "mistakes" you will find that every kind of error has occurred and continues to do so. After all, this is the most mysterious process of all, human birth, and if you try to play God, things will go awry. No one is infallible.'

Subhash nodded slowly, relief spreading over his face.

'I know there have been embryo mix-ups, the wrong ones have been inserted, embryos have been lost and even accidentally destroyed. One really outstanding case happened in the UK, when a white couple gave birth to a mixed-raced baby . . .'

Involuntarily I laughed. 'Now that would have been a real shocker! At least Amelia looks like Susan.'

We seemed to be reaching a joint conclusion. Perhaps what had happened was just an enormous mistake. We were allowed at least one.

Ganguly looked at each one of us slowly once again. 'The best thing to do would be to forget the whole thing. Let's try to get baby Amelia a good home – and not go on trying to investigate what happened, because that might attract undue attention. So far the media hasn't noticed the story – but if we carry on making a fuss there may be some reports on TV, someone might even slap a case against us – and the hospital could shut down.'

Subhash nodded. 'I agree with Ashok. I am worried about it – especially about Preeti – but what can we do? It's a huge mess – but—' He shrugged. 'Let's drop it now and focus on our work. Can we please just close this case now?'

He got to his feet and picked up his stethoscope.

Ganguly appeared relaxed as the two men left the room to attend to some patients. Even Subhash seemed reassured.

Anita, however, wasn't satisfied. When I reminded her about Edward Walters, she wanted me to meet him and settle the matter. Something was obviously still troubling her. And, even more worryingly, she insisted on complete confidentiality.

She urged me to keep it to myself and speak only to her about any new information I might unearth.

'What about Subhash?' I asked, feeling a bit odd about it.

'Definitely not him, because he can't keep a secret – or at least not for long. And for God's sake don't mention it to Ganguly. He hates you anyway and this will make him dislike you even more. *That meddlesome woman is at it again!*'

'Just the sort of thing I love to hear,' I said gloomily.

So here I was in London. Getting angrier and angrier.

I crushed my cigarette underfoot.

If people like Mr Edward Walters thought they could dupe us they should think again. I thought of the helpless baby Amelia, and felt my temperature rise.

Had the milk-drinking, beetle-like Edward appeared in front of me at that moment I would have skewered him and left him to die.

But, of course, instead of that I had to be nice and charming. I had to get him to trust me because I needed to know the truth about his connection with baby Amelia, and for that I was prepared to walk on burning coals.

The truth, as I knew from past cases, was never easy to track down. Even more so because people are never what they appear to be. And so far Edward had seemed kind and gentle, scarcely the sort of person I would accuse of malpractice.

The reality was that despite the problems, the Pandeys had to move carefully and not ruin their relationship with anyone. It was so easy to be blacklisted: all it needed was one negative report to go viral and suddenly it would be on Twitter, on Facebook, and even attached to emails. Reputations could be destroyed in a nanosecond on the Internet.

So, my first stop in London had been Edward. How better to get him interested in me than to pretend I wanted his sperm? To convince him I was so determined to have only *his* child that I was prepared to fly thousands of miles to meet him? A straightforward start to a lifelong attachment! Or so I would have liked him to believe.

I forced myself to call Edward, who messaged me that he was ready to meet tonight if I was. I wondered if another, more sinister SMS message would follow.

I told myself that I must keep an open mind about our encounter and be calm about it all. After all, the man drank milk and rode a bicycle. He looked very healthy

– not like someone who was dying of AIDS or had been HIV positive.

Nor did he seem a crazed assassin.

We arranged to meet at his place.

I was enormously relieved because Sardarji, the landlord where my bed and breakfast was situated, would have objected vehemently to Edward creeping into the house for what would obviously look like a sexual encounter. What would Sardarji do if he knew the truth?

I had planned to record our conversation on a tiny Dictaphone I was carrying in my bag, just in case we needed some evidence. It might not be admissible in any court, but it would help us keep a record of what had happened and how (and if) he knew the Oldhams. In case we managed to get as far as the 'insemination', it would give me a nice dose of DNA, which would go straight into the plastic container in my handbag, and not between my legs, alas.

Anita had also insisted that I record everything because she was worried about me. After our conversation she too had sent me a message, wishing me luck and telling me to be very careful, and not to go too far with him.

She knew me only too well. Despite all my reservations, I took out my only shopping extravagance, Agent Provocateur lingerie in bright red. Old habits die hard. If I were to die in this dangerous cat-and-mouse game with Edward, at least I would be wearing decent underwear!

As I twirled in front of the mirror I thought I didn't look too bad for a woman in her forties. Feeling a little more cheerful I put on a saree – the best attire for a seduction scene – tucked the batteries in the Dictaphone, checked if it was working, collected my Oyster card for the tube I would take later, and left the house without encountering Sardarji. No doubt the whiff of my perfume in the hallway would tell him I had gone out.

Seven months earlier

Kate had been unable to eat properly. Food still made her nauseous, and she was even more sickened to be alive when her reason for living had been taken away from her. For the third time.

Even though it was a month since she had lost her baby she could still feel a slight twinge in her abdomen, almost like a child moving, something growing within her. She knew it was psychological, a phantom pain, but she could not believe her dream had been smashed so vehemently. Instead, she sensed the weight of it within her, the gentle ache at her back as though she were bending a little in order to balance herself, the slight swelling and tightened skin around her stomach . . . It seemed like years ago when she had booked a place in the nursery school, even registered with a website which offered nannies for hire. How happy she had been, walking around looking at children's clothes, selecting armloads – and then the sudden agony, and the collapse.

Her mother and Ben had been at her side when she woke up in hospital. And even as she begged them to say that the child was safe, she knew it was futile.

Increasingly she felt she had failed as a woman and as a wife.

Ben was to confess to her later that, tired of consoling her, he had almost called it quits as well. It was difficult to remember that Kate had once been a strong, independent-minded woman.

He told her that, as he walked home all the way in the rain from the hospital that night, he had tried not to think of the blood. The child who had been just a wretched little scrap, not even visible when it was swept away.

He felt desperately sorry for Kate – and he wished he could make her understand that he did not want to see her suffer, concerned that he might lose her as well.

His mother's death from cancer still haunted him.

But gazing down at the Thames from Waterloo Bridge, he discovered that, underneath the depression, he felt strangely heady, almost carefree. His worst fears had come true and here he was, still alive. Did this unexpected elation mean he was an uncaring bastard?

Oblivious of the downpour, he continued on home and got drunk.

In the middle of the night, he got up and looked in the mirror over the mantelpiece and carefully examined his face. Did it show, this peculiar sensation? How could he have missed it? That odd feeling of liberation he had tried to suppress came surging back.

He remembered what it had felt like before the miscarriage: the worry, the tension, Kate's constant obsession about what to do and what not to do, the lists, the fear.

There had been no time to live, to relax, to have a drink because he just wanted to have a drink. Even to go out or stay at home, sleep or work – everything had been dominated by their unborn baby.

It had been four years! For four years they had been tiptoeing around the whole idea of having and not having children. Of trying and succeeding and then losing. Of coping with checks and medication. Of keeping charts and fertility timetables. He couldn't remember the last time he had slept well, without worrying whether it was the day to 'do' it.

And then after that came another phase of even more extreme stress – of whether Kate would make it through the pregnancy. Ben was used to pressure in the markets: that was easy. It didn't involve his emotions and it pumped adrenalin into him. This was totally different. It was heartbreaking and soul-destroying.

Thus for the past few weeks, he had lived with a peculiar combination of sadness and secret relief. Of course he wanted children but not like this. More and more he wondered if they should simply adopt a child. Slowly the idea took shape in his mind. Perhaps a child who needed a home and parents as badly as they needed him or her? Even one from another country?

But what if Kate insisted on carrying on trying? He had to face up to that possibility, horrible though it was. No, he could not allow her to go through this misery any more. It had stolen their marriage.

If she insisted, he would suggest a trial separation to allow them both to get their priorities sorted out. He would not be able to watch her suffer any more. He would rather leave. It was a drastic measure but it might make her understand how absurdly obsessed she had become with motherhood.

He couldn't think of any other way out.

Then, almost magically, the answer came to him – one evening, when Kate was still in hospital and Ben was at home, while he was flipping through an old family album. At last the jigsaw fell into place. It was so obvious he was astonished he hadn't thought of it before.

And now that Kate was home from the hospital he was ready to surprise her with his marvellous plan.

She came downstairs, still walking a little slowly. The doctor had told him that she was physically alright but that the depression would take some time to go. Ben made some tea and took it to the front room, where she lay curled up on the sofa.

'Cold?'

Kate shook her head, and he placed the tea next to her, drawing up a chair. He pushed the hair back from her eyes and leant forward to kiss her gently on her forehead.

'I worry about you, you know. I hate it that you have to take all the burden. Feel so helpless.'

She pressed his hand gently.

'I do want us to have a proper family. Yes, especially for you, I guess.' Her voice, though tired, was tender.

She always felt sorry that Ben had never had a proper childhood. His mother had died of cancer just after he left secondary school and his father had married again almost immediately. He had hoped that he and his father would come closer to each other, considering the scale of their mutual loss, but instead a new woman entered his father's life, a bottle-blonde Russian, who liked to 'party, party, party', as she put it. They had both dealt so differently with their grief!

'Any news from your father?' she asked, instinctively realizing where his thoughts were.

'Haven't seen him recently or even heard from him.'

'I thought you'd told him about the – problems we've had?'

Ben got up and poured himself a drink. He had opened a bottle of wine yesterday and only now noticed that he had almost finished it. Once upon a time this would have sent a warning signal; now it seemed a mere blip in the larger scheme of things.

'I suppose I should.' But there was no conviction in his tone. He was trying to find an opening in the conversation to tell her, firmly, that they, or rather *she*, must give up on the idea of producing a child. And then he had to convince her about adoption.

'Mum'll drop in again this evening,' she said, making him realize that he didn't have much time to discuss his plan with her.

These days Kate's mother visited more frequently to make sure she was recuperating well. The ice between them perpetually froze and thawed in an almost seasonal variation.

He cleared his throat and bravely threw the dice, hoping that she would not be too angry or annoyed.

'So what do you think you would like to do now? Take some rest, go back to work, take a holiday . . .?'

Kate tried to keep her voice light-hearted. 'It's difficult to decide – my plans were so different.'

Perhaps this was the time to tell her.

'You know, I thought of something we could do together.' He reached over to the coffee table and opened the family album. On the first page was a photograph of his mother with him as a little child in her arms. He still missed his mother and her strong, stoic presence. Right now, he was sure she was the guiding spirit, telling him what to do. 'I've got a great idea. Remember her?'

He handed her the photograph of the Indian woman in his grandfather's *bibighar*. Though she was (probably) long dead, he still felt he owed her something. Strange to feel a debt towards someone whom one had never known or met.

His grandfather's mistress. He looked at the grainy

black-and-white photograph and wondered about his bond with her. Perhaps it was because they were both essentially outsiders, weren't they? She had had to leave the British army officer who could not acknowledge her in public. And he, Ben, was perhaps in the process of backing out of a marriage whose purpose he could no longer understand. Unless he managed to do something about it very soon.

'Of course I do. Where's my photo with the *jhaalar*? Must look for it.'

Kate began flipping through the album.

'So I was sitting here one night when you were still in the hospital. Going through the photographs, depressed. And her picture fell out. Just like that.'

He sipped his wine, choosing his words carefully. He didn't want to say: *I want to spend time with you to find out if this marriage is worth saving.* Or: *For God's sake, there are more important things for us than having a baby!*

He had to be very guarded.

'And then I thought: we've been through so much. We both need a break. Seeing her photograph reminded me how much I've wanted to go to Ambala, to hunt for my grandfather's house, track down his story. And if someone's still there – if *she* is still there—'

'It's been eighty years, Ben. Hardly likely that there's still somebody around, or they would've been in touch.' Contrary to her pragmatic words, there was excitement in Kate's voice. 'So do you want to have an adventure?'

'I certainly do. We both need to do something we would

never do, just a mad escapade – a journey into my family history may just be the best medicine—' He broke off, looking worriedly at her face, wondering if he had said too much.

To his surprise, she nodded. 'I know exactly how you feel.' And she smiled.

Smiled! Encouraged, he sped on with his plans.

'But the best part is that we will get a chance to be together and not worry about anything. So why don't I take a few weeks off, we'll travel to India and—'

But before he could expand on how much he wanted her to recover from the miscarriage, and that they could explore the idea of adopting an Indian child – the doorbell rang.

Ben reluctantly opened the door and Amy, Kate's mother, came in with a shopping basket full of food.

After she too had settled down with a cup of tea Kate turned to her with barely suppressed elation and said, 'Guess what, Mum, Ben was also thinking of an Indian holiday.'

Amy's green eyes opened wide.

'I can't believe this – had you told him? I thought you were saving it up as a surprise?'

Feeling a little bewildered, Ben heard Kate laugh. It had been a long time since he had heard that sound, either.

'No, I hadn't told him. I was waiting to fix it all up.'

Ben broke in.

'Whoa! Hang on – I'm lost. What's the surprise?'

And as Kate told him her own plan, he discovered he had completely misinterpreted her mood.

A sense of foreboding overwhelmed him. It was exactly how he sometimes felt at work when a deal he had brokered slipped through his fingers. But all these years of financial gambling had taught him to remain impassive.

He opened another bottle of wine, offering a glass each to Kate and Amy.

'This is really an amazing coincidence – that's why Mum's so shocked! I was also thinking about India,' Kate said, taking a sip.

Her eyes shone with something other than tears. She seemed happier than she had been for months. Maybe years. Ben felt his heart sink further.

'I've been talking to the doctors in the hospital. Mum knows about it. They've suggested that, given the condition of my uterus and my inability to carry a child, it may be safer to try a surrogate. And listen to this!' Kate looked like she had discovered the secret to life itself.

'Remember that documentary I made a few years ago on medical tourism in India? Well . . .' she paused once again for effect, 'one of the hospitals which was being planned at the time has turned into a huge speciality centre for surrogacy. I've checked the website and chatted with the doctors – and it sounds wonderful. I think that's the answer to our prayers. Or at least *my* prayers.'

She looked a trifle reproachfully at Ben, as she spoke – but her smile came back just as quickly.

Apart from his rush of annoyance that his holiday plans were being hijacked for another bout of baby-making, Ben couldn't help feeling betrayed, as well. Kate had been examining the possibility of surrogacy without even discussing it with him.

This changed things completely, and now he did not want to go to India at all.

He tried to find a way of telling her what he really felt, but how could he disappoint her just when she seemed to be cheering up?

Amy looked at him pleadingly.

He knew she was worried that Kate would never be able to carry a child to full term. Perhaps she too thought that hiring a surrogate was the only way out. Faced with Kate's single-minded determination how could he ever talk to her about adoption? She would reject it outright. She wanted a child with their DNA, their genes, their hair and their eyes – she would never settle for a child who might have nothing to do with them.

He had told her about the first part of his plan: to go to India. Now he knew that the second part about adoption and putting their marriage on firmer ground, could not be voiced at all.

He hesitated and then forced himself to say, 'Give me the number of the clinic, darling, and I'll check it out too. It can't be as simple as you make it sound . . . do you really think we'll just go there and come back with a baby, without any fuss or bother?'

Kate nodded. 'I've met Dr Subhash Pandey before – and I trust him. I'm sure we'll be able to do it.'

He tried again. 'I'm sure we can afford it – but won't it be very expensive? And what about the surrogate? Will she really give up the baby to us?'

'On that last point I agree with Ben.' Amy spoke up. 'Wouldn't it be simpler if you try a surrogate here?'

Kate countered her swiftly: 'There are lots of problems about local surrogates. Recently in a legal case the surrogate kept the baby because the judge thought the parents were too irresponsible. Imagine that! The whole deal collapsed.'

'But that's probably a rare case,' said Amy.

'Mum, it's very complicated. Firstly there are very few surrogates available. Secondly, legally you can't pay anyone, and that makes it all very dodgy. That means the woman has to be someone you can trust, or it can be hell. In India the hospital draws up a contract, and there are lawyers who ensure the surrogate behaves. Thirdly, it costs half the amount. Dr Pandey told me they have over five hundred registered surrogates.'

Kate was in her documentary-film-maker mode, all guns blazing.

'His wife's a doctor too, and she suggested that we stay there throughout the pregnancy; so we can monitor the baby's growth and development ourselves. They will arrange everything. And if you can't be there, Ben, for the full term, I'll stay there on my own and see it through.'

Her calm ultimatum shocked Ben further.

'For nine months! I don't know if I can take that much time off work,' he tried to argue.

'Oh come on, Ben. You know you do so much of your work on the Internet, anyway. Besides – you could take an Indian assignment for a while.' Kate had a ready answer once more.

It was fast becoming a losing battle.

'What if the clinic is in some slum? You can't believe everything they tell you. How can you forget the stink, the garbage dumps? Now be careful, sweetheart, you've already had three bad experiences.'

Kate appeared unconvinced.

'If it's all that bad why do you want to go to India?' she shot back.

'Sweetheart, I'd only planned a small holiday – not this tremendous commitment!'

But he knew that when Kate made up her mind she always had her way. And now he was beginning to feel like a heel, because even as she pushed away his objections, her resurgent, confident demeanour was beginning to crumble. She was on the verge of tears, and Amy already had an arm around her in solidarity.

'I only want to protect you,' he tried. 'It will be terrible if you get hurt, yet again.'

Kate looked miserable.

'I know – but you have no idea how jinxed I feel here. Three times, Ben. You don't know what I've been through. Can't you just humour me – just once more?'

Ben could have kicked himself for making her cry.

But he still did not want to give in so easily. Though he had already booked the tickets and had even brought along a printout of them to show her, he was tempted to cancel everything and walk out. Why couldn't she understand how he felt about it, for a change?

Almost immediately, the flash of temper died down and he realized he would never forgive himself if he did not give her obsession, and their marriage, this last chance.

He forced himself to hand over the tickets that he had hoped to surprise her with.

'So here's to a whole new beginning, darling . . . change the dates as you like. But on one condition. I also get a chance to go to Ambala to find out more about my mysterious grandfather.'

'And what if you find some missing brothers and sisters?' she said, looking relieved.

He shrugged. '*C'est la vie.*'

He consoled himself with the thought that at least he could distract himself with his family history, as well as work, while Kate focused on the surrogacy in India. Somehow he didn't think he would be as involved with the baby this time.

Even though Kate was correct that he could work on the Internet he would have to rearrange his work schedule immediately. He couldn't risk leaving her alone. Apart from the depression he feared she might fall into again, the distances between them would only grow.

He was torn between conflicting emotions.

Ultimately, he realized that if this trip only succeeded in removing the 'jinx' she felt upon her, it might be worth it.

GURGAON

Even though her pregnancy was barely visible, Sonia walked across the room and sat gingerly down in a chair. She had been told to be very careful about the child; otherwise the consequences would be dire. She was nervously gearing herself up for Rohit's visit today. She knew he would not be able to touch her or beat her now, but she still feared him. And it had started so well . . .

After she had told him why she was going to the hospital so regularly, Sonia had been amazed at Rohit's reaction. The normally contemptuous look he gave her had been completely transformed to one of awe. His jaw had dropped and he had sat open-mouthed for a few minutes. She had giggled, and reached across to push his chin up.

'A fly will go in,' she had said. Thank God his mood had swung the other way and she could stop shivering. Her headache had begun to recede.

'Five lakh rupees per child?'

She had nodded, pleased that she had made him happy. For the next few days everything went better than expected, as he let her visit the hospital a few more times. She had been working as a cleaner in the neighbourhood and she also had to give her employers notice before she took on a surrogacy, so that they could make other arrangements.

To her surprise, Rohit continued to be good-humoured. He bought her bangles from Hanuman Mandir, as well as some *sindhoor*, to show that, even though they were not married, he thought of her as his wife. She was a bit worried about this sudden show of affection since she knew how volatile his mood swings were. But who knew, maybe the gods were smiling on her again?

As part of this newfound love for her, he insisted that they went for a stroll in Lodi Gardens one evening after work. They had done this occasionally years ago, after her husband had left and Rohit had entered her life. He bought them both some ice cream and, walking hand in hand, they found their old bench behind a shrub near one of the tombs of the Lodi dynasty, secure from prying eyes. As soon as they sat down, he put an arm around her. They ate their ice cream in companionable silence and Sonia felt a sense of peace, after years.

'*Saala*, I still can't believe it. And did they check you and everything? You can do it, and everything is fine? They won't change their minds, will they?' Rohit was smiling at her, as he had done continually the last few days. He licked his fingers where the ice cream had dripped and then took a huge bite out of her choco-bar.

'Yes, I'm absolutely fine. The doctor said I was healthy and I could have at least a couple of babies.'

'*Saala* . . .' Rohit was looking at her with grudging respect. 'We'll have to look after you now. Dress properly – and eat properly too; you're too thin.'

'They've given me some pills to eat so that I can go in for the pregnancy soon.'

'You'll be there for nine months?'

'Probably. They were saying that it will probably be a *firangi* baby—'

Rohit looked even more excited.

'*Firangi?* Then, *saala*, they must be getting lots of money.' Sonia tried to explain.

'They have to pay for a lot of things, the travel, the hospital, the drugs – the doctors . . .'

'But the main work is done by you, right? So why just five lakhs? Why not more? Don't those hospitalwallahs get paid more? Why do you have to go through them, why can't you go directly? And besides, once they put the baby in you, you can demand what you like. They can't take it away from you, can they? You have the upper hand.' He had obviously been thinking about it all.

Sonia was confused with his excitement and the foolish things he was saying.

'Rohit, listen. Please listen to me. Let's do this properly. This will be a way out for us. I tell you what. I – I think you should keep most of the money, after the baby is born. We don't have to share it. Just give me enough money to go home, that's all. I – I don't want anything from you – just – please let me go home to my children—'

He slapped her. As she recoiled, he quickly looked around. Fortunately no one had seen them as the shrub hid them completely.

'You said you wouldn't hit me any more.' Sonia felt a trickle down her mouth. Her nose was bleeding again. Tears sprang to her eyes.

'You think you're so clever, trying to get away from me, huh? You think I'm ever going to let you go? Let me think about this. If we play our cards cleverly there may be more money in this than you have ever dreamt of in your life . . . and maybe only one baby may be required.'

Sonia started crying in earnest, but quietly. She thought of Preeti, whose husband had been with her earlier in the day. He was so supportive. He had waited outside for two hours or more and then taken all of them for a cup of tea across the road at a *dhaba*.

He had seemed like such a kind and simple man, even saying that Preeti, who was already pregnant, should rest and have a safe delivery while he looked after the kids. Their life would be so smooth, Sonia imagined.

She also remembered the earlier tour of the hospital, those comfortable beds, the television set in every room, the clean bathrooms, and the fact that she would be alone in there for nine months – away from this monster. This motherfucker. Why didn't he just leave her alone? If only she had someone to protect her. She thought of Dr Subhash Pandey at the hospital; he seemed like a nice person, maybe she could ask him.

Rohit decided to be kind. He lit a cigarette and handed it to her. Even though she did not want to, she took a quick drag and then handed it back to him.

'Okay, maybe I shouldn't have hit you. As I said, if you stop annoying me I'll look after you, right? Haven't I kept you with me all these years, even though you are a married woman, with two children? I could have got a younger woman, but I have been loyal to you, right? Go ahead, have the cigarette and relax.'

'I'm not allowed to smoke. I only took a puff to please you. No smoking, no drinking. I have to be clean, totally and absolutely clean. No illness, no disease. Rohit, don't ruin it. This is our chance to get out, our chance of freedom. We can buy things, a big TV, a nice fridge.' She stopped herself from saying anything about her children's education, because she knew it might enrage him again.

Rohit smoked quietly for a while. He sighed.

'We can buy a small car like a Nano for around two lakhs – and then rent a slightly bigger house. Just think – a car and a bigger house! But if we could get around thirty lakhs then we could buy and not rent. Two bedrooms, a nice balcony, kitchen . . . sounds good, doesn't it?'

'It does but it will take six or seven years, five or six babies, and that's not easy. By that time the house prices will have gone up, and who knows – what if I fall sick? Please let's be sensible. I tell you what – I'll have this baby only for you. You take this money – or if you want let's aim for two babies and share the money between you and me?'

'The problem with you is that you don't think big. I do. Look at us today. At least I'm working in the Health Minister's house; we have a nice life. Now we need to think how to use this chance to make a lot of money – then we won't need to do anything ever again.'

'Rohit, ask anyone you like, they will all tell you the same thing. A woman's body is not a machine. I can't go on having baby after baby – and no one will pay thirty lakhs for just one. Ask anyone – ask your wonderful minister, she'll tell you.'

'What will she say? She doesn't have children. What does she know?' Rohit gloomily imagined a rapidly diminishing pile of money.

'Why don't you ask her if she wants to have a child?' Sonia asked with a touch of petulance. But she also wondered if the thought of doing Renu Madam a favour would assuage Rohit's greed.

'Are you mad?' Rohit's eyebrows shot up.

'I mean she might give you something you really want. Money, power, position – if she wants to do this. After all, she has so much money – who is she going to leave it to? And that Vineet Bhai, who hangs around her all the time, will be happy too; they can have an heir. No one will know it's their baby, because I will have it. Maybe we can do one baby for her.'

'Do Indian women do this too?' Rohit was aghast. 'Why can't they just get a man and sleep with him?'

'Sometimes they just can't.' Sonia felt a little strange imparting knowledge to Rohit, who had always inflicted his superior wisdom on her. Mr Know-It-All. 'The problem could be with her, with her womb or her tubes, and not with the man, and sometimes it's the other way round. The problem could be either her or Vineet Bhai, you have to find out.'

Rohit looked very thoughtful.

'You're not as stupid as I thought. The idea is good. Though I think she did have a child once, it's all very hush-hush – he was born mentally and physically *kamzor* and they sent him away. We've never seen him again. Everyone says he is in a home in Chennai. I've heard her talking about children though. I think she may want one.'

'Why would she send her child away then? She's not poor.' For Sonia money could solve all problems. How could a wealthy mother send away her child – no matter what was wrong with him? She herself would have never left her children with her parents if her motherfucker alcoholic husband had not stolen her silver jewellery, run away with another woman and left her penniless.

'She never got married. Besides she's in public life, so perhaps she was ashamed of the child.'

'*Arrey*, that's disgusting. A child is not a piece of jewellery to be used for decoration. She has such a big house,
he could have grown up in some corner of it.' Sonia felt an
overpowering rage at all those mothers who could afford
their babies and did not keep them. 'Look at these *firangis*
coming down all the way here because they desperately
want a child of their own – and this woman has a child
and sends it away. Such people don't deserve children!'

'I don't know the whole story – it's such a long time
back. Anyway, when are these *firangis* coming to India –
maybe we can still find out if this is possible?'

'This week, I think.' Sonia felt like a hunted animal. She
had managed to distract him with the impossible and
almost laughable idea of a surrogacy for the Health
Minister. But now she was worried because he seemed to
be taking it far too seriously.

The only positive outcome could be that the suggestion
would keep him busy for a while.

In the meantime she could get away from him and
escape to the hospital. Or just go into hiding? She
wondered if she could speak to Sharmaji about it.

In fact when Sharmaji had first spoken to her about the
surrogacy, she had pleaded with him not to tell Rohit, imagining that she could have the baby, get the money and head
home to her children. Foolish dreams. Once the process had
been explained to her she knew that eventually Rohit would
find out and could even be a dangerous enemy. And besides,
Sharmaji and Rohit knew each other quite well.

Sharmaji was also a supplier of all kinds of goods to the Minister's house – and that is how, half a dozen times, Rohit had brought him to their room and he had slept with Sonia.

Yet he had never been rough or uncouth with her, or forced himself upon her. He had been a sympathetic listener and always told her that he would try to help her and her children.

Somehow she had imagined a completely different outcome. She had hoped that the offer of five lakh rupees would tempt Rohit and he would take the money and give her her freedom. She did not realize that he viewed her as a perpetual source of income and favours.

Almost reading her mind he asked, 'Who took you to the hospital?

'Sh . . . sh . . . Sharmaji,' she stuttered.

'Sharmaji knows the system? I'll talk to him.'

Rohit took out his mobile phone and dialled Sharma's number.

At that moment Sonia had felt as though the door to the last escape route had been slammed shut in her face. Remembering all that had happened terrified her. And yet, sitting in this hospital room now, waiting for the child to be born, she thought back and realized there was little she could have done differently.

The door to her room opened, and to her horror, instead of Rohit, it was Vineet Bhai. The father of the child inside her, Renu Madam's closest confidant. He shut the door behind him. Purposefully, he walked up and gestured for her to stand. She stumbled to her feet. He came closer, and then touched her abdomen possessively. Through her thin cotton saree, Sonia felt his hand on her body and shivered, nervous about the fate of the child she was carrying.

MUMBAI

Nazir Ali was hurt. He had just received another aggrieved phone call from Dr Anita Pandey. Yet it was he who should feel upset.

In fact, as he reminded Mehta every day, he had genuinely tried to help the lovely Dr Anita Pandey with a fine exchange. He had very honestly told her that he could give her a whole batch of new embryos which were due to arrive within the next ten days. The courier company, who knew that the consignment would not leave customs without special permission granted by Ali, had already alerted him.

But instead of appreciating his gesture, Dr Pandey had turned pale and closed her handbag from where at least a few lakhs of rupees had beckoned him.

She had drawn herself up to her full height and (amazingly) she was almost as tall as Nazir Ali. The corners of her lilac-lipsticked mouth had drooped, even her pale lilac trouser-suit seemed momentarily creased with despair. He had thought she would burst into tears, but instead she was quiet for a few minutes and then spoke slowly, emphasizing parts of her sentences as though to a small child, in case he did not quite understand what she was saying.

'*Mr* Ali, *thank* you for *that* offer. And *honestly*, I do appre-*ciate* it. But the *prob*-lem is – each of those *em*-bryos *be*-longs, you understand, *be*-longs to a par-*ti*-cu-*lar* set of *pa*-rents. It *car*-ries *their* DNA and *their* genes. We *can't* switch *one* with the *othe*r. Do *you* have *child*-ren?' She looked earnestly at Ali and then at Mehta, still speaking carefully, breaking up her words.

Ali nodded, while Mehta shook his head. His wife was still on her chastity drive because of her astrologer, so he was not sure if he would ever have children, unless he were to suddenly become rich or morph into either Lakshmi Mittal or Bill Gates.

'It *is* as *though* over-*night* your *child* was *swapped* for some-*one* else's *ba*-by! How can you ex-*pect* a par-*ent* to ac-*cept* some-*one* else's *ba*-by as *their* own?'

Ali and Mehta had listened to every word thoughtfully. Dr Pandey sounded as if she was giving them dictation, but the rhythmic pitch had become more and more shrill. They looked at each other and then at her. When she stopped and took a deep breath, they nodded vehemently. There was no doubt they had understood every word.

'Dr Pandey, I am only trying to tell you that, er, your embryos are . . . that is, they can't be handed over. Now it's up to you. If you don't want the next batch, that's fine.

You don't have to decide right now. You can go home and call me.'

With her explanation done, Anita's voice had slid back to normalcy: 'I'm catching a flight for Delhi. But here's my card, in case by any chance you can release my embryos. I would be very grateful. We've done nothing illegal.'

She didn't know how she was going to explain the disappearance of the embryos to the anxious commissioning parents. Luckily, international newspapers had not reported this fresh disaster, so perhaps they could find a way to deal with it. She also wondered if she could sue the courier company, but everyone she spoke to said that, as with anything, while consignments did go missing, occasionally, very rarely were they deliberately withheld at customs. And once that happened there could be a time lag. She knew she had to go to some higher authority.

Her only hope was that perhaps some doctor more powerful than she was would pull strings and tweak the rules, and things would work out. In fact, she had received a call from Dr Wadhwani of Freedom Hospital in Mumbai. He sounded like such a nice man. Perhaps he would sort it out. He said he had heard about her problem and that a similar episode had taken place with him as well, and she should not worry. He mentioned his relief that Ali's press conference had been poorly covered.

He was going to take this matter up with the Ministry of Health and Family Welfare, but meanwhile it was better not to make a fuss as it could attract unnecessary media attention and ruin a booming fertility business. Within a few more weeks, he hoped the problem would be history.

A few more weeks! It meant Subhash and she would have to reschedule a lot of surrogacies. Luckily, there were a few Indian ones in the pipeline. Maybe she could fast-track those, or reroute the consignments through Delhi. She must find out why Ganguly had chosen to send the lot through Mumbai.

As Anita's heels clicked down the corridor and the entrance door slammed shut behind her, Ali had turned to Mehta and shrugged once more.

'I was only trying to help her.'

Mehta wanted to say that Dr Pandey seemed like a nice lady and they should have returned her embryos. She had even come prepared with the money – but something in Ali's eyes warned him that his boss would not be too appreciative. He decided not to say anything further at all.

However, a few days later, when Ali called him to his room, he could not help but ask: 'But, boss, where *are* the embryos which Dr Pandey wanted?'

Ali opened the top drawer of his desk. Inside lay at least twenty fat bundles of thousand-rupee notes, neatly tied up.

'That's what the babies grew into!' He laughed and slapped Mehta on his back. Then taking the top two bundles out he handed them to Mehta.

'I told you that there is something you need to do

– remember? This is the payment – in advance. It can only be done by someone I trust and it has to be done very carefully.'

Mehta hesitatingly took the money, but he continued to be puzzled why Ali had been so obdurate about the whole affair.

He still felt sorry for Dr Pandey. It was a shame that he hadn't been able to solve her problem.

'The *gora* babies are in the car downstairs. I want you to deliver them to Freedom Hospital. And don't ask any questions. Dr Wadhwani will meet you there. Just hand him the containers and be very careful with the labels. The labels must remain on them. Wait there till he gives the containers back to you.'

'Will he take the embryos out?'

Ali laughed. 'What do you think this is all about? The bloody milk cans?'

However, Mehta realized that getting the containers back was a smart ploy. If sometime in the future anyone asked for the embryos, Ali would produce the containers and shrug off all knowledge saying that they were in there for all he knew. And if they were not, he would say they had dissolved into the liquefied nitrogen. Was that possible? Mehta made a mental note to find out.

Similar excuses were often used in their department and they always worked. Mehta still remembered the occasion when it was claimed that mice had eaten up a room full of important files.

'When Dr Pandey came why couldn't we have given her this batch and given the next to Dr Wadhwani? I mean, it was very important for Dr Pandey – she had specific parents to whom these embryos belonged. Why give them to someone else?'

Ali sat back and played with his paperweight, listening impatiently.

'Boss, it doesn't make sense. She was also prepared to pay, so why not?'

Ali began to lose his temper.

'*Arrey yaar*, banjo, have you fallen in love with her? Why are you becoming her advocate? Either you do what I am telling you to do or I'll simply call someone else. If nothing else makes sense to you – at least the money should!'

Mehta looked at the notes in his hand and shoved them into his trouser pocket. Ali threw the car keys at him.

'Listen, don't feel so bad. I know you think that the parents will be separated from their children. But these are just eggs and sperms. Plenty more where they came from. Those fucking *goras* will send a fresh consignment and everything will be fine. Whereas what you're doing, banjo, is so important, so important I can't tell you. You're saving lives. That's what you're doing. And the reason why you can't wait for the next consignment is because these *gora* babies have to reach somewhere very urgently . . . Now stop being such a *chootiya* and go!'

But Mehta still hesitated.

Ali sounded bitter.

'Don't be so sympathetic. This is not a Christian problem alone. Let me tell you, even those bloody conservative Arab sheikhs have got into the act. Anyone with money thinks he can use Indian women. Not while I'm alive!'

Something in his tone made Mehta realize that Ali was truly upset. This was not just about settling a score – this was *personal*.

Mehta respected that.

As he left, Ali called out: 'The lot has been put into a black suitcase at the back of the car; and one more thing – don't go in uniform.'

Mehta, like everyone else, kept a change of clothes in the office – usually a T-shirt and trousers – because in Mumbai, especially during the monsoons, you were likely to get soaked travelling back and forth from work. So he quickly switched his uniform for mufti and then went downstairs. After a bit of hunting, he found Ali's private car, a large black SUV, also part of some previous consignment which had been confiscated, no doubt.

In the back was the suitcase. *Saala*, that Ali thought of everything. He opened it and peered in, spotting the milk-can-shaped containers. Shutting the case he got behind the wheel, strapped his seatbelt and drove out.

Malti would be thrilled with the money. Various embargoes against him would be lifted; his life would become simpler. But what Dr Pandey said had affected him, and he also remembered her despair. He didn't quite know where he was taking the embryos and what was going to happen to them, and even though these were not real babies – only a few cells joined to each other at a very early stage of human life – he felt like a thief, a child abuser, a kidnapper.

It was like the story of the cruel King Kansa in Hindu mythology, who had killed every baby born in his kingdom, suspecting that the child would grow up to usurp his throne. He remembered how in that ancient tale each baby was smashed against a stone. Only Lord Krishna, born inside a jail, had escaped, because he was smuggled out at midnight while the guards were sleeping. Mehta felt uncomfortable. Who knew what these children would grow into if they were given a chance?

Therefore how could he just meekly accept a bribe and even behave like an embryo-, no, a *baby*-seller? Did he have the capacity to be evil? Or was he simply amoral?

Yet, he was also puzzled by Ali's claim that he was going to save lives. Perhaps there was something more he needed to find out.

Freedom Hospital was near Colaba, in the heart of Mumbai, and Mehta had to weave his way slowly through the traffic. It was tucked away at the far end of a busy road and when he asked for directions, no one seemed to have heard of it. Mehta thought he had read something about the hospital in some newspaper, but right now it escaped him. He would check up when he got home. His father-in-law had just presented him with a bulky desktop computer which he had, so far, refused to touch. Maybe he would switch it on tonight and get the information on the Internet.

It would be another break with the past. Because up to this moment he had felt demeaned by the manner in which Malti's father just kept thrusting things at him, and had refused to use any of it – except the TV set. And that too was mostly because Malti insisted on her fixed diet of daily soaps. He suspected that the shower of gifts was meant to make him feel insignificant, part of a never-ending ego battle. It was as though the bastard was saying: *Look, Mehta, I know you can't look after my daughter, so I have to keep giving you things. She's used to a certain level of comfort.*

And the reason he, Mehta, said nothing to him, was, of course, due to his own sadness that Malti had still not been able to conceive, even after nearly ten years of marriage. The recent bout of asceticism notwithstanding, and despite the jokes he made about it, she had a long list of things to pray for: his promotion, celebrity status, a better house, more money, a child . . .

Still stuck in the traffic, he wondered if maybe he should have sent Malti along with his parents to Tirupati, and perhaps many of her prayers would have been answered there. He had heard that the *hundi* in Tirupati was very powerful. If you put money in the *hundi*, the gods would listen to you. No doubt his parents were right now flat on their faces in front of the deity, handing over the money, while pandits recited Sanskrit *shlokas*.

Well, if they ever had a child, they would need a larger house. His parents occupied the only bedroom in the flat. He and Malti used the sitting room as a bedroom at night, spreading a thick mattress on the floor, watching the TV Malti's father had given them till they fell asleep. He was a respectful son and so it did not occur to him to tell his parents to sleep in the sitting room. But still they had abandoned their home with him, and were away on a long religious *yatra* around the major Hindu shrines in the country, requesting higher intervention. Everyone seemed to be praying for something better in life – except him.

Was it ultimately his fault then? He felt he had somehow let everyone down. Perhaps he was just not good enough. Because otherwise he should pray too. Or maybe he did not quite understand their pain.

Of course, he also longed for children. But he was uncomplaining. If it was going to happen it would. That's why, now, with this bunch of would-be babies in the car behind him, he felt very odd. All he had to do was rush home with them and maybe present one of them to Malti. He smiled, thinking of the foreign-looking kid that would emerge. Malti was quite pale and had greenish-blue eyes, anyway. So why not?

The money rustled pleasantly in his pocket as he finally located the hospital, reminding him why not: because of what he had promised to do for Ali.

Freedom Hospital was a discreet, white-painted, four-storey clinic, so discreet, in fact, that even the board outside was missing, and there was only a small name-plate at the gate. Yet, as he drove in, he noticed that there was a Mercedes parked in the driveway, and a jeep close by which was bristling with security guards. There was also an official-looking white Ambassador car, with a prominent red light and white curtains on all the windows. Obviously it belonged to some minister. As he was getting out of the car, a silver-grey BMW drove in and Mrs Dhawan, the wife of one of the richest businessmen in Mumbai, emerged, looking very distressed. She swept into the clinic, accompanied by an entourage of private guards and what seemed like family members.

Mehta made sure the car was safely locked. He couldn't afford to lose the suitcase. Going to the reception, he asked for Dr Wadhwani, as Ali had told him to do.

Within seconds, the place became a hive of activity. A surgeon still wearing his operating kit came rushing out and almost shouted at Mehta.

'Ali promised me this two hours ago! Where are they?' He pointed at a nurse standing close by and said, 'Go with him and get them.' A man and a woman sitting near the reception were also glaring angrily at Mehta as though he was responsible for something – he didn't quite know what.

Mehta wordlessly ran with the nurse and wheeled out the suitcase. Together they rushed into the office next to the reception.

The containers were taken out, and the doctor, whose badge identified him as Dr Wadhwani, checked to see that they were all sealed.

'Tell Ali that next time he delays, it will be very expensive. Mrs Dhawan's son is here today. If the operation hadn't been done there would have been hell to pay. Get out now and remember: next time, give them to me a day earlier.'

None of what Dr Wadhwani was saying made any sense to Mehta. What did these poor embryos have to do with Mrs Dhawan's son? All he knew was that the boy had just been in a terrible accident.

He remembered the tragic case of the boy speeding down Colaba causeway in a BMW at night, last week. The family had at least six of those cars in different colours. He was drunk, and after running over a few pavement-dwellers, he had crashed into the embankment. Four children, a man and two women were crushed to death, while his spinal cord was severely damaged. Early indications were that he would be paralysed for life. And he still could be convicted for murder.

As usual, a good lawyer had managed to cover up the facts of the case, and one of the family's chauffeurs (who, rumour said, had been asleep at home with his wife and children) took the rap. Instead of being charged, Mrs

Dhawan's son, Varun, received nationwide sympathy for his terrible injury. The pavement-dwellers were forgotten: no doubt some monetary compensation was given to the 'bereaved families', as the newspapers called them.

And now the boy was in this hospital, while his driver, the poor fool, was going to be hauled to court for negligent driving. Perhaps he too had received a hefty sum to take the blame.

It still didn't explain the requirement for the embryos.

Mehta opened his mouth to ask but the whirlwind of activity had become even more frenzied as the doctor and a few more nurses carried the containers out through the glass doors leading into the main hospital.

Suddenly everyone had gone and only Mehta and the bored-looking receptionist were left behind.

'What do they do here?'

The man shrugged. 'Miracles. Men who can't walk are made to walk. Heart patients get cured. Bad knees are made as good as new.'

'But what happens to the babies?'

'What babies?' The man continued to go through a register, noting down figures and entering them with one finger into the computer. Looking closely at him, Mehta noticed that his face was unusually smooth – and pink, almost like the inside of the fresh salmon Malti had bought that morning. Perhaps it was the light in the room.

'I brought these embryos . . .'

'Let me ask you a question.' Mehta jumped as the voice came from behind him.

A man stood near the door to the reception. He wore a fresh linen suit and smelt like Ali had when he had just 'confiscated' a consignment of perfume. He came closer.

'Let me ask you a question. How old do you think I am?'

Mehta suspected it was a question he asked everyone. There was an impressive spring in his walk. He seemed old but his age was impossible to tell as there was something very youthful about him. His skin was pale and translucent and almost glowed like Malti's did when she had been for a facial. His voice was clear and steady and he wasn't even wearing spectacles.

'Around sixty-five?'

'I'm seventy-five, and you know what? I bet I can race you to the top of Malabar Hill and back again!'

Mehta thought of his own father, who actually was sixty-five and already had blood pressure and diabetes. This man looked so young and fit in comparison.

'Boy, I don't know who you are, but believe me this place is amazing. Look at me. Three years ago I could hardly stand – now I can walk, my knees are fine, and even my eyesight is wonderful. It's a miracle. That's why we call it Freedom Hospital. It gives you freedom. And hope.'

Mehta looked at him. 'You have good doctors here?'

'Absolutely.'

There was something very appealing about the man; Mehta felt he could trust him: he seemed joyous and carefree.

'Sir, if I could ask you a question, please don't mind . . . My boss, Nazir Ali, sent me here with some embryos and I'm just waiting to take the containers back – what is all this about? Why are they needed?'

The man walked past Mehta, obviously heading inside. He paused for a minute at the glass doors through which everyone so far, including the angry couple sitting at reception, seemed to have disappeared. The doors swung back automatically.

'Look, boy, I got involved with this hospital three years ago. It is the best in the country. Maybe even in the world. Ali is a friend who has helped us out in an emergency, but how and why – you don't need to know, isn't it? Yet for your effort this evening let me promise you that if you ever have a problem – any problem, come here and we will cure you. Any problem at all.

'Now, have they brought you a cup of tea?'

He gestured to the receptionist who quickly ordered some tea on the phone from some mysterious source inside the hospital.

While the older man was speaking, the thought occurred to Mehta that perhaps he had seen him before somewhere. He seemed very familiar.

The tea appeared, carried by a young, pretty girl wearing a nurse's uniform. As he sipped it, Mehta walked about, noting the endorsements for Freedom Hospital on the wall. Black, white, yellow faces of all ages and colours, smiling and saying, 'I got cured' . . . 'I got cured' . . . If this was such a famous hospital why didn't more people talk about it? Why was it tucked away like this at the end of a road, with very little to distinguish it from the other buildings in the street?

And where did those poor little unborn babies go eventually? Mehta tried to remember how often these consignments came through customs, and decided that next time he would try to find out a little more, instead of just blindly following orders.

At that very moment another nurse, also as good-looking as the first one, appeared wheeling the large black suitcase.

'This is for you. And goodbye.' She gave a dismissive nod, turned and left.

Mehta opened the suitcase and peered in once again. The containers lay there, innocent and ostensibly untouched. Their labels were in place. But he had no idea what was inside. He was too scared to even think of opening the sealed covers.

Mehta felt sick and anxious. For the first time in his life he had taken a bribe and for the first time in his life he realized the full enormity of that action.

Could he ever forgive himself?

Chapter 4

SIMRAN

Edward lived in a flat on the top floor of a beautifully maintained Georgian mansion near Sloane Square. He told me that it had actually been an artist's studio in the nineteenth century, and light streamed in from all around through the tall windows. The whiteness of the room was accentuated by a judicious use of bright colour. The style was eclectic, with Chinese vases, Tibetan scrolls and deep-red silk curtains. I loved the richly patterned woven cushions and the collection of Conran Shop pottery. I was a recent convert, having been to the shop a few days ago, when I had barely resisted the temptation of breaking my own rules and spending (by my standards) huge amounts of money on crockery which would only get smashed.

My mother wholeheartedly encouraged my infrequent profligacy and was disappointed that I still drew the line at going to Harrods and Selfridges – a status symbol for all Punjabis who came to London. But who knows, after a few more days here I might still succumb. After all, I *had* wandered into Agent Provocateur for lingerie! There was yet hope.

Durga might also make me come back sooner than expected.

Perhaps, later next year. She would enjoy the theatre. We could travel around the country; take a train to Scotland, visit Oxford and Cambridge as well, in the hope that one day she would study there.

Yet right now I was extremely relieved she wasn't with me.

Ever since the morning, I suspected I had picked up an unwanted admirer. Believe me, it was a chilling prospect.

From the time I left my bed and breakfast, right up to arriving at Edward's flat, I had been aware of the same young Indian-looking boy following me. Whenever I turned around, he was there. He made no effort to hide and that was what made me even more worried. He looked quite respectable and nondescript, wearing a brown sweater and brown trousers. I might not even have noticed him.

Except that he also, quite conspicuously, kept staring at me.

I couldn't flatter myself that he had fallen under the spell of my undeniable charm, because another anonymous message had surfaced on my mobile phone: 'WE THOUGHT WE HAD ASKED YOU TO LEAVE. YOU NOSY BITCH.'

The English used hadn't improved.

There were no smiling faces accompanying the message. Not even a number so I could return the compliment. Certainly whoever was sending these messages was no fan of mine. It was odd, because apart from Anita, no one in the hospital had been told I was here. Ma and Durga had been told not to speak about my London visit. Who would be interested enough to hire someone to stalk me? Or to send me these adorable missives?

And who did my present investigation threaten – apart from Edward?

That was the problem.

Had I walked into a perfect trap? Was this case bigger than we had imagined?

But now that I was here, I supposed I would have to simply brazen it out and hope for the best.

From the window in Edward's flat, I couldn't spot the boy who I thought had trailed me all the way here, only the masses of shoppers (despite the recent recession) swarming in and out of the square. Trendy Londoners, the Sloane Rangers. Where could he be?

I imagined him bursting through the door to shoot me.

I didn't know if Edward would protect me, or join in the carnage.

My imagination ran wild; my nerves were definitely jangled today.

Perhaps the morning's episode, and the unsettling message, had reminded me, quite forcefully, that I was alone in London – and if anyone wanted to hurt me, they could do so far too easily. No one would ever get to know.

The uneasy feeling did not leave me, even as I discreetly looked around the flat for any tell-tale signs of a connection with Amelia or her parents. I had learnt that in his day job Edward was a design consultant. Many of his clients were located in this area, so it was perfect for work as well. No wonder he could afford to be philanthropic. Mr Walters was certainly not poor.

The flat had two rooms leading out from the main living area, one of which was an office and the other a bedroom. A large wood-panelled kitchen flowed very naturally into the sitting room. The pots and pans and varieties of herbs and spices indicated that, among all his other gifts, my sperm-donating Facebook 'friend' was probably also a superb chef. How perfect could he get?

I turned to him and admitted that I was envious of this lovely home.

I kept my voice as normal as I could, and hoped I could sail through the evening without any mishaps – and according to the plan I had made with Anita. Which was all beginning to seem more foolish by the minute!

'A complete accident,' he said, with a self-deprecatory smile, 'despite my attempts to wreck it.'

His choice of words, while amusing, did nothing to reassure me. Yet he didn't sound like a crazed murderer, either.

Not that I had heard one before, so how would I know anyway?

And even if he was one, it was probably too late.

I decided to keep the conversation going. If anything did happen to me, at least Anita knew I was here.

'You could never survive in Southall, could you?'

'Never been there, to be quite honest! Now what can I get you to drink? I've got some red wine – and don't worry, I'll join you. I do have an occasional glass of red in the evening.'

'I almost got you a pint of milk!' I said, as I handed him a box of chocolates and a Shiraz I had picked up on my way. While he opened it, I mulled over the fact that he had never been to Southall. It was precisely why I had chosen to stay there.

The different communities were quite divided in London. The Indians in Southall, the Bangladeshis on Brick Lane, the blacks in Peckham, the Muslims in Tower Hamlets . . . and the Chinese, of course, in the heart of town, Leicester Square; everyone huddling close to each other.

Keeping an eye on him, I quickly skimmed through the photographs on the wall. Nothing there. I wondered if I could risk ferreting through the chest of drawers in the sitting room.

'Penny for your thoughts.' Edward stood in front of me with the wine.

'They're not even worth that much!' I laughed a little too nervously perhaps, and clinked my glass against his. 'I'm just intrigued by the segregation, all over the world, between cultures and communities.'

'You're upset about my Southall remark?'

'Of course not, you're just being honest. It's better to go to India and see the real thing, anyway!'

He walked over to the sofa and I followed, at a careful distance.

'That's a point,' he said, settling down, as I sat in the chair across from him 'But tell me more,' he continued. 'I'm intrigued by your story.'

'What story?' I asked guardedly.

He smiled. 'Aren't you worried about breaking a taboo by going in for a mixed-race child? This segregation we speak about is very real. And so you might find you are bringing it into a world which is not entirely kind to children like that. How would he or she be treated in India?'

'Quite well, I imagine. I come from a fairly wealthy family, as I had mentioned to you, so she will be looked after. I have a mother who is desperate to have a grandchild any which way! Even if I don't find a partner – she would be alright with anything! I do have an adopted teenage daughter who would love a sibling. She's very fond of kids. And so you see there will be plenty of family life.'

'And why me?'

Because of an HIV-positive child you've probably infected, I wanted to say.

Or, I could have said, guiltily – *Because you are so perfect*.

Despite all my reservations, I had to admit Edward was looking even better than he had at our last meeting, since he had discarded his all-black Lycra cycling clothes for tonight. His white shirt set off his tan rather nicely, I thought. An interesting scar on the side of his mouth, which I hadn't noticed the other day, gave him a slightly rakish look.

Instead I said, 'I just think it will be better for me to have a child from a man I have met and know rather than some anonymous sperm donor. There's safety in the fact that you have a life here – you won't suddenly follow me back and claim the child.'

'And what about the other way round?' There was a soft and slightly flirtatious tone in his voice. I was a veteran of a hundred love affairs and knew where this was leading. I tried to match his tone.

'Edward . . . or shall I call you Ed?'

I deliberately sat back and ran my fingers through my hair, smiling at him. There was a hint of seduction in my voice as well. Or maybe in all of me. I guess I could have sat Marilyn Monroe style, with my breasts thrust out and waist sucked in, arms behind my head suggestively, but I was trying a more subtle approach: being gentle; making sure I engaged him in conversation. It was important to talk – and I had even remembered to switch the Dictaphone on before I stepped in. I needed him to relax, to confess. To confirm or deny. And for that he needed to feel good about me, to even be attracted to me, perhaps. I was walking on the edge, and I knew it.

For a woman of my age I was at my irresistible best. I'd had my hair styled and put on some makeup. I was even wearing a silk saree with a tiny blouse. In my experience, there is nothing as sexy as a saree. It both conceals and reveals – leaving bare enough parts of your anatomy to stir the imagination. Further, it is the easiest thing to take off, because it is simply one long unstitched piece of cloth. The blouse had a touch of the Kama Sutra; it was the soul of brevity, and had only two strings at the back. A woman could be naked within seconds. That is, if the occasion demanded.

The image of Gurmit, my last boyfriend (why do former lovers pop into one's mind at the wrong moment), and me, lying naked on top of my favourite blue silk Patola saree, floated into my mind. Interesting tableau. I had a large mirror in my bedroom at home and I liked the picture we made, the silk streaming around us, while we tussled and grabbed and bit and kissed, his pale, young, thin limbs entwined around my darker, older body. And then we would fall asleep, spooning each other. But usually I would stare into the mirror across the room and try to imprint that moment into my memory, wondering how long our passion would last . . .

Less than a year, it turned out.

We still cared for each other, but he had gone to pursue Media Studies in New York, and I wasn't quite sure I wanted to date a student at this time of my life. I was also quite sure that a year in New York would change his mind about a fortyish lover in Delhi.

'Edward, please. It's got a nice solid ring to it. Ed is too staccato.'

'Okay, it's Edward then. I like my life, and even if I do fall in love with you, I'm not the sort of woman who will hang around. Besides, once I go home, you'll never see me again, anyway.'

'And why's that?'

'Because I hate flying!'

He burst out laughing.

'I thought you'd give me a more serious answer!'

'It is serious – and I do want you to know that I have thought this through very carefully. I liked your Internet profile, and there is no one else in my life who could do the necessary—' I stopped abruptly, just as he had at our first meeting.

He looked curious. And I was surprised at how comfortably we could converse with each other. I had almost forgotten about the stalker. Perhaps I was too gullible, but my suspicions about Edward were floundering.

'But tell me, aren't there sperm banks in India? I know that there is a huge surrogacy industry there.'

'There are, and I've been there and I don't think you'd want to know!'

'What's wrong with them?'

So I gave him a carefully edited version of what was wrong. How I was helping friends of mine who were running an ART clinic. And how there was a growing demand for assisted reproduction among high-achieving women who had waited until later life before starting a family. And as men were also thinking of having children at a later age, they too found that their fertility was falling.

'And so, yes, you are right, sperm banks have cropped up everywhere, as feeder organizations for the great fertility industry. So I decided to visit one, because I wanted a first-hand experience – to report back to my friends.' I laughed.

To begin with the manager of the sperm bank wouldn't speak to me because I was obviously not a client; I had no real reason to be there. They had never had a woman drop by for a chat. These days, he said, there were so many TV channels around that people like him were worried about a sting operation. He was a little nervous about divulging trade secrets to someone who might have come from a rival organization.

I reassured him by saying that we needed some sperm samples for a woman who had come to our clinic. He wanted to know if we had tried all possible sources.

'What caste are you looking for?'

'Caste?' I was dumbfounded.

'Madam, that's how we like to do it. The genetic pool is kept clean. It is a child of the family. The same caste—'

'How can sperm have a caste?' This was getting more and more curious. 'You can check the DNA but surely not the caste!'

That was precisely what was terrifying the manager: the harmful effect of ART on the purity of the caste system. He said that he maintained his own data quietly on the side, when the sperm was delivered to him, about the caste of the donor.

'Otherwise, madam, you know how worrying it is – lower castes can pollute the Brahmins. I know that in South India there are sperm banks only for Brahmins. No one else can go there!'

'So you try to match the sperm and the client according to caste?'

'Of course, madam, otherwise it will be chaos. Think of what will happen even in the case of college and job reservations. If you give Brahmin sperm to a Dalit woman, how can you call that child a Dalit? He will be a Brahmin, isn't it? So we have to be very careful about these things.'

'And what about religion?'

His eyes became even more round behind his spectacles.

'I note that down as well. Only Muslim sperms for Muslims and Hindu sperms for Hindus. So what religion is your patient? Hindu, Muslim or Christian?'

I had told him that I had forgotten to check, but asked if he had any suggestions as to how we could hasten the process – since I needed sperm immediately – without going through all this rigmarole.

'In that case,' he said bluntly, putting all his files and data away, suddenly not so friendly any more, 'why don't you just get one of your office staff to contribute?'

I thought he was joking. He wasn't.

He told me confidentially that some of the clinics pretended that they had got the sperm from some reputed sperm bank, or that they themselves had stored it carefully. They would say they had noted down everything, including colour of skin, eyes, blood group and even educational levels – but if they were in a rush, they would just ask the attendant or a junior staff member to go into the next room and deliver the goods. How would anyone know? Especially in India, where in any case couples were adamant about secrecy.

Perhaps I was talking too much. Wine usually had that effect on me and I was very anxious that Edward believed in me. After all, if he was HIV positive, and I managed to make him confess – this was the only opportunity I would get with him. Once he knew I was there only to find out his connection to Amelia, I would have to exit very fast. It was a risky plan but it was all I had.

I continued with my narration, smiling at him as cheerfully as I could.

'And so I thought – what if the sperm sample I was going to get came from an attendant masturbating in the next room? And if it was fresh, it could even be–' I was going to say 'it could even be HIV positive', but I stopped just in time.

'It could be totally useless if he had a low sperm count,' I lamely concluded.

Edward looked shaken, but amused. It was time to steer the conversation towards him. My heart thumping loud enough to be heard, I fired the first salvo.

'What is the guarantee that sperm banks are scrupulous here?' I asked him. 'After all, you really have to have faith when you create your baby in a test tube. You know, earlier they used to say that only the mother knows whose baby it is – now, even the mother may not know. Mix-ups do happen. And what if some contamination has taken place?'

Was it my imagination, or did his face flush a little?

'I don't think it's quite as bad here. They don't worry about religion and so on. They are also quite careful about storage.'

'Either way, I would prefer to come to someone like you than risk it in India.'

Edward poured us another glass of wine and then escorted me to the dining table, where he had laid out champagne and oysters, accompanied by a delicious-looking pasta salad.

If the oysters were meant to be aphrodisiacs, they succeeded completely. My mother was right. Instead of listening to my head, I should listen to my heart for a change. If he turned out to be innocent, if he turned out to be 'clean', perhaps a child with Edward was not such a bad idea after all.

'Hey? I asked if you wanted more champagne?'

'Sure.' I broke out of my reverie, drained my glass and held it out for more.

'This has been a great evening,' he said, raising his glass in a toast. 'Thank you, Simran, for coming over! You're a brave woman!'

My heart sank a little at his last words. I had probably drunk too much – and my head felt heavy. What did he mean? I wouldn't have minded if he'd said 'fabulous' or even 'lovely' – but 'brave'? I thought of baby Amelia, lying unwanted in a cot in Gurgaon and I struggled to revive some of my anger, at the same time plastering the sweet smile back on my face. Keep the pressure up.

'So do you think it will be easy?' I asked Edward, trying not to sound too coy.

'What?'

'Our experiment.'

For a moment a shadow seemed to cross his face.

He hesitated and then said, 'Would you like some coffee?'

Why did I get the feeling he was being evasive? Had he found out why I was here? Had I given the game away?

'Yes.'

We moved to the sofa and, feeling a little too comfortable with all that red wine and the champagne, I sat down and leaned back with a sigh. I longed for a cigarette but decided against a puff on a cold balcony. Apart from the discomfort, it would be easy for him to say later that my foot slipped, isn't it?

Edward moved a little closer. His hand brushed against mine. While the feeling was enjoyable, I sensed that I was fast losing control of the situation.

Even if he was the last man on earth, I knew I couldn't afford to sleep with him.

Had I overdone the flirtation?

This was getting more and more dangerous – but I also needed to get that sperm-filled cup before I rushed out of there. Why had I thought it would be simple?

'I've had a great evening,' he said.

'And I'm sure the rest of it will be great too,' I said. His hand wandered over my bare arm and touched my shoulder. I was quite prepared to spring back if he tried to kiss me, overcome (quite properly) with Indian shyness. I knew the HIV virus spread through saliva as well. *All body fluids*, Anita had said, when we had made this mad plan. *Be very careful.*

I geared up to slip his glass into my bag and dash out. I wasn't prepared to go into the full baby-making mode, no matter how attractive he appeared to be. Must be those damn oysters, I thought, a little woozily.

But before I could say anything, he abruptly got up and poured himself some more coffee. When he sat down again he was frowning. 'Would you mind very much if we did this another time? It's been a long day, so . . .'

I was surprised and, secretly, enormously relieved. I hoped the Dictaphone was still on. Perhaps he was about to tell me something.

'What's the problem, Edward?'

'I don't quite know. But you're so different from what I had—' He stopped mid-way, with a puzzled expression on his face.

Had he figured out why I was here? In that case I had

to try to at least get some information out of him. If he was suspicious of my motives, he might not invite me back again. I sat on the edge of my chair, calculating that it would take me less than thirty seconds to make it to the door.

'Are you feeling alright?' I asked him, trying to sound solicitous, wondering about my next move.

'Yes, of course, just a little tired, I think. Though it's been wonderful to meet you and such a fantastic evening – perhaps I'm just a little overwhelmed.'

I was flattered – perhaps my seductive attire had been a little too successful!

'Are you sure that's all?'

'Why?' He seemed surprised.

'I mean – are you changing your mind because of me, anything I said – or is there any other reason . . .?'

How do I get him to say it?

'Look, let's not complicate things. I just want you to have a good experience. We can do this tomorrow, you know.'

Oh no, I wasn't coming back tomorrow. I was still feeling giddy – but I persisted.

'Can I ask you something, if you don't mind? And there is a reason for my asking this, so . . .'

He nodded, still frowning: 'Go ahead.'

I looked at him carefully. And thought of baby Amelia.

'Did you ever know someone called Susan Oldham?'

There are only two words to describe the expression on his face.

Shock. Disbelief.

I felt triumphant. The risk had been worth it, after all.

But almost immediately a warning began to flash in my head. I remembered Anita's prophetic words. I was in a strange man's flat and, thus far, ostensibly ready to sleep with him.

The fact that he knew Susan meant that the likelihood of his being HIV positive, as well as dangerous and deranged, went up by at least 50 per cent.

Edward leant towards me, and my blood ran cold. But there was no desire on his face any more. He looked furious.

I leapt to my feet, moving towards the door. He caught my arm so tightly that it hurt.

As I struggled to push him away, I knew it was already too late. I had made a huge mistake by mentioning Susan. I should have left while I could.

His grip on my arm was unrelenting, as he shook me slightly.

'How the hell do you know her?'

I grabbed my handbag, and pushed him back.

'Don't come near me,' I bluffed. 'I have a gun in here.'

To my horror he shoved me back on to the sofa. I opened my mouth to scream, but he pressed his hand down on my face.

'Don't you dare shout,' he said. 'I knew there was something odd about you. I think we are finally going to have a very interesting conversation.'

Gasping for breath, I was trapped in the chair, unable to move.

Six months earlier

OCTOBER
DELHI

Coming out of the plane into the newly constructed Terminal 3 at New Delhi, both Kate and Ben were impressed with the smoothness of their arrival. Kate hadn't been back for a few years and despite the stories of endless corruption in India that flooded the international media it appeared that some money might have actually been spent on what it was meant for. The cleanliness, the space, the wall-to-wall carpeting and even the modern toilets (though some were still a hole in the ground) were perhaps an indication of a booming economy – as well as improving standards.

'Don't get carried away.' Ben put a cautionary arm around Kate. He was still hoping she would change her mind about the surrogacy. 'You and I know that while these airports are being built, over forty per cent of Indian children go to bed hungry every night—'

Kate cut in impatiently. 'Don't patronize me, Ben.' Then she hid her annoyance with a laugh. 'I've been visiting this country for ages for my documentaries. I know what to look for, and what to believe. At least this is a positive change.'

Ben shrugged and hoped that by the time they reached the hotel her over-optimistic attitude would have been somewhat deflated. He still felt they were rushing headlong into unknown territory. His own painful realization, tinged with guilty relief, that they should not try for another baby persisted. But within a short while Kate was ready to take another risk. He wondered where she got the strength from. His own reserves were totally depleted.

As a pleasant distraction, stored within his laptop and BlackBerry were details of his family history, and as soon as they had visited the hospital and sorted out the details, Ben wanted to start a little expedition of his own, to Ambala.

The last few times he had come to India for work he had been unable to take this step because meetings in Mumbai had consumed most of his time.

Whichever way it all turned out, the journey might help reconcile him to the turmoil in his life right now. He thought of his grandfather making his way across to India in a ship and, after months of travel, reaching a country where fortunes could be made, but at enormous personal loss. Being in a strange land, part of the ruling class and yet unsure of the territory, learning the local customs and beliefs and trying to understand them, coping with the weather, undertaking long and sometimes futile expeditions at a time when the country was rising against the

British, must have been an endless struggle. And so perhaps if he had found affection and love, it would have taken the edge off his loneliness. Was Ben also looking for something beyond his relationship with Kate?

After clearing immigration, they collected their bags and then queued up for a cab. He hadn't realized how warm it still was. Both he and Kate shed their jackets, and slowly he began to relax. The heat always had this effect on him. It was like a comforting hand on his back and neck.

Kate searched her handbag for the sunscreen and after rubbing some on her hands and face, handed it to him. He disliked the touch of the cream on his skin, but took a small amount and pretended to rub it on. Anything to keep the peace.

Kate was sombre as she spoke: 'I never thought I would ever come to India for this. In fact I'd thought that when we came here together, we would have our baby with us. I certainly hope we'll at least leave with our child.'

Ben was silent as they got into the taxi. He was weary of reassuring her. Instead, he sat back, gazing out of the window of the black and yellow Ambassador cab, his mind elsewhere.

They were a leap back in time: these 'Ambassador' cars, Morris Oxford III models which had been discontinued in the UK in 1959, were still found on the Delhi roads. He knew from his last visit that a white Ambassador with a red light on top meant that the occupant was a seriously important person.

In a way it was a metaphor for India. The detritus of past centuries clung on, like dust motes to finely etched glass, blurring the view. Five thousand years of civilization was in a celebratory embrace – but the union did not always make a happy sight.

As they left behind the high-rise glass and chrome sophistication of the airport, little towers of rubble and unfinished structures emerged, scattered all along the road. As though an absentminded emperor had ordered further construction – but abandoned his plans halfway through.

And then the scenery changed once more, to that of garbage mounds spotted with colourful polythene bags waving like flags in the wind. Children scrambled around, hunting for discarded treasure. Emaciated cows pushed their noses into the rubbish, following the scent of a good meal. Many would die after swallowing plastic. This was all just as he remembered it. Ben shut his eyes.

India was a great destination for business – but scored abysmally on all the social indicators. The kind of country with which you could fall in love, but never live in.

As the taxi weaved in and out of traffic, he wondered how he could express his doubts clearly enough for Kate to be convinced.

Her phone rang. It was the hospital, Madonna and Child, confirming their appointment for later. As Kate had told him, it was a one-stop shop. The hospital had been very proactive and efficient: it suggested the accommodation, informed them of the required procedures, provided the surrogate – and even threw in a small holiday on the side.

They had suggested Rajasthan, but Kate had always wanted to visit the Taj Mahal and so that was part of the programme now.

Suddenly, Kate was shaking him gently and stroking his face. 'Ben? Are you feeling okay?'

He opened his eyes and discovered he had slept through most of the journey, and that the cab had come to a halt in front of a small hotel. The doorman, dressed in a lurid red turban and a red faux-army jacket with gold epaulettes, bowed and held the door open for him. Feeling slightly foolish and a little disorientated, Ben scrambled out and followed Kate as she negotiated their way to their room through the plant- and people-crowded lobby.

The temperature had risen further as midday approached and Kate was thankful that the room was air conditioned. There was also a bouquet of roses with a note and a brochure from the hospital. The car would come for them at 4 p.m. In the meantime they could enjoy a free massage, a sauna and a swim in the health club.

'It's like a holiday, isn't it? Just as they had promised,' commented Kate as she undressed and put on a bathrobe to go for the massage.

'I guess they don't want us to feel the pain too much.'

'Ben, don't be cynical,' Kate gently reprimanded him. But she hoped he would drop his reluctance about her attempting to find a surrogate. She really felt exhausted by the effort she had to make these days. It was becoming an extremely one-sided relationship – couldn't he see how much he was upsetting her? And yet he kept insisting that, actually, he wanted to look after her.

After Kate left, Ben opened the bar under the television set and took out a small whisky bottle. He had found that a couple of glasses of alcohol made him less argumentative. By the time she came back, well-oiled and gleaming, he had finished three mini bottles and was sitting in front of the TV, aimlessly switching channels, enjoying his temporary solitude.

Kate pretended not to notice he had been drinking, even though he had arranged the bottles on the coffee table in front of him in a row, like pieces on a chessboard. She tried not to remember that he had drunk steadily throughout the flight to India. His drinking was not the real concern because she knew that he was always very controlled and careful in everything he did. He wouldn't misbehave or collapse. What bothered her was that he was so grim in the way he went about it. She changed into a floral dress and sat down next to him.

They were both quiet as they waited for the hospital car to arrive. A few years ago everything had been so different – they could hardly stop talking or keep their hands off each other – but now they were both lost for words, conscious that a false move might bring them to the end of the journey even faster than they had anticipated.

The hospital bore a strong resemblance to the airport: the high, cantilevered metal-and-glass roof, the large windows and doors and the polished chrome fittings. It looked clean, sterile and antiseptic – and very new.

They were led through a white marble-paved corridor to Dr Subhash Pandey's office, which was large and almost blindingly white in the late-afternoon sunshine. Subhash's highly starched white coat dazzled, and Ben once more closed his eyes – this time against the sharp reflection as the light bounced off the white all around him. When he opened them he noticed that Kate had a disapproving look on her face.

She glanced at him almost dismissively whilst making the introductions.

Since she knew Dr Subhash Pandey from when she had made her documentary, perhaps she felt a little embarrassed by Ben's all too obvious reluctance at being involved.

He sat up straight and decided to participate in the proceedings with a little more enthusiasm. If he treated it like a business meeting, he would be able to cope better.

All he hoped for was that Kate would one day ask him: *Alright, since you want children too, what's your plan?* Right now she wanted to push her own agenda, regardless of the risk – and he would play along as long as he could, since he did not want to abandon her.

He would simply have to hide his resentment.

But given Kate's angry demeanour, it was obvious he was not succeeding. If he loved her, he would have to try harder. Why was life so bloody tough?

Anita joined them, dressed in a formal but richly patterned green georgette saree, with her hair left long and loose over her shoulders. Without her white coat, it would have difficult to imagine she was a doctor. Together she and Subhash made a striking couple, though she clearly stood out with her porcelain skin, and very fine and sharply defined features. He was not as good-looking as her, but his soft bedside manner more than made up for his slightly florid appearance. They both exuded an impressive equanimity and self-confidence.

'How long do you plan to be in India?' Subhash began filling in a form on his desk.

'As long as this takes – we are here for at least nine months.' Kate was firm in her reply though she refused to look at Ben as he opened his mouth to comment and then closed it without saying a word. There was no point fighting in front of this elegant couple – certainly a far cry from the gruff and often crumpled doctors he had dealt with in the NHS back home. The whisky had, in any case, slowed his reactions and he did not want to say anything foolish.

Anita sensed the tension, and quickly decided to step in.

'We have most of the other details with us, so before we fix a time for the procedure would you like to look around the hospital? It's all recently built – and some further expansions have been made because the international response has been marvellous.'

She was thankful now that Subhash had been so particular with the facilities. No one walking around the rooms or the corridors or even the cafeteria – which served only health food – could fail to be impressed. There was even a gym where patients or the family could work out. Seeing the approval writ large on Kate's face, Subhash proudly showed them the space where they were planning to make a giant entertainment area for those who wanted to stay for a longer period. Were it not for the operating theatres and nurses bustling around, the hospital could have been a five-star hotel.

Ben's stress partially drained away; everything seemed better than he had expected. To his surprise it did contain most of the facilities that the Pandeys had promised them on the clinic's website.

He liked the fact that there was privacy for all concerned, and the carefully appointed rooms where the surrogates were going to be kept and monitored seemed comfortable. The Pandeys appeared to have thought of everything. Kate too seemed to be enjoying the mini tour, and when they settled back in Subhash's room they were able to speak more freely.

'About the surrogate – Sonia. Is it possible to meet her? You sent us her photograph.'

Subhash looked through the file on his desk and nodded, playing for time. Sonia, of course, was no longer available and the photograph must have been sent by mistake. But he would deal with that another time, once they had identified another girl.

'Of course, it shouldn't be a problem.'

'Shall we visit her?' Ben asked. 'Instead of her coming here?'

A slight frown crossed Anita's face.

'I think we need to do the introductions, because it is our responsibility to make sure everything goes well. We don't want to encourage interactions, in case, you know, something goes wrong. As we've discussed, since Kate will be ovulating within the next week, I will just check her blood-hormonal level and then harvest the eggs from her and the sperm from you. Only when we are sure of everything will we go ahead. Meanwhile, we'll prepare the surrogate. Your meeting will be arranged very soon and the whole process will begin, fingers crossed. We will do everything to expedite it.'

Anita paused in her sales pitch to ask, 'When would you like to go off for your holiday? It will be good to make the tentative bookings in advance.'

There was an awkward silence and Ben realized that they might have misunderstood his reason for wanting to meet the surrogate. Perhaps they were worried that he might do a separate deal with her or even reject her. But he felt it would be easier to reconcile himself to the process if he got to know the surrogate prior to the embryo being implanted in her. Before he could say anything, Kate spoke up. Her voice was sharper than usual.

'How would you like us to make the payment, cash or card?'

To complete the formalities, Kate was led into a small operating theatre, where Anita ran a test to check whether the fertility drugs she had been taking before her arrival had worked. The result would not be back until the next day, so the decision on how to proceed would have to be taken later.

She explained to Kate that, if the test proved negative, they would have to inject her in the next week or so with hormones to push her body into producing more egg follicles and forcing the ovaries to release the eggs.

By this time, Kate felt her energy draining away. She heard Anita saying something about the side effects of the drugs but it was getting increasingly difficult to concentrate. She signed the consent form, and asked Ben to do the same.

Both Kate and Ben felt the full weight of their exhaustion as they came back to the hotel. Though they were reassured by the hospital, they also felt very alone. Ben was quiet, wondering if Kate would listen to him if he begged her to just have a holiday with him.

'I know I've been beastly – but only because you don't listen to me about any of this. I won't be able to bear it if something happens to you,' he told her, as they picked at their dinner, a rather dismal array of over-spiced vegetables, served with an oily daal.

Kate attempted her usual bravado. 'I'll be alright – why are you getting so worked up? Trust me.'

Lying in bed, later, they read quietly for a while and then, turning away from Kate, Ben went to sleep.

Kate found that even though she tried to get as close as she could to him, pressing her body tightly against his, there was a chill in her heart that refused to go away. It was frightening to think of the risks she ran each time she attempted to have a child. She tried not to admit it, but she was a little scared. Not just about what it was doing to their relationship but also about the possible effect of these hormones she was consuming and being injected with. Even though she knew it was far too soon after her miscarriage, she had insisted on going for the treatment. Her head began to throb as the morning's tension returned. Was it the memory of the child she had just lost, tunnelling his or her way into her mind? She wondered what was happening in that part of her body which was being stimulated into producing the required hormones.

She wasn't feeling too well.

But now there was nothing to do but to go ahead.

DELHI

Looking back over the last three months, Rohit could not stop congratulating himself. It had been a perfect plot so far and everything had fallen into place. For once Sonia had had a brilliant idea – and he had been able to execute it flawlessly. And now like everyone else he just had to wait for the result which was due within the next six months. Sonia was safely in the hospital, pregnant, just as they had planned. But he had to be very, very careful about the next step.

Without revealing anything, he had got all the necessary inputs about the Madonna and Child hospital and the surrogacy offer to Sonia from Sharmaji. He carefully guarded the information that Sonia could have the Health Minister's child. If she wanted one. Now he had to do somehow convey to Renu Madam that this way she would acquire a child who could inherit her genes and her political mantle. At last – a legitimate political heir!

It was obvious, however, that she would be dismissive if he approached her directly – in fact he would be sacked for over-familiarity. Sharmaji was one possibility, because he was a fixer, very useful in politics. But Rohit wasn't sure he could trust Sharmaji.

Perhaps he could talk to someone in Renu Madam's home? He knew from the whispers and gossip around the house that she still missed her child, and sending him away had been a source of huge depression. As often happened, it was a secret from Renu Madam that everyone knew her secret.

When the child was born, she had just started on her political career – and, of course, everyone had said that the father of the child was Vineet Bhai, her political mentor, and leader of her party – though that may not have been the case. Yet he had looked after her during that period. It was also rumoured that the child's birth took place at his home, in 'secrecy', and was never registered.

The curious twist to this story was that Vineet Bhai had taken a vow of celibacy when he was young, stating that he was wedded to politics, and so while Renu Madam and he remained close companions, marriage was out of the question, even if they had desired it.

The child may have been an accidental product of another relationship, but partly because he was illegitimate and partly because he needed constant care, Renu Madam was advised that he would have to be smuggled away. He should not even be mentioned ever again. She could have brought him up in the house as someone else's child but there were many who told her that a child with special needs might be politically risky, as voters liked to see healthy, happy families. Furthermore, Vineet Bhai showed no interest in a baby who was so frail.

He only followed a time-worn tradition in India to hide away or ignore those who were physically or mentally challenged. It was assumed that this child would also 'disappear', as thousands had before. In fact, Renu Madam sent the boy to an institution in Chennai, where she hoped he would be looked after. She saw him infrequently, and eventually all that remained of him in her life were a few black-and-white photographs on her desk. If anyone asked who it was she would simply say, 'A child I had loved very much. I keep these here to inspire me.'

No one asked any further questions, nor did the media bother to follow up the rumours, because in India the media still respected the privacy of the powerful. And Renu Madam was very, very powerful.

Only a few knew the whole story and, of course, Rohit knew, because he made it a point to know everything about Renu Madam. One day he would be able to use that information. And this seemed the right time.

Given that she had not married, and perhaps was fearful that her next child would also have special needs, it was imperative that she be told about the possibilities which existed thanks to ART. According to Sharmaji, only healthy cells were implanted. And for a bit more money the child's sex could be selected as well, if you kept the arrangement quiet and did not tell anyone.

These were made-to-order babies, and this time, Renu Madam would definitely be successful. It would be as though she had borne it herself, but without the bother of a pregnancy. And there would be no gossip, either, because she could just say she had adopted the child.

The more he thought about it, the more he liked the idea.

As Rohit explained to Sonia (quite forgetting that she had first suggested it), 'Offering her your womb will be a great move. Instead of selling the womb to two *firangis*, why not give it to someone who deserves it much more? After all, she is a *neta* – a leader. Your child will be a politician too – think of how important we will be!'

The word 'give' made Sonia uneasy. 'Aren't we going to charge for it? You must discuss the money.'

Rohit was dismissive. 'Of course she will pay – you are doing her an enormous favour!'

And it was not just the money – Rohit hoped that a grateful Renu Madam would offer him a high position in her retinue, as well. Obviously there would be a bond between them for all time, since how could such an act of kindness ever be forgotten? But would her mentor, the savvy Vineet Bhai, MP, agree?

He seemed too involved in amassing a huge amount of money through various contracts for construction work around Delhi to engage in any other activity. There were a few rumours of young girls, and occasionally boys, visiting him, but Rohit had only seen him once, reclining at home, on a sofa, with his arm around someone wearing a skirt and a blouse. The door had been shut in Rohit's face very firmly by Vineet Bhai's bodyguard, so he had not discovered anything useful that day.

Yet Vineet Bhai had always tried to create an image of a scrupulously honest person. He habitually wore white because that was the colour of purity, associated with most Indian politicians who were often anything but pure. He had a white kurta pyjama, a white jacket, a white Nehru topi and even white Nike shoes. He kept a low profile, unlike Renu Madam.

Renu Mishra was a large, domineering woman, with a strident voice which usually could be heard long before she made an appearance. With her short hair and trade-mark salwar kameez, she was a much-reviled, but equally feared, figure. Officials quaked before her, as she was known to strip away the powers of those she did not like. So everyone had to ingratiate themselves into her good books. It was not always possible. Almost every other day headlines would scream about how a well-ensconced offi-cial in the Health Ministry had been transferred to some inconsequential department.

No, she needed to be approached by a person she trusted. Someone who cared about her. He mentally went through the list of people Renu Madam met frequently.

The person who most suited this task was probably Champa. The old crone was a widow and probably Renu Madam's only loyal retainer. Not only did she run the household, she also had unprecedented access to the Health Minister. She gave her an oil massage every day and had been with Renu Madam almost since her birth. Rohit had sometimes helped Champa write to her son, who worked as a cook in a Punjabi restaurant in Manchester. Most of her letters were full of pleas for him to return, saying that she would even accept the 'mem' he was living with as her daughter-in-law. He only replied if he needed some money.

She owed Rohit a favour. Perhaps this information could go through her.

As Rohit sat down, he decided that he would have to explain the whole plan to her very slowly and carefully.

She had to understand that this could make a huge difference to Renu Madam's life – and give her the political heir she craved. Essentially, these days each constituency was like the personal property of the elected member of parliament. Short of leaving it in your will to your children, you had to do everything to ensure it did not go out of your family. Democracy in India actually meant dynastic reign.

And poor Renu Madam's biggest drawback was that she had no child to leave it to.

That was the point at which he started the conversation. How everyone said, sorrowfully, that Renu Madam would lose her hold once the next generation took over. Hopefully there were still twenty years for her to rule – but what after that? She needed someone by her side, not only for her politics but for her wealth as well. She needed to have her own child.

'Ammi, what I am going to tell you is confidential. Please don't ever repeat it.' He leant forward and whispered in her ear. 'Sonia can help Renu Madam.'

Champa, who was the carrier of many secrets, since everyone knew she had direct access to Renu Madam, leant forward in her turn and whispered back, 'How?'

'She is enrolled in a hospital where they can inject anyone's child into her. They take a seed from a woman, another one from the man, and put them into her. She can even have a child for Renu Madam,' Rohit brusquely said into her ear.

Champa jumped back. '*Hai Ram!*'

Rohit calmed her down. 'It's all very dignified, Ammi. Women loan their wombs for other people's children. It's very noble. Because what if other people can't have children? Shouldn't you share what you have?'

He decided that he wouldn't mention the money just yet.

'Sonia was going to give her womb for the child of two *firangis*. But we thought why don't we give Sonia's womb for Renu Madam? She needs a child for the future of her party – and the country,' he added.

Champa wrinkled her nose.

'So they can take Renu-beti's seed – but we also need a seed from a man.'

Rohit looked down shyly at the floor.

'That is for Renu Madam to decide. She can choose anyone. I am sure a lot of men would be very keen.'

Champa sat rocking on her bed, wondering if this could be a feasible thing. Then she thought of how lonely her mistress was – even Vineet Bhai was not a real companion. A child would make a huge difference. She sighed. She had seen a lot in her life and had learnt to move with the times.

As she whispered all her queries to Rohit, the thought that, through this new technology, her Renu-beti could be a mother again slowly began to thrill her. It had been a personal loss when Renu-beti's son had been sent away. She had longed to go and care for him just as she had for Renu-beti, but of course that was just a foolish dream.

Rich people could have children they did not want. The poor wanted them and could not keep them; she felt bad for Sonia, too, who, like her, missed her children every day.

But life ultimately settled the scores – and this was an example. Renu-beti had power and wealth; the world was at her feet – but she had no one to inherit it. And there were further complications since she was still unmarried.

'And so Sonia will bear the child for her?'

Rohit smiled. 'Of course. The hospital has been looking after her. Ammi, if you see her, you won't believe it, she has changed so much! They have been giving her medicines, vitamins, facials, waxing, makeup. Even her hair has been styled properly, and she has some really nice clothes too. Looks like a memsahib. She's not as dark as she used to be – they've bleached her skin – she's become *gori*, really *safed, chitti chamdi*!'

Champa looked impressed with that and then nodded in agreement. It had to be someone they could trust. Luckily, Rohit's occasional attempts to pimp Sonia were known to only a select few, and had escaped Champa's notice completely.

She thought through the idea once more. Could anyone else apart from Sonia be the surrogate? Champa was too old to bear children herself, Renu-beti had no sisters, so Champa saw the sense of Sonia carrying the baby, especially if the hospital had said she could. The best part was Renu-beti could work normally without a break, since, as

Rohit pointed out, she didn't really have to do anything. The main thing was the confidentiality.

'But how will Renu-beti be sure that you all won't go to some TV channel and sell them the story? Remember last year what a fuss was made about that donation money given to Vineet Bhai?'

'There is a proper contract, drawn up by the hospital, with lawyers and so on. No one can misbehave. The whole matter has to be kept very secret, and very few of us need to know. Sonia will go away to the hospital for those nine months, so there will be no gossip. But most importantly, we have a lot of respect for Renu Madam – she is our future leader. How can we sacrifice that for a few rupees?' Rohit ended his speech on a dramatic note.

Finally persuaded, Champa said she would see if she could speak to Renu-beti.

In just a few days, when Champa came across to meet Rohit, it seemed that Renu-beti had shown some interest. And Vineet Bhai as well. She was prepared to discuss the proposal but she needed to know the name of the hospital and review all the legal details herself. Obviously she was worried that there could be some questions regarding inheritance or adoption.

Rohit grabbed his chance. 'Ammi, why don't we first speak to Renu Madam ourselves and Sonia can meet her? But it has to be fast. Those *firangis* are coming to the hospital quite soon and Sonia will be used for their child unless Madam wants her—'

Champa fell for the bait, and interrupted Rohit.

'In that case you'd better meet Renu-beti as soon as possible, and then she can find out everything else from the hospital. I know how much she has wanted a child. Let's pray that now she may find the perfect solution.'

Rohit's heartbeat speeded up. Just then Sonia came back from the hospital, and Champa almost did not recognize her. As Rohit had said, she was now much better-dressed, in a pale yellow saree, with flowers in her hair. The makeup brought a glow to her face and yellow bangles jangled noisily on her arms. She could have passed as a middle-class housewife.

'You've *really* become a memsahib.' It was the highest compliment Champa could pay her.

Sonia came closer, to show her new dangling earrings to Champa. 'Look at these!'

Rohit felt it was time to tell Sonia that the plan was working successfully. So far.

'Remember, Sonia, we had spoken about a child for Renu Madam? Well, now she may want you to go ahead. We have to meet her and Vineet Bhai later this evening.'

The room squeezed around Sonia, as her feeling of well-being was replaced by one of fear. She knew Rohit could not be doing this just out of the goodness of his heart.

She had been looking forward to meeting the *firangi* couple, and had seen their photographs. Doctorsahib had told her about them. And now Rohit was snatching her opportunity from her again. She wished she hadn't ever mentioned having a baby for Renu Madam to Rohit!

He was using her once more – where and how would it end? She felt the sweat break out on her brow.

But for Rohit the entire episode had been a real coup. He looked back on that day with pride. How well he had managed it all! Everything so far had gone according to plan. Now, three months later, with a sense of security, and Sonia safely in the hospital, he began to go through the list of the things he would ask from Renu Madam after the child was born. Or perhaps he could start now?

He picked up a pen and some paper and began to write.

GURGAON

It had been a busy time for Subhash and Anita. Despite the setback from Mumbai after the embryos had been confiscated, they had managed to keep the ball rolling. A few more couples had flown in personally for the conceptions and everything was back to normal. And then twin girls had been born to the gay couple from France.

Subhash found it tough to deal with the two proud parents. Good-looking and young, the two men were constantly touching and stroking one another and Subhash even found them kissing in the men's toilet. The thought of a man's tongue in his mouth made him turn around and rush out abruptly, while the couple barely seemed perturbed by either his entry or his exit.

But now of course, Ludi and Nicolas were totally absorbed with the birth of their children, spending all the time in the hospital and helping the gestating mother with the initial care. Their enthusiasm was apparent as they walked around the corridors showing off their new children.

This case had been personally handled by Ashok Ganguly, who was keeping careful notes and monitoring the children and the mother, hoping to use her again after about six months or so for the next gay couple, who had already registered. He had shrugged off the caesarean-section delivery, saying that the surrogate could cope with it, maintaining that she was twenty-two years old. Only he knew the truth.

Nor was he squeamish about the fact that the commissioning parents were gay.

Anita, too, was relaxed about matters of sexuality. She had been to an all-girls boarding school as a child and remembered plenty of youthful same-sex affairs that took place just because hormones were jumping and the girls often fell in love with each other. Some of the romances outlived school. But given that lesbian affairs were still widely considered taboo, she was unsurprised when the few girls who tried to stay loyal to their partners did finally succumb to a heterosexual marriage. Thus she was quite happy to help these two men achieve their dream children.

'So who will be the daddy?'

Ludi and Nicolas looked at each other and grinned. It had all been sorted out. They had used a mix of sperm, asking the doctor not to tell them whose child it was. When Dr Ganguly had suggested that they go in for a multiple pregnancy, they had agreed, thinking it would be simpler and less expensive only to go through the procedure once. Also, because of the peculiar rules in France, which did not recognize surrogacy in India, they were facing an enervating battle to get their children home. And so to try for more than one child – and get the clearance (hopefully) in one go – made perfect sense.

'I'm going to be called Père – sort of to convey that I'm the number-one father,' Ludi replied.

'And I'll settle for Papa, which sounds informal enough, doesn't it? I'll be the junior dad.'

Subhash smiled feebly, trying to participate in this foolish banter.

'And what does that do to responsibilities? Who feeds the baby, changes the nappies?'

'Oh, we'll both do everything during our paternity leave, so I'll do the first six months and then Nicolas will take over,' Ludi replied. 'Don't worry, we've worked it all out.'

Anita liked their enthusiasm, and frankly she felt it was about time men started participating more in bringing up their children. She didn't care if the men were straight or gay so long as some poor woman could be let off the hook.

As the two men left with the twins, Subhash held his head and asked dramatically, 'What's wrong with these people?'

Anita smiled and leant forward, patting his hand to calm him down.

'I want you to have a look at Preeti and see how she is.'

She had seen his fondness for Preeti but was confident enough not to feel jealous if he showed an undue interest in another woman.

Ever the realist, she knew that even the most loyal partner could get tempted, and she often wondered what held Subhash back. She concluded that he was far too lazy to actually rock the boat. There were men for whom the journey was far more important than where it would lead. But for Subhash, life was only about the destination. And his would always be Anita.

Yet, as almost the whole hospital staff knew, he never needed a second invitation where Preeti was concerned. Anita smiled as she picked up her notes and stethoscope to do a round of the wards.

While the nurse went to call her in, Subhash turned to his computer. He was impressed when he opened the personal histories of surrogates at Madonna and Child on his computer and admired how skilfully their photographs and data had been airbrushed by Ganguly.

Despite his many flaws, Ganguly had become a very useful makeover specialist. He had convinced the Pandeys that a little bit of reinvention was important.

After all, he said, most famous people indulged in it, or their publicity agents did it for them, and no one seemed to mind.

Subhash now clicked the cursor on Preeti, and her smiling photograph flashed up. Impressive. It would be difficult to believe she was barely educated.

The real life Preeti giggled as she entered, wearing a very well-cut salwar kameez, her rather large breasts hidden decorously behind a dupatta. Subhash remembered his excitement when he had first seen her. With grooming, care and a proper diet, she looked even more attractive than she had that day. She was already booked for next year. So if all went well she would earn around ten lakh rupees very soon. Ever protective about Preeti, he had told Ganguly that they should try to keep a longer gap between the babies. But Ganguly pointed to the wretched balance sheet. He had already hinted that Subhash's insistence on a highly sophisticated hospital building meant they would have to cut a few corners to meet the colossal loan repayments.

Subhash sighed and told Preeti to sit down, when there was a knock on the door. A nurse put her head around the door, looking agitated. Always an interruption! Just when he was beginning to enjoy himself. He thought ruefully about those creamy breasts . . .

'What's happened?'

'It's Kate Riley. She's reacted badly to the injections. It's an emergency—'

Telling the nurse to take Preeti to Dr Ganguly, Subhash rushed to the room where Kate had been admitted. A worried Ben stood next to her bed, holding her hand while she lay pale and soaked in sweat, in obvious pain, and nearly unconscious. She was moaning as she moved her head restlessly on the pillow, eyes closed tight in agony.

'Please do something. What's happened to her?' Ben could not conceal his agitation, though he struggled to remain calm.

For him, the entire day was a nightmare from which he hoped he would wake up. All his fears marched out and froze around him, dark figures ready to strike, as he hovered nervously around the woman he loved and towards whom he had been so cruel lately. The very thing he had tried to prevent with his anger and arguments had come to pass. And perhaps now it was too late for her to know – or even understand – why he had been so upset. It was only because he wanted to save her from this – why hadn't he been more forceful and why hadn't she listened to him?

Foolish, stubborn Kate.

The only woman he would ever, could ever, love.

As he explained to Subhash what had happened, the words tumbled out, meaninglessly. He hoped he was coherent, because for the second time in his life, his clever analytical brain was letting him down.

She had collapsed after her morning bath, he told Subhash. Minutes later, screaming from the pain, she had fainted. Unable to revive her and with increasing alarm, he hunted for her pulse. It was so weak and fluttering that he could barely sense it. Sweat oozed from her, and a froth formed around her mouth.

With trembling fingers and cursing his ineptitude at having failed to talk her out of her madness for a child, he had called for an ambulance.

He tied a wraparound dress around her damp body – and held her in his arms. Her breath sounded as though it were stuck somewhere in her throat, and she was struggling to push it out.

He thought of calling her family but was scared about switching his attention from her for a single minute.

Now he stood, as though waiting for his punishment to be announced, head slightly bowed.

Subhash understood Kate's symptoms immediately. There was very little time to waste and he would have to move swiftly if he wanted to save her.

It was an uncommon problem, but a risk most women took during fertility treatments. They were prepared for some of the discomfort and the mental stress, but were completely unaware of the fact that sometimes the drugs given to induce egg production could be life-threatening. Kate was in just that precarious position right now.

After checking her pulse-rate, which seemed to be slowing down even more, he turned to Ben and told him they would have to rush Kate into the ICU. He tried to explain quickly what had gone wrong.

'Her ovaries are probably dangerously enlarged. Let's

take a scan and then decide what to do next.'

Kate was fast approaching a critical stage. Subhash knew that whatever he did would probably result in the end of Kate's dream of becoming a mother. He decided that he would break it to Ben only when and if required.

The ultrasound scan confirmed Subhash's worst suspicions.

'What does this mean?' Ben's usually clear voice was barely audible.

Subhash took him outside the room. Even though Kate seemed unconscious, he did not want to take a chance.

'Tell me what's going on but, for God's sake, please don't let anything happen to her.'

'Don't worry – she'll be absolutely safe. We'll give her some drugs to counteract this swelling. If it doesn't work, I may have to operate. But the bad news is that, either way, after this we may not be able to harvest her eggs – and so . . .' Subhash spread his hands helplessly.

'I understand. Just make sure she pulls through.' Ben's voice was choked and barely audible.

He couldn't believe this was happening. First his mother, and now his wife. Even the reassurances sounded the same: *We'll do our best to save her . . . try not to worry . . . sit down and have a nice cup of tea . . .*

He was jumping with nerves. Why had he listened? This fucking madness would end up killing her, he knew it. A ghastly end to this bizarre adventure. He wished he had managed to convince her not to try for a child again. He even felt he should have walked out of their marriage – anything was better than Kate suffering like this. Anything.

All day he had realized, over and over again, how much she meant to him.

It was just like the last time. Twenty years had passed but here he was, once again, in a hospital hoping that the woman he loved would come back to him, healthy and well.

He remembered only too vividly the final moments at his mother's side. She had admired the roses he had bought for her, saying that the scent reminded her of her gardening days. She was too frail to walk, and the cancer had eaten away her flesh down to forty kilos. She was tiny and birdlike, and knew she would never go into her garden again, or tend to her rose bushes.

She was looking at the bouquet when she stopped speaking.

It took a while for Ben to realize that she was dead. The tears had flowed silently down his cheeks as he held her hand for the last time. That's how the nurse found him, and then gently told him that he should call his father.

Ben sat down outside the operating theatre while they took Kate in. This time he could not even hold her hand, he just had to wait and hope. And hope.

MUMBAI

As Mehta had expected, his wife was thrilled with the money. For once he had the good sense to give it to her immediately. Instead of putting it in the locker, she laid the two bundles of crisp thousand-rupee notes in front of Shirdi Ka Sai Baba and sat in prayer for nearly two days, only taking a few moments out to cook and clean. This was a complete turnaround for Mehta; at last he had seen the light! His guilt increased in inverse proportion to the calls from Dr Pandey, which had become less frequent. He still looked forward to hearing her voice. One day he hoped he would be able to give her some good news, too.

Meanwhile, Malti had managed to tell her father that finally Mehta was doing the right thing, and her father's investment might not have been in vain. She even called his parents and told them that things were looking up and they could return from their tortuous pilgrimage. However, they reminded her that they were also praying for progeny for her and her husband, and till that happened they must assuage the angry gods.

Malti's happiness was instantaneously crushed. It was true. She knew that she must have committed some horrible crime in her past reincarnation that meant she could not even have one child now.

She had undergone all kinds of treatment, including homemade pills and potions, but nothing seemed to work. She had been told that walking barefoot to the Ganesh temple at four in the morning, a distance of five kilometres, would help, and she had done even that.

Now she had learnt that walking was not enough. Other women had actually rolled all the way to the temple, and it was said *that* was the only way. But Mehta, shuddering at this public display of barrenness, would not allow her to do that. He had, on the other hand, said it was alright to eat food without garlic and salt for a month, drink *gangajal*, wear all kinds of threads and *tabeez*, recite mantras of various combinations, feed fish at the aquarium and nearly get jailed for it – but nothing had worked. Their sex, though unadventurous, was vigorous enough to bring them both to a joyful climax, especially when his parents were not around. But her womb remained unresponsive to all stimulants, sexual or otherwise.

Mehta was wondering if one day he could let Malti know about those little embryos. Apparently they were so tiny that they could not even be seen by the naked eye. Would they be of any use to her? And even if he brought them home, what would they do with one? He had no idea how they could be implanted, and decided it was another item to be checked on the Internet. He had also tried to find some information on the Freedom Hospital on the web, but so far his searches had proved fruitless. All he had found was a link which said that the site page had been removed.

Within a few weeks of the embargoed embryos, a new consignment had arrived. This time it was clearly addressed to the Freedom Hospital, even though the courier company was the same as before and it had also come from Mybaby.com in the UK. Again it contained the shiny little milk cans, but this time Ali made no fuss, nor did he make an effort to call the press. He just shrugged and told Mehta that these needed to be personally delivered to Dr Wadhwani, for which a small 'commission' would come their way.

'But why can't the courier company just pick them up, if we're letting them go through?'

'This is a favour I'm doing Dr Wadhwani. Otherwise, if I confiscated the first consignment, I should also confiscate this one. Do you see anyone complaining? Just take your cut and stop whining about it. Wadhwani will hand you the cash at the hospital.'

Over time Mehta realized that the embryos had been turned into a regular earning stream. Ali would be tipped off from the company in the UK when to expect them, and for a fee they would be passed on, usually to the Freedom Hospital.

But Mehta suspected that the real kingpin driving this operation was in Delhi. The boss of BirthingBabies. He seemed to send regular instructions to Ali. It was those phone calls that led to the maximum amount of money being made – mostly from poor Dr Pandey, who then paid once again to get the consignment (which belonged to her anyway) shipped to her.

When Mehta peered into his office, Ali was exercising on the treadmill in the corner. He was sweating profusely, and his straining, sinewy muscles were outlined sharply in the neon lights, since he had stripped down to his waist. Mehta admired his tenacious capacity to work on himself

– most of the other officers of his rank had given up struggling against the avalanche of unofficial perks the job
offered, and allowed themselves to eat, drink and be
merry. Ali, for all his other faults, was a teetotaller and,
oddly enough, said his *namaaz* whenever he could. He
even had a prayer rug in the corner of his office, and
sometimes his staff would have to wait silently watching
while he prayed, even if there was an emergency. No one
was allowed to interrupt when Ali was on a direct line to
God. But the duration of the *namaaz*, which could be one
minute or one hour, depended entirely on what kind of
advice God needed from Ali.

'Okay, boss.' Mehta picked up the containers and
packed them into the black suitcase, following the now-
familiar routine, and lugged them down to the car. As he
drove slowly to the Freedom Hospital, once again he
wondered about the parents of the poor tiny sods inside
the containers.

Of course, he could try to 'kidnap' them. After all, it
was so easy for anything or anyone to disappear in this
country – he could just take a turn anywhere down this
road and find a safe-house for this material – but he
couldn't think of a reason why any Mafia chief or don
would be interested in these blastocysts. Not something
they could trade in.

Only women like Malti might be willing to pay a high
price. It occurred to him that he could take some advice
from Dr Pandey when she next called about it. But he

would have to confess to the fact that he and his boss were trying to make money from 'her' embryos.

The entrance to Freedom Hospital was once again crowded with cars. Though he could not spot Mr Dhawan's car, he saw a few foreigners in wheelchairs being taken inside. On one side were a couple of BMWs and even a Rolls Royce. Not bad for such a discreet hospital. Yet it was very quiet, and there was no urgency of any kind being displayed by anyone, unlike the last time he was here.

As always, he dragged the suitcase inside to the reception. The two foreigners in the wheelchairs had already been checked in and they were taken straight through the doors. Once again he did not notice any young women around who could be the recipients of these embryos. The receptionist, who seemed even younger today with his bright glowing skin, was still painfully calculating bills, as though he were a much older man. He called and left a message for Dr Wadhwani.

'He's just coming down.'

While Mehta was waiting, the man who had said he was seventy-five walked by again.

'Sir,' Mehta called out.

The man stopped and looked at him, puzzled, and then his brow cleared. 'Oh yes, Ali's man. Good, good. How are you?'

Mehta kept thinking he had seen him somewhere other than here at the hospital. Those dazzling blue eyes, that smile. He reminded him of a film actor of the sixties and seventies, Rajiv Kumar, who had developed Alzheimer's and disappeared from public view. The rumour was that Kumar had been kept in hiding by his wife, who did not want the world to see him the way he was, but rather to remember him only as a superstar.

'You know I thought I had seen you before somewhere – are you Rajiv Kumar? The famous film star?'

'You're too young to remember me!' The man was delighted. 'How do you know?'

'My parents used to watch your films all the time on video. But . . . you had some problem? Alzheimer's?'

Kumar laughed yet again. He was such a happy man, an unusual quality in Mumbai, where most people were usually surly, overwhelmed with the struggle of daily life.

Mehta marvelled at his strong, white teeth and ran his own tongue over his yellowing enamel, wondering what toothpaste this man used. Obviously not the one Malti favoured, which she bought just because she loved the TV advertisement!

'Oh no – that was a long time back! After Alzheimer's I got a bad knee, and then I got rheumatoid arthritis! My eyesight started going as well. Don't you remember?'

'I don't, actually. But you look so good now – fantastic!'

'As I said, we do miracles in here, miracles! Bring your parents here sometime!'

He waved cheerily and walked out to the Rolls Royce. Getting in, he drove away. Mehta watched him dumbfounded.

Dr Wadhwani emerged finally and took Mehta to his office. After opening a steel almirah in his room, he took out some cash and, putting it in an envelope, handed it to Mehta.

'Thank Ali. Tell him I'll give him a call.'

'Shall I wait for the containers?'

'No, this time you can leave.'

'Dr Wadhwani, can I ask you a question?'

Wadhwani was just walking out of the room, but he stopped at the door. He wasn't as impatient as he had been last time. Must be a better day.

'Go ahead.'

'What do you do here in this hospital? I just saw Mr Rajiv Kumar – he says he's seventy-five and he looks like he's sixty years old!'

'We help people get better, that's what we do. Simple enough! Did Kumar say he was seventy-five? What a liar!' Dr Wadhwani almost started laughing at the last sentence. 'That man will always be vain. He tells everyone different things. To the girls he says he's only forty. So it's all in the mind, Mehta. See you later.'

Mehta realized he had been dismissed. Once again, as he watched Dr Wadhwani walk through the door, he observed that even he looked so well. He had none of the pallor people tend to get working in hospitals, deprived of daylight. It must be the cheeriest hospital in Mumbai. Everyone looked energetic and healthy – even the receptionist, though he was excruciatingly slow at his calculations. His brow was smooth and he didn't have a single wrinkle on his face. And neither did Dr Wadhwani or even Rajiv Kumar. Wonderful place to work. Or maybe it was to do with the diet. He must ask Ali to check with Dr Wadhwani.

It was while he was driving back to the office to drop off the car and the suitcase that he realized that Rajiv Kumar had been lying about his age, just as Dr Wadhwani said.

In 1970, when he was at the top of his profession, he was already fifty-five years old; Mehta had heard his parents say that often enough. So he couldn't be seventy-five at all.

He must be at least ninety-six.

With that thought Mehta almost crashed into the car in front of him.

Chapter 5

SIMRAN

It had turned out to be a very strange and frightening evening indeed at Edward's home.

The moment he uncovered my mouth and released his grip on me I got out of the chair, and dashed for the door but he pulled me back. We swayed back and forth locked in struggle, while I tried to reach for my bag. My face hurt, and I was worried that he had scratched me.

'Stop this – stop, I won't scream.' I could barely breathe, but I finally managed to get the words out.

My saree had almost come off in the struggle – and I hated the touch of his hands. The thought that I had stupidly put myself in such danger now hit me once again. This was someone who, possibly, had deliberately infected a young child with HIV – he was capable of anything.

'Then be quiet,' his voice was still grim, though soft.

Somehow I managed to mumble 'Will do'.

He released his grip on my face abruptly and I took a deep breath.

A hostile silence fell between us.

When Edward spoke he did not sound defensive –
rather he had an accusatory note in his voice.

'I suspected you right from the start. And what the fuck
is your connection with Susan?'

'I first want your word you won't hurt me.'

He looked at me as though I was from another planet.

'You come into my home under false pretences – and
then say "Don't hurt me". I have every reason to think
you're here to hurt *me*, not the other way round. Who *are*
you? I think I saw a voice recorder in your bag. Has some
woman sent you after me? Is this a paternity suit?'

His eyes narrowed.

'And where did you get Susan's name from?' At her
name, his voice shook a little. He cleared his throat and
glared at me.

I was still shivering from the implications of what had
just happened. I pulled my saree around me and sat
down. It was too late to run away now. Even if he was a
maniac, if I remained calm he might let me go. If he had
looked inside my handbag, presumably he also knew I
didn't have a gun or any other weapon.

'Alright. I'll tell you why I'm here, if you tell me your
connection with Susan.'

'She was a very close friend.'

It sounded like a confession, and I felt a frisson of pure
rage. I thought of baby Amelia, and the true meaning of
his betrayal overwhelmed me. How could he have
fathered her and then abandoned her like that? But was

that surprising? After all, he had told me about it himself: once he had provided his sperm, he moved on, with no attachments.

How many women had he infected?

Could it possibly be he had no idea he was HIV positive? Or, worse, was he seriously unhinged?

I tried to stop panicking. I told myself, *calm down, this can't get any worse.*

Though, of course, it could.

'How well did you know her?' I hedged.

'Before I say anything, where did you meet Susan?'

His tone was firm, so I decided I would have to explain a little.

'In India.'

He looked genuinely surprised. If he was such a good actor, I had to be similarly careful and sharp.

Now the flirtation and the game-playing were over, I needed to ask all the right questions.

While pretending to be looking for my cigarette case, I made sure he hadn't switched off my Dictaphone. I didn't care if he guessed what I was doing.

I took out a very welcome cigarette. I could use him as an ashtray in case he attacked me again, I thought viciously.

Despite my apparent nonchalance, it was irritating to see that my hands were trembling as I tried to light a match.

'You don't mind if I smoke? It's been a long evening.'

He shrugged and said, 'Sure, go ahead.'

I lit the cigarette and, as I took the first deep breath, it felt good.

'And why did you meet her?'

I hesitated and then told him: 'She wanted a child, and the clinic run by friends had arranged for the surrogate mother.'

'When was this?' He still seemed puzzled.

'Summer last year.'

'Really? And then?'

'Look – I've told you enough. I'll tell you everything in detail if you give me your side of the story. Who is Susan Oldham?'

'Why don't you ask her?'

'If you claim to be such a close friend, you should know why I can't ask.'

'Know what?'

I hesitated, and then decided to play along. Whatever his game was, I was sure he knew all the rules.

'Because she's dead.'

He was still standing up. As I spoke, I could swear I saw the shock on his face and the surprising glint of tears. So Susan Oldham had meant quite a lot to him.

His grief seemed real.

I kept quiet, while he made more coffee and, a little cautiously, brought it over.

Did he think I was going to lash out at him? Shouldn't I be the one who should be scared?

Despite the tension between us barely half an hour ago, I could feel the change in him. No longer aggressive. Almost in despair.

'Tell me what happened to her – and tell me the truth this time.'

It was past midnight and we were just beginning to talk honestly with each other. Sometimes relationships are complicated things.

I told him how she and her husband had died in an accident in Rajasthan, and as I talked, he seemed to become increasingly distressed. But I still omitted all mention of baby Amelia or the surrogacy. I wanted that information to come from *him*.

'I can only tell you the rest of the story – if you tell me how you know her,' I said finally.

'Let me show you her photograph first. Let's be sure we're talking about the same person,' he said, getting up.

He went to his desk, and rummaged around till he found an old photograph, dated 1978, and showed it to me. Edward was standing with a group of people – and I couldn't be completely certain, but one of them appeared to be Susan.

'That could be her – the blonde hair matches as well, though it was shorter when we met her.'

'Right. Okay – remember I had told you how I got into this sperm-donating business? That a friend of mine had not been able to have a child and I had helped her out? Well, that woman was Susan. More than twenty years ago, she came to me in this very house – just like you've come today – and we slept together, and then I have no idea what happened. She never came back. I thought, as I told you, she'd had a child. That's why I'm puzzled. Why would she now go to India to try to have another one?'

'Do you have any idea where that first child could be?'

'None whatsoever. I told you that I never keep in touch with the children or their parents. Those are my only terms. I love my independence.'

'Can I ask you a question – and please give me a straight answer, as this is very, very important.'

'Go ahead.'

I thought of Amelia, said a silent prayer, and tried to keep my voice as steady as possible.

'Have you ever tested for AIDS?'

'Every year – along with all other blood tests.'

I looked away and then forced myself to lock my gaze with his.

Steady on, now, I told myself. Just go for the kill.

'Are you HIV positive?'

His tears dried up and his face turned red. He was even more angry than when he had grappled with me earlier. I tried not to flinch.

'Are you fucking out of your tiny mind? Would I be going around donating sperm if I was HIV positive? Do I strike you as some kind of maniac? A killer? A hate-filled monster? I try to help people – not destroy them.'

He was outraged.

I felt my face flush as well. He was right. But could I believe him?

Was his denial enough?

After all, I had thought of him as a monster. A well-behaved, milk-drinking pervert. Someone who wanted to hurt women and children by donating his HIV-infected sperm.

'So you're not?' I persisted.

I could see he was controlling himself only with difficulty.

'Why the hell should I be?'

I finally told him, because, once again, I felt I had no choice.

'Mike and Susan's child, baby Amelia, is HIV positive and we are all trying to understand how it happened.'

Now he fell silent, the anger wiped clean off his face.

'What's that got to do with me?'

His voice shook a little, but the harshness had gone. He almost sounded normal again, even conciliatory.

I got up, suddenly restless, and walked around the room, drinking my coffee, looking to see if there was anything which could give me a hint as to what happened here twenty years ago.

'That's what I am here for, to check out if there's a connection, because we found your name on their admission form,' I continued.

He looked bewildered.

'The poor child doesn't have parents and urgently needs treatment. We're also concerned about the surrogate who carried her. And the strange thing is that Susan and Mike didn't even give us the right address, so we couldn't find out anything about them. I thought they had stolen someone's identity or something, till your name showed up.'

'So you flew to London. All this seduction, this build-up about wanting a child, was just rubbish. Amazing!' He shook his head, but his tone, once again, was not warm and friendly. He sounded cold and contemptuous. From being a supplicant, I was suddenly an enemy. He didn't like where I had put him. Should I leave, I wondered?

Instead I nodded. 'I apologize – but we are really anxious in the hospital because, frankly, not only is baby Amelia now an orphan, but a single case like this can ruin us. I had to find out if you were Amelia's father.'

'Impossible. I haven't seen Susan since that day more than twenty years ago.'

'What do you know about her – or her family?' Perhaps I could find someone else who would lay claim to Amelia.

'I don't know much about her family, because, as I told you, we lost touch after . . . our rendezvous.' He smiled a little sadly, as his anger seemed to fade away. 'We were at university together here in London, part of the same group. Then she went away to get married to someone she had known earlier. She called me when she wanted to have a child; she said her husband was infertile – but we resembled each other, so the baby would hopefully look like it was theirs.'

He stopped and then shook his head once more, as though he still could not believe that she was really dead.

'But now I'm not sure whether she even had the child. If she was with you earlier in the year arranging another child, what happened to the first? Do you know if she had an older child?'

'Nothing was mentioned on our form.'

'Is there any way of finding out?'

As he spoke, my fear receded. I wondered if I could turn this to my advantage. He had fond memories of Susan Oldham. Perhaps, through him, I could find out a little more about her.

'Could you help me contact your old friends? Someone might know more about her, her family, her older child, if any?' I asked.

'I can't promise, but I'll try to contact some of the friends we had in common at the time. What a shame about the baby, though. What's going to happen to her?'

His appeal was a turning point for me. I tried to push my suspicions about him away – and wondered if I could trust him. Or perhaps I could pretend to trust him, and then see where it led me? I didn't see the harm in that. It might even lead to some revelations about baby Amelia – especially if I could meet some friends or relatives of the Oldhams.

Frankly, I thought, as I gazed at him with what I hoped was a sympathetic look, what choice do I have?

I stubbed out the cigarette, lit another one to be on the safe side, and carefully replied,

'That's why we need to find some family for her. You can imagine the urgency – because while we have put baby Amelia on medication already, it will take a while for her to stabilize. And it will be good for her to be somewhere where she is loved, rather than in some strange hospital.'

'But you're sure Mike and Susan were the commissioning parents? You're *absolutely* sure of that?'

'The blastocysts had come from the UK, all ready to be inserted into the surrogate. They were from a clinic here which is a regular supplier to us. Since Mike and Susan had commissioned the child, they also came for the delivery, and they were paying the surrogate, so we assumed that it was their child. But they weren't HIV positive.'

'Which is why you asked me if I was? Because Susan left my name written somewhere?'

'I'm sorry you're so upset, but I had to know. I thought you might have . . . a special connection. Of course – I realize that you may not, because you hadn't met for twenty years.'

He nodded, quiet for a few moments.

'And why were you pretending you wanted a child?' The suspicious look came back on his face. 'I know – don't tell me. You wanted to match my DNA, and also find out about the HIV . . .'

My silence gave me away.

'Fuck! Let me show you my last hospital report. I keep an updated one, just in case some crazy woman like you shows up.'

He fetched a thick file from his office and thrust it at me. Feeling slightly ashamed I flipped through the detailed report. It was a startlingly clean bill of health. Edward Walters had no known disease and was so healthy he ought to have been put in a science museum.

'Sorry – but I had no choice. You are my only link to baby Amelia.' I handed the file back, trying to sound every bit as contrite as I had now begun to feel.

He put down the file and made us another round of coffee. Though I was still nursing my bruises, our animosity was gone, leaving a palpable sorrow in the air. It was almost two in the morning.

After some time we had gone over the various possibilities, but nothing made any sense. There had to be some reason why one of the Oldhams (or someone else) had scribbled his name on that form.

Edward looked at me.

'I think we can talk about this in the morning. Do you want to get some sleep?'

'I would love to.'

His manner had completely changed, from aggressive rage to brisk and matter-of-fact. I think he was slowly beginning to trust me, and I felt the same way about him. Though I still had no way of knowing this for sure, I felt I had misjudged him.

'Now we can drop all pretences, I guess. Why don't you sleep in the bedroom and I can use the sofa?'

My jet-lag had begun to hit me in earnest, and despite my seductive clothes, my mood too had been transformed to solemnity. There was something very odd about this whole incident. It was almost eerie. I kept thinking that there must be a completely different reason for my presence here, and, of course, I had no idea what it could be. Had someone deliberately wanted to bring me here, to his flat?

Anything was possible.

Just earlier in the evening, I had fancifully imagined that if Edward wasn't quite the villain I thought he might be, I would end up in his bed. And here I was, actually in it.

Only I hadn't realized I would be alone.

Five months earlier

NOVEMBER

GURGAON

Kate was recovering well, and Ben had managed to bring her back to the hotel within a few weeks. It had been a terrible scare for both of them, and she needed to recuperate. The thought that she had nearly lost her life made them even more aware of the risks. Was all this worth it?

They watched as other surrogates gave birth, each baby welcomed by its new parents. Almost every week at Madonna and Child, there would be celebrations over new deliveries. Ultimately it was a karmic lottery. Some people could have babies and some were just silent spectators. But this time Kate felt a definite sense of acceptance. She walked around the hospital wards and tried to participate in the joy of the other parents. It was about time she accepted her fate, instead of fighting against it.

While they could have just flown back to London, Kate wanted to stay. She said that she needed time to think what to do next – and if they left too early, she would not be able to take a reasoned and well-thought-out decision.

They had both made the effort of coming to India for a year, just for this, so why not stay a while longer?

It was obvious that, after what had happened, her own eggs could never be harvested, but perhaps they could try something different? Maybe a surrogate could provide the eggs. Ben refused to think about it any more, and told her that not every problem had a solution. It may be best if they left it alone.

Anita and Subhash had insisted that, while they weighed their priorities, they could go to the Taj Mahal as Kate had wanted. After all, it was part of the package which had been arranged for them.

At this stage Ben was reluctant to do anything to upset her, and he decided the best thing would be to use that as an excuse to get away from the hospital. If only he could remind Kate that they could enjoy their life together, even without children, she might change her attitude completely.

They decided that a good compromise would be to go to Agra first, and then to Ambala.

The train to Agra was comfortable and Kate slept throughout. It was already nearly three weeks since her hospitalization, and she was slowly beginning to get some colour back in her cheeks.

Looking relaxed and pretty in her loose printed trousers and T-shirt, she held Ben's hand tight while they had their photograph taken in front of the world's best-known mausoleum.

'Thanks for bringing me here.' She turned to Ben and kissed him.

He kissed her back, but he wasn't as impressed.

'It's a tomb,' he replied. 'Very beautiful, but it's still a fucking tomb built by slave labour.'

It gave him the creeps. While the exquisite marble inlay work and the symmetry of the building made it a tourist trap, he was impatient to leave. White marble reminded him of gravestones anyway. And of the hospital floor.

After eating a hot and spicy meal at a local restaurant, they took a cab back to their hotel. Kate laid her head on Ben's shoulder, feeling very vulnerable and tired.

Slowly Ben allowed himself to unwind. All the love he had felt for her earlier, when he had almost lost her, flowed back. Though this was the end of Kate's dream, it could free them up to be themselves. The thought calmed him down – as did the warmth of her body next to him. For the first time in years there was no pressure or discussion about having a child . . . and that felt good.

It was just the two of them together, gazing out of the cab window at a moon which gazed back unblinkingly at them. Because of the pitch-black sky around, the moon seemed to him like a perfectly circular light at the end of a tunnel.

What a relief! Kate was alive and well – and he must keep her happy. That was all that mattered.

As she snuggled closer to him, Ben wanted to wipe away all her anxieties.

They had changed into their nightclothes, and, wrapping a light blanket around them, shared a glass of wine on their hotel balcony.

Maybe, Ben thought reluctantly, the Taj was actually a unifying force for broken hearts. He laughed at his own sentimentality.

Kate smiled up at him. 'What's so funny?'

'I don't know. I just want us to stop fighting.'

'Yes, let's.'

She still looked a little bewildered by the events of the past few months. She had suffered a lot, and he felt a renewed upsurge of affection.

Also for the first time in many months, he wanted no more than that single glass of wine.

Later, when they were in bed, Ben threw the blanket away, pulling her gently on top of him. The moon through the trees played on her skin, creating a lace of light and shade. He loved the sight of her moving above him, her face full of concentration and her mouth slightly open as she bent over, her tongue sliding around his mouth, teasing and licking. He touched her breasts and her clitoris as she put her head back, seeming almost surprised that her body still could respond to idle useless pleasure.

At last, at last, he felt they were together. There was no child between them, and might never be. It had been a long time since he had felt so close to her and so confident about their love.

The next day, they caught a train to Delhi and then

onwards to Ambala, to track down Ben's grandfather and his *bibighar*. This time round even Kate was cheerful and curious.

The station in the Ambala cantonment opened on to the famous Grand Trunk Road, which in the old days ran all the way to Lahore, now in Pakistan. Mercifully, the stream of traffic which used to block the exit from the station had been diverted on to a flyover. It was now possible to take a rickshaw and swiftly ride past the dusty roadside eateries – or *dhabas* – with their lurid hoardings advertising impossibly plump tandoori chicken, into Ambala Cantt, as it was known colloquially. Just behind lay the Lal Kurti bazaar, named after the red jackets of the British infantry units, which had once thronged here.

Like a true army man, Major Riley had drawn a map of the cantonment where the army was based, and Ben now perused the aged, crumbling piece of paper, carefully trying to find their way around. The British had always strategically kept the army away from the civilian population – out of fear that liberal ideas might contaminate those soldiers taken from among the Indian population.

The residential area of the cantonment was obviously frozen in time – and apart from the renaming of roads after local Indian heroes, everything lay as his grandfather had described it. Even the numbering of the rundown bungalows had not changed, though their conical thatched roofs had been replaced with flat concrete slabs.

Unlike its present rather dusty and dismal status, Ben

remembered that it had been, once, the last staging post for the British on the eastern banks of the Sutlej – as beyond, at the western end, lay the indomitable kingdom of the last great ruler of the Punjab, Maharaja Ranjit Singh.

Established in the early 1800s, Ambala had also been very important for British families. 'After the Indian mutiny in 1857, when Delhi became dangerous,' Ben told Kate, 'it was in Ambala that British women and children took shelter.

'And,' he added, 'it was to Ambala that the viceroys travelled from Calcutta – on their way to their summer capital of Simla.'

A large Anglo-Indian population, the result of liaisons between the British junior ranks and Indian women, also settled down here. Ben had gathered from his grandfather's papers that there must have been a scandal when he, as a British officer, got involved with an Indian. It would have been thoroughly disapproved of by his peers. He may have tried to hide his affair, but the multitude of domestic servants – from his bearer to the *syce* – would have known and gossiped. It would have been quite embarrassing.

Is that why, apart from hints and innuendo, so little was known about the woman? And yet, he knew from his diaries that Major Riley had fallen in love with her. Something had obviously happened to her, and their relationship – as many pages from his journals had been torn out. The story of his tortured romance was tantalizingly incomplete. And, oddly enough, there was no mention anywhere of the battle in which he had fought so valiantly and been injured.

When they reached the once-beautiful St Paul's church, where his grandparents had been married, they found it had been bombed during the Indo-Pakistan war in the 1960s. Many of the gravestones had been vandalized. It was quite different to what Ben had imagined.

Still, Ben refused to be downhearted at what he saw.

'Can you imagine what it was like here when my grandfather was based here? A large, bustling establishment, with a glittering mess and roads full of carriages!'

Kate closed her eyes and tried to visualize the uniformed men and women in gowns and the latest hats, who came by ship to Bombay and then were carried by caravan and horseback to Ambala, among other northern cantonments.

But, walking around the church graveyard, it was apparent that settling here was not easy. The gravestones recorded a sorry tale of women and children dying of dehydration and dysentery, and even the plague – a desperate time, when entire villages in the district had been fenced off by barbed wire – and yet the British families were not able to escape the disease.

They also managed to locate the Sirhind Club, another remnant of the Raj. It was doing quite well. Enthusiastic players of bingo and bridge crowded the card rooms and an equally boisterous bunch sat at the bar.

The Raj was reflected in the furniture, the lithographs

on the walls, even the waiters with their quaint uniforms. But it was clear that many things had been Indianized. Ben thought of the sign posted outside most of the British clubs in India, which he had seen in one of the photographs back home: 'Dogs and Indians not allowed'. He'd always thought it strange for a man who loved an Indian woman, as his grandfather had, to keep that picture among his mementoes.

Now, of course, Indians were everywhere; Ben and Kate were the only foreigners in the club. To their embarrassment, this time it was they who were not allowed in. The bearer was regretful: the dress-code barred shorts and sandals and so both Kate and Ben were politely asked to leave. Even their offer to hastily don their woollen sweaters and jeans did not help.

'I think he looked rather triumphant as he threw us out.' Kate sounded a little miffed.

'Well, we deserved it in 1947, and we deserve it now.' Ben refused to feel discouraged. In fact, he was beginning to enjoy the whole experience. He was on territory where one of his family members had lived and ruled, and it was an exhilarating thought.

Following the map, he found his grandfather's former home next to the old bombed-out church and he wondered if they would at least be allowed to enter here. All he was interested in, really, was the *bibighar* – and he knew it lay at the back of the house.

There was no bell at the gate. Kate and Ben walked in

almost up to the veranda and then stood politely a few feet away, waiting to be noticed by an elderly couple drinking their afternoon tea on comfortable cane chairs. The husband, a white-bearded gentleman, got up on seeing them, his hands folded in greeting.

'*Namastey*. Can I help you?' he asked.

Ben reflexively folded his hands as well.

'*Namastey*.'

He introduced himself and Kate and apologized for the intrusion.

The man, whose name was Vishal Seth, dismissively waved his hand at Ben's regretful tone and said, 'No problem about that. What can I do for you?'

Taking a cue from his friendly tone, Ben took a deep breath and plunged right in.

'Well, actually, my grandfather lived in this house many years ago. He was in the British Army. Obviously he's dead now – and I thought I should drop by and see it, since I was in India for some work. And also to learn a bit about his life here, as I know very little. I hope that's okay?'

'Oh sure, you're most welcome. But you may get disappointed – we bought the house just a few years ago – and so don't really know its history.'

After they sat down, Ben took out his laptop and showed Vishal Seth and his wife a photograph of the house as it had been around eighty years ago, with his uniformed grandfather in front of it. Then he clicked on his favourite photograph – of the woman whom he assumed was his grandfather's mistress. He asked, 'Do any of you know who she is?'

Vishal Seth's wife, Teji, a thin woman with spectacles, scrutinized the photograph carefully and then handed it over to her husband with obvious disdain. 'I have no idea. But there is a family staying in the rooms behind – and the woman, Sheela, says that her family came from Lucknow to Ambala more than seventy years ago. She helps us with the cleaning of the house and may know something.'

She was frowning as she spoke. Her husband understood her implication and he, too, began to sound distinctly unfriendly.

'Well,' he said, 'in the old days a lot of the white sahibs had affairs with local women – that's well known. But many of them were cruelly abandoned.' Mr Seth looked straight at Ben with a stern look on his face. 'Then the British went off – promising to send for them. They never did and the women were left high and dry – but with plenty of Anglo-Indian children who rarely felt at home in India.'

There was a moment's icy silence. Mr Seth might have jumped to the right conclusion, but it only added to Ben's guilt. He could hardly ask, *And were there any Anglo-Indian children, do you think?* Who knew the answer to that?

Ben and Kate looked uneasily at each other. Had they made a mistake by coming here? Then Mrs Seth spoke up.

'If your family was really concerned about this poor woman they should have come here when your grandfather was alive.'

Clearly the husband and wife were no longer prepared to be hospitable. Mr Seth got up abruptly and said he had some work to do and Mrs Seth also remembered a prior engagement.

Trying to contain his disappointment at the way the conversation had turned, Ben asked for permission to look around and take some photographs. Kate could sense his despair and felt sorry for him. He had really looked forward to discovering something about his family's past. The Seths agreed with obvious reluctance.

Following Major Riley's map, Ben and Kate went to the back of the house where the *bibighar* had stood. A young dark-skinned girl sat outside rocking a child to sleep on her lap. As Ben took out his camera, a woman, probably Sheela, appeared, followed by a toddler. She seemed tired, but she smiled and asked them if they would like to have a cup of tea.

'*Chai*, sahib?'

It was easy enough to understand.

To Kate's surprise, Ben nodded and sat down on the mud floor outside in the tiny courtyard, next to the young girl. He looked perfectly comfortable there, waiting for the promised tea. Sheela, though poor, obviously had far fewer qualms about sharing what she had than the much richer Seths.

Kate thought for a moment and then sat next to him on a half-broken, unsteady, three-legged stool, smiling at the curious toddler who stood hiding behind his older sister, while she carried on rocking the baby on her lap.

The woman went inside again to make the tea on an earthen stove lit by a wood fire.

'I know this sounds funny – but I do feel at home here,' Ben said with a sigh. 'Maybe because I've been thinking about it for so long. I always imagined it would be like this.'

'You're just romanticizing this situation, Ben.' Kate's voice had more of an edge than she intended.

'I'm serious, Kate. I've thought of this house so often, and this little *bibighar*. I know it's all totally ramshackle and grotty but I can just feel that something from the Riley past is buried around here.'

Kate tried to be more sympathetic.

'The Riley past ... the Seths weren't too happy with that, were they? Maybe we should have come here a long time back, like he said.'

Ben looked at the children, who had shifted away to a safe distance, staring curiously at these two pale-limbed adults sitting outside their home. He beckoned the young boy to come closer. Uncertainly and, disregarding his dripping nose, the toddler put his thumb in his mouth. His shorts were torn and he was bare-chested. His sister wore a ragged salwar kameez and the child in her lap, another girl, was naked.

Ben wished he had at least brought some chocolates for the children.

'I would love to do something for them,' he said.

'We could give them some money,' Kate suggested, although, as the words left her lips, she realized that this was the easiest option.

Ben didn't quite know how to express himself; it was as though he had been here before, and he knew all about it, but of course that was completely stupid. He had probably spent too much time poring over his grandfather's documents and journals!

A very un-Benlike thought was forming in his mind. He knew what he was going to say sounded all wrong. Kate would misunderstand, but he had to say it. *What if* . . . This place was opening up all kinds of possibilities, especially concerning an idea he had explored when he had first thought of coming to India. Adoption.

He hunted for the right opening. He and Kate had just found their equilibrium, and he didn't want to wreck it.

'I know how much you want a child, Kate . . . so do you think that . . .'

He hesitated again. Kate felt a prickle of unease up her spine. She knew she wasn't going to like what Ben had to say.

Ben tried again.

'I was wondering, do you think we could . . . we could adopt a child from here? One of these kids perhaps?'

Kate almost toppled over.

'Ben, are you crazy? Are you feeling alright?'

'Why not? You've been going on and on about having children, and here this woman has three. She can barely cope.'

Kate looked at the little baby in the young girl's arms. She had to talk Ben out of this mad enterprise. These were not some long-lost cousins, for God's sake! And then what about the child's own mother? She might not agree! What was Ben thinking of? You couldn't just walk into a house and say, 'I want this child!' It wasn't like going into a department store, she thought, annoyed.

But Ben was already on his feet. He went inside the tiny room which was the sum total of the *bibighar*.

When she heard his triumphant shout a few minutes later, her heart sank further. She really wasn't enjoying this any more.

She walked in and saw him standing in front of a photograph hanging askew on the wall. It was half covered with fungus, and hidden behind cobwebs, but Ben's grandfather and his 'mistress' were clearly discernible.

Had Ben actually found his long-lost relatives?

Kate's head began to pound with dread. This was going to be very tough if he felt there was a genuine connection to this family.

GURGAON

Sitting in her office, going through the day's reports, Anita was pleased that Preeti's surrogacy for Mike and Susan Oldham was going well.

Preeti had turned out to be a perfect choice. She was smart and quick on the uptake, obeying all the instructions that had been given to her. She had even learnt enough English to communicate, and she could talk to Susan over Skype with confidence. She was the ideal candidate.

In fact, Ashok Ganguly had taken her pregnancy on as a special case, and was recording it in detail. It was important, he said, to keep these records and analysis, as many assisted reproductive techniques and practices were still new and no one knew if there were going to be any consequences later. So far, the children born had been normal, but only time would tell if there were any far-reaching implications of this new technology.

Anita sometimes had a feeling that Ashok Ganguly was not as careful about data as he made himself out to be. But he was right about the need to take on cases in order to study them, and so she agreed when he asked for permission to monitor Preeti.

It meant that Subhash no longer checked up on Preeti or interacted with her as much as he used to. Initially he felt a little resentful that Ganguly had taken over his pet project, but the pressure of work was so high now that even if they all worked 24/7 they would find it difficult to keep up with the demand. So, like a lot of other things in Subhash's life, Preeti also sank into the background.

Meanwhile, Mike and Susan were planning to come to India within a few months, closer to the delivery. They were happy with a normal delivery and had not requested a caesarean. Updates on the mother and baby were being sent to them regularly, and they could also speak to Preeti whenever they wanted, as she was going to be in the hospital for the entire nine months to ensure nothing went wrong. Anita still remembered a case from another hospital when the woman went home for the weekend and miscarried within days. No one quite knew what had gone wrong but they suspected domestic violence. That was when Subhash had decided they should keep the gestating mothers in the hospital. In retrospect, it had been a wise decision.

Going through the records, Anita realized that in a few days' time a lesbian couple from Germany was going to arrive, and she had a quiet laugh thinking how her husband would react. Probably insist on fumigating the premises! She was amused at his paranoia regarding homosexuality, but hoped that as the frequency of these requests increased he would begin to treat them normally. The world was changing very fast, and some-times Anita felt that even she and her daughter Ramola were living on two different planets. Half the time she could not even understand the emails and messages her daughter sent, the abbreviated words making little sense. But she coped as best one could with a teenager who was connected to the worldwide web and had a thousand friends on Facebook. The learning never stopped.

As she worked through her files for the day, checking the progress of each surrogate, Anita was happy that, except for Ben and Kate, the other planned surrogacies had been successful. In all, the hospital would have delivered eight more children through surrogacy in the next few months. A few more local requests had come in, and she must tell Ganguly to make sure that all arrangements were made for the next day, so that the IVF procedure could be carried out.

She also made a note that she should ask him about the fresh lot of missing embryos, because he had been coordinating it all. He was in charge of securing the consignments from Mybaby.com in the UK, from where they were shipped to his own company in Delhi, BirthingBabies. Annoyingly, every time she tried to broach the subject with him he would cheerily point out that, considering the scale of the operation, some problems were natural. What they were doing was pioneering work. Who would have imagined a few years ago that sperm and eggs flown in from all over the world would be turned into babies in India? It still sounded bizarre!

By now it was late evening. She just had one patient left to check up on. Sonia. It was such an odd pregnancy! She remembered the hullabaloo in the hospital four months ago, when Subhash had burst into her room.

'Hurry up and come to my office. It seems the Health Minister of Delhi is paying us a visit.'

A little nervous, even though they and the clinic did not

come under Renu Mishra's jurisdiction, Anita had jumped up and, grabbing her white coat, dashed after Subhash to his room.

Renu Mishra had swept in regally, surrounded by her security escort and accompanied by her mentor Vineet Bhai. Settling into Subhash's office and accepting the offer of tea, she dismissed all her security guards as well as her personal assistant from the room.

Anita and Subhash leant forward to hear every word, because, quite uncharacteristically, the Minister had decided to lower her voice. This was going to be very confidential. She came straight to the point.

'I understand that you provide surrogacy here, right? That's what I've come to discuss. Firstly, I would like to have a child. Secondly, I need to be very sure that it does not suffer from any physical or mental disability. Thirdly, the child should carry my and Vineet Bhai's genes. Fourthly, this should be kept a secret. Now tell me if all this is possible.'

Without waiting for an answer, she added, 'I need to do all this for the future of my party – I don't have a political heir and this has become very important in recent days.'

For a second Subhash allowed a grin to creep on to his face, thinking she was joking, and then realized (too late!) that she was very serious.

'Yes, yes, madam. All this is possible,' Anita said quickly.

But Renu Madam kept staring at Subhash till he looked down at the floor sheepishly.

'Dr Pandey, you might think it is funny, but you know this country is run by dynasties. Those of us who don't have children spend our whole lifetime building up our parties and our political legacy just for some foolish person to fritter it away. All the other political parties are handing over the seat to their children. Vineet Bhai and I are unmarried but we have a power-sharing agreement, and after we have done our bit hopefully our child will take over. I will bring him up as an adopted child. We will get a Dalit woman as a surrogate, so everyone will think it is her child who we have adopted. We are both Brahmins, but what better *punya* than to raise a Dalit child? The only reason I am telling you all this is that right now we need your help to see it through.'

There was a small silence. It was as though the queen had spoken. Subhash could imagine her pronouncing the last sentence at a political rally and being greeted with wild applause.

Vineet Bhai leant forward.

'We know that certain genetic qualities are important. Is there any way you can ensure that? Most importantly, it should have Renuji's sagacity and my intellect; the rest we can teach. The looks are unimportant, but the child should be fair in complexion, because fairer babies do better.'

He paused, took a sip of water and carried on, before Subhash could interrupt about the 'fairness' criteria. This was a hospital, he wanted to say, not a bleaching factory. But as Anita shook her head ever so slightly, Subhash bit his tongue.

'All this, as you know, is very distasteful for me,' Vineet Bhai continued. 'I took a vow of abstinence at the age of twenty-five. But for this cause, to create a child who can be a great politician of the future, I am willing to make a small exception. Just this once.'

He too was very serious in describing his own credentials for becoming a parent to a future politician. They were an impeccable double act.

'Vineet Bhai is my mentor and my guru,' said Renu Mishra. 'With such a powerful combination of nature and nurture, no one will ever be able to defeat our party. And one more thing, please ensure that it is a boy. I know I should not say this, as it is illegal, but women politicians have a very difficult time in India. If Indiraji did not have Pandit Nehru as her father, or I did not have Vineet Bhai as a support, where would I be?'

It was also important, Subhash thought, that both of them belonged to the same caste. It was diabolical: they were both Brahmins, but they were going to pretend the child was a Dalit. It would appeal to multiple vote banks throughout the country.

'One of your potential surrogates, Sonia, lives in one of our servant quarters. I would like her to carry the child. As I said, she is actually a Dalit, and when the child is born, I will take it from her.'

Renu Mishra had thought of everything.

'For the sake of authenticity,' Vineet Bhai said, 'we are prepared to forgo the issue of racial purity. Strictly speaking we should get a Brahmin girl, but politically that doesn't seem like a good idea. This will be a masterstroke. But if any news of this ever gets out of the hospital, it will create a big problem for me, but a bigger problem for you.' Vineet Bhai's eyes narrowed and Subhash got the message immediately.

There was little hope of either Subhash or Anita surviving any such mistake.

'We would like to do this immediately. The whole thing should be over by the elections; we need to pull in the Dalit vote bank. The child should do it. There is barely a year left. Please make the arrangements as soon as possible.'

'You mean you want the child by next year?'

'Elections are in April. The baby must be with us by then. Thank you, now we must go. I will be here early in the morning.'

As suddenly as they had come, the couple leapt to their feet and marched out. There had been no discussion of payment or any other arrangements. It was assumed that now that the orders had been issued they would be executed. If the Pandeys did them a favour, no doubt it would be returned one day. Renu Mishra was known to help those who stuck by her and ruin those who dared to obstruct her. It was better to be on her side.

Anita looked stunned.

Subhash sighed and sat back. 'What have we done to deserve this? Luckily Sonia is still available.'

Before Anita could answer, Renu Mishra's secretary thrust his head into the room.

'Madam will be here at nine a.m. Please make everything ready. We will bring Sonia with us. And, please, you both must handle it yourselves. We do not want anyone else involved. And regarding Vineet Bhai, the sample will be ready tonight. You can send a nurse to collect it. Is that clear?'

Subhash gulped and said, 'Perfectly clear.'

What a palaver they had that evening! And now, four months later, as she went to Sonia's room to give her a quick check-up, Anita wondered why Subhash's normally suave voice had sounded so shaky on that day.

Was it the thought that perhaps the future Prime Minister of the country was going to be born in their hospital?

MUMBAI

Mehta found himself standing in front of Freedom Hospital a few days later. Ali had sent him there with another consignment and he was increasingly reluctant about entering. Why did he find this place so terribly strange? He got goose bumps thinking of the 96-year-old actor. It sounded too weird to tell anyone, so even when he spoke to his parents he did not mention that he had met their favourite star, Rajiv Kumar.

Perhaps the man was an imposter? People used plastic surgery these days to look like famous people, and it was possible that the hospital was providing some surgical procedures.

Meanwhile, there had been a couple more consignments for Dr Pandey's clinic too, which Mehta had spotted. Ali had made a phone call (Mehta guessed to BirthingBabies) to check what to do with them. After he received a green signal, he allowed them to be collected privately, and Mehta was not involved. Many more of these consignments went to the Freedom Hospital than to Delhi. Mehta wondered if Ali had forgotten his conspiracy theory and was sending the blastocysts all over, getting money from everyone. Mehta only knew about the Wadhwani connection; maybe other people were involved in the other operations? He knew that the consignments were still 'illegal' – according to Ali – thus these clandestine arrangements had to be made.

As Ali had always told Mehta, you have to pick your battles, and Mehta understood. His wife was happy with the occasional commission and he was not a greedy man himself.

Over the months he had understood that Ali was not just making money – he had been conducting a private jihad against surrogacy ever since his sister had been lured away by that rich sheikh. This meant holding up consignments and trying to obstruct their smooth delivery – but did it mean anything else?

Idly going through the papers, he had read just this morning that Varun Dhawan, the rich businessman's injured son, whom he knew was probably being treated by Dr Wadhwani, was making a 'very slow and painful recovery' and it might be years before he started walking again. It dealt once again with the story of the accident that night. How dreadful it was that the driver's mistake had not only killed the five people but also left the boy, in the prime of his life, with his spine severely damaged. He could not even attend the court case, but in any case the driver (whom everyone still swore, *sotto voce*, was innocent) would have to serve the full jail term.

The only mitigating factor, in defence of whoever had been driving the car, was that since it was night and the roads were badly lit, the victims would not have been clearly visible. Thus his prison sentence would probably be reduced (right now it was three years) while the families of the victims had also been heavily compensated by the father, Mr Dhawan. There was, as a grim reminder, the distressing photograph of the crumpled car, and a picture of Varun – a handsome boy staring into space, with his hair ruffled by the wind. It had probably been taken in happier circumstances.

Today, it seemed that once again his family was at Freedom Hospital. People were running about, in and out, and Mehta saw the boy's mother go inside, accompanied by her usual entourage.

To his surprise, he saw that the boy himself was being wheeled inside in front of his mother. In fact he did not look too bad at all. Mehta rubbed a hand over his eyes to make sure he was seeing clearly. Then he watched in astonishment as Dr Wadhwani came out of his room and the boy got up to hug the doctor. It was an astonishing sight. Just this morning, the papers had said that he would be paralysed for life. This place was amazing – barely had someone been felled by a terrible misfortune than the Freedom Hospital had made them hale and hearty, before you could say Hare Krishna!

Mehta dragged the black suitcase to the reception. As he waited he considered how odd it was that while almost every week he delivered embryos from all over the world, yet he hadn't spotted a single pregnant woman. Last week alone he must have brought five consignments. And every time he found some miracle cure being pointed out to him, usually by the receptionist, whose job it was to tally the registers and punch numbers into the computer; only occasionally did he take a phone call. None of this made any sense to Mehta.

It wasn't as though Mehta was peddling guns or cocaine, or even underage girls – all that was regular *dhanda*, and he could understand that. But trading in these embryos was difficult to explain to anyone.

After depositing the embryos and driving back to the office, he decided to call Dr Pandey and reassure her that a fresh consignment was on its way. He also thought she might be able to shed some light on what was happening to the embryos he was taking to the Freedom Hospital.

Dr Pandey thanked him and asked him if there was anything she could do for him. Over the months, Anita had stopped being angry with Mehta, as she realized that he was only a symptom and the malaise lay somewhere else. It was also good for her to have her own contact with customs, just in case she needed to cross-check anything that Dr Ashok Ganguly told her.

What Mehta did not know was that the prospect of losing the blastocysts was not her only headache. Almost all the recent implantations done by Ganguly had led to miscarriages. Was this just a coincidence? Her instinct kept telling her something was wrong somewhere. Everyone knew that while implanting an embryo, time should be allowed for it to warm up from the freezing temperatures in which it had been stored. Was Ganguly following that procedure? Or had the embryos been tampered with?

She had shared her fears with Simran, but not anyone else. More miscarriages meant more blastocysts were needed, more IVF treatment and more expense for the commissioning parents. So it was important she kept track of the blastocysts and made sure, with Mehta's help, that they came in without any problems.

Mehta plucked up his courage. 'Dr Pandey, can I ask you a question?'

Her voice carried its usual warmth over the phone. 'Sure.'

'I know a place in Mumbai where I have been supply-ing embryos every week. As in your case, we try to help them out. But I haven't spotted any pregnant women, so what could they use them for?'

There was a silence. 'Where are the embryos from?'

'Mostly the UK – just like—' Mehta bit his tongue. He had almost told her that her confiscated embryos had been deposited there, as well.

'I wouldn't be able to say off hand. Maybe they have a storage facility – so the embryos can be implanted later? Why don't you ask?' She did not sound too concerned. 'Sometimes hospitals do that, you know.'

He realized how foolish he had been. Of course, such a simple solution. Why hadn't he thought of it earlier?

'What is the hospital called? If it's bothering you, let me do some asking around to see what I can find out.'

'It's the Freedom Hospital in Mumbai.'

'I know it,' Dr Pandey said. 'I think they specialize in surgery, especially brain surgery, but they may do some fertility treatment – I remember once speaking to Dr Wadhwani there – but I'll check on that. Thanks.'

As she rang off, Mehta was wondering if he could also seek her advice about his wife's inability to conceive. With his parents away, and half of Malti's prayers answered, they were now at it like rabbits, but nothing seemed to change the mood of her unyielding uterus. Or maybe it was his fault. Perhaps he should also get his sperm count checked. Now that he knew a bit more about infertility, he no longer blamed Malti for their childless state.

He was fairly sure that there was a sperm-bank near his home. At least in checking his sperm count he would be making some progress towards fulfilling the other 50 per cent of her dream.

Chapter 6

SIMRAN

I stood in front of Mybaby.com. As I had learnt from my Internet search, it had once been a corner grocer's shop, and was just a few minutes' walk from the busy Tottenham Court Road. Now it was an ART clinic with a grim-faced receptionist answering phone calls and guarding all access to the main facilities like a stout *yakshi* in a temple forecourt.

It took me a while to get her attention, as she seemed intent on answering every phone call before she looked up. Her tight orange dress, long nails covered with glittering varnish, and dark hair in an afro frizz made her look like a lost member of the Supremes. I resigned myself to a long wait, and compared our spacious new reception in Gurgaon with the rather cramped area here. Of course, this was the heart of London and so land was at a premium. After years of admiring facilities in other countries, it was good to know that some Indian hospitals could easily compete with the best in the world.

The waiting area was covered with posters and photographs of smiling babies and a few women sat in silence, looking sorry for themselves. I knew from my experiences at Madonna and Child that fertility treatments could be quite unpleasant and I did not envy any of the potential mothers. Apart from the many discomforts they suffered, there was also the risk of giving birth to more than one child, which took its own toll on the women.

The receptionist finally got off the phone and I told her I had an appointment with Dr Maria Hansen, the doctor in charge.

After about twenty minutes, Dr Hansen came out of her room and asked me in. She was a petite blonde with clear blue eyes and an impatient expression.

Her room was completely wiped clean of both paper and personality. Obviously she was either very efficient or had very little to do.

'How is your hospital coming along?' she asked abruptly, after I had introduced myself.

'Very well,' I replied. 'Every year there is a big jump in the number of babies and surrogates, and we are also in the process of increasing the storage capacity for the blastocysts. Our rates are extremely competitive, so things are looking good.'

'Yes, I know.' She was smiling, but the smile didn't quite reach her eyes. 'You're taking away a lot of our customers. Why would they have fertility treatments here if they can do them for a quarter of the price in India, even if they risk picking up the New Delhi bug?'

I shrugged. 'Every year a new bug is discovered

somewhere. More people are killed by going to hospital than if they stay out.'

It was meant to be an example of my black humour, but Dr Hansen had apparently forgotten how to smile.

'So. What can I do for you?'

'Well, we have had a few problems with some of the blastocysts sent to us. One of them turned out to be HIV positive—'

'I think we have already told you it had nothing to do with us. The sample we sent was perfectly fine. We also know that India has issues with the surrogates, who tend to come from lower-income groups, and who may not have been thoroughly checked.'

'Dr Hansen, I'm here merely to ask you to examine your records to see if, by any chance, the sample could have got contaminated – or indeed the donors were HIV positive. We have Mike and Susan Oldham listed as the parents, and now we find even their address is incorrect. It could be that there was a mix-up—'

It was clear that Dr Hansen believed completely in her own infallibility. And she wasn't going to allow a resident of the Third World to come into her office and accuse her clinic of slipping up.

'I've already done a check, and we've no idea why and how the address was incorrect. In any case, Mike and Susan were killed during a sightseeing trip organized by *your* hospital. If I were you I would be pleased that people are not making complaints against you.'

I realized what she was doing and I wasn't about to let her pass the blame.

'No one has come forward to claim the child, and she's HIV positive. It is *very* worrying. And I've good reason to think that Susan had another child earlier, when she was only in her twenties, so there must be some family we can contact. I need an address so that I can make sure the child has a home. She needs to be looked after.'

Dr Hansen looked irritated.

'Do you think we didn't check everything before you came here? We've gone through all our records and found nothing wrong. We followed all the procedures and I've no idea why the Oldhams decided to keep their address a secret. I can't help you with this. Is there anything else?'

'There is. As you know, some of your consignments have been held up at Mumbai airport, and it's causing real problems. We need to sort it out.'

'As far as I know that was just once; all the paperwork was correct from our end. And let me tell you I send regular consignments to the Freedom Hospital in Mumbai and another one called NewLife in Delhi – and nothing seems to happen to them!'

At the last sentence her voice rose several decibels and she seemed to be saying, So there! If she could have, she would have stuck her tongue out at me. I was bewildered by her attitude. I had thought that we were partners in this, working together – instead of which she was being totally and quite needlessly unhelpful and rude.

'Has Dr Ganguly already explained the situation to you? As these issues can be a problem, we don't want patients here getting upset.' I thought that mentioning Ashok Ganguly, who had been working with Mybaby. com for a while, would calm her down.

I also surreptitiously put my hand inside my bag to make sure that my trusty Dictaphone was recording everything. This was a crucial moment.

For the first time a small smile came to her face. At last I had met a person who seemed to like Ganguly!

'We're in regular touch. In fact he has not sent me a single complaint of any kind so far.'

That was odd; I had personally asked Ashok to write to her about the Oldhams and a few other cases.

I hesitated and then pushed on regardless. 'But there is one last thing. Is it possible for me to go through your records in case I can find some kind of match for baby Amelia or the Oldhams? Maybe someone else who came in that day, just in case the samples got mixed up?'

'That would be violating doctor–patient confidentiality. My advice to you would be just let it rest. I know it's sad about baby Amelia but these things happen.'

I took another deep breath. I must be careful not to lose my temper.

'Can you at least give me the dates of when they came in and when the samples were sent to India?'

'I remember that they were in a rush – let me check.'

She looked through her laptop rapidly and said, 'It was the first of May last year, and the samples were couriered to you that week itself.'

'One last request: do you know if the couple came into the surgery themselves?'

'I remember her, blonde hair sharply cut, and I remember thinking that Mr Oldham looked quite young compared to her. That's all. So they must have come in and given their samples – and yes, that's what it says here, too.'

I thanked her and started to get up.

'Miss Singh, can I give you a bit of advice? I think you're creating a huge amount of fuss over nothing. It's important to bury these cases quickly – if the press gets hold of the story your reputation will be destroyed. Think of the facilities you've set up. They will all be wrecked. Okay, someone made a mistake. Maybe it was a contaminated needle, or a blood transfusion, or the surrogate – or maybe it was carelessness – but either way the deed is done. Let's all learn a lesson from it, right? An HIV-positive case is a very serious thing. Your hospital may be forced to shut down, which no one wants. In the US there was a very public court case which became extremely expensive for the hospital concerned.'

She leant back in her chair. 'Do you know what this industry is actually worth if you can do what Ashok says is possible in India – an army of surrogates producing children for the Western world? At least a billion pounds. So don't mess around with it.'

There was an urgency and a threat in her voice, and I realized that she had completely exempted herself and her clinic from any blame. The story would go to the papers if I did not shut up and go home. I would also be responsible for wrecking Madonna and Child's reputation. And everyone would lose a potential billion pounds.

I decided to be completely soft in my response, to take the sting out of hers.

'Thank you, Dr Hansen, and I am *so* grateful for all your help and your advice. I'll remember it.'

I walked out feeling I had wasted a whole morning. The only thing I had was a recording of Dr Hansen's voice in my handbag, but she had said nothing remotely helpful, and so even that was a waste of digital space. I switched off the Dictaphone and walked briskly to Leicester Square, where I was meeting Edward. We had met a few more times after that disastrous evening in his flat, and had found, to our mutual surprise, that we quite liked each other. My distrust of him had completely receded, which meant he was off my list of suspects, much to the annoyance of Anita, who would have liked to see a neat ending for baby Amelia's story. I was now hunting for fresh evidence as to who was responsible for the HIV contamination. And also for any family links to the Oldhams. Edward was helping me with names of people I could meet – which meant that, despite my present despair, I would have to spend a few more days in London.

My progress was slow so far. I was beginning to worry that I might never find baby Amelia's family or even a nice home for her. Especially after meeting the annoying Dr Hansen, I felt I had spent enough time in the UK over this and it was time to go home. I was missing Durga, and even my mother's constant nagging about getting married.

If only I could go home by ship, instead of flying! Better still I should take Edward home with me and present him as a potential suitor. He could also hold my hand through the flight.

Edward had said he wanted to visit India, and my mother would be thrilled, even though he was a *gora*. No harm in a bit of daydreaming. As I dwelt on the fantasy my heartbeat quickened. A thought struck me: was I in denial about Edward? Had I become fonder of him than I would like to admit?

I called him to let him know I was near the Apollo Theatre on Shaftesbury Avenue and would be with him in five minutes. From the corner of my eye I saw someone come up to me – I thought it was the same Asian boy I'd feared was following me the other day.

He said something that I could not hear.

I turned towards him to ask him who he was and just then the back of my head crumpled in agony. I fell on to the road, hitting my face on the tarmac; I could feel a trickle of blood down my nose and a sudden sharp pain on my forehead. There was a pressure, as though some-one was pushing me, on the back of my neck, and I knew my trousers had torn from the knees as the tarmac scraped into my skin.

I struggled to get up but my legs refused to obey, and though I tried to call for help, my voice was stuck in my throat, as in a bad dream. I thought of my mother and Durga, while my head exploded. Before I shut my eyes because of the unbearable pain, I saw a car speeding towards me, but I was like a butterfly pinned on a drawing board. That was just before I passed out.

Four months earlier

DECEMBER
MUMBAI

Nazir Ali, of the Customs and Excise Department, Mumbai branch – Diwan Nath Mehta's boss – had six children and the seventh one was on the way. He said that it was because he had led such a pious life that Allah had granted him six sons. Otherwise who could be so lucky? He often joked that he was planning to start a football club with his kids, but since his father had fourteen children, he still had a few years before he could break that family record. And then he would find the time for football.

Mehta used to listen to this banter without any envy. But these days he felt restless when his boss spoke about his children. The unfairness of the universe began to dawn on him, and some of his happy acceptance of things-as-they-are disintegrated. He spent an increasing amount of time in self-castigation.

For instance, why had he for so long been uncaring of Malti's prayers for a child?

He had simply assumed that it was her duty and responsibility to ensure that children came along. And she had assumed that role, since (whatever his other failings) Mehta was her *pati parmeshwar* – his semen would, like that of Lord Shiva's, always be potent.

It was understandable. Right from childhood she had been given dolls to play with and told that these toys were children to be fed, clothed and bathed. And from that she assumed that children would be her responsibility alone. He thought of the stories he had read in school, in which invariably the woman was a home maker, happiest when with her children and husband. So what was a childless woman supposed to do? How would she react when she was called *baanjh* or barren, and treated as a stubbornly wanton, careless woman, who had betrayed her family? Her crime was seen as another form of infidelity.

So perhaps he was not entirely to blame, if he too had begun to believe this all-pervasive propaganda. Yet his anxiety and guilt grew every day. Was there something he should do about their childless state?

Listening to Ali's anecdotes about his sons, he was puzzled that a man could be so affectionate towards his own children yet so callous about another person's. It made no sense to him. Here was Ali sending off embryos to the Freedom Hospital while parents somewhere else would be grieving. Just because these were tiny little cells, not yet fully grown – they did not have teeth, or hair, or feet, or even a brain or a heart – did that make them dispensable?

He thought back to what Dr Pandey had said about them simply being stored in Freedom Hospital, but he couldn't square that with the sense of urgency he felt when he delivered the cans there. Were they meant to go somewhere else? Why did Ali insist he do it personally? Were there other hospitals, like this, where embryos were needed in the same way?

Perhaps if he rescued a few of these containers – could they one day be reunited with their real parents? And – if he kept them with him – he would also have some evidence for that nice Dr Pandey, whom Ali particularly liked to trouble and fleece. They would be proof of Ali's secret jihad.

So when the next batch was given to him, he delivered five of the containers and kept one back in the car, and later dropped it off at his home. Over the course of the next few consignments, he started keeping one container in the house, and told a puzzled Malti not to touch it. To keep the stolen collection safe, he put them inside his cupboard along with his trousers and shirts.

'But what are they?' Malti asked, looking at the shiny milk cans and wondering why she wasn't allowed to touch them, as they proliferated all over her home.

Mehta told her that he was trying to bust an international conspiracy. That was alarming enough to silence Malti, for once. These canisters, too, all bore names of foreigners: Thelma and John Macey, Brigette and Ike Thornton ... but one he got a special pleasure from 'saving' had an Indian name pasted on it: Arun and Jo Sengupta.

Unfortunately, apart from the name of the parents and that of the clinic, Mehta knew little more. Ali had been careful not to share too much information with him. Even the papers in the office only had the London clinic number. Sometimes at night, when it would still be early evening in London, Mehta wistfully thought of calling up these deluded parents. If only he had their personal phone numbers. But then he thought of Ali's anger and gave up on the idea. Besides, he was complicit, as well, wasn't he?

All this talk about the embryos reminded him about his own sperm count. On the Internet he confirmed that there was a sperm bank close to his house, and thought that perhaps if he went there he would be able to find out if indeed the fault lay with him. He knew that Malti would soon take a vow to shave her head, as the temple priest had told her, and leave her beautiful jet-black curly hair as offerings to the deity. Mehta was going to miss those locks, as he loved the sight of them cascading like a black river against the whiteness of her smooth back. Even better, he admired them dressed with mogra flowers on a hot summer night. The scent of the flowers always made him crave to be in Malti's warm and comfortingly plump arms.

Somehow he had to prevent Malti from sacrificing her hair.

But, she said, such an acknowledgement on her part

that she was shorn of all vanity might encourage the gods to bestow a few favours, i.e. a child or two. It seemed the stars were quite well-placed right now for the fulfilment of her wishes.

Mehta knew all about these scams and warned his wife that all she was doing was giving a wigmaker some income and that her hair would probably be exported to China where it would adorn a bald Chinese man, but she was adamant. She had to try every possible fertility rite and ritual because, even though her mother-in-law did not say so, she was wondering (in her heart of hearts) if Mehta might divorce her and marry a more fertile bride. It was why her father kept up a steady supply of gifts – the latest was a microwave oven that would arrive in the next few days.

She knew her father would bluster and try to tell Mehta that he was gifting all these things only because he, Mehta, was so useless and could not buy his daughter anything – but the real reason (in *his* heart of hearts) was that he was worried his childless daughter would be sent home.

A baby was meant to be her anchor – otherwise she might lose her home and her husband. Losing her hair was of no consequence.

So, rather urgently – since the hair was to be offered within the next few days – Mehta found himself at the sperm bank, facing a bored middle-aged male nurse, who shoved some forms at him.

'Are you a donor? If you donate we will give you two

hundred rupees?' Almost every statement of the nurse sounded like a question.

'No, sir, I just want to test . . . My wife and I have been married for ten years and there is no child, so—'

'Okay. You pay us one hundred rupees? Go into that room and leave a sample?'

There was a row of cubicles like changing rooms in garment stores: some had doors and others just had curtains. From behind the curtains came grunts and moans and even gasps. One curtain shifted and a young man, barely out of school, with adolescent pimples still on his face, staggered out, zipping his trousers and holding a cup in his hand. Despite his dishevelled appearance he was smiling happily. He placed the result of his efforts on the table, wiped his semen-stained hands on his trousers, took the money, signed the register and left.

The nurse rang a bell to remind the inmates of the cubicles that twenty minutes were over.

'Sometimes,' he whispered to Mehta, 'they have such a good time, they do it twice? But we can't allow them to spend more than twenty minutes? Otherwise they would be here all day?'

'Why do you take such young boys?'

'That one is educated, he has just joined Elphinstone College – there is a big demand for educated boys? And he is a Kshatriya – we don't often get sperms from that caste? We are well stocked on Brahmins, though.'

Carefully putting on his gloves, the nurse went inside

to give the sperm sample to the technician who would run it through various tests for diseases and motility and then store it.

Mehta walked into the tiny room, which was just big enough for a man to sit down in and, if he wasn't too tall, stretch his legs. There was a chair in the corner of the cubicle, where he gingerly placed himself, putting the sterile cup on the small table on the side. The table had a pile of blackened magazines, mostly in Hindi and Telegu. They were obviously much thumbed, and the edges were torn. Some dated back at least five years, but the content was still relevant: plump, well-endowed women with their breasts falling out of their tightly cut brassieres were on almost every page in all kinds of situations. There were schoolgirls being spanked, housewives being disrobed, topless bathing beauties who were all at sea, surrounded by men – Mehta was completely bemused. He had never had a chance to see these kinds of magazines before and for a while he quite forgot why he was there. His Customs and Excise brain took over, wondering if he should confiscate these publications under the censorship act.

In Ali's office, when pornographic material arrived it usually went straight to Ali himself. He was careful to go through it personally, all the while clucking at how reprehensible it was. He then usually repackaged the magazines and forwarded them to his own boss, whom everyone knew had a special interest in these things.

Occasionally Ali would hold closed-door viewings of the pornographic films, saying that he wanted to know if they should be censored, at all. Usually these difficult decisions needed a few viewings before he concluded that they had to be sent to the appropriate authority, i.e. his boss. Therefore Mehta and his colleagues only got a few tantalizing glimpses.

Confronted with a whole pile of erotica and just twenty minutes to absorb it all, he decided to throw away his inhibitions and enjoy the first sex he had ever had with any woman apart from Malti. It turned out to be more fun than he had imagined.

Now he just had to wait for the result.

GURGAON

Ben and Kate were back at Madonna and Child, and they were barely on speaking terms. Ambala had, finally, been a disaster – and more depressing because after they had briefly rediscovered their love for each other, they had ruined it all by fighting again.

Ben, who had seriously thought that Kate would understand that his desire to adopt one of Sheela's children provided them with the best compromise possible, was shaken up by her rather violent rejection of the idea. To him it was a beautifully simple solution. He had naively imagined that, because the children had some kind of a connection to him, the idea would appeal to Kate.

But Kate dismissed his suggestion as foolish romanticism.

Yet he had only been trying to be completely honest with her.

While they had been in Ambala, drinking tea on the floor of what could have been the *bibighar*, Ben had finally been able to speak to Kate about how his family history was like a burden upon him. While Kate laughed at his post-colonial guilt, he told her that, however illogically, he felt responsible for his grandfather's actions. He constantly wondered about the woman left behind by his grandfather and now, recalling scraps of information from his diaries, was certain that his relationship with her was deeper than his family had acknowledged, and must have led to many problems. It would not just have meant embarrassment for him, but placed her in an awkward and insecure situation. Especially when, around her, Ambala was witness to so many similarly abandoned women.

In his diaries his grandfather had described his night-mares about her, immediately upon his return to England: she would be sitting by a riverside, when suddenly the water would rise and engulf her. Or she would be riding a cloud, hair flowing freely and with many arms like a goddess, hurling bolts of lightning down at him. Or she would be all alone in a room, and he would be trying to reach her, but the floor would continue to expand and expand . . . and she became smaller and smaller till she finally disappeared. At any other time these images would have seemed funny to Ben, and he would have laughed it away – but now it all seemed very serious. It had always puzzled him why his grandfather had been haunted by her till the end of his life. He remembered her so well, describing her honey-coloured eyes, and long, gently tanned limbs, the white cotton saree she wore, her black hair always dressed with jasmine flowers ... without really revealing his own relationship with her. Obviously he had done something to her which was unforgettable. Perhaps even unforgivable. Now Ben had finally begun to comprehend what it could have been.

He wondered ruefully whether, just as Kate had developed her baby obsession, he had defensively become obsessed by his grandfather's story, hoping that one day he would be able to piece together the mystery. Kate was right that his grandfather's act of betrayal had become his burden.

Yet, how could it be wrong if he now wanted to do the honourable thing?

His grandfather may have been disloyal and selfish, but Ben would be kind and caring.

Kate looked at him with a deep cynicism.

'You want to start collecting children to lift them out of poverty? Who do you think you are? Madonna? Angelina Jolie? For God's sake, Ben, get real!'

'I am being real. You want children. So just look at these children – what kind of life do they have? Now if we take one of them back with us to London, we can give her or him a good education, a great school, a wonderful university . . .'

'Ben, your grandfather left India a very long time ago. We're not even sure he had any children with that woman. All you have is a photograph and a whole lot of family rumours. You don't have to feel guilty about it, for God's sake!'

'You're making it sound stupid. Please – as I said, you want children. So do I.'

As Kate raised her eyebrows, he amended his statement.

'Alright, I admit I want to adopt a child *now*, after Ambala. But I *have* been thinking about it for a while. It would be too dangerous for you to have them now. We should just look around and find some child we can give a better life . . .'

'Ben.' Kate's voice was cold. 'This is not a financial take-over, either. Let's not play mergers and acquisitions.'

They argued bitterly from the time they left Ambala and caught the bus back to Delhi till they reached their hotel.

Now they sat in the hospital, waiting for Subhash to arrive. He had to make sure Kate was recovering well, and suggest future options.

Knowing how obdurate she was about having their own child, Subhash had hoped to give them some good news. But the results of the recent tests were quite disappointing.

'Kate, I'm sorry, but I think you will have to forget your dreams of IVF for the time being,' Subhash said, after giving Kate a quick examination using the ultrasound scanner. She had had a narrow escape and there was no point taking another risk.

Though she had been prepared for it, it still took a minute or so for Subhash's words to sink in. Thus, she thought, do dreams die. She recollected her optimism when Ben and she had first planned on having children. How misguided she had been! The simplest things are often the most complicated. She longed for Ben to hold her in his arms, so that she could allow herself to cry. But instead she closed her eyes to lock in the tears.

'What alternative do we have?' Kate asked, finally.

Ben heard the tremor in her voice, and instinctively – despite their recent fall-out – reached out to hold her hand.

'You sure you still want to go ahead?'

She nodded.

'Well, the next step is that you could possibly use Ben's sperm and eggs from someone else. But not every woman can adjust to the idea that the child is her husband's and not really her own.'

'At least it would belong to one of us!'

Ben visibly flinched at her wounded tone. Subhash remembered how reluctant he had been throughout about assisted reproduction. He sympathized with him, knowing only too well that at every stage there were ethical and physical hurdles to overcome.

'Ben, you've hardly said anything in all our interactions – and I'm not sure what you really want. A child is a big responsibility and both of you have to be ready for it.'

Kate opened her mouth to say something and then closed it. She didn't want to discuss Ben's latest fixation.

Ben threw his hands up in the air and got up. He stood, staring down at the floor, half-turned away from Kate.

'I don't know, Dr Pandey. I have a completely different way of looking at this. I think we should adopt a child – but Kate is the one who wants it to have our genes and our DNA. So I guess the decision has to be hers. Can she live with it being only half ours? Or do you think we should consider adoption?'

Subhash nodded thoughtfully.

'Unfortunately we only deal with adoption if it's to do with one of our surrogates, or a child born here. Why don't you talk it over with each other – and if you still want to adopt, I'll put you in touch with a social worker, Simran Singh, who will be very happy to help.'

Kate refused to look at Ben. She had tried to explain that the whole idea of her going through IVF was to gift him a child that bore his DNA. Now she was even willing to step aside and let him create a baby with another woman's eggs. It was a sign of her love for him. Why would she want someone else's child? If she had, she would have adopted a baby years ago.

Just then Anita walked in with a box of sweets. She immediately knew something was very wrong: Kate sat sobbing and Ben looked like he wanted to be anywhere but there.

Subhash glanced quickly at Anita and gave an imperceptible shrug as if to say, *Why is this couple always so much on edge? Why can't they be calm and have a reasonable discussion?* Anita toned down her breezy greeting.

'What's wrong? Kate . . . hope you're feeling okay?'

'Just a little shaken. Subhash just told me I can't go in for another round of fertility treatment. It just feels horrible – after all this, nothing to show for it . . .'

Silence fell upon the group.

Kate wiped her tears away and looked at the box of sweets in Anita's hands.

'What's that for?'

'Well – this isn't great timing – but I've got some really wonderful news!' Anita hesitated once again. 'Though I'm not sure this is the right moment for an announcement—'

Ben shrugged.

'Life won't stop just because the Rileys are falling apart. Tell us – we need cheering up, too!'

'Alright – then first have a piece of this.'

Anita opened the cardboard box of sweets and passed it around to Ben and Kate, who each took a tiny piece of the grainy yellowish *ladoos*.

Relieved at the lessening tension in the room, Subhash took two. 'Hope I'm allowed one extra for having made a small contribution towards the celebration?'

'Go ahead.'

'We've just had a brand-new baby boy in the Magnolia room. The parents have been trying for a child for ten years. This is their third attempt – they are over the moon. So please join us at around five o'clock at the cafeteria to celebrate?' Anita said, hoping for a swift exit.

Ben and Kate realized it would look ungracious if they allowed their private battle to dominate a festive moment.

'Sure.' They spoke together, and then inadvertently exchanged glances. 'We'll be there.'

But the distance between them grew by the minute.

GURGAON

Preeti sat near the Magnolia room, listening to the barely audible cries of the newborn baby. She was waiting to go in and congratulate the surrogate, Reena, who lived close to Preeti's home in Uttar Pradesh. Reena, like Preeti, needed money, but for different reasons. Her husband was unemployed.

Because of their common background, the two women got along very well and understood each other.

Though Reena had told the Pandeys that she had one child, in actual fact that child had not survived illness and poor nutrition. She had died before her fifth birthday. No one in the family had been perturbed, since deaths of baby girls were a routine occurrence.

Sharmaji's net was spreading ever wider. He knew someone in Reena's village who, after taking a commission, had suggested her name. He had brought her to Delhi to join the 'army' of surrogates that Subhash had wanted to create.

Preeti sympathized with Reena as she had discovered early on that she had been quite nervous about the delivery. To begin with, like her, she was far away from home, and she was also alone, since her husband was still in the village. He had been told to come to fetch her only after the delivery, as Sharmaji was concerned that he would give the game away.

He was an emaciated and dedicated tobacco-chewer.

It was the only thing that kept him alive.

Besides, even Sharmaji knew that his broken, paan-stained teeth and dirty nails would have required too much cleaning up for him ever to be presented in front of commissioning parents.

Reena had had a difficult pregnancy. She'd constantly suffered from morning sickness; her blood pressure had also shot up, and over the last few months her water retention had been worrying.

The situation was so bad that Anita and Subhash had asked their nurses to monitor her day and night.

Looking at her multiple problems, Subhash had wished Ganguly luck with his artificial womb where children would be incubated, painlessly. In his own ideal world, women in white gowns would be placed on a bed of flowers where, almost in their sleep and totally relaxed, they gave birth. He always wondered why, with all the scientific advancement, no one had found a way to remove the agony.

Personally he hoped there would also be a medical breakthrough to shorten the human gestation period. His motives were not all altruistic. After all, he said, if someone could cut the nine months down to three or four, wombs could be used with greater frequency, increased profit and less discomfort. Subhash hated to see anyone suffer – which is why Anita always asked him why he had become a doctor in the first place. And to make matters worse a gynaecologist!

Even after nearly twenty years he still got extremely distressed when women in his care were unwell or sick – or, though very, very rarely, died.

The contract they signed with the commissioning parents now included a clause covering the possibility of death, and a few insurance agencies had also stepped in to cover the surrogate during the period of the pregnancy, but only for the princely payout of two lakh rupees. *Only two thousand pounds? Is that the price of their lives?* questioned some concerned parents. He had to explain to them, sadly, that, though it wasn't very much, it was some compensation at least. He knew that women's lives in India were worth much less than that, and maternal mortality was extremely high.

So they kept a special eye on Reena and it was an enormous relief when she finally gave birth, despite all the complications she had suffered. However, now new problems set in. To begin with, Reena wanted to nurse the baby quietly and in private, without the presence of the Australian parents. She had given birth to a beautiful baby boy, and the Pandeys gave in because there was no doubt she was quite emotional about him.

Anita said that it was probably post-partum depression combined with anxiety about giving the baby away which was making Reena so possessive. After all, it was the first time in her life that she had received this kind of attention and been made to feel important. The Australians had been very thoughtful throughout, and even now they showered her and the baby with gifts. Was there a fear that once she gave the child up, she would lose her newly established identity as a mother?

At the same time the Pandeys had to be careful not to get tough with her or upset her, as the stress might lead to her breast milk drying up. So time and again she was left alone with the child. They hoped that within a few days her tear-filled outbursts would be over – and in any case the child had to leave by the end of the week.

Preeti listened carefully outside the Magnolia room and it seemed to her that the baby had stopped crying; it had probably fallen asleep. Before anyone else came in, she thought she would go in and see Reena. She wanted to know how the whole experience had been for her. Even though Preeti had two children, and her husband had said that he would, along with her sister, look after them, she missed her home. This new, shining, squeaky-clean hospital was beginning to overwhelm her. She missed the freedom of roaming around in the marketplace in her village, chatting to her friends and playing with her children. She missed the sunrise over the rice fields, the sharp clucking of the hens, the loud lowing of the cows at milking time. She even missed the dirt roads and the smell of the cow pats. She was homesick and worried because there had been a long silence from her sister. Hopefully nothing untoward had happened – she did not trust her husband alone with another woman in the house. Just as she did not really trust Dr Ashok Ganguly. The money would be excellent at the end of this confinement but not worth it if she lost her husband or if the doctor did something bad to her.

Inside the Magnolia room, she found Reena hurriedly packing a small suitcase, while the baby lay asleep in the cot. She was dressed and ready to leave.

'Where are you going?'

Reena burst out crying and flung herself into Preeti's arms.

'I can't give him up, *didi*. I don't have any children, as you know. I would rather have this one than not have one at all.'

'Don't be stupid.' Preeti sat down on the bed and firmly held her hand. 'You'll be in deep trouble if you try anything like that. They'll come after you and take the child away. You've signed a contract – and don't forget about the money. You'll lose all the money!'

'I don't want the money. This is my child; I know it. He is a gift from God to me. *Didi*, don't stop me, let me go.'

Preeti opened her mouth to speak again – but what could she say? She knew that Reena was distraught and not thinking things through. But at the same time, she could be charged with kidnap. The baby, fair and blue-eyed, was obviously not hers. No one would believe her story.

Yet, Preeti was sympathetic. In the lessons they had been given in the hospital they had been clearly told that they had to divide their heads from their hearts, and realize from day one that they should have no emotional attachment to the child in their womb. But was that really possible? After all, they had carried the child for nine months, fed it with their blood.

So she sat silently and watched as Reena picked up the sleeping child and her suitcase and walked out of the door.

Preeti sighed. For some time she just sat there and imagined a happier future for her friend. Reena, at home, garlanded by her neighbours, feted for having given birth to a beautiful baby boy.

But she knew it wasn't possible.

Wiping away her tears, and feeling like a traitor, she went to the phone by the bedside and dialled reception. She reminded herself that she could not afford to lose her own goodwill in this hospital. Her husband had already decided how the money would be spent. It would mean freedom from working in menial jobs and better schools for their children.

Hopefully, in another few months, she would be on that train going home to a life she recognized and understood. One which was real and not make-believe like this one, where she was going to give birth to a child which would never belong to her.

She walked slowly back to her room and lay down with her face towards the wall, while Reena was brought back and sedated.

The hospital had sprung into action and people were rushing about busily, and concerned whispers filled the corridors.

The Australians were called and asked urgently to take the baby as the mother was feeling unwell. Sharma was also called and Reena was handed over to him, with the money. She was put on the first train home. That was it. Her job was over. She had been cashiered from Subhash's army. A rogue soldier.

Preeti ran her hand over her abdomen protectively. She knew that running away was something she could never do. For her this child spelt comfort and freedom. She had to keep going.

Anita came in and touched her shoulder. Wiping away her tears, Preeti kept staring at the wall. For the first time she felt she didn't like Anita-didi either. She used to like

Dr Subhash and had thought he cared about her, but now he had abandoned her to that terrible Dr Ashok.

Dr Ashok, who liked to call her names she could not repeat, fumbling between her legs, touching her breasts. It made her uncomfortable, and it was sometimes painful, but he was careful not to leave any marks on her or do anything which would hurt the child.

But every time he called her for a check-up, it made her feel terribly ashamed, almost unclean. It was something she could never talk about. He said he was doing some tests on her but she did not quite believe him. Like Reena, she too wanted to run away, though perhaps for different reasons.

Anita hovered awkwardly over Preeti's bed, slightly disconcerted by the woman's determined silence.

'Thank you for telling us,' Anita said, 'or she would have disappeared with the baby. We found her at the back of the hospital, getting into an auto-rickshaw.'

Preeti kept her back turned to the doctor. She was suddenly feeling very weary.

'You should keep the children under lock and key,' Preeti said to the wall, in a dull undertone. 'Women do this all the time, especially if it is a baby boy. Someone almost stole my son, too, when he was born. You get a lot of respect if you give birth to a boy.'

'We'll be more careful in future. Why don't you go on and have your dinner? I've asked them to keep a special piece of chicken for you.'

The hospital was very particular about her meals and exercise.

'I'll go soon. I'm just feeling quite tired today.'

For some reason her tears kept trickling down. She was gripped by a premonition that something bad was going to happen.

Not too far away, from the opposite room, Sonia had watched the whole episode unravel from her vantage point where she, too, lay listlessly on the bed. It was dinnertime but she did not really feel like eating, either. She knew she had to, though, or else both Vineet Bhai and Rohit would come after her.

Rohit. He was still taking almost too much interest in her pregnancy and she hated his possessiveness about it. As though he was doing everything and she was only a puppet.

Because in the end, it was Rohit who had pushed her into it. He had forced her to go to the Health Minister's residence that night. Her crazy idea had come to fruition. She would never forgive herself for her own stupid suggestion. And this meant her dreams of going home as a free woman were over, for sure.

The memory of standing in front of Renu Madam and Vineet Bhai, that evening five months ago, still made her feel naked and embarrassed. She thought about it every day. If one had to carry the child of a total stranger, it was bearable. But to carry the child of someone on whose wrist she had even tied a *raakhi*, along with all the other Dalits in the area ... it was despicable. Besides, though there were rumours to the contrary, Vineet Bhai had always maintained he had taken *sanyas*, and would never have a sexual relationship with anyone.

Sonia knew that Vineet Bhai projected himself as a universal brother, the saviour of the poor and the defenceless, and especially of the minorities and the Dalits. Because he was a Brahmin, the Dalit votes were high on his agenda. Anything to bring them into his fold was worth trying. She had understood all too well why she had become such a valuable commodity a few months before the elections.

'Are you healthy?' Renu Madam had asked her. 'No aches and pains? No problems?'

She had shaken her head.

'You know what is going to happen? Have they explained everything to you? The most important thing is you have to stay in the hospital till the baby is born. Do you understand? And no one must know whose child it is – have you understood?'

She nodded once more, still looking at the floor.

Vineet Bhai beckoned her closer. She could smell the whisky on his breath.

'I have heard things about you. But now you must behave yourself. The doctors say that you are ready to carry the child?'

She nodded again.

He looked at Renu Madam. 'I might need to spend some time with this girl. You carry on with your meeting.'

Renu Madam looked as if she was going to object. Then she said, 'Remember the nurse is waiting outside.'

And she left the room, dismissing Rohit, who followed her without looking back. Sonia and Vineet Bhai were alone.

Vineet Bhai had got up and walked around her.

'What a joke, the mother of my child, a bloody Dalit.'

She kept her eyes down, wondering why he hadn't let her go.

He drew the curtains and locked the door. Now she began to understand.

'It's been a long time since I did this – I've been a *sanyasi* for twenty years. Take off your clothes.'

Sonia undressed, and saw that he had taken off his white shoes and trousers, and sat down again. His penis hung fat and flaccid between his thighs. He put a hand on it, and massaged it slowly. It began to stiffen.

'Come here.'

She came close and he pushed her to the ground, till she was kneeling in front of him.

'You know what to do. Just make sure you don't swallow it, or Madam will cut your throat.'

Later on, she had dressed and left the room. The smell and taste in her mouth made her want to throw up.

Outside she became aware of the curious eyes all around. Only Rohit, waiting for her, seemed unperturbed, even triumphant. The nurse went in and emerged with a sealed container inside a plastic packet, which was rushed to the hospital.

Rohit and she walked back to their tiny room. He asked her what had happened, but she refused to reply and lay in bed for a long time, angry and unable to sleep, wishing that she could have had a chance to have a child for the *firangi* couple for whom she had been selected. Now she would never meet them. Why was her life so complicated?

And so here she was in the hospital. Already five months pregnant, and waiting for the child. Renu Madam hadn't met her after that day. Vineet Bhai came over quite often these days. He would drop by to make sure she was taking care of his child.

She felt like an animal with no feelings, as far as he was concerned. How could he have any respect for her anyway – she was only a stupid Dalit woman.

She was also worried that no contract had been signed. More and more the realization was dawning on her that they were all using her. The hospital doctors, Renu Madam, Vineet Bhai and Rohit. Everyone was getting something out of it, but her.

The only person who was a total loser was Sonia. And watching what had happened with Reena, she realized that she couldn't even run away.

Just like Preeti across the room, Sonia wept.

Chapter 7

SIMRAN

Nursing a bruised shoulder, grazed knees, a bump on my scalp and a nasty cut on my forehead, I was sitting at the computer in Edward's home, while he was away for a client presentation. It seemed that my discomfort only increased every day whilst trying to unravel this case. But luckily he had left me with a well-stocked bar and I would help myself to a glass of wine every time I remembered those awful moments. Which meant that I went through a lot of wine in the days I was recovering from my 'accident'.

Apart from many bottles of alcohol, I owed Edward a huge debt for saving my life. I'd fainted, so had little memory of what happened. Fortunately, since I was on the phone to him as I stumbled, he heard the squeal of a car and my shout as I hit the tarmac. It seems he had raced across from Leicester Square where we were supposed to meet and made it to where I was, near the Apollo Theatre, in five minutes. The benefits of a milk-only diet!

The car had missed me by inches, though it had whizzed off by the time Edward arrived. Two youngish men, who could have been Indian, were trying to lift me, but when he asked what had happened, they said they were only helping me, and abruptly left. He had no reason to try to stop them. Later, I did wonder if one of them had pushed me.

Some things simply did not add up.

When Edward put me in a taxi and took me to the nearest hospital, St Thomas's, where I regained consciousness, I found a mysterious, painful bump at the back of my head.

The doctor thought someone had assaulted me, but no witness had come forward to tell Edward anything. And since I could not turn it into a police matter, I told the doctor that I had stumbled and rolled over on the kerb, hence the bruises on my face and the back of my head. Apart from looking a little curiously at me and Edward he asked nothing more.

Luckily nothing was broken, though my trousers were torn and my shirt had ripped from the shoulder.

I kept wondering – who were the two men? Were they really helping me? Was one of them the man who had followed me to Edward's house? Had I really been hit on the head and pushed down on to the road – or was I being paranoid?

At home that evening, Edward settled me down, the strain clearly etched on his face. I thought I must share my fears with him – after all, I was living in his house now.

'I didn't want to worry you,' I said, 'but for a while I've

suspected that I'm being followed. An Indian-looking guy has popped up far too many times. I've ignored it so far because I thought I was imagining things – but there could be a few people who would be happier if I disappeared.'

Edward looked very concerned. 'Well,' he said, 'then there are some questions you must answer and some things you must do.' He counted off each point on his fingers as he spoke. 'Firstly, bring all your stuff from Southall and move in here for the rest of your stay. Secondly, tell me if there's anything dangerous about this investigation that you're doing . . . Thirdly, is there someone who would *really* want to kill you, as you say? And lastly, should we go to the police at this stage?'

He picked up a pad and pen to note down my answers. Obviously he felt that we needed a serious discussion. I remembered the morning with a tingle of fear. He was right.

I didn't need to think for too long. The answers were in front of me.

And so was one big question. Should I really discuss this case openly with him? Hadn't it become more dangerous than I had imagined? Swallowing my misgivings, I decied to confide in him.

'Fine, then – let's start with the suspects. Firstly, Dr Hansen. I think she would be really happy to get rid of me, in case I ruin her billion-dollar business. It's odd that this happened *just* after my visit to her. Someone wants to prevent me from finding out anything more about baby Amelia's background. And that surprises me, because I haven't told anyone what I'm really doing here.'

Except you, I thought, but I did not say it aloud as I wondered whether it was safer for me to stay here or go back to Southall? Worse, I wondered whether my attacker had got information about me from Edward?

Edward had a lot to lose. His reputation was also at stake. Yet he remained my only hope of getting to the truth. And oddly enough, I had to stick even closer to him now, because that was the only way I would be secure. So long as I was staying in his house, he could hardly get rid of me. By now, he was aware that Anita and my family knew I was here.

Edward almost read my mind. 'While you figure out what's going on you should move in here with me, as these guys could be connected to the man who followed you from Southall. Remain indoors and rest for a few days. '

He added cheerily, just to make me feel better, perhaps, 'Hansen may be trying to bump you off – but if you go underground for a little while, in a few days I'm sure they'll get tired of waiting for you – they may think you've given up and returned to India. In fact that's what you should tell anyone who knows you are here – so that they, too, support the story.'

Was he trying to create a case for my eventual 'disappearance'?

Middle-Aged Social Worker Vanishes – Thought To Be En Route To India. I could just see the headlines.

'How long can I hide? ' I said carefully. 'I've come here to find out more about Amelia's family. I have to go out.'

'In that case wear a disguise! Get yourself a completely new look! I'll get you the wig of your choice. Any colour. Pink, green, yellow, red, brown – and I'll also get you a skirt and a top. Transformation will be therapeutic for you – and confusing for anyone who is hot on your heels!'

'And make those high heels!' I said, trying to be jolly about it all.

What if that person is you? I wanted to ask, but decided to accept his offer – both to let me move in, and to get me a disguise (though a far more conventional one than he had suggested).

Even though Edward was trying to keep everything light-hearted, while, curiously, seeming worried about me, I had to be careful not to demonstrate my own emotions. I realized that in my vulnerable state I might begin to trust him too much – and that could mean disaster.

However, because I did not want my friends or family to be worried about me – or others to be alerted to my whereabouts – I kept the news of my predicament to myself. Only to Anita did I mention that there had been an incident, and keeping in mind that baby Amelia was still in hospital, they must ensure a fulltime nurse for her.

Her security was paramount. After all, if people wanted to get rid of me just for conducting an investigation – they might want to remove the last piece of evidence, baby Amelia herself. It was a very frightening thought.

I told her about my hope to return within a week or so, with some more credible information. She emailed back, puzzled about how anyone had known of my address in London – we had chosen Southall particularly because I could get lost quite easily in the crowd, even though London as a whole, I realized, was more full of Indians than I remembered.

To everyone else (including my mother and Durga) I said, as cheerfully as I could, that I had stumbled on the pavement, but all was well, Edward was looking after me – and I would be on my return journey shortly. And in the meantime – what could I get for them?

I only wished that my optimism wasn't too misplaced.

And that is how, a few days later, I actually began to leave the building in a skirt, lots of makeup to cover the bruises, bright-red lipstick, dark glasses, and a hat! Edward's 'disguise' for me. Even without a wig, my own mother wouldn't have recognized me. No shabby jeans, no crumpled silk saree. I have to say it was fun to have a whole new identity in what was a largely dismal scenario.

Besides, it was a fact that the sinister messages that had been arriving on my mobile phone had stopped as mysteriously as they had begun. My hunch was that my would-be assailants, when they left me unconscious and bleeding on the street, were sure they had got rid of me. Perhaps even permanently.

Many questions continued to trouble me, though.

Had Edward looked relieved when I told him that we could not go to the police? Anita had warned me many times to be careful and keep a low profile. Why hadn't I followed her advice? Had I been too open in visiting Edward in my colourful sarees – or in going to Dr Hansen's clinic?

Even as I asked Edward to remove my luggage from Southall, and bring it to his flat, the doubts remained as to whether I should have been more concerned about the fact that he had arrived by my side far too quickly after my accident? And how did he know exactly where I was?

To preserve my sanity I decided to accept the situation at face value.

After all, I was slowly recovering from the shock of near-death, and still trying to hunt for the truth about the Oldhams. For all of those reasons I needed Edward more than before, and he seemed happy to offer all kinds of support.

But bearing in mind that I couldn't afford to be complacent, while he was away I did rummage around his house looking for any evidence of his involvement with baby Amelia's case. Since I didn't immediately find anything I presumed his innocence, for the time being.

Having said that, I still slept with the light on and kept a chilli spray under my pillow. Physically I might have kept myself safe. But my mind was playing all kinds of games.

The worst part was, I continued to be attracted to Edward.

Under different circumstances, perhaps this forced proximity would have ended quite differently for me. His protective attitude enhanced my own uncertainty. I wondered if he noticed my ambivalent feelings towards him? Especially when he caught me staring at him. Or when, quite by accident, our bodies touched in passing.

I wasn't used to being looked after – and this was a whole new feeling. It was the little things he did which began to matter: he made sure I had my medication on time, and that the fridge was stocked for me before he left for his meetings. To reciprocate, I began to cook meals for us, and to any outsider we could have passed off as a couple joined in domestic bliss. He also asked me to call him whenever I felt worried or anxious or had a query, and took care to ask how I was two or three times a day.

And so is it surprising that for a few days I quite forgot that he too was on my 'dangerous' list? Possibly I did not want to believe anything negative about him.

Today, I forced myself to stop dreaming about him and began slowly trawling through the Births, Marriages and Deaths registers, searching for all the Oldhams in the Highgate area.

According to Edward, Susan Oldham had met an old friend for a coffee in Highgate, a few years ago. At that time she had said that she lived close to Highgate cemetery.

Edward had been carefully tracking down all his university friends to see if any of them had kept in touch with her. I hoped that it would bring us closer to the truth.

As the days passed, Ma became concerned, once more, about my delayed departure, so I decided to share the bare minimum with her. Once more I did not mention the attack, just that the investigation had reached a very sensitive point and I did not want anyone to know where I was in case the evidence was messed up. The only circumstance which brought her some relief was that, whilst still in London, I was spending a lot of time with Edward. Little did she know that all Edward and I were doing was trying to unravel the mysterious life of Susan Oldham and her family. Nor did she guess I was worried about his involvement in this murky business, as well.

Edward had been told by another mutual friend that Susan had become a bit of a recluse and was not seen very often. She had spoken about some domestic problems, but had not elaborated on them. The friend thought she had mentioned a grown-up son; again there was very little clarity.

Whenever we could, Edward and I tried to put together whatever information we had collected thus far and think of reasons why Susan could have wanted another child so late in life, if she already had a grown-up son or daughter.

One possibility might be a second marriage, and that she might have wanted a child with her new husband. But it was merely a hunch, as nothing so far supported this theory.

I helped him go through his entire phonebook, calling everyone he possibly could find to ask about her. I would then take a tube, bus or train to the address mentioned and personally check if they knew of Susan Oldham. Of course, after the attack on me there was no time to waste. London had become treacherous – and I had to get back home to India as soon as possible, and to those who were dependent on me.

Edward did not mind my somewhat vigorous investigation. In fact he seemed to want to be involved in this whole case. He said he was increasingly worried both about me and the fact that so little seemed to be known about Susan. I confess I had begun to believe him. Perhaps much of what had gone before, right from the phone number on the hospital form to his rescuing me from the accident scene, might have been just coincidence – and destiny had led me to him.

People on the verge of falling in love often get muddle-headed.

And I was no different.

As I got to know him better, I thought I saw his resolute independence undergo a gentle transformation.

Susan's tragic death had actually made him wonder about the fate of the child she may have had with him. I think he was beginning, for the first time, to feel responsible for someone he had never even thought about as his own. I could see it was an uncomfortable sensation, but somehow my presence helped him deal with it. He could talk to me about that part of his life which he never ever shared with anyone. And for me, it was good to have someone with whom I could discuss the investigation. Quite unconsciously, in different ways, we became dependent on each other.

So you might wonder why we maintained our restraint towards each other?

He never made a move – and my concern for baby Amelia drove me on.

It was an old habit; I have often been accused of having a one-track mind. Once I get into something, it is difficult for me to just let go. Each time I swear never again, and each time I am sucked into the vortex. And the thought of the tiny sick child back in Delhi drove me on.

Very rarely we would slip into a softer mood, deciding we were exhausted and needed a small break, going out to the theatre, followed by dinner. On those few evenings we got along extremely well and frankly, if it weren't for the fact that we needed to find out more about Susan, perhaps we could have spent a lot more time together doing things which were no fun to do alone.

The more we talked about it, the more the questions and doubts seemed to multiply.

After the violent attack on me, I wondered if, before

coming to London, I should I have examined the deaths of the Oldhams myself.

That evening I ran my suspicions past Edward.

'Look at how it all happened. Baby Amelia is found to be HIV positive, and Mike and Susan die shortly afterwards. No evidence is left behind – everything is as though they had never existed.'

'Right,' added Edward, making some late-night coffee for us (instead of milk he had decided on decaf with soya milk; mine was instant, black). 'You also said that the surrogate vanished overnight. Then you go for a meeting with Dr Hansen, question her about the HIV issue and about the Oldhams – and a few minutes later someone pushes you.'

'Perhaps, to protect Dr Hansen's reputation, someone is more than willing to eliminate a few troublemakers. Like me. After all, this is a multimillion-dollar industry and lots of reputations are at stake. My life wouldn't be worth more than a few quid.'

'You're sure it's not someone from India? After all, Madonna and Child could also be in trouble. Maybe lose its licence – get sued, who knows? This may not even be the first case – but it's the first one you've got involved with.'

He was right. Had I been blind to the failings in the hospital simply because I had so much faith in the Pandeys? I had believed that they must know the whole story, or at least have shared everything with me. I tried to recollect what had happened, piecing together the sequence of events after the deaths of Mike and Susan as best I could.

I remembered how enthusiastic Ashok Ganguly had been about going to Rajasthan and how smoothly he had sorted everything out: the disposal of the bodies, the police report, the UK High Commission. Or so he told us. And nothing reached the press, for which the Pandeys (who had already suffered some intrusive TV cameras the previous year) were immensely grateful. It was the first time I felt a grudging respect for his efficiency – and his clockwork precision in saving the hospital from disgrace.

It was he who had informed the Pandeys that Mike and Susan's passports and their belongings had been destroyed in the resulting fire. And of course, since he was their colleague, no one had bothered to check whether he was telling the truth. At that time everyone was actually a little distracted with the crisis of baby Amelia. Thanks to my social-work background, and NGO-*wali* status, I was called in to help supervise the care of the orphaned child, and occasionally even brought Durga in to play with the baby, cuddling and looking after her. Subhash was away on a marketing blitz as usual: talking about the hospital and getting more work (as well as funding for Ganguly's planned medical miracle – the giant womb!). Anita was overseeing the other surrogates and births which, quite in contrast to this one tragic case, were going very smoothly.

Suddenly I sat back and stared blindly at Edward.

He was right.

Anita and Subhash were my friends but did that mean I could trust them implicitly? They, too, had a lot to lose.

Edward began, quite seriously, to make a list of the people he thought might have wanted to push me under that car. As the list grew longer, I began to feel like a hunted deer.

'What do you know about Dr Ashok Ganguly?' he asked.

'Not very much,' I mumbled nervously, helping myself to a glass of red wine. Edward had stopped looking disapproving. He knew I needed to steady my jangled nerves.

'Okay, let me think,' I said, referring to my notes. 'He's helping to make the hospital one of the biggest for surrogacy in South Asia. He's also urging the Pandeys to set up a separate unit on stem-cell research and surgery. He's told them that it's going to be worth billions and it's a natural corollary for a fertility clinic.'

Edward interrupted. 'That last bit sounds crazy to me. Is it legal to make that connection?'

'I'm not sure, but a lot of things go on in India under the radar. Embryonic stem-cell surgery is definitely banned and there's a lot of caution about using other stem cells, but doctors are experimenting with all kinds of things. They want to be ahead of the game when the permissions finally are given.'

'So have the Pandeys fallen for the investment bait?'

'Not as yet. Ganguly has some partners with whom he

has floated a company to do this, which is already listed on the Mumbai stock exchange. I've always thought that he was ambitious and smart. From what the Pandeys have said, he's more of a businessman than a medical saviour.'

'So how would you describe him?'

'He's a bit of a creep, to be honest.'

Edward looked sceptical. 'Let me play devil's advocate here. Do you think they're using you for a cover-up? Ganguly could just be a scapegoat – they need someone like him: street smart and savvy as well. It benefits all of them. Are you sure they don't know more than they've told you?'

I wondered, once again, if Ganguly had actually sent that letter to Dr Hansen? I realized I didn't know much about the relationship between Mybaby.com and his own company BirthingBabies, except that the embryos were routed through it.

Perhaps the time had come to examine the mysterious Dr Ganguly more closely, as well as his connection with the Pandeys. I sent an email to Anita to ask what exactly Ganguly had said about the accident in Rajasthan when he got back, and what he had told the High Commission. I also asked her to send me a scan of the form that Susan and Mike had filled in, as I was wondering if there was anything on it which I could use while trying to find them. I had all the details noted down, but was there something I had missed out? No longer sure whom I could trust, I kept the tone of my email as casual as possible.

Then I set off for one more address that had been given to me by Edward. This was another long-lost friend, who had some information about Susan; he said he had met up with her just around one year ago. Leaving the comfortable flat, I thanked God for the Edwards of the world, who not only helped women by donating sperm to them (free of cost!) but also gave them a perfect disguise when needed.

As I stepped on to the street I looked around carefully to check if anyone was following me. Thankfully, London commuters tramped past the woman in a short skirt, stilettos and a hat without any interest. I felt safe at last as I climbed on to the bus. The man I feared most did not seem to be around.

Preston worked in an estate agency in Dulwich, and had asked me to join him for a coffee in between calls, at a café with pavement seating. Originally from Uganda, he had settled in South London, and had known Edward and Sue, as he called her, from their days together at university.

Their meeting, last year, had been purely coincidental. She had come to his estate agency looking for a three-bedroom flat in the area. Pleasantly surprised, they were happy to meet again, and she had taken him out for lunch at the local pub.

She said she needed a house with a bedroom on the ground floor, because her son had been sick recently. He sometimes needed help, and could not climb the stairs unassisted. She had rented a house, but now thought she should buy.

So Edward was right: there *was* a son!

'How old is he?' I asked.

'I never met him, but he was at university at that time, so he must be about nineteen or twenty I suppose.'

'Any other children?'

'No, that's the only one, as far I know.'

'So what happened? Did she buy the house?'

'No. She said her son had taken a turn for the worse, and she wasn't sure if she would need the place any more.'

'And then what happened?'

'I don't know. I have to say I was busy and I just forgot to chase her up. It's funny that you should turn up here now because I was looking at her papers just the other day, wondering if I should chuck them away.'

'Could you give me her address? Or phone number?'

'I'm afraid I won't be able to do that . . .'

I reminded him that Edward had put us in touch, and this was needed for a very important reason.

He looked uncomfortable.

'But Susan might get angry with me. Perhaps she doesn't want to be in touch with anyone, not even Edward.'

That was closer to home than Preston would ever know. During her lifetime, Susan had kept to her promise.

I decided to tell him the truth, as gently as I could. 'She won't be angry,' I said, hesitating to complete the sentence, and then forcing myself to do so, 'because she's dead.'

Preston was shocked into silence.

'That's . . . that's unbelievable!' he said after a while, gazing down at his coffee cup.

I lit a cigarette and passed him the pack. Both of us smoked quietly for a while.

'How did it happen?'

'She was in India, which is where I met her. She and her husband died in an accident in Rajasthan.'

'So why are you looking for her? I mean, why are you here?'

'Because – we just need to find her family members and tell them. The address we had was incorrect. That's why I need to know. And her son has been sick, as well – I mean, now you know why Edward and I are worried.'

I decided not to tell him about baby Amelia. I had no reason to believe that the information would in any way be useful to him. The less people knew about the child, the better.

I had said enough to persuade him and he gave me the address. He must have had mortality and not mortgages on his mind when he went back to work that afternoon. When he was at university with Susan they would have thought they would live forever. Or at least long enough. Poor Susan had not had that chance.

I caught the train back into town. Getting off at Victoria Station, I walked slowly. Either it was the spring showers, or a morsel of Preston's grief had got under my skin. I felt depressed.

My phone rang; it was Anita. She had been calling me every day since my accident.

'When are you coming back?' This time she sounded very upset and even tearful. Much more so than the other day, when she learnt of how I had narrowly escaped death. I stopped walking and stood on the side of the pavement to hear her better. I forgot my suspicions about her and Subhash. My heart was pounding so loudly it almost drowned out the traffic sounds. For some reason I thought of my mother. Had something happened to her? Or to Durga?

'What's up?'

'It's Amelia. Today . . . we had a huge shock. There was a bit of an emergency. The nurse had stepped out for some water. There was no one in her room, but when she came back she found that the child's drip with the medication had been pulled out. It's terrible to think someone can be so callous. And why?'

'Maybe the nurse forgot to put in the drip in the first place?'

'She is our most conscientious nurse – we've never found anyone better than her – so I am imagining the worst. She's the one who reported it. But ever since you said there may have been something we missed in the deaths in Rajasthan, I've been trying to keep a strict watch on her.'

My mind raced through the possibilities, trying to get an idea of what was going on. This was worrying news indeed. It fitted with my fear that anyone who was connected with baby Amelia or her case was at risk.

'Do you think it's worth keeping an eye on Ganguly?' I asked cautiously.

'Whatever for?' Anita was genuinely surprised. 'He is as upset as us over this, if not more. In fact he's trying to find out whether someone came into the hospital from outside. No one actually working here would do such a terrible thing to a little baby. Oh no.'

Perhaps Edward was right: this was an even more malevolent conspiracy, with many more players, than we had initially thought.

I assured her that I would be back within the next few days. I only needed to check up on a few more addresses and people, and would do it immediately. It could be that the real story was in India – and I had made a big mistake coming to London.

While we were speaking she agreed that I would come back via Mumbai. I could meet the Customs and Excise officer there and talk about the missing embryos.

I called my travel agent and booked my ticket. Then I took a quick cab to the address Preston had given me in Hyde Park, where Susan had hired an apartment. It was an apartment block, and her flat was on the fifth floor. Before entering the building I called Edward. I did not want to be alone when I finally met her son. I just felt that someone should be with me. Besides, Edward may now be interested in meeting the boy who was, in all probability, his son.

He must have sensed my urgency because he said he would be there in fifteen minutes. As I stood smoking on the pavement, waiting for him to arrive, I shivered at the thought that someone wanted to harm baby Amelia.

By the time he arrived, I had a severe headache from the stress. I told him about my meeting with Preston. I also told him how someone had tried to harm Amelia. The thought of facing another traumatic situation was almost too much for me. I slipped my hand through his arm, gaining some comfort from his presence.

He understood perfectly. We entered the lobby. But my run of bad luck wasn't over yet.

We went up to the concierge and told him that we had come to meet Susan Oldham's son.

'They don't live here any more,' he said. 'Miss Susan gave up the flat after her son's death last year. '

The blood drained from my face and I felt giddy. Perhaps I hadn't quite recovered from my fall. Taking a few deep breaths to steady myself, I looked at Edward's shocked face. It was my turn to feel sorry for him.

Now Edward would never meet him. I did not know what was worse: never to have even made the attempt, or to have made the effort and discovered the futility of it. Perhaps this was why it was best that he never sought out his children. It was impossible to tell what sad stories would emerge.

'How – how did he die?' His normally clear voice sounded choked.

'All I know is that he had a very long illness.'

'What do you think it was?' I knew I should not press, but this might be crucial to my investigation.

'Madam, it is not our business to enquire,' he said. God, this was such a polite, non-interfering society. Respect for privacy prevented everyone from finding out anything. In India we would have shouted about all these issues from the rooftops. There was no problem too big to be gossiped about.

But slowly a picture was forming in my mind. There was one place I could think of where the mystery might finally get sorted out, and that was Mybaby.com. I wasn't sure if Dr Hansen would help me, so I would have to think of a very creative solution.

As we left, I looked up at Edward's face and was horrified to see how grey and drawn he looked.

Life can be very strange indeed. My heart broke just looking at his silent grief. I forgot all my resolutions and, reaching up, planted a kiss carefully on his cheek. We walked out into the night hand in hand.

Three months earlier

Mehta now felt ready to take on the world. He had confronted his own devils and managed to survive. After all, what could be worse for a man than to actually confess the fact that his sperm count is low? It was as bad as admitting impotence. He even stoically accepted the fact that his mother had probably been right when she had told him not to cycle so much or wear those tight briefs when he was a teenager. He might have wrecked his chances of parenthood forever. For what? A silly childhood fad! But he was able to face up to it. *It is always better to know, than to die in ignorance.* Some famous man must have said that – unless it was an original witticism from Diwan Nath Mehta. He grinned when he thought of that. He would be famous one day. He had started keeping a notebook to jot down these weighty thoughts.

In fact, ever since that fateful day that Nazir Ali had asked him to deliver those *gora* babies, his own personality had begun to change. He was more thoughtful, more concerned about what was happening around him. And more interested in Malti's wellbeing.

He was on his way back to the sperm bank to pick up the final report. Malti was also in a better mood this morning, and he thought he would take her out for a stroll, and some snacks on Chowpatty beach in the evening. She'd had a reprieve since his parents had said they would return a few days later, and for the time being at least, she had even given up the idea of shaving her head. He kept telling her that perhaps there was another way, that he was working on it.

He was also trying to persuade Dr Anita Pandey to come to Mumbai and look at Freedom Hospital for herself and she had promised to try. That was good news – both because he wanted to clarify his doubts about the place and because he hoped to get some medical advice from her.

Why did he have so much faith in her, when no doubt he could find someone equivalent in Mumbai?

Mehta found himself unable to answer that question, apart from the fact that when she had first appeared in front of him in her lilac-coloured suit he had found her very admirable. Perhaps she made him think of a better world out there, which must exist, and to which one day his children (if he ever had them, and educated them well) would belong.

So now he thought he should try to smuggle out from Ali's office the (possibly empty) containers of the consignment which had been confiscated originally. It was evidence of what had been happening over the past few months. She had a right to know the truth. Even if most of the embryos had been removed from the containers, Dr Pandey would be able to understand, no doubt, why the consignment had been kept back.

As Ali always told him, it was important to bring the containers back. Just in case there was an official inquiry, he could produce the containers and prove that the confiscated consignment was still languishing in a locked cupboard. In this case he had even hinted to Mehta that not all the embryos had been used by Dr Wadhwani and that some containers were intact.

That was it. He was going to return the whole lot to Dr Pandey and take her to Freedom Hospital. Something was going on that he did not quite understand or like. The last time he was there he had actually seen Mr Dhawan's son get up and walk a few steps. For someone who had been declared bedridden, it was eerie.

He had also seen some people far too poor to afford the hospital fees being taken in for treatment. A beggar who had been blind from birth. A woman who was mentally unstable.

That was even more bizarre.

But it was the embryos which were depressing him most of all. He had recently read in the newspapers that a paedophile ring was operating in Mumbai. He knew that sometimes the children preferred by these perverts could be mere infants or even newborn babies. Now Mehta wondered whether Ali's original claim of human trafficking might not be all that far wrong. Perhaps that was why the embryos of foreigners were disappearing inside the hospital, and why it was so secretive. Could the embryos be implanted and the resultant newborns trafficked or used by paedophiles? It was a wild theory but anything could happen these days.

Mumbai, as all cosmopolitan cities in India, had become a hub for child-trafficking under an indifferent government. The children were usually forcibly taken from one state to another, or were voluntary 'runaways' coming to the 'big city' in search of a better life. Once their identities had been ripped away by gangs who cruised the streets and railway platforms for these vagrant waifs, they would vanish into the hordes that crowded Mumbai. Each year more than half a million children in India were 'lost' forever. If the gangs acquired them from birth, they would be very useful. Fair-skinned children, especially, could be worth a lot of money.

Even more worrying was the prospect that these children could be inducted into brothels or drug havens. If they were brought up in that environment they would never be able to escape. It had to be stopped. Somehow he had to get inside Freedom Hospital – all the way inside.

He remembered Rajiv Kumar saying that if ever he needed any kind of medical treatment, he should come to Freedom Hospital. Perhaps the time had come to accept that offer? How else could he get in?

At the sperm bank, the nurse, Mohan, was very sympathetic.

'These things happen?' he said, questioning fate generally.

Even though Mehta had prepared himself for it, he waited anxiously for the blow to fall.

'It is oligozoospermia, I'm afraid?' Mohan pronounced sadly, still ending each sentence with a question mark. 'You were right about the low sperm count?'

It was the third sample that Mehta had given, and now finally this musical title had been bestowed on him.

'Oligozoospermia. It sounds like the first line of an A. R. Rahman song.'

'*Jai ho!*' Mohan said, smiling indulgently, but his tone was gloomy. 'This means that there are less than twenty million spermatozoa per one millilitre of your ejaculate . . .?'

It was there in black and white. The certificate that said he could never be a father. He was surprised at his own feelings of despair. It was as if that thing between his legs had become just a useless appendage. Which was odd because he had used it quite briskly inside Malti just that morning. He had been ready for bad news but this made him feel as if it was only good for peeing. Maybe not even that. For the first time he really understood how Malti had felt all these years.

Mohan carried on explaining, with a chart and some diagrams, what Mehta could do.

It was too technical for Mehta. And besides, he thought rebelliously, surely that was quite a substantial level of spermatozoa, actually! Twenty million! And still not enough?

No, according to the nurse, not enough. Finally Mohan put the chart away.

'Do you have a brother?'

Mehta shook his head.

'Then what about your father? Is he alive?'

'Yes.'

'How old is he?'

'Sixty-five.'

Mohan leant forward so that they would not be over-heard. He spoke in a loud penetrating whisper which Mehta was sure was audible in all the cubicles. His ears turned red with embarrassment.

'Bring him here and we will take his sample? If it's healthy we will store it? This is a list of hospitals where IVF is done and we supply the sperm? Later, if you take your wife to any of these hospitals it will be injected in her? Simple? That way you will maintain your racial purity, your child will carry your DNA, and neither your wife nor your father will know that it is not your child, but his? It will be your secret? And ours!'

Mehta's head was reeling with the information, and he felt even worse. But he always liked to get the entire picture, no matter how much it hurt.

'And what do I say to my father to bring him here?'

'Whatever you like? Tell him it's a test for prostate cancer? Or, if you feel confident you can tell him the truth . . .?'

Mehta imagined telling his father the truth. It wouldn't work.

Yet, this man was right, in a way. The alternative would be to get the sperm of a complete stranger. And then he remembered the pimple-faced adolescent boy he had seen here the last time. What if someone like that were to be the sperm donor? He was appalled by the very thought.

As though to scare him completely, a curtain shifted and this time it was an older man, one who looked just like Nazir Ali, who emerged. Mehta almost jumped out of his skin. He was just as broad-shouldered and macho. He deposited the sample and strolled out, after collecting the money. He seemed well-dressed and not someone who needed to be here, in these grimy surroundings.

'Why does *he* come here?'

The nurse shrugged. 'As I told you earlier, we get all kinds, and we also get all kinds of demands. We encourage people like him to come, because some people are only looking for tall, well-educated men? Others want their children to look like themselves, so we also need to give them a wide variety to choose from?'

'What about getting him to donate for me?'

'*Arrey baba*, he is a Muslim, and you are a Hindu? No, no, we don't encourage that because later you can say we gave you wrong advice?'

Mehta suddenly thought of all those embryos lying

inside his cupboard. If he had to choose a stranger, why not just take one of those blastocysts? Besides, since they were all from foreigners, they were without caste and many without religion, too.

He thanked the nurse and walked out, trying not to think of the bad news he had just received. Their barren status was his fault and not Malti's.

Deliberately diverting his thoughts, which were making him more and more depressed, he began plotting how he would get the half-dozen containers out of Nazir Ali's office. Maybe his audacious move would make the whole operation grind to a halt. It was worth making an attempt anyway.

Suddenly he was exhilarated by his proposed action – his *real* role was as an embryo liberator! What a shame that this was one story he could not share with anyone – expect perhaps the honourable Dr Pandey. He imagined her standing in front of him, looking grateful in her impeccable lilac suit. 'Thank you, Diwan,' she would say. 'Without you my embryos would have been lost forever. Now they will be reunited with their parents and lots of children will be born.'

For Mehta the dilemma now was – how could he get hold of Dr Pandey's containers without making Ali suspicious?

Perhaps he could somehow get Ali out of his office. Or perhaps he could say there was an emergency of some kind and Wadhwani wanted the embryos. But what if he managed to get the containers and Ali decided to call Wadhwani to check? The answer struck him just as the clock hands in the office hugged each other announcing noon. Wadhwani's surgery hours were from twelve to around 4 p.m. He would not be available at this hour. Picking up his courage, Mehta walked tremulously into Ali's room. This wasn't going to be easy. Very few people could get anything past Ali. He just had a nose for bullshit.

Ali was on the treadmill, sweating profusely as he ran, so Mehta realized he wouldn't be able to get him to leave the room. He had yet to exercise with the dumbbells and the weights.

Spotting Mehta hesitating at the door, Ali looked a little annoyed, possibly because he had his iPod plugs in his ears, and his favourite Bollywood number 'Munni Badnaam Hui Darling Tere Liye' was providing a nice hot tempo. This was how he relaxed and stayed cool. Even his own boss left him alone, knowing it got the best results. Ali would eventually deliver – if allowed to carry on at his own pace.

Mehta tried to look anxious but found his face was already frozen in a tense frown. His voice sounded higher pitched than normal as he spoke.

'Boss, Dr Wadhwani is really worried because he urgently needs some containers – but no deliveries have come in today.'

'So?'

'So – boss – those embryos you had confiscated, no, the

first time? Remember? They are still lying here – I had brought them. He didn't take out all the embryos but you had asked for all the containers back. Can't I give the unused ones to Dr Wadhwani?'

'Smart boy. These days, banjo, the extra diet of those Reserve Bank of India notes is making you very smart. Lot of vitamins and brain power in that paper. A little more and you'll become like Einstein.'

'Yes, boss.'

'Banjo, let me tell you something,' Ali patiently repeated what he had told Mehta the other day, 'those *gora* babies are our security. What if that original consignment is ever asked for? And what if anyone comes to us in an emergency? If you give them away what will we have left?'

'Boss, this is an emergency. What will it do to our relationship with him if you say you can't provide any embryos to him when he needs them?'

Ali looked thoughtful.

'You're right – I can't lose a client. The funny thing is he normally calls me. What's happened this time?'

Mehta spoke quickly: 'He's busy, boss – he's in the operating theatre. Now can I take them? He said he'll settle the accounts later.'

He sidled up to the grey Godrej cupboard and opened it, revealing the shining canisters. His old friends, he remembered every name – Betty and Alexander Smith, Susannah and Peter Wimpole, Kevin Franzen and Hannah Jacobson . . . He brushed his hand across the top of the rocket-shaped cans and hoped the children still inside some of them were safe.

While Ali watched and wiped his face with a hand towel, Mehta quickly put them into the familiar black suitcase to get out of the office before Ali asked any more questions.

He was almost at the door when Ali called: 'Wait! Let me check with him. This whole thing is a bit odd.'

Turning around slowly, Mehta stood at the door and, with his heart thumping, watched Ali stroll to his desk, wipe his face and hands with a towel and sit down to dial Wadhwani's number. The minutes slowly ticked away. The phone rang and rang.

Ali shrugged and put down the phone, getting back on to the treadmill.

'It's okay, banjo, you win. Take them away.'

Almost collapsing with relief, Mehta wheeled the suitcase out and took it into the car. This time he treated the containers like porcelain. As he put them in the cupboard at home, he made up his mind to tell Malti the whole story. It may not be long before Ali found out about his secret stash.

It was about time she got to know the truth about those milk cans.

GURGAON

Sonia had the same nightmare again – these days her

sleep was disturbed and full of frightening things. She dreamt she had lost the baby and Renu Madam had locked her up in jail. The bars were too heavy to open so, changing his shape like an amoeba, Vineet Bhai squeezed through, his penis thrust before him, a giant protuberance which danced before her eyes and bit her cheeks till she cried.

Restless and hot, she woke up to find herself in the silence of the hospital. Apart from the usual mewling of a few newborn babies, there was the soft whirr of the fans, and the hushed footsteps of nurses walking about, checking temperatures and giving medication. There were obviously no emergencies tonight.

She had had no problems as yet, and the child inside her seemed to be doing well. Her stomach was enormous, and she felt a slight discomfort when she walked. She looked around and found the remote for the television; switching it on, she kept it on mute so that she did not disturb anyone in the other rooms. This was her one great luxury, to lie in bed and watch television just like one of those madams in whose homes she had worked: sweeping the floor, washing the dishes and the clothes, and cleaning and clearing all the things they would never deign to touch. A few of them prevented her from entering the kitchen because she was an 'untouchable' and 'unclean'. They would even separate out the glass she was allowed to drink from. If she entered their prayer room by mistake, they would wash the whole place out, muttering curses upon her. She found it ironic that she was now carrying the child of the country's most prominent Brahmin power couple. Her main regret was that she would never be free to speak about it to anyone.

She drank some water and through the half-open door she saw the dim light in the room across the hall.

There had been so much excitement earlier in the evening, when the girl, Amelia, had been born. Since she had been slightly premature, she was placed inside an incubator in the room, and she seemed fine. Everybody had been rushing around and there was the usual erup-tion of joy when a surrogate mother delivered successfully.

Then, a few hours ago, the mood had completely changed. It seems there was some trouble, because the doctors had gone into the room for a detailed discussion. When the nurse saw her standing outside, she drew the curtain at the doorway so that Sonia could not see the activity inside the room.

She tried to find out if Preeti was alright but the nurse in charge was quite grim and told her to go back to her own room. And when she walked down to the dining hall, she found that Susan and Mike, the baby's parents, were talking softly to each other, looking worried. They had always been nice to her, and she smiled at them, wanting to congratulate them. But for once they just continued their conversation, barely noticing her.

Dr Ganguly came and told them he had got 'the tickets'.

They argued with him about something. Sonia was shocked, because no one ever argued with Doctorsahib; everyone was scared of him. She remembered how Preeti dreaded going for her health check-ups.

Still looking upset, the Oldhams left with him for Dr Subhash's office. Sometime later, they came back to peer through the door at baby Amelia and Preeti and then they left, as well.

Sonia assumed they were going out of town, as the hospital often arranged trips to tourist sites for the parents. Susan and Mike did not seem very interested in leaving, though Dr Ganguly was trying to persuade them.

From the little she could understand through her newly acquired English, they were having a heated debate about the money and the child. The rest she could not make out.

Now that the hullaballoo was over, out of curiosity, she stepped out and found the corridor was deserted. Since she could not sleep anyway, she thought she would go into the room and see if the baby and Preeti were alright. She still missed her own children terribly and she loved to watch these babies, which reminded her of her own. Often she would pick them up and hold them close, and at that point, pure happiness would spread from her heart all over her body. It tingled, but like a soothing balm. It took away all the hurt and pain she had felt for so many years.

She was keen to see Amelia – who would she look like?

Preeti had told her she wouldn't leave until the baby was a week old, because they had earlier wanted her to nurse the child for at least a little while. It would be nice to talk to her if she were awake.

Going to the door, Sonia tried the handle, which to her surprise was locked. Short of making a noise, there was little she could do. She knocked softly on the door and whispered, 'Preeti, open the door.' But there was silence from inside.

A little frightened, she walked back to her bed and drew the curtains at the door, leaving them slightly apart so she could keep an eye on the door opposite. Her instinct told her something was wrong.

She must have fallen asleep because when she woke up with a start, a few hours later, she noticed a shadowy figure go inside the room opposite. She could not make out who it was. She dared not get up, but lay very still and saw in the dim light of the corridor that Preeti was being brought out in a wheelchair. She seemed unwell, as her head drooped to one side, and her arms hung loose. The attendant, who looked familiar, wheeled her swiftly away down the corridor.

Still half asleep, Sonia struggled upright, aware that the child inside her was kicking. It took her a few minutes to swing her feet on to the floor and cross the corridor. By that time the attendant and the wheelchair had vanished from sight, but the door was slightly ajar.

When she walked in, the room was deserted. The baby

was lying on her side and was breathing heavily but peacefully inside the incubator. There was a drip in her arm. Sonia sat on the chair on the far side of the room and thought she would just stay for a while and wait for Preeti to come back, when her eyes started to close. But before she could doze off, the door opened once more. Some instinct made her pretend to be asleep, her eyes almost closed.

It was Dr Ganguly. He came closer and looked at the child. He bent and began to lift one side of the incubator.

For some reason, perhaps remembering how Preeti had been wheeled away, Sonia grew nervous again. Forgetting her habitual reticence, she called out, 'Doctorsahib, is the baby alright?'

Ganguly whirled around and, for a minute, Sonia felt she was back in her nightmare. All alone and with no one to help her.

But then his expression changed. His face broke into a warm and familiar smile.

'Sonia, you really frightened me. I thought the baby should be looked at since the nurse wasn't here. I didn't see you in that chair. What are you doing here?'

He came closer. His hair flopped over a broad forehead, and his eyes shone with good cheer behind his spectacles. Though Preeti vehemently disagreed with her, Sonia thought that Dr Ganguly could make everyone around him feel as though there was no one else in the world that mattered apart from them. That was why one had to be careful with him. He had huge quantities of natural charm, and his plump face and chubby cheeks were disarming.

'I saw the door open.'

It was odd that he had said nothing about Preeti. She wondered if she should ask.

'And how are you? Is the baby giving you trouble?'

His easy but slightly intrusive manner made Sonia a little self-conscious. She had still not got used to the fact that here they treated her as someone special. It was because of the child, of course, but nevertheless it felt strange.

'No, I am fine, Doctorsahib.'

But he didn't move, and for some reason kept looking at her. That steady unblinking gaze started to make her feel a little uneasy.

'Would you like to go to your room and rest? I need to check on Amelia.'

'Doctorsahib, what's happened to Preeti?'

His usual bland and happy expression remained unchanged. He did not answer, as he flipped through the papers near the child's incubator.

'What's happened to her? Where is she?' she asked again, her voice thin with the strain of questioning some-one who was obviously far above her status.

The question did not seem to interest him.

'I haven't seen her. Perhaps she's gone home – she had mentioned that her husband had called and said the chil-dren needed her.'

Sonia wondered if the sight of Preeti in the wheelchair

belonged to her nightmare. She decided not to say anything to him about what she thought she had seen.

'Tell me, have you told anyone that you are going to have Renu Madam's child?'

'I won't tell anyone, Doctorsahib. Renu Madam made me promise.'

'Let's hope not! You do realize that it's a secret – if you tell anyone she will get very, very angry and the hospital will also lose faith in you. You do want to be a surrogate with us for a little while longer, don't you? After this one I will make sure you get good money.'

'Yes.' Sonia had no idea where the conversation was going.

'Don't worry, I'll look after you. If you help me keep a little secret . . .'

'Okay.' A shiver of fear went down her spine. What did he mean? She definitely wanted to come back and have another child so she could earn some money. She did not want to upset anyone.

'If you see me coming into this room, don't mention it to anyone – I am looking after the child because she is sick, and I want to help Subhashji. And then I won't tell Renu Madam you told me it was her baby.'

'But, Doctorsahib, I never told you – you asked me.'

He laughed and wagged his finger at her, as though at a stupid child.

'You didn't have to tell me, even if I asked. Why did you tell me? The mistake is yours and not mine. You know

334

you are not supposed to mention that to anyone. So you keep my secret and I will keep yours.'

He smiled and walked out. Sonia tried to understand what he had just said. Having survived all forms of oppression throughout her life, Sonia could recognize blackmail when she saw it. There was nothing to laugh about in what he had said, even if he had said it so cheerfully.

She went over to the child and watched her; she seemed fine, and was sleeping undisturbed.

The nurse came in, and Sonia started to tell her what had happened and then thought better of it.

'Is the baby alright?'

The nurse was relaxed, checking the drip and bustling about.

'Yes, darling. What are you worried about?'

'Nothing.'

Sonia stood nervously for a while.

'Please check if she is really alright.'

The nurse stopped and stared at Sonia.

'I think you should go to your room and sleep.'

Sonia wanted to ask the nurse about Preeti – but then thought better of that too, fearing she might inadvertently reveal that she had seen Dr Ganguly with the baby. She had to be careful. Just as he had told her to be.

Slowly Sonia left, but with a feeling of dread. She kept wondering what kind of treatment he was carrying out and should the Pandeys not know about it? She trusted them more than she trusted Dr Ganguly, but why would anyone pay any attention to what she had to say?

She left her door wide open, so that from her bed she could keep her eyes on the door across the corridor. That was all she could think of: if he came back, she should be able to see him. Perhaps she ought to move into baby Amelia's room?

She desperately wanted to protect her.

AMBALA / GURGAON

Ben, meanwhile, had not given up.

While working on a financial report for a Mumbai-based company, out of their hotel room in Gurgaon, he was still thinking of ways and means to persuade Kate to come around to his point of view.

Adoption was the answer. And why look further than Sheela's three children?

His mind went back to that day in Ambala.

The photograph on the wall of Sheela's shabby little room had come as a sweet assurance. He was on the right track. He wasn't completely crazy to have made the trip.

He had looked at it closely again.

'Who is this? *Yeh . . . kaun hai?*' He struggled with his Hindi, pointing to the woman in the photograph.

'*Mere pati ki badi bua.*' My husband's great-aunt.

He looked at Kate helplessly. Her Hindi was much better than his. But she didn't want to help, standing at the door of the small room, enraged. This was turning into a farce. She had never thought they would find anything. Now it seemed the shadowy woman in Major Riley's life had a very real role to play.

'Please.'

Kate sucked in her cheeks, pushed back her annoyance and came in.

Between them they finally sorted out the story.

The woman in the photograph was Sheela's husband's great-aunt, who had committed suicide when she was young. It was over that *angrez* in the photograph, Sheela said. He was a *pardesi* and he said he would take her back with him, but he got married to a memsahib. So she had jumped from the top of the church while the wedding ceremony was going on. She was pregnant when she died. This photograph was all that was left of her.

It was all told in a matter-of-fact way, and Sheela's children gathered around as well. It was obviously a story they had heard before, but they were still enthralled by the bloody dénouement.

Ben felt small and humiliated over his grandfather's actions. None of this sounded heroic, at all. Was this the reason he had left Ambala so quickly after his marriage? Not because of the hand-to-hand combat with local rebels which had left him wounded – as Ben had been told? Now the secrecy about him, and the gossip, hushed up by his stern grandmother, made sense.

'What was her name?'

'*Nahin maloom, sahib,*' replied the woman, shaking her head, now squatting down on the floor and fanning the burning twigs inside the earthen stove. On it sat a blackened tin utensil in which water and milk with tea leaves bubbled.

'She says she doesn't know,' Kate translated, also surprised and rather shocked at the revelations.

At this point he dared not tell Sheela that the man in the photograph was his grandfather, and he could feel Kate's eyes boring holes into his back. He knew she was wearing a slightly ironic smile.

'Why don't you tell her who you are? This is why you came, isn't it? The grand reunion?'

Ben refused to be pushed.

As they sipped tea from chipped cups, Ben desperately wondered how he could repay her generosity, at least.

Finally he took out some money from his wallet and pressed it into her palm.

Her smile froze.

'*Nahin, sahib.*' She pushed the notes back at him.

He had been in India long enough to deal with that. Now he thrust the money into the hand of the toddler, who was swaying from side to side, snot still running down from his nose. The money stopped his drunken movement and he sat down with a thump, promptly putting the notes in his mouth.

Everyone, including Kate, burst out laughing.

'*Hum . . . vapas . . . aayenge.*' Ben carefully put the words together. We will be back.

But on the way back to Delhi, his effort to persuade Kate that adoption was the way out led to a flaming row.

'You don't adopt to do penance. You adopt because you want to be a parent to that particular child. Ideally you should adopt out of love, not your own need to be noble. Besides this may not even be legally possible!'

Kate's words hurt – especially since there was a kernel of truth in them.

As he sat in his room, putting together the report, and simultaneously trying to think of a cogent argument to present to her, there was a knock on the hotel-room door. Kate still wasn't back from sightseeing, so Ben opened it.

Outside stood a man with a large paunch, a bright blue blazer and a file under his armpit. Despite the Delhi chill he wiped his forehead, over which a few hairs had been tugged forward and plastered across, before speaking.

'Myself Sharmaji, are you Ben Riley?'

'That's right – do I know you?'

'I heard about your problem from Dr Pandey.' Sharmaji, ever the salesman, dropped his voice slightly, but came straight to the point.

Ben was surprised because Subhash hadn't mentioned that he would be sending someone to him.

'What problem?' Ben asked cautiously. Right now he had too many to enumerate.

'I was told you are looking for a child to adopt?'

Sharmaji shuffled past a surprised Ben and sat down on the sofa.

'Do you work with an adoption agency?'

'Sir, I work everywhere. Whatever you want – I can do for you. Now, I brought this form with me: what kind of child do you want? Black, brown, white? Girl, boy? Young, old? Chinese-looking or Indian? Any religion or caste? Some people specially ask for discarded baby girls. Very popular with foreigners. Just fill this form. I have some friends in orphanages and they can check – and we will fix a meeting. If you like the child, we can take it forward – if not, no problem. And in case there is any *particular thing* you want, we can provide that too.'

He handed over a form to Ben. Looking through it, Ben thought he must clarify the situation.

'I will do this, but I must point out that nothing is certain yet. I mean, I would like to adopt but we may just go ahead and still try for a child through a surrogate.'

Sharmaji's face brightened perceptibly.

'That's interesting, sir, because we can help you there as well.'

'Yes, thank you, but as you know we are already enrolled with Madonna and Child.'

Sharmaji smiled and said, 'That's alright, sir, and I am the one who brings all the surrogates there – but if there is anything special you want or any *particular thing* you are looking for, let me know.' It was the second time he had said that, and Ben began to wonder what Sharmaji could possibly mean.

And had he really winked at him?

Even though their meeting with Simran Singh had gone quite well and she was looking into various options for them, Ben thought he should find out something about the adoption process from Sharmaji, since Subhash had recommended him.

'Are infants or newborn babies available for adoption with you, or does one have to go for an older age group?' he asked.

'Sir, it's a little difficult to get newborn babies, but I'll try. However, sir, there are always a lot of problems for couples from abroad who want to adopt. So my advice to everyone, especially if you want infants, is to go in for surrogacy, because then you have a legal right, and also the courts now are quite sympathetic. You can easily take the child back with you. But adoption takes much longer. You know they worry about child-trafficking, paedophilia and so on.'

Ben thought of Sheela once again.

'What if I give you the name of a woman whose child I want to adopt?'

A sly smile broke out on Sharmaji's face.

'That's what I meant, sir, when I asked if there was anything *particular* you were interested in. I had heard about that woman in Ambala from Dr Ganguly. Some family relationship, I believe. It can be done, sir, anything is possible for a payment. Where do I find her?'

Ben was a little hesitant, as he wrote the address down.

'I'll give it to you – but please don't mention this in front of Kate, my wife. She gets quite upset.'

Pocketing the piece of paper, Sharmaji gave a distinct wink.

'Your secret is safe with me. But this is also why I would suggest you also look at other options, come and see our clinic, you may change your mind.'

'Are you still suggesting surrogacy after all?'

'Don't rule out that option. If you use our facilities then you can get the same service as in Madonna and Child but for half the price. I hope you don't mind my speaking frankly, sir. Subhash sahib is my best friend, but then business is business, am I correct?'

Ben was mystified. There was a certain manic charm to Sharma, though he obviously had no qualms about stabbing his best friend in the back the first chance he got.

'We are helping Subhash sahib to set up his hospital and make it one of the biggest in Asia for surrogacy, but, sir, you have to provide for all kinds of needs, right? So we have set up another clinic and whatever Subhash sahib cannot handle is sent to us. Dr Ganguly decides. We are smaller, but more efficient and more flexible. Our surrogates are very good, sir. You must come and see, sometime. In fact we could have helped you right at the start. Instead, you been here for months, your wife has been unwell and the hospital has just been taking large amounts of money off you. In our case you need not have travelled so far at all. We have all kinds of facilities; our brochure is getting ready – but I have a leaflet here.'

Sharma whipped out a page covered with dancing babies, which said, quite clearly:

> Don't Worry Be Happy
> Just Come to Collect Your Baby
> Use our Courier Cryogenic Service
> At 100 per cent No Risk

> Only Send Us Your Sperm
> And You Will Learn
> That We Can Get You Egg Donor
> Any Way You Want Her

> Big, Small, Slim, Tall
> Its Your Call
> We Also Find the Surrogate
> At Very Good Rate

> Soon She Will Be
> Pregnant With Baby
> You and Wife Can Take Rest
> NewLife – Cheap and Best

Sharma looked rather pleased.

'You like it, sir ? I wrote it.'

Ben couldn't resist a smile, even though he was a little

shaken by the poem – and not only because of its quality. He had been told that some couples at Madonna and Child had sent their blastocysts in advance. But for a clinic to do everything – including finding a surrogate and an egg donor, without the commissioning parents even bothering to meet these women personally – was a little difficult to absorb.

'Do people really do this?'

'Oh yes. It used to be done at Madonna and Child as well, but at NewLife we have a high success rate.'

'Don't people want to come and see the surrogates?'

'What for, sir? We will send you the photograph and you select – after all, you are interested in the baby, right? But if someone cannot afford to come immediately, that should not halt the production of their child. All we need is the sperm. Our girls are very good. Some of them are very pretty too, so there is no problem with the donor egg.'

Ben was silent, feeling a little awkward about the whole situation.

'So would you like to come over , sir?'

How could he just switch to another agency, when the Pandeys had been so helpful? Especially Subhash, who had been particularly sensitive to him?

Just when he was deciding what to do with Sharmaji, Kate came in. She was beginning to look so much better. Despite the stress, her face was glowing as she sat down and dropped the parcels she had been carrying on the floor. But the tension between them still persisted.

Ben introduced Sharmaji to her, and was careful only to mention the proposal of finding an alternative surrogate and egg donor. Surprisingly, she seemed interested in the thought of going elsewhere. Perhaps the long delay and the amount of money spent without any concrete result had made her tire of Madonna and Child. While the surrogate could be managed quite easily, they had still not found a suitable egg donor at Madonna and Child – and Kate had met and interviewed at least twenty in the past few weeks.

She shrugged: 'Why not? We might have better luck with the donors at Sharmaji's clinic. '

They agreed to meet at NewLife in the coming week. As a memento, Sharmaji left behind a calendar with pictures of various embryos dancing in the womb, and a DVD with a computer-generated embryo performing gymnastics and clicking his fingers, endorsing the clinic. It was leaping about in perfectly choreographed moves – to the beat of Sharma's lyrics set to a popular Bollywood tune.

It was meant to set their minds at rest.

At least it made them both burst out laughing.

GURGAON

Subhash and Anita had quite another kind of crisis on their hands. As they had suspected would happen, the gay French couple were not being allowed to take the twins back home because France did not recognize surrogacy. Their court battle with their own country was becoming a very public case. On the other hand, the Indian judge was sympathetic, and was happy to settle the case in their favour.

But more worryingly, outside the hospital a full-scale demonstration was going on, led by a local militant organization, Pratha Suraksha Sansthan. They opposed surrogacy overall – but for gays in particular.

'A Husband Cannot Be a Wife' said one banner rather prosaically.

'Up Up Hindu Culture! Down Down Gays!' was another one being waved around, with a cut-out of a man who looked like George Bush. Even though he had been out of power for years, George Bush had become a symbol of everything wrong with the Western world. But the fact that one day he would be a gay icon was something even he may never have dreamt of.

'Gay Sex – *hai hai*!' shouted the motley assortment of men, women and even children.

Subhash was aghast. If anything proved to him yet again that he was not alone in his fight against homosexuality, this certainly did – but he wasn't quite sure he wanted this rag-tag army of fundamentalists and their offspring on his side.

Worse was to follow.

Anita received an email detailing all the children born in the hospital whose parents were gay. By name. And this time it wasn't a Hindu group but an Islamic organization denouncing their births. It seemed they too were worried, because they had learnt that a gay American couple, who were Muslim, had registered with them.

'How did they know?' she asked Subhash. 'This is really very odd.'

'Obviously someone has been leaking our hospital information. Now all we need is Al Qaeda to send in a suicide bomber.'

Subhash was only half-joking. In this febrile atmosphere anything was possible. Usually the organization sponsoring a protest like this did it for the publicity. If any office or institution was vandalized during a 'protest', TV cameras were sure to arrive and publicity for the group concerned was ensured. Even if the cause was forgotten.

'Simran was scheduled to come in today to take a look at baby Amelia. Perhaps I should ask her to help us out,' Anita suggested.

She marched out to get Simran, while Subhash sank further into his chair.

Ganguly came in, looking a little pleased with himself, surprisingly. It may have been due to the fact that last night he had managed to persuade the Oldhams to leave for a small holiday.

'Be careful, Subhash, don't dismiss this lot as a gang of loonies,' he said. 'The Sansthan has many supporters, including government officials, politicians and now even godmen and vigilantes.' Ganguly looked out of the window at the sloganeering bunch, which burst into a fresh frenzy when their leader, Swami Ganga, arrived. 'We might have to rethink our policy towards gay parents.'

'Bhaiyo aur behenon,' began the 'godman', standing on the steps of the hospital in his orange toga, striking a regal pose, much like Caesar on the steps of the forum. The chanting stopped. 'The Sansthan believes homosexuality is a sin against nature. Not only is it against religion and against God, all religions – including Islam, Hinduism, Christianity – condemn it. If gay couples are stopped from following this path in India perhaps the rest of the world will also be halted from using India as a child-production factory for gay parents.'

'Gay sex – *hai hai*!' chanted the group around him.

As Subhash and Ganguly watched the events unfold outside of the window, Anita re-entered the room, and said that Simran was on the phone to Ludi and Nicolas and would join them shortly.

Subhash responded to Ganguly in an aggrieved tone: 'Look, I've always thought our involvement with gay parents was a bad idea. In fact out of all of us I've had the maximum problems with it. But we've already started the fertility treatment in about five cases – another six women are already pregnant. Bit difficult to suddenly make all these women and children vanish.'

It wasn't his fault at all, and in fact till his surprising turnaround today, it was Ganguly who had most vociferously championed the cause of gay parents. Usually because of the extra money used to pay off the huge loans. What had happened to the man today? He was washing his hands of any responsibility.

Anita said, 'I agree with Subhash. We have to be rational, because so far we've always helped gay parents. Ashok, I don't think we should take the demonstration too seriously – these are just a bunch of goons.'

Ganguly would usually argue back, but now he looked completely unmoved by Anita's words.

'Sure, it's up to you. Let's carry on. After all, from our end we earn much more from these cases and couples like Ludi and Nicolas have had a very good experience so far. So why would we stop? But this could escalate into a real problem. Don't say I didn't point it out.'

Subhash was shaken by Ganguly's thinly veiled warning.

It made no sense to Subhash, who hated any kind of controversy.

'This is a real reversal of roles. That's usually what *I* say – and you've been pushing us to go down this route since it's good for business. Now that we're in trouble – you're coolly saying that we should back out? We must have a consistent policy on this—'

Before Ganguly could answer, Simran, in her usual crushed-cotton saree, with a big bindi in the middle of her forehead and short curly hair, came in, frowning.

'Nicolas and Ludi are on their way here. It seems one of the Sansthan men came around earlier in the day, asking for them, and they got nervous. They felt that they would not be able to protect the twins in case something happened. I've asked them to come in through the back door, and wait in Anita's office.'

Almost immediately behind her, brushing away the security guards, the godman Swami Ganga entered Subhash's room, and sat on the chair with his feet off the ground, in the lotus asana. Two of his followers stood behind him, silently. The three hospital guards who had entered with him looked at Anita for further instructions. She dismissed them, and they left visibly relieved. Swami Ganga was too powerful politically not to be treated with respect – though mild disagreement was permitted. After a few minutes of mumbling some mantras, he fixed Anita with a ferocious glare.

'Mother.' Anita knew he addressed all women as 'mother'. 'Don't you know better? Don't you have children? How did you have them? And how did you bring them up? God created men and women to marry each other – what you are doing here is evil!'

Having been a recipient of Swami Ganga's vitriolic mail and text messages for a long time, none of this was new to Anita. She listened patiently.

Subhash however was not so sanguine. He felt that he should openly side with Swami Ganga. He had told Anita and Ganguly months ago that he did not want to accept these kind of cases, and he resented being put in a difficult situation by them.

Unlike Ganguly, who had only spoken up for the first time today, he had even previously pointed out that Swami Ganga had many sympathizers among the local police, who also sent their 'undercover' sleuths to check what was going on in the hospital. He was worried about the possible day-to-day harassment of their patients and knew the situation could get dangerous.

None of them, however, could have predicted that one day Swami Ganga would turn up at the hospital to demand that the French couple give up the twins.

But Subhash found that he was ready to capitulate even to that demand – until he saw Anita's determined face. Knowing that Swami Ganga and his hoodlums were quite likely to be rude to a woman, even if they called her 'mother', it was best that the discussion was curtailed as soon as possible.

He looked rather helplessly towards Simran. Perhaps she had an idea how to deal with this situation?

'Swamiji,' Simran swallowed hard, and spoke softly so that she did not annoy him too much, 'these people are the parents, not just any two men. These are their children, whether you like it or not. And the children will be orphaned if those men are not allowed to take their children back to France. The girl who gave birth to them can't afford to give them the same lifestyle as they would in France. There they will have a good education, good food, and a lot of love.'

'Mother, you are meddling with nature. You are

sending these two girls with two men. What do they know about bringing up children? These children will suffer. You are ruining four lives, not two.'

Simran thought of arguing back, but then decided to placate him by appearing to switch completely to his side. She knew that at least Subhash would agree with her ploy. The crowd outside was getting restless and anything could happen. She did not want the hospital premises to be invaded by them, as was likely to happen.

Choosing her words carefully, but without promising anything, she said, 'So, you would only be happy if we ensure that a man and a woman take the children? Or if we can arrange for a mother for the children? Or if one of them promises to go back and get married to a woman?'

Swami Ganga looked pleased.

'Best will be if we actually give them to the birth mother. *Asli ma ka haq banta hai.*' He clutched the toes of his feet with both hands and massaged them happily as he spoke. 'That will be the proper way to do things. Let these men repent and let the mother have the children.'

Anita looked at Simran aghast and shook her head vehemently. But glancing at Subhash's grim face made her realize that this was not the time to say anything. At least Simran's suggestions could provide them a temporary reprieve. They should *look* as though they agreed with Swami Ganga and his absurd arguments.

Swami Ganga then uncrossed his legs, got off the chair, and said he wanted to bless the twins.

Ludi and Nicolas, who had arrived and were hiding in Anita's room, were asked to come through. They brought the children out reluctantly and stood there while the Swami recited some Sanskrit *shlokas* over them and waved his arms around.

'Reform yourselves,' he told the startled men in Hindi. 'Reform and leave this life of sin before it's too late.'

Then he turned around and looked sternly at Anita and Subhash.

'We will never allow this practice to flourish in our country. If you pursue and support this trend, soon everyone will be doing it. Girls will marry girls and boys will marry boys. Your test-tube babies will replace natural birth – and what will happen? *Kalyug!*'

He walked out and Ludi burst into tears.

'What did he say?'

'He said that if we carry on like this we shall create hell on earth.' Subhash sat back and stretched his arms wearily. This was one area of medicine where everyone had a view accompanied by a different set of ethics. It was never straightforward or simple, like heart surgery or a hip replacement. ART was an ongoing, lifelong struggle. And, despite the high stakes, he was getting quite tired of the battle.

'So do you think he'll do something to stop us?' Nicolas helplessly stroked a weeping Ludi's back as they each cradled a child close to them.

'Are you at all in touch with the birth mother? She might actually be the answer,' Simran said finally.

Ganguly looked annoyed at the suggestion. 'I think we need to look at other solutions.' His gruff tone drew everyone's attention. 'I would suggest that one of you adopt the twins as a single parent. Then the issue of being a gay couple will not come up. Otherwise you might face some embarrassment.'

Listening to Ganguly's proposition Nicolas reluctantly nodded.

'We'll think about it.'

'Remember that we are also likely to get a phone call from Father Thomas about this, so you can expect a barrage of emails from the Church as well. Christian fundamentalism is not unknown and the Vatican has just spoken against IVF! It may be better to just do what either Simran or Ganguly is saying. We need to make you feel secure – till you get back to France!' Anita pointed out as gently as she could.

Of course this wasn't the end of the story. Anita thought of the lesbian couple booked to come in, but decided she would not remind Subhash right now. They would have to find out who was constructing careful lists of gay parents.

'Luckily we can manage the situation. Ashok, you better make sure that Ludi and Nicolas leave the country as soon as possible; please get the legal issues all sorted out.' Anita tried to placate everyone, especially Subhash, who was looking particularly troubled.

'I'll check on it,' said Ganguly, his tone truculent.

Simran was thoughtful and she deliberately reiterated her point, looking at Ganguly all the while. 'I still think we should find the birth mother and persuade her to be with the baby. At least till the court order comes through. She'll be like a firewall. Seeing the children with a woman will make all the difference.'

Ganguly's usual insouciance had faded completely, as his pleasant expression changed into a frown.

'I don't think that's required at all. We'll get the adoption papers ready for either Ludi or Nicolas—'

'What's the problem?' Simran looked directly at Ganguly once again, uncaring that Ludi and Nicolas were still in the room. 'Don't tell me we don't know where the birth mother is? Wasn't her name Radhika? Or has she disappeared the same way that Preeti did last night? Don't you think it's odd that in many of the cases you exclusively deal with, the women seem to vanish?'

Ganguly looked grim for a minute and then forced himself to smile.

'Simranji, you are always trying to bring your social-worker activism into our hospital. I would like to state that we do know where the mother is – but she may not be available for this.'

'Is there any harm in us meeting her, or Ludi or Nicolas discussing it with her? After all, she will earn some more money, and all she needs to do is be with the babies.'

'Believe me, it's not required. It's better that they stick to their plans rather than all this subterfuge.'

Ganguly abruptly got up but his cheery expression was a little strained as he spoke to the French couple, who were worriedly following the argument with the twins in their arms.

'If you come with me I'll escort you to a cab.'

As Ganguly left, Anita turned around and stared at Simran.

'Now what was that about? I know you two don't like each other, but for once I have to agree with him. Bringing the woman back will serve no purpose and she may get too attached to the children.'

'You asked me to check into this and so I did.' Simran got up and shut the office door firmly, leaning against it. 'He's not telling us the whole truth. I went outside and met some of the demonstrators. When I started talking to them they said someone from the hospital had asked them to come here and agitate. They didn't know the name. I wonder if it was Dr Ashok Ganguly. I don't know what he's up to, but I suspect he is behind this. They also told me that Radhika's father had been quite upset – apparently she's only sixteen – and that Ganguly has brought her back into the hospital for another pregnancy. Now that can blow up in your faces in a big way. Why did you allow Ganguly to do this?'

Subhash leant over to comfort Anita, who had let out an audible gasp.

'We never allowed any of this – nor did we know about it. She's certainly not enrolled for another surrogacy with us. It's barely six months since she had the twins. I know you're cynical about us – but even we're not so mercenary!'

'And you're quite sure she is not in the hospital anywhere?'

'Perfectly sure.'

'Then perhaps this is just a rumour – but I think you have to keep an eye on him. That's why I was insisting that he brings the girl back, so we can see if any of this is true. I was also told her husband had a bad fall at a building site and Ganguly said he would take care of him. But no one has seen him for a long time, either. And the fact she's underage can make it very tough for you!'

'To be fair,' said Anita, 'many of these girls are not very truthful – often they themselves don't know their own age.'

'But a doctor should be able to tell.'

'We must run a proper check on all this,' added Anita. 'It's crucial we find out who's giving away our data. That could be dangerous – and destructive for us.'

Meanwhile, as Ganguly left the room, he struggled to keep his temper in check. He took charge of Ludi and Nicolas, assuring them they needn't worry about Simran's suggestion, because he, Ashok Ganguly, was the chief troubleshooter. The manager of Madonna and Child.

He told them he didn't mind the extra responsibility at all. In fact he wouldn't have minded running the whole operation by himself. It would make things less complicated in many ways.

As he waved the couple off in a taxi, Ganguly was irritated at how hard he had to work, and how little appreciation he got for it. Subhash was a dreamer and whined too much, and Anita was far too idealistic. And that foolish Simran – why did she have to keep showing up? He would have to do something about that.

He wished the Pandeys would understand that to run a hospital which had the potential to become a multimillion-dollar enterprise required hard-nosed business acumen. Which he possessed in great quantity. Recently he had received a request for ten surrogacies from the UK. These were all from gay couples. He could handle them. And there was no need to tell Subhash or Anita what he was doing, as they would simply fuss and wreck the business.

Besides, now that they were under pressure from all these political organizations, it was unlikely they would want to get involved so he could divert the ten requests elsewhere.

All of this suited him very well indeed.

He must thank Sharma for a job well done.

He would just have to ensure that that bitch Simran Singh did not come snooping around his office.

The less anyone knew, the better all round.

Chapter 8

SIMRAN

This situation was beginning to enter the realm of cloak-and-dagger subterfuge. I was sitting outside a café down the road from Mybaby.com, having a very politically correct decaf coffee with soya milk. Some of Edward's habits were beginning to rub off on me.

But I was also smoking a very politically incorrect cigarette, while I spoke to Ma on my phone. Soon I would be on that plane going home. My usual pre-flight jitters were upon me, tinged with a touch of sadness. So many things were still left unresolved. I hoped for Amelia's sake that I made a bit more progress over the next few days. Or did my sorrow over leaving have anything to do with Edward?

Edward had parked his bicycle down the road and gone inside the clinic.

I had come by bus. There are a few things I will draw the line at: cycling in London with enormous double-deckers passing by was something I simply refused to do. It undermined my confidence.

This was a last-ditch plot we had hatched. The only way to get some proper information from the clinic was to send Edward in, claiming to be a cousin of Susan Oldham hunting for her address. Hopefully, they had less reason to refuse to give it to him. I had warned him to try his luck with the receptionist rather than Dr Hansen, who was likely to stymie him.

Meanwhile I was talking to Ma to steady my nerves, trying not to think of the looming flight.

As my scars had healed in the past few weeks, I had begun to lose my fear of London streets, though I was still staying with Edward, and still cautious when I went out. The men who had attacked me hadn't showed up again.

Ma said her blood pressure had been quite high that morning and was making her feel unwell. Luckily Durga had come home early from school and cheered her up. Ma loved Hindi films and Durga had discovered the cure for her hypertension by suggesting they watch the latest blockbuster at the nearby multiplex. Miraculously, Ma's blood pressure plunged down to normal as, happily distracted, she was getting ready to go out.

However, I was a bit concerned about Durga seeing a film which had violent scenes in it. We had been careful, so far, not to expose her to anything that might remind her of the past.

Ma was scathing. 'What world do you live in? There's violence everywhere. Just this evening on the news we have had a story of a family of eight being burnt alive over a land feud in Uttar Pradesh. One girl has been stabbed to death and another shot outside a college in Delhi and a minister has just been hauled up for rape—'

'Okay, Ma. I get it. But remember Durga is still a little vulnerable.'

'I know, but we have to be robust about it. She has to live in the real world, and you can't keep her wrapped in cotton wool.'

It was odd that someone as hard-nosed and liberated as me was being so conservative, while Ma was behaving like a woman of the world. What was wrong with me? Recently I knew I had been behaving in a romantic way towards everything. A bit woolly-headed. Was all this talk about babies and motherhood making my iron-clad soul a trifle rusty?

And that led to other questions. Did my softening up have anything to do with Edward? Was I in love? Not again!

'So how is Edward?' I noticed the coyness in Ma's voice. She could not enquire about any man in my life without imagining that perhaps *this is the one*!

'He's just gone to the IVF clinic,' I could not help teasing her. 'I've just donated an egg and come out.'

'Simran!' I could not make out if she was horrified or overjoyed.

'Ma, don't yell. Your blood pressure will go up. I'm only joking. He has just gone in to check up about baby Amelia's mother.'

I could tell Ma was weaving dreams in the air. Now that she had a granddaughter in Durga, it was time I got a husband, too. Like everything else in my life I was doing things the wrong way round. But that didn't matter to her (she was used to it). What mattered was that I should settle down. I could hear her thinking thousands of miles away in Delhi, *Why won't she try harder and get that man?*

Little did she know that I was, for once in my life, trying – but getting nowhere. Perhaps it was the circumstances under which we had met, or the colour of my skin, or the fact that he had never really been involved with a woman since his girlfriend's death – but something made Edward keep his distance, even though we were spending a lot of our days and most of our nights together. Under the same roof, but of course in different rooms.

My own reaction surprised me. As I said, I thought I was tough, someone who had earned her medals in the battlefields of love, so why was I disappointed? I knew I was not naturally flirtatious and no one could accuse me of being too charming either. But I had an interestingly dusky look, and was not unattractive. Especially now, since (though I had dropped the complete disguise) I continued to wear shorter skirts when I went out! My legs might not make Victoria Beckham envious – but they were quite well-shaped and slim.

And yet Edward had made no move towards me. I told myself not to care about it; he was right. There was no point getting involved. I would fly back to India, very soon, and his life was here. Once we had sorted the case out, what was there for us together? Nothing. We came from completely different worlds.

And I am probably the kind of woman who only wants the man she cannot get. Once she gets him, she probably does not want him any more.

Thinking about my past affairs, I quite forgot to look out for Edward. He stood in front of me with a triumphant look.

'I must say I quite like playing James Bond.'

'Why – did you get it?'

'I had amazing luck. I walked in and that Supremes number you had told me about was at the reception. I really acted completely helpless. Everyone loves a helpless man, upset over losing touch with his favourite cousin. But the best part was that Dr Hansen was out of the office.'

It was the first bit of good news I had heard in a long time!

'So she hummed and hawed and then said, okay, what the hell. She was very sweet, you know. Really nice woman.'

I was getting a little envious at all this lavish praise.

'And then?' I could not help sounding impatient.

'And then she actually left her phone and went to pull out the records. She photocopied them for me. Here they are.'

With a flourish he took them out.

'I think you deserve a nice hot glass of milk! You are a genius!' I ordered his milk and then spread the photocopies in front of me.

Luckily I had asked Anita to scan and send me the forms from India and straight away I realized that there were quite a few differences. In the Indian form many things had been scratched out or overwritten.

To begin with, the father's name had changed from Martin to Mike. In fact, in the Madonna and Child form, the name had been overwritten and only the 'M' was visible, which we had assumed stood for Mike, Susan Oldham's husband. Martin's age was twenty-one. In the Indian form it was fifty.

The mother's age and name were the same in both forms: forty-two. Susan Oldham.

In fact, now that I looked at the Indian form I could see the address had been scratched and smudged, and was obviously incorrect. I could clearly read an altogether different address of a flat in Islington in the original form. So there were a lot of things that Dr Hansen had hidden from me that day.

'You are a complete genius!' I spontaneously leant over to kiss Edward's cheek. He slightly turned his face and our lips brushed together. I felt my face turn red. Perhaps it was a pre-menopausal hot flush. I quickly took out another cigarette and lit up.

He took it from my hand and stubbed it out.

'You'll have to give up all of this, you know. It's not good for you. And anything that's not good for you is not good for us.'

I was lost for words. What did he mean? Was he making a pass at me? Considering that I was just moaning about his decided lack of interest – why did this sudden initiative fluster me so much?

'I know it's not good, but—'

He leant over and kissed me again.

'I mean it will get in the way if I ever want to kiss you.'

'Oh God. Is this how people stop smoking?'

'I'm doing this for the sake of your health!'

His milk arrived and as he drank I quickly went through the forms once more – which also allowed my flushed face to stop burning.

Obviously these anomalies meant that the clinic could have made a mistake and sent us the wrong embryos. But that still didn't help baby Amelia and we still needed to find her family. Was there something in this form that I had missed? I began to scan it once more for clues.

'I'm feeling so relieved.' Edward was smiling again. 'I was really worried that this woman was my Susan, but it's probably someone else. Thank God. The moment I saw that it was a younger man who was the husband I realized that it probably wasn't her at all. I know for certain that Susan's husband was much older than her, and I have no idea who Martin is. Thank God we came here! I am so happy I could kiss everyone in the café and on the entire street!'

Okay, stop my foolish heart! He hadn't fallen in love with me after visiting Mybaby.com, he was just expressing his relief, his happiness. That's the way the cookie crumbles, I told myself grimly, as my racing heart started

pumping slowly again. But I could deal with this disappointment. Oh yes, I could.

'Fantastic, I know. But we still need to check this address
– just to be one hundred per cent certain.'

'Sure. Would you like me to come with you?'

Now my heart really splintered. Did this mean that all
his interest, all the time he had spent with me, was only to
find out if the woman killed in India was the Susan he
knew? And now that the possibility had dimmed he was
willing to dump the project (and me) and walk out? Not if
I could help it.

'This woman could still turn out to be the Susan you
knew, Edward. After all, your name was on the form I saw
in India. I admit it isn't on this. Someone must have added
it later – but we can only find out more by going to this
address. Shall we try it?'

A shadow crossed his face at my tone. But I did think
that there could be a link, and despite his history of abdi-
cating responsibility he would have to come with me to
find out.

Not looking as happy as he had been a few moments
ago, he got up and put on his helmet. He briefly glanced
at the address.

'You're right. Let's find out and hope for the best. Shall
I meet you there?'

Once I got the bus route from Edward, I, too, set out for
Islington. With luck we would both reach it around the
same time. But given the way the traffic was moving

today he would probably get there before I did. I watched him from the bus, weaving deftly in and out of the traffic. His figure became more and more distant as I gazed at him from my perch on top of the double-decker.

I had thought we were growing close to each other. It had been nothing more than a foolish dream. Spring was in the air and evening was already beginning to fall. I was homesick and tired of wandering around London's streets. The sky had turned grey and a light drizzle began to fall, accompanied by a cold breeze. Though it was cosy inside the bus, the raindrops slid across the window, wiping away any reason to stay on in London.

As always before a flight my thoughts turned to my first love, Abhi. Today was no different. Perhaps, I thought bitterly, if he had not been so badly injured, we would have grown up together and built a life together. I wouldn't have been enchanted so easily by Edward.

Or seduced so easily by so many men before him.

To distract myself from thinking about Edward, I began to make a mental list of the men in my life.

Had any of them been worth it?

Two months earlier

FEBRUARY
DELHI

Ben and Kate stood outside what seemed to be someone's home in Green Park in South Delhi. It said 'NewLife Fertility Clinic' on a large board. But it didn't look like a hospital or even a clinic. It was a three-storey-high red-painted building, which was not even very well maintained. The paint was chipped and peeling in various places – very different from the highly polished chrome, glass and marble finish of Madonna and Child.

Outside the gate, a guard in a shabby blue uniform woke up from his siesta on a broken grey plastic chair, and asked them who they wanted to see.

'We're here to see Sharmaji,' said Ben, feeling a little foolish.

'I hope he gave us the right address,' Kate muttered under her breath. 'He seemed a bit flaky, didn't he?'

The guard took them inside the drive and pointed to the front door, asking them to ring the bell. A uniformed nurse opened the door, and with a sense of relief they went in. Perhaps it was the correct place after all.

Sharmaji was in a tiny sitting room. He was talking to two men, one of whom seemed extremely worried. Perhaps, Ben wondered, they were also looking for a surrogate. The men would occasionally speak to each other in French, but softly, so that neither Ben nor Kate could understand. She thought she had seen them somewhere before.

Sharmaji asked Ben and Kate to wait while he took the couple into another room. 'They want a mother for their babies,' he said with a wink. Ben was now resigned to his over-familiar manner, and bad poetry.

He had been reading in the newspaper about the problems a French gay couple had with taking their child back to France. Perhaps these were the same men. He looked at them with idle curiosity. This transfer of embryos, babies, surrogacies and multiple parents was creating quite a confusing web of relationships, and governments still did not know how to deal with it.

Kate's voice – sounding somewhat subdued – broke into his thoughts.

'This is why it's so much cheaper, Ben. Look around, this is really the bottom end of the pyramid.'

'Get real, Kate. This is still better than how most of the surrogates live and you know it. You're the one who is so keen on surrogacy and this is the real thing. Not that fancy place we've been at all this while. But this is the nuts-and-bolts place. This is how women are really treated here – and why don't we just join the exploitation? Perhaps it might make a good documentary one day: *Exposé! How to Have a Baby With an Indian Surrogate!'*

There, it was out.

Ben was shocked he had actually said it. The words he had been avoiding all this while because he did not want to sound exalted – superior, holier-than-thou. He had lost that right – God knows how much damage he and his family had done already. But here he was, doing it all over again. Using some poor, illiterate woman. What was the difference, then, between him and his grandfather?

Kate was furious.

'How dare you say that! You know the money we give them will change their lives forever.'

Sharmaji walked in, luckily, before they started arguing again.

His sandals slapping against the cement floor, he sat down and made a big 'V' in the centre of the sofa.

'Those poor boys. We are trying to help them – they have a big problem. Some local organizations are troubling them so we are trying to see if the woman who gave birth to their children can go home with them.'

Ben nodded: 'So will she go?'

'She would like to but she is already pregnant again. I know I can be frank with you. Sometimes these women come back again and again. The money means a lot.'

Ben looked at Kate, who shrugged helplessly. They would just have to be more careful about whom they chose as a surrogate.

'This is not five star, and you know it. But the girls are just like those at Mother and Child and they are looked after the same way. Only the rates come down because you don't pay for the frills. Treatment is the same, storage facilities for eggs and sperm etcetera are the same—'

'Can we look around?' Ben cut into the sales pitch, abruptly.

'Sure.'

Sharmaji took them into a tiny cramped room where about seven women in different stages of pregnancy were sitting or lying down, idly talking to each other. The scene reminded Kate of chickens in a coop.

'Are they allowed to go out?' She felt she was asking, Are they free-range or not?

'Of course, exercise is very important. They go to a park close by and do yoga every day and walk around. They can even go home if they live locally, and if the commissioning parents don't mind. But most of them prefer to stay here, where the parents can contact them regularly and we can look after them. You know, many people prefer to have these women in a safe environment. Unlike at Madonna and Child we don't pretend that they are middle class, or that they are educated. Many of them are not, and yes, they are poor. We tell you as it is. Now, if you like this, I can call some six or seven new women for you sometime soon and you can see them for yourself.'

Sharmaji launched into another list once more: 'Just tell me your requirements: tall, short, fat, thin, straight hair or curly hair – because you also need the egg from her, right?'

The women had fallen silent as the trio stood there at the doorway. A few of them smiled and greeted them with a 'namastey'. Kate replied to their greeting, feeling a little odd as she looked at their cheerful faces.

The women were dressed almost identically in colourful kaftans. Though the room was clean, it was sparsely furnished. There were a few scattered chairs and a couple of mirrors framed in plastic hanging on the walls.

Their belongings were either hanging from hooks, or shoved in suitcases under the bed. A television set was placed strategically in the centre so that the women could all view it together. Most of them had returned to viewing the serial that was being shown, losing interest in the visitors. No doubt they were used to being looked at every day, by people from all over the world.

Kate could feel her enthusiasm for surrogacy fading away as Ben's words rang in her ears. This world was completely different to the sophistication of Madonna and Child. The atmosphere made her uneasy.

Was she really exploiting them?

She had thought she was helping them and in return getting a child. But could she be disrupting their birth cycles? What if whilst giving birth to her child something went wrong and the woman was unable to have children again? Many of them did not look particularly robust.

She knew that only those women who already had complete families were permitted by law to participate in surrogacy, but she also knew that women could be tempted by the money to forgo their own children. How would she be able to live with the knowledge that some woman could not have a child because she, Kate, had wanted one? What if the woman died? Anything was possible here.

Her eye was caught by one of the surrogates who seemed asleep on a bed in a corner. She had a bandage over a part of her forehead. She looked familiar. She reminded her of Preeti, the woman who had been baby Amelia's gestational mother. Everyone had said that she had disappeared, and yet here she was.

'Isn't that Preeti?'

Sharmaji looked puzzled.

'Who is that, madam?'

'The woman who gave birth to baby Amelia. You know, that poor child whose parents died in Rajasthan?'

'No, madam, that's not Preeti. That woman went home.'

Kate knew she was being brushed off. She went up to the sleeping woman.

'I never forget a face. This is her.'

'Ma'am, this woman is Kunti, and she had a slight accident. She just arrived today. We're sending her home this evening.'

Ben pulled Kate away. All the women were now beginning to look at the couple curiously. A few of them began to giggle at Kate's confusion, though they could not follow what was being said.

Embarrassed, Kate freed herself from Ben's steady grip and they walked back to Sharmaji's office.

'Now. If you like we can find a nice surrogate for you.'

Ben raised his eyebrows and looked at Kate. She was reluctant to admit defeat so easily.

'Shall we think about it?' she said.

Sharmaji escorted them out with the same breeziness as he had first met them. He was undismayed with their noncommittal answers. Ganguly had recently told him to find ten more surrogates for some gay couples from the UK. He was wondering if he could just recycle some of those in the room, or would he have to find new ones? Six months should be a large enough gap between pregnancies.

DELHI

Rohit was furious. After all that he had done for Renu Madam, she had had the cheek to sack him. All because she had found him on the kitchen floor with that new maid. What was he to do? It was lonely without Sonia and it wasn't his fault that she had been locked up in the hospital while he had to fend for himself.

No one understood that he had to do all the housework in his own home because she wasn't there. And neither was she there at night when a man needed some company.

It was astonishing how ungrateful people could be. Here he was, allowing his woman to have someone else's child: wasn't that the biggest sacrifice a red-blooded man could make for someone else?

And that new cook they had got in Renu Madam's house had totally seduced him.

'Rohit,' she had said, coming up to him, swinging those hips of hers and staring at him with her large bewitching eyes. 'Champa-ma is asleep and I want some money for vegetables for tonight. Do you have any?'

Rohit smiled at her, just like the actor Rajesh Khanna in the film *Nauker*. Head slightly tilted to one side.

'What sort of vegetables do you want, Raniji? Round-round tomatoes or long-long cucumbers? Or tiny-tiny peas?' He accompanied each name with an appropriately obscene gesture.

Rani laughed. She was used to his teasing.

'Shut up or I'll take the money out myself.'

'Just try,' he replied, arms akimbo.

Of course he had meant it in all innocence. It was just a game they were playing. Nothing serious.

And then she had slipped her hand into his trouser pocket and, well, one thing led to another.

Still playfully struggling, they fell on the floor. Her body had felt soft and warm under him. Normally no one came in the afternoon, and Renu Madam was in the office. God knows what made her walk in just when he had unzipped his trousers.

He had quickly got up and pretended to be hunting for something on the floor, but was startled by a loud shriek.

'He's trying to molest me,' the girl said, crying loudly and flinging herself at Renu Madam's feet. 'I was trying to push him away and he wouldn't let me get up . . .'

And suddenly he was out of the house and that wretch was laughing at him.

But he wouldn't let anyone get away with this. He was sitting in his room drinking, and wondering how to get his revenge. Didn't Renu Madam know that he could ruin everything by telling everyone whose baby it really was? What if he went to the press and sold them his story? The more he thought about it the more he liked the idea.

But if he did that, he would lose his trump card forever. In fact, he had kept quiet over it for months because this was the time for him to benefit from it all – just a few months before the baby was born. This was when Renu Madam was going to select him for an important post because he had sacrificed so much for her. He had even sent her a letter requesting an appointment, when he was going to present his list of demands. Instead of which she had sacked him. At the time, he hadn't wanted to say anything in front of the other people present and had gone quietly.

Now he was worried that perhaps they would even kick him out of his home. Where would he go? And besides, Sonia was his woman, wasn't she? How could he leave her? She needed him, and he needed to be there to guide her and look after her. Even if she had originally had the idea of having the child for Renu Madam, he had planned it all. Renu Madam thought that she could wreck his life – well, he would just show all of them.

He needed some kind of protection too, in case something went wrong or anyone got tough with him. So maybe he should go to Sharmaji. Delhi was full of country-made pistols, and Sharmaji knew where most of them came from. Besides, now Sharmaji owed him a favour. That day, hadn't he managed to get Preeti out of the hospital? And he hadn't said a word to anyone – not even to Sonia. Even after she had told him that she was worried about baby Amelia, and how Dr Ganguly had come into the room and threatened her.

And nor had he said anything when Preeti had fallen out of Dr Ganguly's car. Poor thing, she had been such a pretty girl, and what a lovely body she had, too. Enough to arouse any man, and who knew what that Ganguly wanted to do with her?

He was owed something for keeping that secret, and a gun might just be the payment he deserved.

Finishing the last drop of whisky in his glass (usually the stock was replenished from Renu Madam's bar) he called Sharmaji. This would be the moment to settle all the scores.

Chapter 9

SIMRAN

We met near the flat in Islington. Edward was definitely looking cheerful, though my own black mood continued.

It was disconcerting to find that perhaps I had completely misunderstood Edward's friendliness. I knew he was aloof, but I had always thought that once this detective work was over, our meetings would have far more significance. Thinking back, of course, it was true that while we had enjoyed our evenings together, there had been nothing in them which bore a hint of romance. I suppose I had also been very careful with him: partly because I always knew that he had a history of disengagement, and partly because his extra-curricular business meant that he would always keep the company of women, not just me.

Perhaps he was totally committed to this lifestyle.

Yet I couldn't stop hoping.

I forced my attention back to the problem before us. Even though Edward would like to think he had nothing to do with the case, the question remained: why was his name on that hospital form? There had to be some kind of a connection between him and baby Amelia. He might prefer to dismiss it as a case of mistaken identity, but I had a hunch we were inching closer to the truth. Perhaps we would find it here.

We stood outside an end-of-terrace house divided into three flats, and Edward pressed a security buzzer for the second floor. After a while, to our mutual relief, someone actually answered.

'We're looking for Susan and Mike Oldham.'

'They aren't at home,' said the male voice after asking who we were. 'But come right up.'

I was staggered. Finally there might be a glimmer of light.

We climbed up to the second floor, and a young man, probably in his twenties, opened the door. He looked like a student, dressed in jeans and a T-shirt. He had messed-up curly hair and a gap-toothed attractive smile. From his paint-spattered clothes, he could have been an artist.

We introduced ourselves once again and he cleared the books off the sofa, making room for us to sit. Peter Brown obviously lived alone.

'Any particular reason you are looking for Mike and Sue? Are you friends of theirs?'

Edward glanced at me, and I slid forward to the edge of the sofa. This was important.

'I knew Susan very well when we were in college, but haven't met her for over twenty years. I hope you don't mind our dropping by like this. It's quite urgent. I'm here purely as a friend of Susan's and Simran is from a Delhi hospital. We really need to know how you know them – and if we can get in touch with them.'

Peter looked concerned.

'You're from Delhi? Has anything happened to them there?'

'Our apologies,' Edward cut in. 'Before we discuss anything further, could you please tell us a little about your relationship with them?'

A sad expression crossed his face 'They had a son – Martin. I was his partner.'

'What happened to him?' I asked, thinking, *That was the father's name on the Mybaby.com form. Martin.*

'He died, last year.'

At least some information seemed to match. Not looking at Edward at all, I pressed on.

'And both of you lived in this flat?'

'Mike and Sue had rented it. We all lived here for a while, together. His parents would shuttle up and down between here and their flat in Hyde Park – and Martin occasionally spent time with them there.'

The simplicity of his answer took us both by surprise, and for a minute, we had little to say. Some things were definitely falling into place.

I stole a glance at Edward's face. The happy, relaxed expression had been wiped out and he looked worried, once more. He had hoped that his child was still alive somewhere, and that this was a case of mistaken identity – and that hope was now being stamped out.

'How did he die?'

'It wasn't pleasant – he was HIV positive. He didn't tell anyone till it was too late for him. I met him just after his diagnosis. His deterioration was so rapid, we didn't really have much time together.'

We both knew in that instant that the story was more complicated than we had thought, and that we *were* probably talking about Edward's son.

'Do you have a photograph of him?'

Edward's voice was low.

'Sure.' Peter brought a photograph from the next room and showed it to us. It was of a bright-eyed, thin, smiling boy with soft brown hair. There was something in his intense expression which reminded me of Edward.

I put the photograph down, but Edward picked it up again and ran his finger over the face. This was probably a child he had made with a friend one afternoon and forgotten about for more than twenty years. How did he feel now, when they would never be able to meet?

'Do you have any idea where Mike and Susan could be?' I asked, because we had to be certain this time.

'Well, I last heard them planning a holiday in India. But after that I just don't know. I've called them a couple of times but their mobile phones are switched off, and they're terrible with emails anyway. Maybe they've gone into the mountains. Sue was always a bit of a free spirit – into Buddhism and so on.'

'Did you know whether they wanted to have another child? Or did you and Martin want to have a child?'

'That's a pretty personal question, isn't it ?' For the first time Peter seemed to physically withdraw.

Edward sighed.

'I know it is. But the answer to where they would be right now depends on this question. So please – forgive me, but we need to know.'

Peter took Martin's photograph back from Edward and placed it carefully on a table next to him.

'I'll take your word for it, though this conversation is really very weird,' he said. After a short silence he carried on. 'Yes, we'd certainly discussed a child. Martin and I – though I wasn't very keen. I think his mother took him to a clinic to do something about it. She wanted to keep some kind of memory of him alive – you know, have another kid, maybe use his, umm, you know, sperm. Martin was her only son.'

'But wouldn't that pass on the HIV virus to the child?'

'No. The clinic had told her that they would wash the sperm carefully, and separate the HIV virus. A lot of HIV-positive people have managed to have children this way. So the clinic was going to do this – and if it all went well, they were going to use a surrogate. That's all I know. Then Martin died, and Mike and Sue went away to India. I haven't heard anything from them for months. It's a bit odd, but I just assumed that they were busy or didn't care.' Peter got up. 'Would you like some coffee?'

I could have done with something stronger, but I accepted the offer, as did Edward.

'So the clinic botched it up?' I said softly to him, as Peter made coffee for us in the kitchen. No wonder Dr Hansen had wanted to throw me out the moment she saw me. It was not something she wanted to be reminded of, and it was so much easier to blame the poor systems in India.

'I suppose so. Why didn't they take care to remove the HIV virus?' Edward wondered.

I needed to check the taped conversation with Dr Hansen again, but I think she had said the blastocyst had been sent within a week to India. That would have been far, far too soon if the HIV virus had to be removed; and quite apart from that, the normal procedure was to keep it for a few months, and run some tests on it, before sending it on.

'It's odd that they probably were rushing the whole thing through.'

I remembered, now, that Dr Hansen had also mentioned that Susan's husband was much younger than her. Perhaps it was Martin who had gone to the clinic with Susan?

'So this was the second time round that Susan decided to try IVF – using her son's sperm. Surely it wasn't her own egg?'

Peter had come back from the kitchen with our coffee and so I swiftly addressed the question to him.

'Do you think she used a donor egg?'

Peter hesitated a little before replying, 'As far as I know, she had planned on a donor, and it had been harvested. But as I said, since I did not go along with them to the clinic, I have no way of knowing the truth.'

Once again I avoided looking at Edward's face. I remembered only too well that the clinic had named her as the mother.

Was this then another strange twist in the life of baby Amelia? Could this be incest in a way that only ART could make possible? She might have wanted to ensure that there were no problems when she brought the baby back– as re-entry into the UK would be smoother if she were the mother. Or had Susan found a donor and requested MyBaby.com to put her name on the form as the mother? We would never know – and poor Amelia would never know either.

A key realization dawned . . . it was while Preeti was pregnant with baby Amelia that the consignments from Mybaby.com started being confiscated by customs, and when some simply vanished. Was someone trying to ensure that no evidence ever came to light – in case any other embryos were similarly contaminated?

We sat quietly while Peter served the coffee. There was just one more thing I wanted to clear up.

'And what about you, were you keen on having the baby?' I asked him. I wanted to check if he was interested in looking after baby Amelia.

'Please don't misunderstand, but I didn't really care, one way or the other. Look, I'm leaving for Brazil in a few weeks. I'm starting a new life there. Had Martin lived, we would have both gone and perhaps things would have been different. But he's dead, his parents are probably not coming back, and I can't afford the rent here any more. So in a way it's a good thing there's no child to look after. I certainly wouldn't want a child right now. No way. Maybe in another ten years or so.'

He looked at us frankly, but with sorrow.

'The child was something Susan wanted, she was keen on it. I think she was doing it for him, really – he loved children, and wanted a family – but it was far, far too late.'

Given the circumstances, it made little sense to tell him about baby Amelia. Yet I felt that, for Martin's sake, I should. He was a little embarrassed and depressed, but at least he had been honest.

And he was right; it wasn't his problem. What could we do anyway? We were not his parents – and his relationship with Martin was, from what we could gather, quite informal and not a civil partnership. In fact he had only known him for a year before he died.

After I explained the circumstances of baby Amelia's birth, he merely shrugged and said there was no point him getting involved in any of this. Peter Brown had decided to move on.

But I wondered how much of all this was known to Dr

Hansen and to our own hospital staff, especially those who had dealt exclusively with Mike and Susan, like Ganguly.

Someone had obviously taken care to score out as much of this information as possible from the hospital papers in India – but someone else (and my hunch was that it was Susan) had outwitted everyone by leaving Edward's name on the file. A reminder of a debt still to be collected. Perhaps something had alerted her in time that things could go wrong, as she had scribbled the name in a corner.

It was a last message for Edward. Would he now finally reach out over the chasms of life, death and birth and finally hear her out?

Couldn't he see that she had kept her promise while she lived – but after her death, she wanted him to know about baby Amelia?

Perhaps, like me, she too had fallen in love with this strange and reticent man.

To me it began to seem as though the removal of the correct name, the deletion of the proper address and the deaths of Mike and Susan might be more closely linked to the fact that baby Amelia was HIV positive than any one of us had initially understood. Now I had to figure out whom this cover-up had protected and why they had taken these extraordinary steps. Once again I wondered if the obvious suspects were my friends, Subhash and Anita, but I quickly pushed that out of my mind. They would be foolish to involve me in something where the finger of suspicion would point to them – unless, of course, they had depended on me to find an alternative villain? At this stage I had to think of everything, I told myself grimly.

As we left, I asked Edward: 'Do you realize this means you're probably a grandfather?'

Edward still looked pale, but a slight smile did reach his eyes.

'The thought just struck me too.'

'So what are you going to do about it?'

I was hoping he would say that he would come with me to India and look up baby Amelia. That is what Susan had hoped for. In case something happened to her. But to my enormous disappointment, he remained quiet.

We walked for a while in silence on the pavement as he wheeled his cycle alongside.

He knew I was waiting for a proper answer. This would be important for me, and I needed to know both for baby Amelia and for myself, before I left for India.

Finally he said with what seemed like regret: 'Simran, I know you would like to change me. But I can't. I'm not careless, but I'm not prepared for a big responsibility. I hate being tied down, as you know. I didn't want to know about any of the children that I may have fathered, and till you turned up I did not even want to know about Susan, Martin and baby Amelia or anything.'

But surely, now that you know, I wanted to say, *you might want to change your mind?*

'Look, I told you right at the start, I don't want to hurt you,' he said. 'You come from a different culture, you have different expectations. What can I say that will make this sound any better? It's bad enough as it is.'

I understood what he was saying, but I still didn't want to give up.

'Why don't you come with me? You can meet baby Amelia and then decide whether you want to be involved or not. She's really beautiful. And she needs someone to look after her, very, very badly.'

Edward stopped walking and looked at me, shaking his head.

'You don't get it, do you? I wish I could come with you, but I can't. I'm not who you think I am, Simran. I don't think I could ever be.'

I think you could be who I think you are – you just need to try a little bit. I almost said it out loud.

He saw the disappointment in my face.

'Look . . . I'll help you with everything. Now that we know who baby Amelia's parents are, we'll find out more. Perhaps we could set up a trust, make sure she is looked after. But that's all I can do, I'm afraid. These are the rules of the game, and I told Susan that as well.'

He planted a quick kiss on my forehead, gave me a hug, and then, strapping on his helmet, quickly rode away before I could protest any more.

As he cycled off, he turned around once to shout, 'I may not see you before you go. I have a late dinner and you'll probably be asleep when I get back. Have a safe trip!'

And that was it.

I was leaving early the next morning. Edward obviously had other plans for tonight. This time, when I opened the bottle of red wine on the flight home, I would be drinking not just to smother my fear of flying and my memory of Abhi, but also to bury my realization that Edward had understood, all too well, that I needed much more than he was prepared to give.

And I would also drink to bury the hurt that baby Amelia would never meet her grandfather.

One month earlier

MARCH
DELHI

Ultimately, Kate had decided to go back to NewLife, despite Ben's cruel jibe, as she was still intrigued by its environment. It seemed much more gritty and real than the pastel-tinted atmosphere at Madonna and Child. Sharmaji had promised her a new batch of surrogates and possible egg donors today. Ben said he had other things to do, as he had taken on a few more local assignments, and could not accompany her – so she decided to go alone.

Meanwhile, she had browsed through a few articles about UK surrogates on the Internet. Their lives seemed remarkably dissimilar to those in India. One case she remembered vividly was of a woman who'd given birth to nine children – all to give away. She had no children of her own, nor did she even have a boyfriend. She was now forty-four years old and was still a surrogate, fulltime. The only difference was that, whilst earlier she could use her own eggs, now she was using donor eggs.

Having these children was an addiction, she confessed; she felt incomplete unless she was carrying a child. She had even been suicidal and depressed in between pregnancies. Kate wondered if this kind of mental instability could affect a child while it was in the womb?

Even though it was illegal, this woman had informally charged a fee for her expenses and yet was able to rent out her womb fairly quickly. Many of the women Kate had met so far in India were quite the opposite of this surrogate: they were docile and submissive, becoming surrogate mothers not for themselves but for the betterment of their families, whilst maintaining their anonymity.

Another key difference was that fear of public ignominy seemed to bother few of the UK surrogates; they were not unduly embarrassed that they were carrying someone else's baby, unlike most of the Indian women.

She wondered whether the newly recruited surrogates at NewLife would be any different, and if she could select someone that Ben and she might agree upon.

She also wanted to take another look at the girl she thought was Preeti, if she had recovered from her accident and hadn't gone home as yet. Since she was a fair-skinned, pretty girl, Kate felt there was a strong resemblance between the two of them. They shared a snub nose and a rather generous figure. She could be a likely egg donor.

What other characteristics should she look out for? It was a difficult choice, as Sharmaji pointed out, since most of the women, no matter what the hospital claimed, were usually poorly educated and displayed few talents. She tried to check on Preeti on the Madonna and Child website but was surprised to find that both her picture and even her name had disappeared.

She hailed an auto-rickshaw, as any Indian would, having discovered this form of transport was cheaper and quicker than a cab. She had even learnt how to bargain with the rickshaw drivers, in her broken Hindi, when they tried to overcharge. With her long blonde hair tied in a ponytail, she wore a T-shirt and harem pants and long dangling bead earrings. She looked completely different from the woman who had once worn business suits and efficiently put together PowerPoint presentations to raise money for her films.

Sharmaji was at the clinic, waiting for her, looking dishevelled and cheerful, as always. His plump face bore a huge smile of welcome as he ushered her into the tiny sitting-room-cum-reception.

Keeping up a cheery onslaught of platitudes, he offered her a sweet, hot cup of tea. Resignedly sipping the milky brew, she wondered, once again, if the Pandeys had any idea about NewLife. Or if Simran Singh, the social worker who had discussed adoption with them, knew about it, either. Somehow she doubted it.

Kate and Ben, too, hadn't brought the matter up with anyone at Madonna and Child. Ben had been too busy to go across in the past few weeks – and Kate had decided to be discreet and not mention it to anyone there. She knew that, officially, she had been discharged from the hospital

– and there was nothing unethical about going to another surrogacy clinic – but she still felt a little uneasy about it all.

'Are the Pandeys involved with this in any way?' she asked Sharmaji.

'Oh no, madam. This has been set up very recently and, please madam, don't discuss it with them. The two hospitals are totally different, with different clientele. In fact you're one of the first to have come from there to us. Only because you said you were looking at other options.'

'You said you were going to bring some surrogates for me to look at today?'

Sharmaji grinned even wider – and almost winked at her. Ben had warned her to watch out for that – and not misunderstand his friendliness. Perhaps it was a facial tic, as he had suspected.

'Sure – they are here already. And I have a special surprise for you, as well. '

Kate backed away from him. He seemed to be standing a little too close. What 'surprise' had he got for her?

Kate thought of the girl with the bandage. She would be perfect. But remembering the consternation she had caused the last time, she decided to bring up the subject of the 'Preeti lookalike' gradually. Meanwhile, she would simply go with the flow, as they said!

So instead she said, 'What's the surprise?'

'Your husband wanted someone special. He isn't with you, so maybe we should save it up for when he comes

– first I want you to meet the surrogates we had already called in.'

Puzzled at the reference to Ben, and feeling as though she was about to inspect some thoroughbreds, Kate went into an even smaller room on the side, where four women stood uncertainly in a huddle, talking to each other. Two of them seemed a little older than Kate, though she knew that often it was not age but a life of deprivation that made Indian women from a certain class seem older than they actually were.

The women introduced themselves, and one of them, who was particularly thin, with curly hair tied in a bun, quickly came forward and, wiping tears from her eyes, started speaking rather rapidly to Kate in Hindi, while the others looked on shyly.

Even though Kate had been learning the language, she could not follow the woman's dialect, and ultimately turned uncertainly to Sharmaji, who stood beside her, patting the woman on her back sympathetically.

'What's she saying?'

'She says she would love to carry your child. She needs the money because her mother is very sick and requires urgent treatment.' He shook his head at the girl. 'The problem is that she thinks she will get the money straight away. She doesn't know that it will take nine months.'

'Can't the money be given in advance in special cases?'

Sharmaji was tempted to say yes, and then thought better of it. She could always check it out with the Pandeys.

The fact was that no hospital could afford a risk (or 'riks' as Sharmaji pronounced it) like that.

'What if she takes the money and runs off? That way you will never be able to recover anything, and we would lose money all the time.'

That reminded Kate, and she glanced across to the door behind which the gestating mothers lay.

'I was wondering about one of the girls I saw here the last time. I'd mistaken her for someone else at Madonna and Child. She's very pretty and I thought she might be a close match with me because she's quite light coloured.'

A frown crossed his face.

'As I told you last time, we normally never keep any girls from Madonna and Child here.'

Kate did not bother to contradict him directly, but pressed on.

'She looked like Preeti, and you said she'd had a small accident. I would really like to speak to her and perhaps select her – unless there is something wrong with her medically?'

Sharmaji's affable expression seemed to fade a little as she spoke.

'I don't know who you mean. Accident? No, no madam. You must be thinking of some other hospital.' He wiped the sweat from his brow.

Kate was equally adamant. She was taken aback by his complete denial of the incident.

'I clearly remember I saw her here. Just one month back. In fact, I thought she would be better now. She had a bandage on her head, you said she had fallen and that you would be sending her home.'

Ever the TV producer, she began marching towards the room where she had seen the woman.

Sharmaji blocked her way.

'Please. There is no such person there and you are wasting your time. We only have women who are pregnant in there, and they are of no use to you. I don't want to disturb them.'

Short of shoving him away, there was little she could do. Something in his face warned her that this was not going to be an easy battle. Obviously he could not 'riks' her entering that room – else why would he try to hide a surrogate from her? What was it that he didn't want her to know?

'I think, madam, if you don't like any of the surrogates I have shown you, it would be best if you left. Perhaps Madonna and Child will suit you more.' Sharmaji was not being rude but the more he asked her to leave, the more anxious she became.

Kate looked over her shoulder and found the four women staring at her. She could see fear in their eyes; somehow they knew that something was not quite right. They, too, could sense danger in the air, and latent aggression in the way Sharmaji was opposing her. His fawning manner had vanished.

Unsure and yet angry, worried about the women, Kate felt she had to diminish Sharmaji's power over them – and make some kind of gesture to tell them to get away from him. As fast as possible.

She walked back to them. Pulling a bundle of notes out of her handbag with slightly trembling fingers she pushed it into the hands of the woman who had said her mother was unwell.

'Go home, *chale jaao*,' she said in her broken Hindi. '*Tumhe khatra hai* – this place is not safe.'

Suddenly she felt Sharmaji's hand on her shoulder.

'Madam, what are you doing? Please, I think it's best that you leave. Why don't you understand these women can easily be booked for someone else – I was just being nice to you by trying to help. I must insist you don't disrupt our working discipline here.'

He sounded annoyed and upset as he steered Kate to the door. A nurse had come to stand beside him, blocking Kate's way back into the clinic. She felt small and humiliated, but her face was still flushed with rage.

Turning the handle he stopped and looked at Kate pityingly.

'You've really upset our women today. No wonder your husband asked for that woman in secret. Why would he want you to know – the way you are behaving? Screaming at our surrogates! I was keeping it a surprise for you – but perhaps it's best you don't meet her at all. You may say something to her which is not good.'

Kate's heart jumped into her mouth.

'What woman?'

She was beginning to feel sick. *Ben?*

'It doesn't really matter. She'll make a good surrogate for someone else, as I doubt if you would want her. And, in any case, she doesn't like you either. After all, I know your husband's family doesn't have a very good record with Indians, do they? She was so worried you might misuse her – that you wanted to take away her children. I had a very difficult time persuading her to come.'

He almost had shut the door on her, when Kate began pushing her way back in.

'Who is this? Sheela?' Her voice was high pitched and she didn't care whether people on the street were beginning to stop and stare at her. The image of Sheela and her three children in Ambala, generously serving them cups of tea, floated back into her mind.

'Ask your husband,' said Sharmaji with a sneer, as he closed the door firmly in her face.

She stumbled out into the sunshine, angrily close to tears and wondering why she had created such a fuss. If only she hadn't got so upset – she might have managed to meet Sheela. And why had Ben asked for her – without telling Kate?

Was Sharmaji right – was she becoming hysterical and out of control?

Still agitated, she walked down the road, wondering if Sheela was now trapped inside that dilapidated building, and what would happen to her, since it was doubtful that Sharmaji would now ever permit her to meet the Rileys again.

Would she disappear like Preeti? After all, half a million women died in childbirth in India. Shivering in the sunshine, she longed to be with Ben – but at the same time was furious with him. Why had he suggested Sheela's name, for God's sake!

Suddenly scared, she started running along the crowded street, anxious to get away from the clinic as quickly as possible. The voice of the surrogate begging her for money rang in her ears, sounding louder and louder.

DELHI / GURGAON

Rohit had spent the last month acquiring a gun from Sharmaji and planning his revenge. He was now completely convinced that he should kidnap Sonia and not let her go till Renu Madam and Vineet Bhai came to their senses. How dare they treat him so badly, when he had messed up his own life to help them out? He had tried to meet Renu Madam many times but Champa, that old witch, kept saying Madam was still angry with him.

Initially Sharmaji had convinced him that the gun should not be used on anyone. He had advised Rohit to try to meet Renu Madam and apologize for messing about with the maid, explaining that it wasn't his fault. He wasn't the first man to have been trapped by a conniving woman! Though Rohit had not told Sharmaji about the child Sonia was carrying, he had a feeling that there was very little Sharmaji did not know.

Rohit had followed his advice and left messages for Renu Madam – and in fact had managed to explain a little about what had happened that afternoon to Vineet Bhai. Despite that, he got little sympathy and his job wasn't handed back to him either.

Now Champa had completely stopped talking to him – while that bitch who had got him sacked was still working in their kitchen. All that meant he was no longer being given the respect he deserved. So he would simply have to grab it back. He needed to assert himself. Perhaps a little bit of blackmail would not do any harm. He had seen enough of that going on in Renu Madam's office.

Catching the Metro to Gurgaon he realized that it was seven in the evening and visiting hours at the Madonna and Child hospital were over. Surely, however, they would allow him in to talk to his woman? After all, he was the one who had told her to go there. The world thought it was his child anyway – who was to know that it had anything to do with Vineet Bhai or Renu Madam? Once he took Sonia away they would have to beg to get the child back.

What a marvellous joke it would be if it was he who ultimately brought up the child destined to lead the country? And if anyone disbelieved him, he had the child's

DNA to prove its lineage. Rohit had learnt enough scientific terms since Sonia had gone in for the surrogacy.

When he reached the hospital, to his intense irritation, the guards at the gate said he could not enter. Rohit shouted at them, but did not take out his country-made pistol because he did not want to raise any alarm before he had actually entered the hospital. He saw Dr Ganguly's car drive past. Bastard! He did not even stop, yet a while ago he had been so grateful when Rohit had got Preeti out of the hospital and into his car. And when she had tried to escape and hurt herself, once again Dr Ganguly had expressed his thanks for Rohit's help, accompanied by a few thousand rupees. These people were all *chootiyas*! Exploiting the poor! Wait till the truth came out and the shit hit the fan!

Enraged by Ganguly ignoring him, he yelled at the receding headlights.

'Fuckers, don't you know my woman is in there? It's my baby!'

The guards looked at him curiously and then gestured at him to move on.

Unknown to him, Renu Mishra had already called Anita and explained to her that Rohit might come looking for Sonia. It was imperative that he not be allowed to go in. Renu Madam had dealt with many Rohits in her life: after a bit of a roughing up and firm handling, they soon understood whom they were dealing with.

Realizing that they would not allow him into the

hospital, Rohit pretended to lose interest and strolled away, looking back at the building from a distance. Obviously he should try another entry point.

He walked around to the back of the hospital and found the service entrance, which was shut because entry and exit were possible only with an electronic ID card. Fortunately a nurse was just leaving and had buzzed open the door; he quickly slipped in and she, intent on leaving, barely gave him a second glance. It was almost as easy as the last time he had entered from here.

He followed the corridor up to the changing room. He had been here before, too. He found a green overcoat – normally worn by the hospital attendants – and put it on. Taking a wheelchair from the emergency unit, he began purposefully wheeling it towards Sonia's room.

His adrenalin was pumping. He felt he had to teach everyone a lesson, including Sonia. She had dreamt up these stupid ideas just to make him suffer. He was going to screw her for going away when he needed her. He was going to beat the shit out of her. And if she lost the baby it would teach Renu Madam and Vineet Bhai a lesson. Or hang on, perhaps his earlier plan was better – he should take Sonia away with him, refusing to give up the child till Vineet Bhai and Renu Madam begged him for forgiveness and asked him to come back. Ideas chased each other furiously inside his head.

He was comforted by his pistol snugly parked in his jacket pocket: this meant he could take Sonia hostage. It made perfect sense. He stopped in front of Sonia's door and pushed it open.

Sonia was lying on the bed, resting.

She found it increasingly difficult to move around, as she had gained much more weight than in her last two pregnancies. Perhaps it was not even a normal pregnancy, but she would soon, hopefully, be freed from this child.

Strangely enough, while she rejoiced when others had children, longing to hold them, playing with them whenever she could, this child did not interest her. It was simply a chore and a duty she had to carry out. She hoped she could get it over soon so that she could start planning the next child, which would at least earn some money for her.

The door slammed open and her heart almost stopped beating. It was Rohit, in an attendant's uniform, pushing a wheelchair. She was reminded of Preeti on the night she had seen her being taken away.

'What are you doing here?'

Rohit left his wheelchair, shut the door, and walked up to her.

'I was missing you, my darling, and I've come to take you away. Aren't you pleased to see me?' He pulled her up towards him.

Sonia panicked. Anita Madam had warned her already that Rohit may come to see her and she was supposed to call the guards if he did. He had tried to molest some woman in Renu Madam's home and she was very upset about it.

Seeing him suddenly appear like this, with that wheel-chair, made her feel even more unwell. Now she knew why she had thought it was a familiar figure, that night, taking Preeti away. It must have been Rohit. What was going on? Had he killed her?

'Why are you here, Rohit? Please go away, it's only a few more weeks now and I'll be with you.'

He slapped her.

'How many times do I have to tell you not to try to send me away? You and I are going to enjoy this child. This will be our child and that fucker and his mistress can watch us bring him up ourselves. I will never let you give this child away, you whore.'

Sonia felt her head spin, and she thought she might faint. The baby moved uncomfortably inside her. Rohit had locked the door, but someone was knocking on it. Maybe someone had spotted Rohit and alerted security. Sonia knew there had been a special eye kept on her right from the start. The knocking on the door grew louder and louder.

'Sonia! Open the door – this is the matron. Is there some-one in there with you? Don't worry – I have a guard with me.'

'I won't fucking open the door,' Rohit shouted back. 'My name is Rohit and tell Renu Madam and Vineet Bhai that I will not leave this room or let Sonia go free unless they promise that they will take me back and give me the job I deserve. And be careful, I have a gun!'

He took it out and brandished it, turning to Sonia, who had staggered back towards the bed.

'Get on to that wheelchair. I'll blast that door open if I have to and take you with me.'

Frightened about being hit again, Sonia tried to obey his orders, but could barely move. She couldn't even breathe. Collapsing on to the floor, she felt a sharp surge of pain. She dimly heard Rohit shouting something but the agony of her contraction made him sound like he was far away. As a familiar wetness spread through her clothes, she realized that her water bag had burst; the pain was now coming in waves, and her uterus was pushing outwards in almost involuntary spasms. She knelt on the floor, in a puddle of water, dragging the bed sheet and the pillow towards her. Instinctively she knew what was happening and she had to be prepared.

The hammering increased in volume and Rohit shot a bullet into the wall as the police sirens blared and her screams grew louder and louder. Rohit tried to put an arm around her and pull her up – but with almost super-human strength, she pushed him away. He, too, backed off when he saw the puddle of water around her, and her bare thighs, as Sonia, moaning with the contractions, pulled up her saree.

By then, she had forgotten about him and the swelling on her face where he had hit her.

She withdrew into her private space. Now it was only her and the baby. If she was screaming, she did not know or even hear it. She felt the contractions come faster and faster, and she struggled to breathe in tandem, as she had been taught in the hospital. Rocking with the spasms, she tried to remember what she was supposed to do. When she had given birth earlier she had had her neighbour by her side, an experienced midwife, and her own children had been born quickly without any problem. Sonia had also helped her mother in the village during the birth of her siblings. So she wasn't scared of childbirth. That gave her some confidence. Besides, what choice did she have? She knew that Rohit would never let her leave the room. She had to do whatever she could on her own.

In the same way as she had given birth earlier, she squatted on the floor and pushed downwards. With each contraction she focused on her stomach muscles, using all her strength; sweat broke out on her brow and she felt it trickle all over her body. Her clothes clung to her and unthinkingly she pulled off her saree, stripping down to her blouse and thin petticoat. That gave her more freedom. She could feel the child come down a little more with each contraction. It was almost like the baby was forcing its way out impatiently into the world. It simply could not wait any more.

It seemed like hours, but must have been much less than that. Later, she would have no recollection. All she was doing was pushing and praying that the pain would cease.

With one particularly agonizing contraction, she screamed for help and unconsciously reached for Rohit's hand. Startled, he knelt down next to her.

'Push harder,' he shouted over her screams, completely forgetting why he was still there – watching, awestruck, as the child's head emerged. He had never seen a live birth before, even though he was the eldest of four children. He had always been told to go out of the house when his mother was in labour.

'Push a little more – you're almost there!' he said instinctively, as the child emerged bit by bit. Sweating with the effort, Sonia laid her head on his lap, her hands now clenched around his.

Even as the door was being broken, Rohit's excitement grew. His attention was completely diverted.

Then suddenly when she thought her strength was depleted, she could feel the child slipping out. Immense exhilaration overwhelmed her as she saw a baby boy, covered with blood and vernix, fall neatly between her thighs on to the pillow she had placed on the floor. He contorted his face in a lusty yell, and shoved his hand into his mouth.

Exhausted and uncaring of what Rohit was doing, she smiled with relief. She barely even noticed the contractions that expelled the placenta. The boy looked just like a monkey, with his wizened face, but he was completely normal, as she quickly checked his toes and fingers. And if those cries were anything to go by, his lungs were fine too!

She pulled him towards her. The umbilical cord made it difficult for her – and the child was slippery.

A strange kind of joy coursed through her, burying her enmity towards Rohit.

'Don't just sit there, you fool,' she said, gasping for breath. 'Give me something to cut this with.' She pointed to the cord.

Out of his pocket Rohit sheepishly brought the knife he had got along with the gun (just in case things got out of hand).

With the last of her strength, she cut and knotted the cord securely. Rohit bent further down to help with the child who was squirming and crying. He had forgotten about the incessant hammering on the door and the phones which rang nonstop. There was even someone at the window, prising open the shutters.

Pulling the boy on to her chest, Sonia unbuttoned her blouse and let him suckle. At last the battle was over. There was no victory or defeat, but simply life which had to be celebrated. The quarrel about whose child he was faded from her mind.

It was just a little baby who belonged to her. At least for this moment.

Rohit watched helplessly, his hand still on the child's damp head, as the boy sucked furiously, as though deprived of months of nourishment.

'*Kitna bhooka hai re,*' he said, admiring the newborn's single-mindedness. He is really hungry.

'Leader *banega,*' replied Sonia with pride. He's going to be a leader, alright.

As the noise around him became audible once more and Rohit came back to reality, he knew he should do something or shoot someone, push Sonia on to the wheel-chair and drag her out – but he just couldn't. He had thought he would beat her but he couldn't do that either. Instead he sat on the floor, next to her and the baby, one hand around her. Protectively. When he needed it the most, his anger had deserted him.

The blows on the door had grown louder till it was broken down. Along with the matron, nurses and security personnel, Anita and Subhash entered to find a strangely quaint family tableau. Sonia lay on the floor with the child at her breast, and Rohit was beside her, her head on his lap. His gun lay abandoned next to him. He was gazing down at Sonia and the infant as though enchanted.

Subhash picked up the gun and handed it to the guard. He wasn't quite sure how to deal with Rohit, but knew he would have to call Renu Madam and tell her the child had been born and that her political dynasty was safe.

MUMBAI

Mehta found Ali was in a foul mood. For a minute he was nervous, thinking that perhaps Ali had found out about his 'kidnapping' of the embryos that belonged to Dr Anita Pandey. Perhaps Wadhwani had called him and they had chatted, discovering to their horror that the demand was bogus.

In that case Mehta could be sure every bone in his body would be systematically broken, a threat that Ali issued every day to his 'enemies'.

Fortunately, however, there was an avalanche of problems that was worrying Ali. The aftermath of the attack on Mumbai and the trial of the lone Pakistani militant captured, Ajmal Qasab; the situation in Kashmir . . .

But a fresh article in the newspaper, with a picture of smiling Indian surrogates, revived his fear that thousands of Indian women were being bribed by the Western world to have their children. So, he told Mehta grimly, there would be growing numbers of Western kids, soon, with Western lifestyles – and a corresponding decline in children growing up with Eastern traditions and culture.

He was pounding away on his treadmill, getting more and more furious with each step.

'After all, banjo, why would a woman want to have a child for free when she can buy a house or a colour TV or educate her kids with the money she gets, don't you think? All she has to do is lie on her back and the baby just grows. No hard work in that either. This is a *sin*, banjo, a *sin*. There has to be a law against it. Why doesn't the government wake up?'

Ali's passionate outburst had been provoked by the article stating there was a 'specific and rising' demand now for Muslim women to become surrogates for clients mainly from West Asia or the Arab countries.

'*Specific and rising!* And all these rich Arabs! Invaders! *Taubah taubah!*' Ali clutched his ears in anguish. '*Arrey,* Mehta, *meri biwi ka kya hoga?* What will happen if this trend continues? Will my wife refuse to sleep with me and say get me an embryo and that will do? And we will get rich that way?'

'I don't think your wife will say that, boss.'

'Banjo, do you know my wife?'

'No, sir,' Mehta replied quickly.

'Then don't pretend you know what she will say. Women can say anything. We men are idiots. You know my own sister—'

Ali abruptly stopped.

He changed the speed on the treadmill and then continued, 'I mean one of my distant relatives has just gone to Dubai to be a womb for a fucking sheikh. And her husband puts on bangles and watches helplessly. Is he a fucking eunuch?'

Ali began lifting weights and breathing heavily as he worked his way through the argument. At times like this Mehta felt quite unfit and flabby as he sat drinking his sugary tea from a plastic cup and reading through the newspaper, cutting out stories and filing them away neatly while his boss pumped iron. He wished he too could be as passionate as Ali in everything he did.

'Could even conservative women like my wife ever be tempted to do these things?' asked Ali rhetorically.

This time Mehta gave an unequivocal answer.

'Exactly, sir,' he said. It meant nothing and it was important right now to remain neutral, while Ali was exercising and being exercised.

'This is a difficult battle,' he told Mehta. 'We have to wake up the nation. But how can I fight it alone? Maybe we need to get an association of people like us united against this ceaseless exploitation. What do you think?'

'As long as people have money they will think of these things, boss,' said Mehta pragmatically. 'How can you prevent them from wanting to have children if science can help them?'

Mehta thought sadly of his own situation. Sometimes over thirty-two embryos were created for one successful implantation, he read, as he cut another article out. And in UK one fertility cycle cost over four thousand pounds! That was more than three-and-a-half lakh rupees! Perhaps he could use some of that money his father-in-law had given him. For once black money would be put to some good use. He had already, in preparation, got rid of his tight underwear and even his jeans and had started eating – as Malti had done for years – all kinds of potions made from cow's urine, elephant dung and tiger's bones. Could, by some miracle, his sperm-count be pushed up?

And more importantly, could he tell his parents to pray for his potency? He wondered how to break the news to them.

'Bloody bullshit! But then why don't they stay in their own country and use their fucking science in that country alone? We have to find a way to dissuade the entire world from coming to India looking for babies. Banjo, I have found my real purpose in life.'

Ali crunched his biceps dangerously – fighting off imaginary hordes of embryos flooding into an unsuspecting nation.

Meanwhile, the file grew fatter as Mehta clipped the 'bad news' to prepare a defence against surrogacy for his boss, just in case he was caught and suspended or had to fight a legal battle.

Ali knew that his jihad had raised the hackles of many in the medical profession – and soon someone could slap criminal proceedings against him.

Fortunately he had received clandestine support from religious organizations which had learnt of his endeavour, and which were not only against the idea of surrogacy – but also the fact that babies were being provided for gay couples, something that redoubled Ali's efforts. It would soon become a rainbow coalition of religious organizations and right-thinking people.

He was planning to throw his battling hat in the ring, to rescue misguided women like his sister. If he had to give up his job, so be it.

In the process, Mehta's world view expanded. Today in the folder dramatically named 'Jihad Against Surrogacy' (JAS) he filed the information that there were very few women in countries such as Germany who were prepared to have children.

'Soon the world will be divided between those countries that can afford to commission babies and those who can't. Only the rich and the Western world will be able to afford them. The poor in our country will have to do without children.' Like a modern Cassandra, Ali would make gloomy pronouncements and ask Mehta to write them down or preserve them in the JAS folder.

Every day the scenario grew more and more bleak.

And slowly Mehta realized that Ali simply wanted the embryos destroyed, because he never answered his persistent question. 'But what does Dr Wadhwani do with the embryos?'

'Banjo, I told you: he is saving people's lives while I am saving the women of India from this foreign invasion,' he would reply obliquely.

Could it be that simple? Shouldn't there also be a law preventing Dr Wadhwani from permanently removing the children from their 'parents'? It must be equally unethical to do that. Mehta hoped that Dr Pandey would come soon and he could discuss this confusing situation with her. Without, hopefully, getting into trouble with his boss.

What worried him was that by then it could be too late. He had tried to 'liberate' as many embryos as he possibly could, hiding the cans in his cupboard, in the kitchen loft – but he was running out of space, and Malti was complaining.

To calm her down, he told her how one day they would be able to reunite the embryos with their real parents. It was a romantic and encouraging thought: he and Malti surrounded by hundreds of chubby, rosy-cheeked babies and their grateful parents. And an elegant Dr Pandey in her lilac suit, standing applauding him from the side.

Chapter 10

SIMRAN

The flight had been a nightmare and I was barely able to cope. I drank so much red wine to calm down that my head started spinning, and instead of helping me, the combination of an airborne plane and alcohol made me feel seriously unwell. I got increasingly maudlin over my London trip, wondering why I had not been able to express myself properly to Edward, even when I went back to spend my last night in his flat. Perhaps I should have woken him up before I left.

And why hadn't he understood that a relationship with me could be hugely enjoyable – because hey, I was such an entertaining person! Anyone should be able to see that. I wouldn't tie him down, I would free him up!

Images of Abhi and the plane crash also floated through my mind once more, and at one stage I became convinced that our flight was going to similarly dive into the sea. I described the entire scene in great detail to the terrified passenger sitting next to me, a grandmother going back to Delhi for hip-replacement surgery. She took out her prayer beads and began reciting the *gayatri* mantra, convinced, after my vivid description, that Armageddon was nigh.

It was fortunate that no one I knew was travelling on that flight back to Mumbai, otherwise they would have never let me forget how I tried to enter the cockpit to warn the pilot about faulty altitude detectors. To everyone's relief I took a sleeping pill and finally crashed out.

The terror I feel on a flight is difficult to explain but I can only request that my exceptionally bad behaviour may please be excused. If there were a way to carry me on board, sedated and on a stretcher, it would be better for all concerned.

However, one positive thing about my London trip was that now I had a fairly good idea of what had happened not only to baby Amelia but also to her parents. I thought I had even cracked the mystery about the missing embryos. No doubt I would learn a little more when I met Diwan Nath Mehta in Mumbai before I went on to Delhi. The answer no doubt lay in the peculiar routeing of the embryos via Mumbai to Delhi, set up by Ganguly.

Prepared for the worst, Subhash and Anita had informed me a few months ago that they were now encouraging the couples to come in person for the initial cycle of fertilization, as even a single mishap regarding the couriered packages was far too many.

Ganguly was the only one who remained unfazed by it all. 'Why worry?' he said. 'We could explain away the need for more embryos by simply saying that the implantation had been unsuccessful and the surrogate had miscarried. The commissioning parents are too far away to check whether the consignments ever actually arrived.'

'That's a rather dubious and dishonest way of handling it,' I had objected. And as usual it had led to a clash between me and Ganguly.

'Look – it can take up to five or six cycles for an embryo to be successfully implanted. We already know that, and so if we ask for a few more consignments – why not?'

There were far, far too many reasons why Ganguly and I continued to argue.

I remembered him making surrogates agree to a paltry sum of two thousand pounds as insurance money, in case they died during pregnancy or while giving birth. Two thousand pounds! I remembered him harvesting eggs from a very young girl in the basement of the hospital. But he had dismissed all my concerns as meddling.

And now he would try to shut me out once again, no doubt.

As soon as I walked out of the airport, I spotted Diwan Nath Mehta. He had emailed his photograph to me from the computer he said his father-in-law had given to him. He had taken leave for the day and I had thought we should hire a car from the airport and go wherever he wanted.

He took me home first, where I met his wife Malti and he showed me some of the embryo containers that he had been asked to deliver to the Freedom Hospital.

'This is evidence, madam. These containers should have gone to you many months ago, but instead I took them to Dr Wadhwani. He must have given Ali more money than even Dr Pandey, because she was prepared to pay. I don't know why or what happened, but you can see that the names of the parents are still stuck on the side.'

There were a few more containers scattered about the house, concealed in the loft, even under the bed and behind a sofa.

Malti echoed his disapproval.

'It's not fair that the parents are being cheated like this, madam,' she pointed out squarely. 'Look at us. We have no children and we long for them. Such a waste to think of these babies who are not being allowed to be born.'

I called Anita and checked with her about the other containers I had found. But barring a few, none of the other consignment details seemed familiar to her.

'I'm not sure why these were being sent to Freedom Hospital, Simran. I know Mehta has asked me before. They could be redirected embryos harvested from unsus-pecting parents, or they could be surplus blastocysts taken with genuine permission, which Mybaby.com was offloading on to Freedom Hospital. It's a strange business.'

I realized that because a single fertility cycle sometimes created many embryos, once the hopeful parents were caught in the process they depended on the doctor to decide how many embryos were used and how many discarded. It would be difficult for them to know for sure how many eggs had actually been fertilized successfully in the laboratories. Even if a few were frozen and stored, the rest could be easily shipped off and used – but for what?

Mehta had a dramatic theory about baby-trafficking. He thought that these embryos could be implanted into women to produce fair-skinned children who would then be inducted into the sex trade. It seemed a fine if bizarre explanation, but it would also be expensive, complicated and unnecessary in a country like India, where so many babies were already available off the street. When children of any colour – black, brown, yellow, white – could be bought for less than the price of a handbag. I didn't think this was a persuasive argument.

Taking Malti with us, who was also curious to see this place which had so fascinated her husband, we therefore decided to drive to the Freedom Hospital to unravel the mystery a little more. En route, Mehta told me about the amazing recovery of Mr Dhawan's son. I was astonished that he was doing so well. The news of his improvement had obviously been kept out of the newspapers. The court case was still carrying on, and information about his recovery may have mitigated the sympathy factor for him and perhaps even led to a fresh examination of the case.

Curiously, Mehta said that recently he had also seen obviously poor people go into the hospital for a free cure. But he wondered about the authenticity of the treatment, as a few of them seemed to have incurable diseases. One, for instance, was afflicted with Parkinson's, and another had been blind from birth. Could there be a permanent cure for these ailments?

'But, madam, the receptionist said they would be fine, and Dr Wadhwani was working on it. It all seems very good for these people because they are so poor they could never afford this treatment,' he said.

Call me cynical, but it sounded too good to be true. It was well known that the medical profession had conducted illegal experiments on the poor and vulnerable in the past as well. One memorable case was when some multinational pharmaceutical companies tested new contraception methods on unsuspecting women without their permission, leading to all sorts of complications. Recently, there had been huge consternation when it was discovered that mentally ill patients in state-run hospitals had been injected with experimental drugs, unrelated to their condition.

As we approached the hospital, I suddenly sat up, curious. This road, the buildings around, the entrance to the hospital were all beginning to look familiar. My life in Mumbai as a young girl began to flood back. I had been on this street before. *Why did it all seem as though I had been here many times?*

Memories I had long buried came flooding back. Feeling nauseaus and sick, I stared around at the once-dreaded road. In a dream-like state I remembered a

12-year-old girl, crying all the way to this very address. Her prayers and laments – all unanswered. Her friend lay beside her, almost lifeless, his face frozen in a mask of pain, his eyes wide open, and apart from the sound of the ambulance siren and her sobs, there was silence. Always total and complete silence. Even the noise of the traffic, and what her father said to her was wiped out by memory.

The area was practically unchanged: the winding roads, the crowded pavements. I shivered, thinking of that day, thirty years ago, overcome with a sickening sense of déjà vu. And, as we approached the hospital I remembered its discreet facade only too well. In fact, it was due to its nondescript exterior that even the hired ambulance driver did not know the way and my father had really had to hunt for it. Everything was exactly the same.

This is where, with the siren wailing overhead while I crouched next to Abhi holding my father's hand, the ambulance had brought us that evening.

Of course, we had lived at the other end of Mumbai, near Bandra, but as bits of memory kept flashing through my mind, I slowly recognized the area. With growing excitement I realized that, on that blustery day, Abhi's injured and frail body had been carried into this building. It was the oddest, most peculiar coincidence.

And as the car swung in – the entrance was hauntingly familiar, too. So many tearful evenings had been spent here while we waited for news. Put it down to destiny, fate, karma – but this was definitely the same hospital in which I had last seen Abhi.

A shiver of anticipation ran through me. I had been so caught up in baby Amelia's case that I simply had not thought I could even accidentally find Abhi, or a connection to him, even if I came to Mumbai. But if life could spring such an amazing surprise on me, I should at least allow myself to hope!

All those years ago, he had been in a coma. Yet miracles are known to happen. What if there had been changes in the interim? What if he had recovered?

I had not made the connection with Abhi because the hospital name had changed from Bella Vista Clinic to Freedom Hospital, as Mehta now told me. He had researched it very well during his visits.

And as a young girl I remembered overhearing that my father had brought Abhi here because it was known for its wonderful surgeons.

Looking at it with tear-filled eyes, the only difference that I could pinpoint was that as a child it had loomed over me like a vast and frightening place from which my friend would never emerge. Dauntingly enormous. But now I realized that it was really a very small hospital set in a cul-de-sac.

Perhaps I could ask Dr Wadhwani about Abhi, and if, miraculously, he was still here? I was still reeling from the surprise – struggling with unexpected happiness – but wondering if I could really hope for an absolute miracle.

Could Abhi have lived on – for thirty years? And what would he be like now?

Since this hospital was reputed to specialize in revolutionary medicine, anything was possible.

The fresh-faced receptionist, as Mehta had warned us, was endlessly punching numbers into a computer program. He said that Dr Wadhwani was busy in an operation but could meet us later if we were prepared to wait.

As we sat down, I shared the story of Abhi's near-death with Mehta and Malti, and the remarkable fact that it was this hospital where I had seen him last.

I also called my mother to check what she recollected about those few weeks following the plane crash. She was thrilled that I had found myself at the Bella Vista!

'This is fabulous news!' Her voice lost its usual composure and she sounded as emotional as me. 'But darling, don't get too upset by whatever you learn there. Be prepared for the worst, but hope for the best. You know we lost touch with his grandparents, because your father was very worried about the effect it was having on you. Which is why we didn't even talk about it ever again. As a child all you did was cry and cry, every time anyone mentioned his name.'

'Was there a Dr Wadhwani around at that time?'

'There may have been, but, honestly, why don't you just ask the hospital staff if they know anything about him? Let's hope he got better! Wouldn't that be wonderful?'

Trying not to become too hopeful, I walked around the waiting room, admiring the large number of endorsements from people all over the world who had been helped to recover from all types of diseases. It seemed to be doing very well – but I couldn't see any photograph of the familiar beloved face with the soft brown eyes. Though in my memory Abhi was only a teenager, I knew I would recognize him if I ever saw him again.

Trembling with anticipation and sick with worry, I wondered what I was about to find out? I wished I had a glass of whisky to calm myself down.

Instead, I took a deep breath, leant over the receptionist's desk and asked: 'Do you keep a record of previous patients? I had a friend who was here in the seventies but I don't know what happened to him.'

He asked for the name and handed me a brochure while he searched. I started going through it. There was a glowing report about the hospital from the famous actor, Rajiv Kumar (who had probably been airbrushed because he looked amazingly young) and of course from Dr Wadhwani. Mr Dhawan, whose son was being cured, had just endowed a new wing to the hospital. They all spoke of the unique surgical procedure at the hospital, which was helping the whole world. They mentioned how India was at the forefront of this technology because in many parts of the world it was still controversial. Stem-cell surgery.

From what I remembered, stem cells were harvested from bone marrow and other parts of the body. The use of embryonic stem cells, however, was banned in many parts of the world, as in India.

So far, there was strong resistance from many on ethical and moral grounds, especially from those who said that embryos were the beginning of life. It was a disturbing debate because embryonic cells were the miracle cure. They had the power to take the shape of whatever damaged part of the body they had been injected into and provide a replacement. This was not without its risks. Early experiments on mice had shown that sometimes tumours also resulted. Or the wrong part of the body might suddenly grow instead of the part that was being cured. This was not to say that this was not cutting-edge technology, but people were still cautious with its use.

But in India a close connection had been found between fertility treatments and embryonic stem-cell surgery in a few hospitals, because the one could provide the wherewithal for the other.

One enterprising clinic in Goa claimed that it had taken a single embryo donated during IVF and used that to create many more. They had 'patented' the system of doing this and so far no one else was able to actually find out the methodology for duplication. The clinic also claimed that, among other miracles, spinal damage had been rectified and blind children had recovered their sight.

I had also met some older people who'd had stem cells

injected straight into their bloodstream – and said it felt like a shot of adrenalin.

Now the penny was beginning to drop. Were our embryos being 'rerouted' here to address urgent cases? On the next page of the brochure I found our own connection with this hospital. There was a wonderful tribute from Dr Wadhwani to the doctor from Delhi whose time and investment was making Freedom Hospital into such a successful operation.

It was accompanied by a smiling picture of the suave Dr Ashok Ganguly.

It was entirely because of him that Freedom Hospital had now floated shares on the Mumbai stock exchange – and the price per share was already a thousand times its face value.

Dr Hansen had been right. This was a billion-pound industry, in many more ways than I had thought possible.

As I was mulling over these details, Dr Wadhwani walked in.

He was a tall and good-looking Sindhi with a pencil-thin moustache, and I was struck by his almost military bearing. It was impossible to guess his age.

He ushered us into his office and asked us if we would like some tea, or a cold drink.

I told him I had just arrived from London that morning and had been eating and drinking all night. I thought that it was important to let Dr Wadhwani know, in an indirect way, that I could pay for anything I might want.

My little Dictaphone in my bag was already switched on.

'Dr Wadhwani, I have come here with two problems. I have a friend who was almost in a coma, following the terrible *Emperor Ashoka* crash. In fact, I've just found out he was admitted here.'

Like Ma, my voice was shaking again and I could feel the tears start in my eyes. *Please tell me he is alright?*

I cleared my throat and then carried on.

'I know its a long time bac, but I would like to know if he recovered and what happened to him. And secondly, Mehta tells me that you have been getting a regular consignment of embryos and sometimes he has been delivering them here himself. Is that right?'

He looked a little taken aback but quickly recovered to nod his head. 'Yes, that's right.'

'I took the liberty of bringing Mrs Malti Mehta with me. She would make a wonderful mother, but pregnancy has eluded her. So would it be possible to check her up – and enrol her for assisted reproduction?'

'I think you've misunderstood. We don't do any IVF here. But we might have been able to help your friend if he was admitted here, as we have a surgical unit and we perform all kinds of procedures. You may have read that in the brochure you have with you.'

'I see. So why do you need embryos? I thought these are meant only for IVF?' I tried to be as charmingly confused and helpless as possible.

He laughed, and I looked across at Mehta – who no doubt remembered that carefree chuckle from previous meetings.

'Is that what Mehta told you? Well, he was trying not to give our secret away. He and his boss have helped us out quite a few times. You know, Simranji, we often use bone marrow and umbilical-cord stem cells for serious cases – but in very special cases we also use a tiny number of embryonic stem cells because they are more adaptable. There have been some amazing results. But please be sure that this is confidential.'

'And illegal,' I pointed out.

'So what?' He shrugged. 'Our approach in India is far too cautious. We must take a few chances for science to advance.' He even sounded like Ashok Ganguly.

'But what about the parents, for whom these embryos are very precious?'

'Simranji, look at the bigger picture. Instead of destroying the embryos you are using them for a greater good, you are saving lives. It's like for your friend – you won't deny him the treatment, will you? You're not going to ask too many questions at that time – all you need is results.'

I could see Mehta nod vehemently at the term 'saving lives'.

I also realized what he said was true. If Abhi was one of the recipients, would I change my mind?

'But hopefully you do get permission from the parents about using the embryos for research or surgery?'

'Most of these are surplus embryos so they would have been discarded anyway.' He shrugged once more.

Like so many things in this country, his confession about using embryonic cells must be an 'open' secret. If Mehta had been paid for bringing the embryos, he too was involved in this crime, even if unknowingly. That made him complicit – and so no wonder Wadhwani felt safe talking about it to us.

He turned his computer screen towards us and played a little video which featured Mr Dhawan's son, once-upon-a-time a young playboy.

'This is something I share only with those I can trust. I kept this video diary to record what I think is a miraculous recovery. A life-threatening accident which left him paralysed less than nine months ago, and he is already taking his first few steps. People don't realize the power of embryonic cells. But of course, please do not tell anyone outside. We only do these things to help the patient – and only in extremely special cases, I must stress that.'

That is, he was only stealing embryos occasionally, and not all the time. Could that be a good defence?

The video ended with Dhawan junior standing up, taking a few shaky steps and then looking into the camera to give a thumbs-up verdict. It was impressive.

'So what about someone in a coma?'

'We can certainly give it a try. We've done some work already with a few people who have had serious head injuries. But do tell me your friend's name?'

'Abhinav Joshi,' I said, suddenly finding that I was getting choked up, and fighting back tears at the memory of what had happened to him.

Dr Wadhwani gave his memorable laugh once again. It was deep and nonchalant. I could imagine that nothing would ever ruffle him or upset him. More and more like Ganguly, actually. No wonder they were partners.

'Well, well, well. Isn't that amazing! Then I think I can help a little.' He was hunting for something on his computer.' I haven't seen this for a long time – but yes, here it is . . .'

As they say, you always think you are prepared for the worst, till it happens to you. And it is also true that you may want something desperately and find that, when it is handed to you, your desire increases and does not diminish. Over the next few moments my feelings were fluctuating between these two states.

The video was difficult to watch for more than one reason, and I was badly unprepared.

I almost collapsed with the shock of it. But at the same time I could have watched it forever.

It showed an emaciated figure, almost skeletal, on a bed, and his head seemed too large for his frail body. Swaddled in white loose garments, he lay staring at the doctor who hovered over him.

It was when the camera moved into a close-up, and the man turned his large eyes towards us, that I remembered them, very clearly. The same chocolate-fudge centres. They were completely expressionless, but slowly he raised one hand to hold a paper cup, and drink some water, while the doctor encouraged him to do so.

'Now, this patient had been in a deep coma for many years, and had been admitted here initially in the late seventies. After that he has been looked after by his grand-parents at home, interspersed with hospital visits when he regressed. But the moment they heard about our new research, they brought him back to me around three years ago and we have been working with him once more. He is slowly beginning to recognize words – or at least we hope so. See, he is able to move his hand to grasp the cup; he wasn't able to do that in the past. We don't know if this will be successful – but . . .'

Once again he smiled, and switching off the computer, swivelled his chair around to face us.

I seemed to have stopped breathing. I clearly had an ethical dilemma before me – but right now I could only think about my long-lost friend.

'That . . . that is *definitely* Abhinav Joshi, isn't it?'

My voice shook, and Malti pressed my hand in sympathy.

Dr Wadhwani nodded. 'You've come to the right place.'

'Hare Krishna!'

I was startled at the invocation but Mehta's voice was sombre. He, too, was surprised at what we had learnt and seen today. In a way, Ali was right. They were saving lives at Freedom Hospital – but on the other hand, this was not strictly legal, was it?

'So his family brings him to you?' I asked.

As I spoke I realized that, actually, I couldn't afford to be too sentimental about it all, or my investigation would get completely derailed. I had to force myself to stop wanting to know about Abhi and instead focus on the real issue before us. Freedom Hospital had been involved in bribing officials and conducting illegal experiments. And Madonna and Child was being wrongly blamed for losing consignments. There was also a human cost to this. I must remember that.

'That's right – off and on. They live in Bangalore and so they bring him back for a fresh dose of therapy whenever they can.'

'Is all of this very expensive?'

'Well, depending on the ability to pay, sometimes we just do these things for free.'

You mean you can also bring in people from the street to experiment with? Perhaps because of the jolt I had just received, I said nothing accusatory. It seemed wiser. I just hoped Abhi was not part of some ongoing experiment.

Though I was sure if I asked Wadhwani he would produce a fully completed consent form. All possibilities would have been covered. The only thing that would not be mentioned in the form would be 'embryonic' stem cells.

I also had to be careful what I said as Mehta was with me and he could lose his job if word went back to his boss. So I kept my tone casual.

'But isn't this like Frankenstein medicine? What if something goes wrong?'

'Simranji, don't worry. We have been working in this field for a long time.'

It was the usual argument employed by those who will never admit that the lack of strict regulation in India gave them many loopholes to exploit. And so, not only was there little danger of being caught – if there was any accident or death, no one would ever find out.

'But do you always use imported embryonic cells like the ones Mehta gives you? Why not cells from India?'

'Not all patients are fussy but a few are worried. You know, about caste and religion and so on. They don't want to be contaminated. So sometimes, to reassure them, we get embryonic cells from abroad. Don't worry, if anyone prefers Indian embryonic cells, we can get them from our sister hospital in Delhi.

'I can show you some work they are doing on a patient in Delhi, who also had a head injury – she fell out of a car.'

He clicked on another film clip and played it.

A woman lay on a hospital bed surrounded by wires and clamps, being monitored by various machines. Her eyes were closed.

'Now this patient came to us very recently. We are using Indian embryonic stem cells on her because she is from a poor background and cannot afford the imported ones. But she is showing signs of improvement already.

The damaged part of her brain is beginning to grow again.'

He clicked on two more images to show us the woman's brain before and after, and where the signs of activity were beginning to be manifest.

It was odd but I thought I had seen that woman some-where before, but I couldn't be sure. In any case, right now it was better to say nothing.

He took out a piece of paper and scribbled something on it.

'And regarding IVF, I would recommend an excellent hospital in Delhi that our partner, Dr Ashok Ganguly, is involved in.'

I waited for him to tell me about Madonna and Child.

Instead he handed me the paper, which said clearly: 'NewLife Clinic, Founder-Patron, Dr Ashok Ganguly'.

'Incidentally, they also do stem-cell surgery – and that's where the second video is from. Abhinav of course is our patient, but in case you want to recommend it for anyone else?'

I should have guessed. It was all falling into place.

But before I left, I told Dr Wadhwani I wanted to meet Abhi.

For the first time a shadow fell over his eyes.

'Simranji, I would be very happy to take you to see him. But his grandparents are very strict about it. They have been protective about him from the start. Let there be a bit more progress and then we will definitely fix something up.'

I tried to plead that I was leaving for Delhi, but obviously he either did not want me to meet him, or Abhi's grandparents really had given strict instructions that he was to be left to recover in peace. He would not even tell me if he was in Mumbai at the moment. Obviously the work they were doing was meant to be kept under wraps.

Making a note that this time I would not lose touch with Abhi, I left to catch the plane to Delhi, depressed and confused.

But as I swallowed a bunch of pills to stop my flight jitters, I realized that I still had a nuclear option that would destroy Dr Wadhwani's equanimity and give me some bargaining power. I hadn't told him that some of those 're-routed' consignments from Mybaby.com might have carried HIV positive embroys. Was he aware that Dr Ganguly might have kept this crucial information from him? I wished I could see his face when I told him that. I also wondered what his VIP patients would do to him when they found out they would have to be tested for the AIDS virus!

And the day after . . .

My mother had grown a little thinner in the three weeks I had been away. She said her water retention had reduced as Durga had put her on a salt-free diet and they were going for walks every evening. They were also practising yoga together in the park and so her blood pressure was coming down every day as well.

We were back to enjoying our evening ritual of watching TV and reading and chatting desultorily. I had told her about the details regarding Abhi and she was as pleased as I was that we had managed to track him down. But she too was distressed about his precarious state. Something had to be done about him, eventually.

Meanwhile I had to sort out baby Amelia.

I was back on the sofa in my favourite position, a glass of whisky glinting alluringly in one hand.

After a while, my mother could not resist asking: 'So what exactly happened with Edward?'

I sighed and took a long deep breath of cigarette smoke. It was nice to be back home where I could put my feet up and smoke whenever I liked, rather than in the UK where you were made to feel like a pariah if you lit up.

'He wasn't my type at all. He drank milk and liked to cycle. He was too healthy for me. I want a man who drinks and smokes and lies around uselessly, just like me,' I told her.

Durga, who was sitting close by and reading, burst out laughing. She also seemed more relaxed than when I had last seen her. I beckoned her to sit close to me, so I could smell her freshly washed hair, a scent I particularly loved. I had not realized how much I had missed her. Sometimes you just take love for granted – and it can be found anywhere, not just with a man. And sometimes this kind of love is simpler, sweeter and nicer. It comes without any strings attached. I kissed her cheek and noticed that her skin was glowing. It was apparent she had used my new night cream from Boots. What are daughters for, after all?

And mothers too. I sighed with contentment yet again. It was good, perhaps, to have a household without the disruptive presence of men. Soon Sharda, who had recently begun to smile again, would come down and join us and our circle would be complete.

The day, however, had not been so peaceful.

Instead of going to Madonna and Child I had decided to visit the NewLife clinic. Before I met Anita and Subhash, and started telling them what I had discovered, I thought it would be sensible to find out what exactly Dr Ganguly had been up to.

I had also dwelt on the details given to me by Kate when she had visited the place before I had left for

London, around a month ago. She had been extremely upset following her visit to NewLife, but I am afraid I did not take her account too seriously, at the time.

She had complained about Sharmaji and said that she had seen someone who looked like Preeti there. We all knew Sharmaji was a supplier to many clinics and so I wasn't shocked to learn he was with a downmarket clinic in Green Park as well. I did not think it needed any special investigation, or even a second thought

Poor Kate. Since I had only seen her rather emotional side, once or twice, I had dismissed her version, putting it down to the fact that she seemed to be on edge, and very highly strung. And worse, when I spoke to Sharmaji, he supported my view wholeheartedly – and in fact was quite rude about her.

But now I knew that she had a very good reason to be so upset.

I wished now I had at least gone there before I had left for London. So much would have been easily unravelled. I was also curious to know who the woman was in that video I had seen in Wadhwani's office.

Once more I checked my recording of what Dr Hansen had said, and she clearly mentioned that the blastocysts belonging to Mike and Susan had been sent to India within a week.

This by itself was an incorrect procedure. Why the rush? Perhaps it was to get embryonic stem cells to Dr Wadhwani as fast as possible? As his work took priority over everything else. I was beginning to think that the money he paid was probably much, much more than I had imagined, both to Mybaby.com and to customs. Perhaps to Ganguly too. The sheer illegality of their operations forced the prices to go up.

How simple this was – just to get the embryos rerouted, and if they disappeared because of courier mishaps or customs confiscations, no one would be the wiser.

All samples sent to India would be as fresh as possible, as within the first few days of harvesting they were more pliable and could take any shape. Obviously there had been enough traffic of blastocysts for Ali to have spotted a business opportunity and put an extra levy on them. He made money, and placated Mehta by pointing out that assisted reproduction was actually a dangerous trend, and that he was launching his own jihad against it.

From the information Dr Wadhwani had shared with us during his presentation, embryonic stem-cell surgery was soon going to overtake even IVF as a medical business opportunity, and India would be at the forefront of it. Unless the law took cognizance and actually enforced the ban. From past experience I knew that once an illegality was permitted it was difficult to stop. There were always 'sympathetic' doctors like Dr Wadhwani who would be eager to help VIP clients and experiment on poorer ones.

And the world was full of sick, ailing and ageing people who would prefer to go in for what seemed like a permanent, if not instant, cure than spend a lifetime in hospitals or on medication.

Of course none of this would have ever been known to us if, in their rush to supply the embryonic stem cells, Mybaby.com had not included, by mistake, an HIV-positive blastocyst. I hoped that it was the only one – and it was ironic that, in fact, it had actually reached its proper destination at Madonna and Child.

But of course there was a very real possibility that some of the re-routed embryos sent to Dr Wadhwani might have been similarly contaminated. Or, I wondered, was Ganguly deliberately importing these HIV positive embryos to experiment with? Knowing this penchant for data, that too was possible.

Thus Ganguly must have thanked his stars that Mike and Susan died before anything more was found out.

By all accounts (including the eyewitness reports gathered quietly from Sonia and some staff members by Anita in my absence) they were extremely angry about poor baby Amelia and perhaps were ready to sue both MyBaby. com and Ashok Ganguly for not ensuring that the blastocyst had no trace of the HIV virus.

Or, as I was now beginning to suspect, had they been killed? In a billion-dollar business anything was possible. It was time to confront him and his work. I was more and more convinced that someone had tried to get rid of me and baby Amelia too.

The one precaution I took was to ask Anita to send me

the car and driver to take me to the NewLife clinic at four o'clock, from where I would emerge in exactly one hour. I wasn't going to take any more chances.

It was now four o'clock. I would have one hour here and I hoped that would be enough. The car and driver being present would also ensure that I would be able to get out of there safely if I ran into trouble.

The NewLife clinic was shabbier than I had imagined. Obviously the idea was to make the maximum profit possible. It was amazing how small the operation appeared – and yet I could hear a babble of Spanish as a man and a woman walked through the door. Impressive that it, just like the Freedom Hospital, had an international clientele.

A young woman with blonde hair in a wheelchair was leaving as I went in. She did not look like a candidate for fertility treatments, though on the exterior of the building it was the IVF facility which was clearly advertised. Obviously the more controversial side of the business, embryonic stem-cell surgery, was not going to be up in neon lights. But in tiny print on the side of the entrance gate I found the name of Viva-Bio, one of the larger international pharmaceutical companies known to be working in the area of stem-cell medicines. So could they be the main sponsor of what was going on?

I told the sleepy-looking guard that Dr Ganguly had sent me, keeping my fingers crossed that I would not run into him. As far as I knew he would be on his evening rounds at Madonna and Child. If he came here at all, it would be in the mornings. He had clearly planned his involvement in both clinics quite carefully and, on the face of it, there was no connection between the two. I had realized after talking to Anita that she did not even know that NewLife was cannibalizing their hospital.

The clinic was actually a three-storey residential building in Green Park converted into a hospital of sorts. This was one of the most crowded areas of South Delhi, with a market close by. I walked to the reception and, to my consternation, I saw Sharma talking to the couple who had walked in before me. Before he saw me, I quickly turned around and almost bumped into a nurse. Behind her, on the wall, I spotted several calendars with 'Viva-Bio' printed on them in a tiny font. There was a connection – but so discreet I wasn't surprised no one had noticed it. Even I would have missed it, if I hadn't come prepared to check every scrap of evidence.

I told the nurse that Dr Ganguly had sent me here as I was undergoing fertility treatment and I wanted to look at some possible surrogates as I was prone to miscarry.

I hoped she believed me. Fortunately she had no reason not to.

She told me that Dr Ganguly was not in, but another doctor was on his way, and that if I waited he would come to check me over. She tried to herd me back into the reception, but I said I wanted to use the toilet.

I quickly shut myself in and waited a few moments.

After some time, sure that she had left, I walked down the corridor, opening a few doors randomly as I went by. One room was full of pregnant women. Most of them were dark-skinned and thin. They looked like the surrogates Sharmaji had brought to Madonna and Child before Ganguly started them on a high-protein, vitamin-packed, fresh-food diet and bleached their skins. Obviously none of that was really required here.

And the thought occurred to me how very convenient indeed this arrangement was. Sharma didn't have to go into the villages and hunt for surrogates as he often told Anita he was forced to do. He could simply rotate some of the more robust women between the two clinics – and take commissions at both ends!

It was a crowded and noisy room, a far cry from the soft hues and elegant environment of Madonna and Child. 'Viva-Bio' was printed on the wall clocks and the calendars in this room too.

It was a cut-price version of the Madonna and Child hospital, and I recognized at least one woman, sitting there deep in conversation with another surrogate.

Radhika. The woman who had been used for the gay French couple. She was obviously pregnant again. This could be dangerous, because the twins had been born through a caesarean section quite recently. What the hell was Ganguly up to?

I took out my mobile phone and pretended to be dialling a number and speaking while I took a quick video of the room, taking care to upload it as soon as it was done. The women barely noticed me as they were drinking their tea and chatting to each other.

Seeing Radhika there had made my temper rise, but I decided to explore further before I said anything.

On the second floor I found the stem-cell unit, according to the sign hanging outside the door. 'Viva-Bio' again. There were three small rooms. In one lay a blond, white patient who was perhaps being treated for a spinal injury. Checking the file hanging from the foot of his bed, I learnt he was Australian. He was asleep, and a wheelchair stood next to his bed.

In the next room lay a well-dressed man who, according to his papers, was eighty-five. A blood-transfusion bottle was attached to his vein – and I realized that stem cells were being pumped directly into his system. His coat and shoes lay neatly by the side of his bed. Obviously he, like the Australian, would leave as soon as the treatment was over.

But it was the next room which puzzled me. Here a man and a woman lay in a catatonic state. They were completely still and were being monitored by a plethora of machines. It was exactly like a scene from the video shown to us by Dr Wadhwani. I thought I recognized the arrangement of the bed and the other furniture in the room.

If this experiment succeeded, no doubt Dr Wadhwani and Dr Ganguly would be sitting on a gold mine for Viva-Bio (and Madonna and Child was inadvertently helping him bring in the loot). It was all preparation for the pharmaceutical giant to break into the world of stem-cell surgery and surrogacy worldwide. No wonder Ganguly went on and on about the 'giant womb'. Who knew what other experiments were ongoing? We thought Ganguly was crazy with his obsessive data-collection and his mania for donor sperm and eggs, but he was also obviously planning for the future.

Approaching the bed I looked closely at the man. He was dark-skinned and thin. Somehow I did not think he could afford this treatment. The card at the foot of his bed said 'Pyarelal, head injury, fell from a scaffolding 2010'.

More than a year ago. Something told me that this was poor Radhika's husband. Even though Sharma had told her he was in the hospital, she had begun to think he was dead, as there was no news from him. She had no idea he was just one floor above, pumped full of medication.

I took out my phone and took photographs, quickly emailing them to Anita and Subhash.

On the other bed lay someone I knew would *definitely* not be able to afford the treatment.

It was Preeti.

Why hadn't I guessed?

She had a bandage on her forehead as well. At the foot of the bed it said 'Found on road, victim of a car accident'. There was no name on the card.

No wonder the woman in Dr Wadhwani's video looked familiar.

I photographed her and sent those off to the Pandeys as

well. How had we ever collected evidence before mobile telephony came along? I knew I had to ensure I could defend myself. With concrete evidence.

My instinct turned out to be correct.

Hearing a noise I whirled around – and to my horror I saw Ganguly marching down the corridor accompanied by Sharma. A nurse was pointing towards me agitatedly. I should have realized that the place would have security cameras.

I knew I couldn't run away, and this was going to be an uncomfortable meeting.

Ganguly stopped a few feet away with an unpleasant expression on his face, as though he had found excrement on his doorstep.

The feeling was mutual.

'What the fuck are you doing here?' he asked. His voice was shaking with anger. All niceties were gone. There was no 'Simranji' here.

Sharma looked mournfully at me. 'Madam, you shouldn't be here. This is a private ward.'

'A private ward with a labourer and a poor woman we all thought had run away? Who exactly is paying for all this? And is this man Radhika's husband? Does she know he is right here?'

'None of your bloody business,' said Ganguly roughly. 'Now get out of here, before I throw you out.' He reached across to pull me but I evaded his grasp.

'Too bad your thugs couldn't get rid of me in the UK.

That was a nice try though – to push me on to the road. I could have joined these two on a bed out here.'

I took a chance as I said that, trying to taunt him into replying. My phone was recording it all.

'Too bad you got away – if only your stupid boyfriend hadn't shown up. We won't miss this time, though.'

'Don't touch me, *Dr Ganguly*. I asked you who's paying for all this – and I can already see that NewLife has a joint venture with Viva-Bio.'

Ganguly stopped in his tracks.

'If you touch me you can be sure that there will be demonstrations outside your clinic tomorrow morning. I am quite sure there is no permission for embryonic stem-cell surgery. Viva-Bio would be very interested in learning that – if they don't already know. This place will be shut down in no time at all.'

Even as I spoke as calmly as I could, I wondered if he would kill me anyway. I had no illusions about how cheap life was. It could always look like an accident, just as they had planned that the attack on me would look like an accident, and I would join Preeti on the next bed. Another candidate for experimentation. My heartbeat raced. It was stupid of me to have come alone. And then I remembered my safety net.

'And I should let you know that Anita and Subhash know I am here. Her car is downstairs. In fact, she is on the mobile phone right now, listening to every word. I suggest you take a deep breath and cool down, and we can meet tomorrow at the clinic. Let's keep this civilized.'

There was silence as the two men thought over what I had said. Ganguly opened his mouth to speak but I cut in.

'Besides, I must tell you that I have already emailed all the pictures of this clinic to the Pandeys. So getting rid of me will only incriminate you further. I think you're in enough trouble already. I doubt if Viva-Bio would like it if you tried to actually kill a social worker.'

I knew that Rohit had procured his gun for the near-shootout at Madonna and Child from Sharma, so no doubt one of them was carrying a weapon. Looking at what they had done to Preeti made me realize that the stakes were very high indeed. I tried to stop trembling.

Ganguly's phone began to ring, and I knew it was Subhash calling him.

After a moment's hesitation, Ganguly looked down at his phone and then indicated the door.

'Get out – you bloody bitch.'

I walked out with my head held high. But as soon as I reached the road, I exhaled and tried to breathe normally once more.

The car was waiting for me outside. All I could think was that I must remember never to be alone in the same room with Dr Ashok Ganguly ever again.

And the day after . . .

GURGAON

My meeting with Subhash and Anita was a long one. I played some of my recordings to them, and told them about what had happened during my London trip – and later in Mumbai and Delhi. They had already seen my clips from yesterday, and had listened to some of the conversation between me and Ganguly.

Subhash was pale with shock, while Anita looked as if she had half been expecting this betrayal from Ganguly.

'Why did he do all this?' Subhash said, astonished.

'More money. Plus he's setting up his own hospital – and then he has probably got this enormous grant from Viva-Bio. They know India is a big surrogacy centre and it would be the best place for them to route their experiments. But more importantly the HIV infection was something he had to bury. That was something which could have destroyed him, and his arrangement with Dr Hansen as well as Viva-Bio. They could have pulled out their investment. So I am quite sure he got rid of Mike and Sue. Perhaps if we hunt for the driver we may learn something.'

'And this whole embryonic stem-cell stuff? Why didn't he just tell us what his plans were? I trusted him totally – and allowed him to manage the whole hospital. He knows everything about us. I even gave him access to my bank account.' Subhash was full of self-recrimination.

'Didn't you wonder about the Mumbai connection? It was such odd route – to send blastocysts for a hospital in Delhi, via Mumbai. Initially when he was setting up his own business, his link with Freedom Hospital must have been good for him. Then he continued to send the embryos through Mumbai, using you as the excuse if needed to bring them to Delhi. But once he established NewLife, and Viva-Bio came in, he got greedy and tried to cut you completely out by saying you were inefficient – while the consignments carried on going through to NewLife.' I finished speaking, got up and walked about restlessly.

Anita was pragmatic as always. 'Apart from surrogacy, once this whole business of embryonic stem-cell surgery becomes legal they will have built up enormous experience working in that area as well.' Science was removing old taboos so quickly – soon this debate over embryonic stem cells would be probably passé.

Later, in that context, I would tell them about Abhi – but not right now. It was still something I had to deal with.

'I think we should call Ganguly in and ask him what exactly has been happening,' I told them. 'Before you do anything drastic, let me make one thing very clear. We have to keep it all very quiet – it must not leak out or become a big issue, because it will wreck your reputation. This is a dangerous and ambitious man and he is capable of anything, possibly even murder. And I have a first-hand experience of it in London – which he did not deny yesterday.'

As I told them of the attack on me, the magnitude of what was happening at their hospital hit them once again. We sent for Ganguly, wondering if he would confess to anything.

Ganguly came in unperturbed, looking relaxed and happy. Despite our unpleasant encounter yesterday, he was back to addressing me as Simranji. It was astonishing. It was as though he were a completely different person.

Subhash began the charge – but to our surprise, even as the accusations mounted, Ganguly continued to look cheerful, though a little pained that we were doubting his integrity – after all, hadn't he done so much for the hospital, brought in business, worked hard? His defence was that he had done nothing wrong. He had never kept it from Subhash and Anita that he was interested in stem-cell surgery, and in fact he had been importing embryos from London long before he tied up with Madonna and Child.

'But,' I interjected, 'it's illegal to use embryonic stem cells—'

Ganguly was quick to retort: 'We have all the permissions from the parents of the embryos as these are all surplus at Mybaby.com. If they do not mind them being used for research or to help someone, we as doctors shouldn't be so squeamish about it.'

I thought of my friend Abhi and I found my eyes tearing up. What the hell was I supposed to do? I was so quick to question others but whose side was I on?

He had looked directly at Subhash when he said that – because everyone knew that Subhash was the true conservative. But at least Subhash was upfront and honest about it all, I wanted to point out, and then decided to stay silent. It was best to let Ganguly speak his part and then find another way of resolving the problem.

Ganguly had a lot to say.

He told them that he had also made it no secret that he found their reticence about it all a little prehistoric. We had to think progressively. Regarding his own clinic he said he had never taken any patients from Madonna and Child because his clientele came from a different income group. They wanted cheaper services – and now he was also providing surrogacy for the gay community, as Subhash had so often raised objections about the practice.

'In fact, I would like to remind you that you were in deep trouble over the French gay couple and their twins. Remember the threats from the Pratha Suraksha Sansthan and those emails from Father Thomas? Well, they were going to organize a big media conference about all this – and it was I who advised the boys to have some photographs taken with a couple of women and the babies to appease them. We convinced the Sansthan and the protesters that the couple was straight and then it all blew over. I'm not looking for gratitude, but you seem to be reading too much into a couple of coincidences.'

This was hardly deserving of high praise – but I didn't remind him that he had organized the protest against us in the first place to hijack the 'gay' surrogacy business from Madonna and Child. He had played upon Subhash's fears and got what he wanted.

Following the protest, all the gay couples registered for the future had been cancelled.

But getting Ganguly to confess to any wrongdoing and attempting to harm the interests of the hospital could prove almost impossible.

He sat in front of us, his usual jovial self, completely at ease. It seemed to me that he was almost turning the tables on us, and instead of us making him feel guilty he almost succeeded in the opposite.

'That's a bit too smooth,' I interjected. 'What about Radhika? You made a 16-year-old girl undergo surrogacy twice with only a gap of six months. I find that indefensible.'

'I didn't know she was sixteen, Simranji. You have always disliked me and are reading all kinds of motives into whatever I do. It is people like you who prevent scientific advancement in this country – always trying to find some silly reason to hold up everything. Everyone makes mistakes. Why just pick on me?' Now he sounded like a martyr.

'What about Preeti, then?' Subhash asked. I could see that he felt sick and angry that he had swallowed the story that she had gone home, when actually she had been lying injured and in a coma at Ganguly's clinic.

'She had an accident and her family wants me to cure her. In fact I am spending a lot of money on her. If the embryonic cells work, she will be out and about very soon.' He looked at me. 'I know you think I am doing something illegal. But don't you want me to save her life?'

Then he added softly to me, 'I've learnt that you have a friend undergoing embryonic stem-cell treatment – don't you want him to recover, either?'

I felt my blood run cold at his words. Was I really blocking Abhi's path to recovery?

He was far too slick for either Subhash or Anita. He had enough ammunition to make us feel guilty. Even if we were not.

Witnessing his Oscar-worthy performance, I was completely convinced that Mike and Susan had been murdered. If anyone could have pulled it off without a single hitch it was this man in front of us.

Thinking back, perhaps the only time he had been nervous was when he had been unable to persuade the Oldhams to remain quiet about the HIV-positive child. He simply did not want his very lucrative tie-ups with all these various individuals and companies to be exposed. Had they sued him, or MyBaby.com, a lot of dirty secrets would have come tumbling out.

'Tell me, what would have happened if the HIV-virus story had become public? Why did you want to conceal it?' I asked him. 'Were you worried that Viva-Bio would pull out or that Dr Hansen would be sued – or that the investigations would show up your dealings with Wadhwani, with Ali, and expose the whole web of deceit?' I, too, had a long list of accusations. 'Is that why you wanted me attacked, and perhaps even killed, just like the Oldhams?'

Anita broke in quietly: 'Let me add something. Sonia told me that the night Preeti went missing you went to her room and you were fiddling with Amelia's drip. That is really a sick thing to have done.'

'That's a lie. You know I was Preeti's doctor. It was perfectly legitimate for me to check if the child was okay. After all, she was premature and her mother had left. And as far as Simranji's many accusations are concerned – all NGOs have a problem with globalization and I know you don't like surrogacy. Don't use me as an excuse for your prejudices.'

But it was Subhash who finally managed to unnerve Ganguly.

'Just answer this question, in that case. Why did you induce Preeti's delivery? Once you found she was HIV positive and may have picked up the infection from the child she was pregnant with – did you want to get rid of her? Tell me why you went in for the c-sec? I remember how much she was bleeding. If I hadn't come into the theatre, she would have died.' He finally spoke up.

'Are you crazy? I didn't know about her HIV status – because, by the way, all the initial tests were done by you! She came to me only later – remember?'

But Subhash had done his research properly. 'Then why did you book the theatre in advance? Susan had asked for a natural birth – they had timed their arrival accordingly – Preeti was fine. How did you know she was going to have the baby on that day?'

I hadn't known that either – and I fell back on my chair. This was the most convincing argument we had heard so far. For a minute even Ganguly looked nonplussed.

Slowly, Subhash continued, 'I think you had always wanted to get rid of her and the baby somehow. Mike and Susan, in fact, had come here earlier than expected, and perhaps you got stuck and couldn't find a chance of bumping her off because they were already here. So you waited till that night – you got Rohit to take Preeti away.'

Ganguly's voice, however, was steady: 'That's all rubbish. The only reason I conducted a caesarean was that the baby had come down. She was experiencing discomfort. And I thought we should do something about it.'

Subhash argued back, 'But you booked the theatre one month in advance. It was impossible for you to know at that time.'

Ganguly was stubbornly sticking to his stand. 'Say whatever you want. I'm telling you what happened.'

I realized that he could afford to feel he had got away scot free because, very conveniently, there seemed to be no one with any stake in baby Amelia's life to take up the issue, or to complain about the procedure.

Or perhaps there was one person.

'You know you think you've got rid of everyone, and no one can say anything about baby Amelia and the HIV virus? Well, I've got news for you. Baby Amelia has a grandfather. And he is going to sue Dr Hansen.'

Even though I had made the last bit up, it was fun to watch Ashok Ganguly's face. He looked as though someone had hit him hard in his groin.

'What does that have to do with me?'

'It has everything to do with you. We have all the admission forms, and the Indian ones have been clearly fudged – only you would have the motive to do so, because only you will benefit if the case is kicked into the long grass. But then we also have the DNA samples; we have the recorded statement from Martin's partner that he was HIV positive, and that the clinic was supposed to remove the virus from the semen; we even have Dr Hansen's admission, which I also recorded, in which she admits that the samples were sent within a week – which is never ever done. What more do you want? We can even prove you messed with the evidence and arranged for the murder of Mike and Susan.'

I think Dr Ganguly would have, if he could, dragged me to the NewLife clinic and lobotomized me.

Subhash threw up his hands.

'Look. This is becoming a nightmare. No, hang on, it's worse than that.' Subhash paused and groped for the appropriate words. 'You have abused our hospital and our confidence. And all sorts of horrible things have happened. Ashok, why did you do all this?'

Even though a frown creased his broad forehead, Ganguly still tried to bluff his way through.

'I think you are all making a fuss about nothing. The whole point is we have a very successful surrogacy operation going on. Let me make you an offer. Let's become partners in the embryonic stem-cell surgery and take it forward. And let's forget all this HIV stuff? After all, mistakes happen all the time!'

There was silence in the room. Slowly his furrowed brow cleared.

'Besides, I will take all of you down with me if you try to accuse me, or Dr Hansen. Your hospital is where Preeti was for nine months – I could just as easily prove it was a contaminated needle.' He was still intent on protecting himself. And we knew he could do it. All it needed was for him to 'create' a single eyewitness who said the hospital had not followed safety procedures.

Anita spoke up at last.

'I think, Ashok, instead of accusing each other, the time

has come for us to part. You should leave and let's call an end to all of this.'

I decided not to be hostile, because at that moment a very interesting thought crossed my mind.

'I agree with Anita,' I said. 'Let's just drop the whole thing. If there is a police case, there will be more bad publicity. Let's just agree that all of you have different styles of working and that's it.'

Ganguly looked relieved, and Subhash looked confused.

'So that's it?' Ganguly could not believe his luck. He had ripped us off, and he was being allowed to walk free.

I waited for him to leave the room before I turned to Subhash and patted his hand.

'Don't worry, he's not going to get away with it.'

I sighed.

Why were people such complete bastards? He deserved to be hanged and quartered – and he was a *doctor*. I gazed at Subhash and Anita, thankful that at least they were different.

'Look, as I said, we are not going to let him get away with anything, but we shouldn't be the ones to do anything to him, because he is a vicious bloody man, in a hurry to get rich.'

They nodded in agreement. Subhash looked as if he was ready to give up everything and go home right at that moment. Anita looked grim.

'Remember we still have a friend in the Health Minister? She owes you a huge favour. You saved her

political dynasty free of cost. Call her and tell her everything. She has the power to destroy him – and it will be
so subtle that no one will connect it with you. Get her to
revoke his licence, and conduct a raid on his hospital. She
should charge him with illegally taking away the
embryos, and of conducting embryonic stem-cell surgery.
Tell her about the surrogacy scam and Radhika. But tell
her you want to stay out of it all. Screw his happiness so
badly he'll never practise again. Try to get Preeti and
Radhika out of there.'

I paused and looked through my notes.

'Regarding Dr Hansen: it's a contract; you can tear it up
and never have anything to do with her again. Only one
warning: you will have to find an agent other than
Sharmaji and he mustn't find out what happened.
Remember where Rohit got his pistol from – even though
Renu Mishra eventually forgave him?' I shuddered.

There was silence in the room – and suddenly, with a
whoop, Anita gave me a big hug.

'You're a genius! Now I owe *you* a really big favour.'

I had already thought about that, as well.

'Actually there are three big favours! Firstly, I want
you to try to find out where my friend Abhinav is. Dr
Wadhwani is treating him – once you turn on your
charm, he will, I am sure, give you the information.
And secondly . . .' I took out Malti's file and handed it
to her. 'You owe something to Mehta too – his wife
needs IVF.'

But there was still one more point. We had to ensure that Ganguly's ties with Dr Wadhwani were snapped forever, and that the latter also realized the pitfalls of illegally acquiring embryos from Ali.

I looked straight at Anita.

'You will also have to inform Dr Wadhwani that some of the consignments he received might have contained HIV positive embryos . . .

She gave me another hug, her relief clearly visible. After this Ali would never be able to conduct his jihad again! As for me, even though I empathized with his mission, I obviously disapproved of his methodology . . .

It was a good feeling when I saw baby Amelia that evening. At least we had sorted out her past – now we had to do something about her future.

Later at home I carefully went through all the possibilities with Durga and my mother. After all, this was a question of Amelia's life. It was Durga who suggested the solution.

And the next day . . .

GURGAON

Out of the mouth of babes . . . and it had been in front of me all along.

I met Ben and Kate, to explore all the possibilities, and to make sure the proposition would appeal to them.

It was obvious that, after Kate's experiences at the NewLife clinic, there was already a huge trust-deficit between them and Sharmaji. Though they did not know the truth regarding Ashok Ganguly, the two of them seemed exhausted from having looked at so many different possibilities, including surrogacy, without any resolution.

So, fortunately, they were now seriously considering adoption.

However, Ben was still feeling guilty that, unwittingly, he had pushed Sheela into surrogacy. I sighed and made a mental note to ask the Pandeys to try to get her out of NewLife as well.

Though my own feeling was that now, if she had already been offered a job as a surrogate mother, it would be tough to extricate her. The money would be too good to refuse and no matter what help Ben offered, it would still not match up. She would probably prefer to keep her children and not send any of them away with the Rileys.

It was doubly sad because, while Ben had thought he would wipe out the memory of any historical indiscretion by his grandfather, in Sheela's eyes he had become equally culpable.

He was determined to help Sheela's family but I told him gently that it might be a while before she would be willing to meet them again. Once Sharmaji had managed to find a new recruit, it was difficult to extricate them. Of course, the Pandeys would do their best, and offer her another surrogacy with their own hospital – but the whole situation would take time to evolve and stabilize. And Ben's plans would have to be remoulded and reshaped accordingly. As I spoke, I could see the relief on Kate's face.

So I took the fact that they were still waiting for a child as a good omen. The timing was just right, all around.

I mentioned to them that baby Amelia needed a home desperately. She also needed medical care. If they were willing to adopt her it would solve so many problems.

It turned out to be simpler than I had imagined.

They thought about it and, to my intense delight, after spending some time with her, agreed. One of the clinching factors was the fact that it was unlikely she would get a home in India, where the prejudice against HIV would ensure she led a marginalized existence. Already I could see the difference in the attitude of the nurses – who, as they realized what her illness was, wanted little to do with her.

It had been a painful year in many ways for Ben and Kate, but sometimes one has to travel the whole road to find out what love and parenthood really mean. For me, too, it had been a long and troubling journey. But if we all put our hearts into it, this was probably the best outcome. I surrendered any thoughts I might have had about baby Amelia's grandfather, letting go of whatever hopes and dreams I had erroneously nurtured.

Even if Edward ever did show up or enquire about her, I had finally accepted the fact that, given his history, he would not be able to sustain a long-term interest in a child – and besides, how could he raise her or look after her? She needed constant monitoring and, given his carefree lifestyle, he would not want to be too involved. I agreed with what he had said. Perhaps I had been hoping he would change – but honestly, in reality, that was too much to expect.

It would be best, though, if I discreetly informed him of our decision. I sent him an email, and hoped he would understand. The good news, I told him, was that the child had parents now and would be in London – and he could participate in her life whenever he wanted. I had already told Kate and Ben and they did not mind at all. They quite liked the idea that baby Amelia was starting her new life with a grandfather as well.

Besides, the solution fitted in with my philosophy completely. Why bother to bring more babies into a world which already had plenty of them who needed love and good homes? Despite frowns from Subhash, who hated it when I destroyed his business, I would carry on assisting with adoptions whenever I could, connecting needy parents with abandoned waifs.

And the next month

GURGAON

And so now the time had finally come to say goodbye to Amelia, the innocent catalyst of so much turmoil.

The paperwork was done, and in another week, she would be gone with Ben and Kate.

I went into her room in the hospital and picked her up. She smelt pleasantly of milk. She had been sleeping well and was much healthier than when she was born. She was out of the incubator and thriving, ready for her life in London.

Going up to the window, I cradled her in my arms and planted a kiss on her forehead. She meant more to me, in so many ways, than I would ever be able to tell her. I held her towards the sun so that I could see her dark blue eyes better and apologized to her.

Her tiny fingers curled around my hand and her sweet pink mouth formed a perfect 'o' as she yawned sleepily.

'Darling,' I told her. 'I tried very hard. I tried to find your real home. I tried to find your real family. I went all the way to London. I tracked down your grandfather – but what can I do when he is so stupid he doesn't want a lovely little thing like you—'

'Who says I don't want her?'

The familiar voice sounded close enough to give me goose bumps. I didn't turn around in case I was hallucinating.

'He's a very silly man,' I continued determinedly. 'He pretends to be sensible, drinks milk and rides bicycles – but now I've found you a set of parents who will look after you and love you for who you are.'

'Just as your grandfather will do, along with them.'

I still couldn't believe he could be here. Baby Amelia smiled toothlessly at someone over my shoulder.

I finally turned around and saw the tall thin figure silhouetted against the doorway.

Tears jumped into my eyes as Edward took baby Amelia from my arms.

'She's every bit as beautiful as you told me she was. In fact there were many things you told me which are exactly the way things actually are.'

It was a cryptic statement which made perfect sense.

He lifted her up and then put her against his shoulder and put his other arm around me.

And his body next to mine felt exactly the way I had thought it would.

Acknowledgements

This book had a slightly bumpy conception (all puns intended) and would not have been possible without the constant love, support and critical comments of my husband, Meghnad Desai, my parents Rajini and Padam Rosha, as well as my children, Gaurav and Mallika Ahluwalia.

And how can I ever thank Clare Hey? The marvellously capable and very insightful editor who has not only been unfailingly patient and understanding, but has also guided the book to a miraculous delivery along with the wonderful team at Simon & Schuster. Will Atkins, Rahul Srivastava and Shireen Qadri, especially, many thanks!

And I must also thank the gorgeous Caroline Michel, my agent, for her sagacity and wisdom.

Thanks are also due to V.K. Karthika, Simon Petherick, Ryan Davies, Julian Friedman and the team at Blake Friedmann for their support and inputs.

There are many friends who have been patient with my long absences, whilst writing: expecially Abha (Bunty) Sawhney, Shaila Mishra, Deepa Mishra-Harris, Shailja Bajpai. Habiba, (the late) Mario Miranda, Pankaj and Sujai Joshi, Shekhar Gupta and Neelam Jolly, Vivienne and

Brian Henry, Megan . . . It's a long list, and will be contined in the next book!

I also would like to thank Naren (Lord) Patel and my brother Dr Deepak Rosha for their careful scrutiny of the medical details in the book.

And last but not least, I would like to thank Ravinder Kaur for her suggestion that I explore the complex issue of surrogacy in my next book – *Origins of Love* is the result!

Author's Note

As in my first novel, *Witness the Night*, most of the cases
and stories examined by my heroine, Simran Singh, in
this book, too, are based on reality – but have obviously
been changed and fictionalized not only to protect the
characters but also to weave them into a single narrative.
Even the bizarre seizure of embryos at the Mumbai airport
actually took place, and is not a figment of my fevered
imagination.

Declining fertility both among men and women all
over the world have led to some solutions – IVF, surrogacy and so on – none of which are without pitfalls. But I
leave the reader to agree or disagree with Simran Singh,
as she is now already into her third, equally difficult,
investigation!

Read on for an exclusive excerpt from
The Sea of Innocence, Simran Singh's
next adventure, out soon.

Chapter 1

The girl in the video did not look older than sixteen, a pale flame flickering amongst the four dark-skinned boys who crowded around her, raising her hands and moving to the music. The boys merged together in the dim light as they jostled to get close to her. They may have been older than her but since they were all dressed in T-shirts and bright shorts, and two of them had their hair tied in ponytails, they seemed quite young. The girl was tiny in a yellow halter-neck top and short blue skirt and they circled her, dancing with eyes closed, mesmerized by the hypnotic beat.

The low-ceilinged room was lit by a single bulb covered with a red scarf, the light spilling in splashes of blood onto the swaying figures. Familiar-sounding trance music bound them in a robotic movement. Curtains lined the walls, and in one corner a circular window was visible.

The video was possibly shot on a cell phone; the images were grainy and no effort was made to adjust the quality or to zoom in.

One of the boys suddenly said something vehemently to the girl. It was difficult to distinguish the expressions on the faces and though the tone of his voice was shar the words were muffled by the music. From her relaxed manner, it seemed the girl knew him well. She shook her head and pushed him aside as he tried to say something into her ear. It was obvious she was confident of herself. Without even opening her eyes, she carried on dancing.

The boy slipped his arm around the girl and cupped her left breast. The other boys stared and the dancing came to a standstill. Nervous laughter broke out as the girl slapped him and one of the boys blocked the camera view, momentarily trying to stop the fight, perhaps. He was pulled away by the boy next to him and, as though made aware of the camera lens, he looked over his shoulder and stepped alongside the girl. The girl threw her long curly hair back over her shoulder and struggled with the boy who was still groping her. He managed to untie her top, exposing her breasts.

The other boys became absolutely still.

She quickly pulled the two ends of her top back behind her neck, retying them. And then she lunged at the boy to hit him. But he ducked and caught hold of her wrist. There was a momentary pause as though the script had gone wrong and someone had given instructions to redirect the video.

'Oh come on!' one of the boys said. This time both the d their implication were clear.

, you idiot,' the girl replied, and then giggled 'don't be stupid.' Oddly, she didn't sound

The screen went dark. Then when the video started again three of the boys and the girl were on a bed. One of them was lying on his side, speaking to her.

'You promised. You can't be . . .'

The audio was once more as blurred as the visuals, and even the little conversation which could be heard was jagged and unclear.

The girl was obviously immune to his persistent, persuasive tone. She lay flat on her back, still in her halter-neck top and short skirt, staring at the ceiling. Her legs were crossed but her feet were moving in time to the music.

The camera was shakier than before. Earlier the phone might have been placed strategically on a stable surface and now someone – maybe the fourth boy? – was possibly holding it, and moving closer to the bed.

'Come on . . .' An off-camera voice was more aggressive, louder and shrill, and the girl looked directly into the phone lens. But her eyes were completely unfocused. She pushed herself up, perhaps trying to obey the instructions. She was moving with unnatural slowness, and finally slid back, as though the effort was beyond her. Was she drunk? Why didn't she get up and leave?

'Just take off her skirt,' someone said, loudly with a clear voice, with a distinct Indian accent.

The lens moved still closer to the bed and hovered over the girl, scanning up her pale legs and then the screen went blank again.

The video did not last more than three minutes.

I stared at the small dark screen of my cell phone, in a state of shock.

Amarjit, an old college friend of mine and a police officer presently based in Delhi (while recovering from a high profile divorce), had sent the video clip through.

It was accompanied by a message saying he wanted to speak to me. After his ex-wife had threatened to name me as a co-respondent in their divorce, there had been very little reason for me to communicate with him recently. In fact, I had stayed away from him for the past three years.

So was this some kind of horrible joke? A schoolboy prank? A lewd video sent to intrigue me and break the ice instead of a bouquet of flowers? Hook me with a mysterious and disturbing message, and then reel me in?

I wasn't falling into that trap again.

I answered politely, suggesting that he tie his feet to a 500-kilo weight and drown himself in the Arabian Sea.

But despite my flippant reply, the video had an unsettling effect. Its very visible sexual overtones and the vulnerability of the girl upset me more than I had realized. I was also puzzled and angry that Amarjit had cho___ to send me the video, especially now.

As ___ probably knew, since he was still in touch with ___r, I had come to Goa for a holiday, to lounge on ___s beaches and watch the sun spread its golden ___ water. Not for this.

I sighed and chucked the phone into my bag, already overcrowded with guide books and sunscreens, and made my way back to the beach. I wanted to join Durga, my sixteen-year-old daughter, as quickly as possible, nervous that she had been left alone even for a short time.

Durga, meanwhile, was sitting happily on the sand getting a henna tattoo of broken hearts in a daisy chain painted onto her arm.

'Too depressing; why broken hearts?' I asked her briskly, deliberately not looking at her, not wanting another argument. Though we always made up, I didn't want to risk an all-out war, which was so easy on holidays, when you're supposedly meant to have a good time. 'Try something else.' My stentorian declaration could have been incorrect, but how was I to know? After all, I was thirty years older than Durga and anything but trendy. Even though I now lay next to her on a sunny beach I was wearing a flimsy pink sarong over my daring black swimsuit to hide any unseemly bulges.

'How about a string of paisleys around your arm, like this?' I tried to inject a happy note into my voice. I waved my own plump arm with its intricate paisley henna tattoo (which looked quite nice if you ignored the accompanying bingo wings) in her face.

'Perhaps you should have got a dragon tattoo,' quipped Durga as she presented her other arm to Veeramma, the canny beach vendor who had attached herself to us for the past three days, showering us wit endless compliments in fluent, if ungrammatical, English, French and Russian, as well as her native Kannada. 'It's more suited to what you've been up to.'

She was teasing me about my penchant of trying to solve difficult crime cases, even though my avowed profession was that of a social worker. And there were many who described my voluntary work as annoying interference in matters that didn't concern me.

Having developed a thick skin over the years, I ignored the taunts, and plodded on, regardless. Often at my own peril. So I just laughed at Durga's little jibe and said 'Touché!', mindful of the fact that we still had a week left of our holiday.

I wondered how Veeramma and her gang of fellow beach gypsies walked around all day, barefoot on the hot sand with a swathe of elephant-print sarongs on one arm, a bundle of silver jewellery dangling from another, and a patchwork embroidered bag slung over one shoulder. She smiled and smiled, used to dealing with camera-clicking, sensation-hungry tourists from all over the world.

I had a feeling she was humouring us, sharing a wink with her sister-vendors who now gathered around us in a good natured crowd. In India, a *tamasha*, a spectacle, could be created within minutes.

Right now I had drunk too much beer to bother about the women's apparent interest in us. I lit a cigarette, marvelled once at the slow pace of Indian governance, as the long-proposed ban on smoking on the beach still had to be implemented.

I blew smoke rings into the air, to the delight of the women surrounding us. At any other time their proximity would have made me suspicious and withdrawn, but it was a lovely December day and I wasn't going to let anything ruin it. Or so I thought.

I watched Veeramma deftly dribble another thin line of black henna on Durga's arm. Obviously she knew who was more likely to win the battle of the broken hearts – if I dared to fight it out, that is. I sighed and fell further back into the sand. Why argue when Durga wasn't going to listen anyway? I tried to synchronize my breath with the rise and fall of the waves instead.

Veeramma had squatted comfortably on the sand next to us, while the other six vendors edged closer to me and began complaining about their husbands and their mothers-in-law. They asked me, half-teasingly, to take them all, or perhaps at least one of them, back with me to Delhi, as they said they hated their lives of wandering around on the beaches all day. They longed to be inside a house, cooking and gossiping and squabbling like the over-dressed housewives in the TV soap operas they watched at night. They did not even mind being hired as domestic help. Anything, so long as they were not seeking out customers all day, often turned into objects of ridicule, treated almost like untouchables, shooed away from the shacks serving food and drink which lined the G‍

beaches. Yet these beach vendors had been here from the time hippies had first discovered Goa, and were now possibly the most exotic part of the landscape, earning more through their sales than they would back in Karnataka.

'What we do, madam?' one of them said to me with a sweet smile. 'My husband bastard boozer. I like here, no like home.'

'Take her Delhi, madam,' rose a chorus of giggling voices. 'She care your daughter, make you nice *idli-dosa*, give good massage every day.' Their staccato sentences were communicative and crisp.

'Sounds super, Mother. Maybe we should. Nani would love that, wouldn't she?' Durga's eyes lazily smiled at me at last. She sipped her fresh pineapple juice, looking relaxed now with the cool touch of the henna on her arm.

I glanced back towards the row of beach shacks: temporary thatch-roofed, sand, cement and wooden structures that dispensed a steady supply of food and drink to the tourists, unique to the Goa beaches. Barring a few, they would be removed every monsoon and then reconstructed in the high season, the licences given to them providing an additional income to the government babus who gave th___ ___mp of approval to these prized allocations. They ___ ___eir own economic and social environment and ___ ___asionally death) on the beach depended on ___ you attached yourself to.

___tting close to the water because, according to

well-practised beach apartheid, these women were not allowed near the deckchairs that Durga and I had occupied in the past few days. So we had to walk down to them, crossing the Lakshman Rekha, the invisible dividing line between the haves and have-nots which even existed where naked skin would make it impossible to guess who was rich and who was not.

'Bastards no let us come up to deckchairs, still taking *hafta*,' Veeramma grumbled under her breath.

I had already learnt that the cops who gave them permission to sell their wares took their cut. In the few days that Durga and I had been in Goa, we had realized that a well-oiled, systematic food chain existed. The tragedy was that no matter who postured as the biggest fish, there were others still larger than them.

Reluctant to get up, I gestured to the waiter near my erstwhile deckchair to bring my beer over as it seemed too far away to reach in my flip-flops.

The sand was soothingly warm against my back while Durga's tattoo was completed. Veeramma had wanted a thousand rupees for the work and later settled for five hundred. Even though I love to drive a hard bargain, I had succumbed to all-pervading *susegaad* – a delightful expression frequently used and directly connected to Goa's Portuguese past, which meant 'taking it easy'.

Still in a beer-induced haze, I noticed that Veeramma's hypnotic movements over Durga's arm had tempora stalled as she stared towards the sea, her eyes glued to a young girl in a bikini, running past us, her blonde hair bouncing behind her.

I felt my stomach knot in tension. She reminded me far too much of the girl I had seen in the video less than an hour ago.

Veeramma said something to one of her friends who was also closely watching the girl. I couldn't follow her comment, but both of them burst out laughing. Puzzled, I watched the girl speed over the sand, light-footed like a gazelle. She seemed no different from all the other tourists who crowded the beach and were swimming in the water. Why had she caught Veeramma's eye?

'What's so funny?' I asked her.

Veeramma shook her head. 'Nothing. She new catch, I think.'

'Caught by whom?' I asked.

A silence followed. Durga moved uncomfortably as Veeramma's grip on her arm tightened slightly. Then Veeramma looked up and smiled. The smile did not reach her eyes.

'Some beach boys like fish.'

oman sitting beside her cut in swiftly, 'They sell

added, 'And make tasty curry.'

la fry! Chop chop! *Bon appetite!*' giggled the

o her, saying the last few words in a perfect

French accent, bowing slightly towards me and present-
ing her palm as though serving a culinary treat, while the
other arm looped the air.

Watching her, all the women laughed out loud, and
almost by a hidden signal they started gathering their
things and stood up to leave.

'What do you mean?' asked Durga.

'Forget it, baby. Enjoy holiday. Many things on beach
you don't want to know.'

'Gou, Goa . . . Goa, Goa.' One of the woman got up and
swung her hips in time to the chant, as she pirouetted on
one heel.

Veeramma poured a bit of oil on Durga's henna hearts
and told her, 'Don't rub this off just now. Only after thirty
minutes then the tattoo stay on for few weeks.'

I handed her the money but couldn't help asking, 'But
how do you know that girl?'

'I did tattoo, madam,' she said, suddenly looking shy.
'But private place.' She quickly placed her hand just below
her belly button and darted a look at Durga, who was
listening fascinated. 'Not you, baby. Shut eyes, ears,' she
added. Even though Durga was as old as the teenager
who had just run past on the beach, Veeramma made the
classic blunder of thinking that, being an Indian adolescent, she would be more innocent.

A tiny shiver of unease ran through me while I remembered the permanent tattoo that Durga had once on her
arm which we later had removed, at her request. Little

did Veeramma know what Durga had been through in her young life.

Perhaps I had made a mistake bringing her here; perhaps it might bring back difficult memories. The care-free feeling which had been somewhat dented by the morning's video suffered further erosion.

It was also becoming apparent that the naivety which once existed on Goa's beaches seemed to have disappeared long ago. Even in the short three days that I had been here I kept thinking that there was an uncomfortable dichotomy between life on the beach and that on the rest of Goa. At times this seemed almost like another country which was ruled by its own laws of behaviour, not all of it pleasant. The picture-postcard beauty of serene cosmo-politanism, offering a variety of sea sports and other simple pleasures, had a creeping darkness crumpling the edges. Shades of it had been apparent in what Veeramma said about the girl, but I had also glimpsed the dead eyes of some of the beach boys and the cynicism with which they looked at the near naked bodies strewn on the beach.

In contrast to the beaches, mainland Goa seemed almost puritanical, despite the proliferation of the liquor shops and bars. But then there was an equal (if not greater) number of churches, temples and mosques put together that would give the merry-makers instant absolution. And thus, contrarily, prevent them from permanent absti-nence. Why bother if you could swing dizzily between partying and penance?

Durga smiled back at Veeramma.

'So why do you think she had the tattoo done down there?' Durga asked, trying to look as though she hadn't understood. 'No one would ever see it then.'

'Only fish in sea,' Veeramma quipped. Many days later I would remember our laughter and realize how eerily accurate Veeramma's answer had been.

But right now I said our farewells as I paid her and the women walked away.

'She's quite clever, isn't she?' said Durga, looking at Veeramma as she pulled her bag over her shoulder and joined her friends.

'You have to be, I suppose, if you want to survive on this beach.' I thought once more of the video I had seen in the morning. Her comment about the beach boys made me think of the identities of the men in the video. Could it have been shot around here, and did the clue lie in the casual attire, the shorts and T-shirts that everyone wore around Goa? And that accent? The fact that Amarjit had sent it to me might not be purely coincidental.

'I wonder who that blonde girl was?' Durga asked while we trudged back to the restaurant under the thatched roof, up on the higher ground.

I shrugged. I was already worried that our holiday would get ruined with our occasional squabbles, and now I had another reason to be concerned.

Urging Durga to order some king prawns drenched in

garlic butter sauce, which she loved, I lit a cigarette and ordered another bottle of chilled beer.

I decided that I was going to stick to my plan of holidaying with Durga. I would erase all memory of that girl in the video, and stop worrying about what happened to her. It was not my problem.

Famous last words, as they say.